Dea

by K. J. T. Carr

Cover art by Neil Rankin.

For Emma, for believing in me when I did not.

PART I

Prologue

Avatar Age, Year 820
Bulwark

Assen felt a familiar rumble through his armoured boots. The usual shriek pierced the air, echoing from the rent in the cliff side. The Daem horde approached.

The rain-dappled scene was like its hundred predecessors. Stone walls flanked the long killing field that stretched to the cliffs. Tips of longbows peeked above the parapets, hundreds of archers at the ready. A few feet ahead, a platoon of squires blocked the exit of the killing field—the poor conscripts unlucky enough to have drawn spearman duty this morning. Behind them, flanking Assen, stood a dozen of his Deathless comrades. The final line of defence.

Eighty years had passed since the day he died.

The day he made the foul pact to become Deathless. Eighty years of defending Bulwark, and what had changed? The earthworks had given way to wooden walls and finally stone. Armour became more refined. Weapons were formed of stronger steel. But the men and women before him still shook with the same fear. The air was filled with the same stench of sweat and blood and piss. And always, the Daem-ans still flooded through.

The assault was heralded by the overpowering odour of sulphur boiling from the cliff face. Before his death, he had hated that odour, now it felt calming, like returning home. Then, with the sweet and dreadful wail of the damned, the Daem-ans poured from the cave. Black, twisted shapes scrambled across the well-trodden field, asymmetric limbs built from mismatched bones, all draped in a too-tight skin, black and cracked as half-burned corpses. Some towered eight feet tall, enough to put pause in the hearts of the Ash-an squires holding the spear line. Other Daem-ans were no larger than a Greml-an, scuttling under the hoofs and claws and tendrils of their larger brethren. To the sane—to the living—they were abominations, horrors. To him, they were also marvellous. A discordant mob, united by a common desire.

To destroy.

Arrows rained down into the charging throng, felling the beasts. Fresh, beautiful monstrosities piled into the killing field. Dozens. Hundreds. Through sheer force of numbers, the Daem-ans pushed forward, clambering over their own dead to bear down on the line of spearmen.

Shrieks of pain. Howls of fear. The slap of a severed limb striking mud. The crack of a shattering bone. The smell of blood.

The Daem-ans were more numerous today. The hundred squires stood no chance, taking only a few of the beasts down before being ripped apart. A hundred men and women, drafted from all corners of the world, thrown away in a matter of minutes. It was horrendous. It was glorious.

Assen and the Deathless advanced, drawing their mismatched weapons. They plunged towards the weakened Daem line, expertly swinging spears and swords and flails. Eighty years of war—eighty years of ceaseless training—had honed them into unparalleled warriors. They did not tire as the battle raged, had long grown accustomed to pain. They were unstoppable.

But they were not immortal.

As the dust settled, as the last wounded Daem-ans were dispatched with uncaring thrusts, one fewer Deathless stood to hold the line. The survivors gathered around Garrek's mangled corpse. No doubt that poorly-healed collarbone had slowed the man. Decades of injuries took their toll, even on Deathless.

No one mourned. There were no keens, no tears. Garrek's true death had been sixty-five years previous, the day he had given up his soul for a second chance to defend his homeland. Now, that broken body was an empty vessel, finally brought down. The fate that awaited all Deathless.

Something moved on the killing field. Assen turned, sword ready, expecting to see a Daem-an struggling to its feet. Instead, a young Ash-an stood on shaking legs, her lethal head wound already fading.

The Deathless stared at their new comrade. They knew the sacrifice she had just accepted. The damnation she had just committed herself to. The decision all Deathless came to regret.

For her, Assen wept.

Chapter 1

Avatar Age, Year 1238
Vandar Forest

Xia leapt from tree to tree, twenty feet from the ground. Her anti-grav belt flared to life with each jump, letting her clear the distance between the pines with ease. Even from this height, her Elf eyes picked out the trail carved across the forest floor. Grinning, she kicked off another tree in pursuit of her prey.

Digging her clawed fingers around the rough bark of a particularly wide old pine, she paused to look behind her. Startled birds broke cover as her brother came crashing through the forest. Eight years younger than Xia, Eddan had just turned ten and started to learn the art of the hunt. As he slammed from trunk to trunk, knocking loose bark and branches, Xia knew the boy had much to learn.

As Eddan landed beside her, the old bark trembled, his claws—barely worn—disturbing the bark, releasing a waft of the rich woody scent. He panted, sweat slicking back his hair, and grinned.

Father always said they looked alike, but Xia could not see it. Sure, they had the same pine-bark hair and the pale skin of all central Elf-ans, but the similarities ended there. Xia kept her hair neck-length, neatly tied into a crowning braid. Eddan roughly hacked his down whenever it grew more than an inch long. Xia was tall for an Elf-an, at just over five foot. Eddan was small for his age, a good foot shorter. Her hands and feet were thickly calloused from almost a decade patrolling these branches, her claws hardened and worn. Eddan's skin was almost as soft as on the day he had entered this world.

Of course, their greatest difference lay in their abilities. Regrettably, educating the child was now Xia's responsibility.

'What do you see?' she prompted.

'Trees.' His lopsided grin met a stony glare. 'Erm, tracks?'

'Good, where?'

He glanced around the forest floors, then shrugged with a broad grin.

Not for the first time that day, Xia rolled her eyes. 'Avatars' sake. Are you sure you weren't switched at birth? A Hum-an with oddly pointed ears?' She sighed at the hurt on his face. 'Look down there. See the broken underbrush, all bent in one direction? It makes a track, a path. Those leaves? They're bent, but not discoloured. This track was recent.'

'So we're close?'

'We'll see when Rikk returns.' Xia scanned the endless trunks ahead, finally catching the rapid movements on their hunting companion. 'There.'

Xia pointed towards the approaching vulfik. Where Eddan's motion had been lurching and cumbersome, the hunting beast's leaps were precise, elegant. Half the size of a wolf, the creature moved with the agility of a bird of prey. It launched itself from the trunks, flaring a furred membrane to glide between trees, highlighted by the odd sun ray that broke through the thick pine canopy. The little height it lost on each jump was quickly recovered, sharp claws effortlessly scurrying up the thick bark.

Its darting motion soon brought it to Xia's tree, the impact barely perceptible through the bark. Vulfiks had hollow bones, strange for a predator, but few creatures survived the initial ambush from those long claws. In pre-history, vulfik packs tormented the forest, striking fear in animals and 'an alike. These days, the only vulfiks in Vandar Forest were companion animals like Rikk.

Xia gave the furred creature a welcoming scratch on its canine head. Rikk nuzzled her in greeting, then let out a series of excited clicks and chirps—he had found the deer they tracked… or an unguarded picnic. With Rikk it was hard to tell.

'Lead us,' Xia commanded. Rikk bounded back in the direction he had came, pausing a few trees down to wait impatiently for his Elf-an to follow. Signalling Eddan, she took off after the creature.

They progressed rapidly through the forest. Xia could not kick off with the speed of the vulfik, but she lost far less height with her grav-belt and so spent far less time climbing compared to Rikk. Occasionally, the beast still had to pause to let her catch up, huffing with displeasure. Eddan trailed far behind.

Reaching a trunk next to Rikk, Xia frowned at the animal's pose. Body pressed against the tree, pointed downwards, hair flattened, teeth exposed—a vulfik's ambush posture. But there was no deer in sight.

Scanning the ground, Xia wondered if the idiot animal had led her to some small rabbit or fifil. Then she saw it. Down in the undergrowth, mostly hidden by broad leaved ferns.

Blood.

Frown deepening, Xia released the tree, turning the power down on her belt to allow herself to drop gently to the forest floor, dry leaves crunching underfoot. The glorious odour of greenery mixed with composting leaves flooded the air, tainted with fresh blood.

She picked her way into a thicket. There, she found her quarry. A buck, big one, fine set of antlers.

The deer was cleaved in two.

With a thump of shattering twigs, Eddan landed beside her, peering curiously into the thicket. 'By the Avatar!'

'Don't blaspheme,' Xia said, distracted, examining the corpse. Deep gouges criss-crossed the halves. Entrails still linked the two bloody masses.

'Wow.' Eddan whistled. 'You think it was feral vulfiks?'

Slowly, Xia shook her head. 'You watch too many horror shows. Besides, a vulfik couldn't rip a monkey in half, let alone a deer.'

'A pack of them could.'

'Why would they? They'd just cut the throat in the first pounce. Besides, there's no bite marks. No way a vulfik pack would leave a fresh kill without feeding. You ever seen Rikk pass up on food?'

'Good point.' Eddan grinned. 'Then what? Bear? Ogre?'

'I don't know,' Xia admitted. 'Whatever it is, it must be close. This kill is fresh.' She walked around the corpse, examining the broad line of shattered bushes left in the wake of the mystery predator. Its tracks were easy to make out, but like none she had ever seen. Deep gouges flanked a trail of footprints looking like talon marks of some enormous bird. She shook her head, realising the left claw was smaller than the right. 'I've never seen anything like this.'

'We should go home.' Eddan's enthusiasm had evaporated.

'No.'

'But Father said...'

Xia glared at her brother. 'No. This is our responsibility. We're forest wardens. That means we have a duty to keep the forest in balance. Whatever did this will do so again.' She could think of the notoriety she would gain for taking down an ogre. Maybe even an invitation to the high-wardens of Enall. '*I* will not let that happen. I'm going on. Go home if you want.'

Eddan sighed, but stayed put. Xia unshouldered her rifle—an EG-25, Greml metalSinging partnered with Elf shooting mastery. The polished rosewood frame surrounded an intricate steel core, topped with an electric sight. The rifle had been Xia's most prized possession since her mother had gifted it on Xia's tenth birthday. Looking at the huge and asymmetric tracks, Xia had never felt so relieved to hold the weapon.

She set off on foot. Picking her way through the underbrush would be slow compared to leaping between the trees, but she wanted to keep relatively hidden, and needed her weapon ready.

Green stalks creaked underfoot, twigs snapped, dry leaves crunched. Through the thin rubber of her climbing shoes, she felt every stone, every branch, every thorn. The slim shoes were designed to give sure grip on trees, not to protect against rocks and brambles. Thankfully, an active lifetime had given her feet a thick sole, and the stabbing thorns had no hope of drawing blood.

The trail, at least, was easy to follow. Whatever creature had come this way had not been subtle. Bushes had been crushed, green ferns stamped into the soft soil, the earth cleaved down to the tree roots.

Xia crouched, examining a marking in the dirt. A footprint, but one far more familiar than the tracks she was following. The smooth print looked nearly identical to those she left. Climbing shoes.

'What is it?' Eddan whispered.

'Someone else is following these tracks.'

'Another warden?' he offered.

Without answering, Xia stalked forward. Light bloomed ahead. The thick pine canopy opened up, allowing the sun's rays to pour over a wide clearing. A cold wind greeted her, blowing through the breathable material of her tunic and shorts, bringing the scents of wildflowers and something else. Something foul. Sulphurous.

Both sets of tracks lead into the sunbathed tall grass, stalks flattened in a path that stretched across the field.

And there, half way across the clearing, a figure crouched, speaking, the voice just audible to Xia's Elf ears over the chirps of birds and rustle of wind through the leaves. Xia could not make out the words, but the accent sounded Southern.

Darkness fell over the landscape—the midday eclipse. Xia glanced up to see the last of the sun being swallowed by Watcher, the gas giant their world orbited. The daily occurrence would leave the landscape in twilight for the next hour.

Xia turned on her scope, looking down the digitally enhanced sight to get a better view of the stranger. Short. Pointed ears. Definitely Elf-an. The black hair and tanned skin marked the stranger out as a Southern Elf. Matched the accent.

The hesitant voice continued, though Xia could see no one else. Zooming her scope, Xia made out a headset. The stranger was communicating with someone distant. Maybe they were a high-warden from Enall, sent to trail the beast?

Silence descended. No chirps from birds, no screech of insects or howls of monkeys. Even the leaves seemed to still. Dread grew in Xia's stomach.

Then she heard it.

A rumbling sounded from the far tree line. Branches shattered. Wood snapped. A cloud of debris tore towards the clearing. Then a wail pierced the air, a terrifying cry like some poor beast in its death throes.

The stranger's yell filled the clearing. 'It's here!'

A black mass thundered into the tall grass, at least eight feet tall and just as broad. Xia could only watch, frozen with shock. Two shots rang out, accompanied by a flash of light from the stranger, but the black thing barely slowed. The mass slammed into the stranger, a spray of crimson spiralling into the air, raining down over the grass stalks.

Hands shaking, Xia looked through her scope. The creature paused over the body of its latest kill, giving a clear view. What she saw shook her to her core. The massive beast was wrapped in a blackened and broken skin, red cracks littering every inch, as if the beast had been partially cremated. Great wings flanked an emaciated torso, each capped in a viciously curved talon. A sinuous neck led to an ugly head, all fangs and beady eyes, looking far too small for the rest of the creature.

Xia had watched enough historical epics with her father to identify the monstrosity—a Daem-an.

Hundreds of questions rushed through Xia's mind. Was this a nightmare? How did a Daem-an get so far west? What was the stranger doing following this thing? Had Bulwark been breached?

All questions died as that stub of a head snapped towards Xia.

With another soul-chilling screech, the thing started to charge. Its movements were ungainly, limping on the shorter hind leg, barely supported by wing tips acting like over-sized crutches. It struggled to build momentum, its mass too large for those daft legs. The absurdity somehow made it all the more terrifying.

'We need to go,' pleaded Eddan. He tugged at her arm in desperation. He was right. They needed to move. Get high. The thing didn't look like it could climb.

Why wasn't she moving?

She stared in shock as the Daem-an tore across the field. Her weapon dangled from limp hands. Legs rooted in the soft soil. Even as Rikk jumped down, snarling as it put itself between her and the monster, Xia could not move a muscle. She felt like a cornered fifil, frozen before a predator, staring helplessly at the approach of death.

The roar of an engine drowned out the creature's unsteady claw-falls. The air shook, debris sent flying as a hoverjet cleared the treetops and slewed to a rest just off the ground, blocking Xia from the Daem-an.

Xia squinted against the dirt blown into her eyes by the jets of the silver-plated craft. The air filled with the thick odour of ozone and aviation fuel.

The Daem-an screeched at the ten-meter-long hoverjet. It clearly realised it was outfaced, and took off at a gallop towards the far tree line, flattening stalks beneath its wing-arms.

The hoverjet's flat landing legs extended to meet the grass. The engines wound down as the back of the fuselage opened. Another stranger burst out, at least as tall as the Daem-an had been. Xia had no time to make out any features before the figure disappeared behind the craft, towards the bloody mess marking the centre of the clearing.

By the time the figure strode back around the polished silver frame, Xia had managed to move, if only to drop to a crouch. The blood seemed to drain from her head, and she was forced to cling to her rifle for support.

As her terror subsided, embarrassment and annoyance took its place. Xia was a warden, meant to maintain the forest, keep the balance—trivial in these days of plentiful food, transcontinental travel and high-powered rifles. She had long dreamed of some way to justify her role. An ogre from the south. A pack of tretts from the west. Some challenge to overcome. Anything to show that she was worthy of succeeding her father, that the wardens were still relevant. And here she had been handed a Daem-an—a legend, a myth to make her mark on the world. She would be the only warden to have killed a Daem-an in almost five hundred years. And what had she done?

Stood there. Helpless.

It was a wonder she hadn't pissed herself. She was weak. A coward. A fool. An amateur. Everything she despised.

Her self-recrimination would have to wait. The tall stranger came to a stop a few paces away, clad in a dark Kevlar suit. The woman before her was musclebound, her grey skin completely hairless. Xia recognised her race from history class, but the Ash-ans were extinct. Her questions were forestalled as she met the woman's stern eyes—completely black, no iris, no white.

'You're a Deathless,' Xia breathed.

The Deathless grunted. 'Are you injured?'

Coming to a stand, Xia shook her head. 'No. I'm fine. There was someone in the field...'

'Cattin, my scout,' the Deathless replied, her stony voice strained for a moment. 'Dead.'

Eddan staggered forward. 'Was... was that...'

'A Daem-an?' the Deathless finished. 'Yes.'

'How did it get into Vandar Forest?' Xia asked. Bulwark had kept the Daem-ans bottled up for centuries.

The Deathless glanced towards the far tree-line. There was no sign of the beast. 'That's what I'm here to find out.'

'Then why aren't you following it?' Xia scratched Rikk behind the ears, trying to settle the beast, which was still standing before her in a protective stance. Daft, loyal creature.

'My scout has just been killed.' The Deathless's words were void of emotion. 'I cannot track.'

'So you're just going to let it go?'

The Deathless nodded. 'Until I can find a new scout. What were you children doing out here?'

'I'm not a child,' Xia said defiantly. Those black eyes stared, impassive. 'I'm a warden. Eddan here is my brother. I was training him when we found the Daem-an's trail.'

'A warden?' The Deathless cocked her head to the side. 'So you know how to track a creature through this forest?'

'Of course.'

'Excellent. I have need of a new scout. Track the beast for me.'

'What?' Xia scoffed.

A frown crossed the Deathless's face. 'I have need of a new scout. Track the beast for me,' she repeated, slower.

'No, I heard you. In why in the Avatar's name would I do that?'

Black eyes blinked. 'You do not have to do it in the name of any Avatar. You just need to do it.'

Xia shook her head. This was like talking to a computer. 'It was just a figure of speech. Why would I come with you to track a Daem-an?'

'To stop the Daem-an,' the Deathless replied as if the answer was obvious. As if she was proposing a stroll through a the trees. Not suicide.

'I'm a warden, not a Deathless, not from Bulwark. Killing Daem-ans is your job.'

'I do not need you to kill the beast. I need you to find it. *I* will kill it.'

Xia barked a laugh. 'No, I understood you. You're insane. I'm not going anywhere near that thing.'

'You're a warden—sworn to protect the forest.'

'Not from Daem-ans.'

'But the Daem-an will kill again if it's not stopped.'

'That's why we have you Deathless.' At Xia's raised voice, Rikk bristled, softly growling at the grey-skinned stranger. 'Why we have Bulwark. Vandar pays its tithe. It's your job to defend us. There must be a hundred scouts at Bulwark.'

The Deathless glanced east. 'Bulwark is six days round trip in the hoverjet. In that time, more will die.'

Xia raised her chin. She would not be dragged into doing the Bulwark's job. 'Then you best get going.'

Painful seconds passed as the ashen face regarded Xia, unmoving. Finally, the Deathless grunted. 'You disappoint me. Once the wardens were noble. I see even your order has forgotten this world's true threat. I hope you have the luxury to continue to live in ignorance.'

Spinning on a heel, the Deathless strode back into the waiting hoverjet. The rear hatch closed after her, and the engines began their high-pitched whine. Xia shielded her face against the debris blown outwards as the vessel pushed itself from the ground, the winged oval craft smoothly rising from the clearing. With a roar of its jets, the vessel accelerated, disappearing beyond the tree line.

'Holy shet,' Eddan breathed as the roar subsided.

'Don't swear,' Xia said, distracted.

'A Daem-an. A Deathless. Dad's not going to believe it.'

Xia groaned at the thought of explaining all this to her parents. Their dear Eddan put in such danger. Xia would get chores for a month for choosing to follow those tracks.

'Come on,' she said, weary. 'We best get back. Stay high up the trees, in case that thing's loitering nearby.'

Eddan needed no more encouragement and began to scrabble up the side of a nearby pine. Xia turned, looking over the forest. She had made the right choice refusing the Deathless. Fighting Daem-ans was for the Bulwark. She had a duty to the forest, sure. But not against monstrosities from the underworld. The Deathless would find the Daem-an without her help. This would pass as some minor note for the local news, nothing more.

Yet throughout the journey home, she felt hateful eyes watching, waiting.

Chapter 2

The pine canopy hid the sunset. After hours of jumping between trees, Xia and Eddan reached Ethelan Village, home. The steady glow of electric lights twinkled between the upper branches. Ethelan, like most Elf settlements, was built amongst the treetops, traditionally to be safe from forest predators, these days mostly to allow rooftops to peak above the pine needles and bask in the sun and reflections from the planet overhead.

The buildings were formed from the trees themselves. Elf lifeSingers manipulated the living wood, melding trunks and branches to form walls, floors and ceilings. Homes stood at bulges in the upper trunks, bristling with an outer layer of pine needles. Schools, offices, workhouses and shops occupied the cooler lower levels, bark-covered growths mid-way up the trunks. Branches intertwined to form paths slung between the buildings and ladders draped through the village.

Plastic-coated cables intruded on the natural aesthetic, standing out from the greenery. Those cables wound their way down to the powerhouse dug among the tree roots, where the village's family of Gobl-ans took shifts chargeSinging to generate electricity for the city. All for a fee, of course. The Greenok family were the richest people in Ethelan.

Xia clambered down a trunk as she reached the outskirts of the village. With a grav-belt, it was far quicker to leap between trees than navigate the web of walkways.

Below her, the last offices were turning off their lights for the night, tired workers clambering their way home. Most were Elf-an, whose clawed hands scaled the rough bark with ease. A few other 'an were dotted around. Krendik and Eccol, the workhouse's Greml-ans. Yadeen, the Hum schoolmaster. Even a Drak policeman, Kriss. Ethelan was the sort of village where everyone knew everyone else. Small. Quaint. Dull.

Smells of cooking drifted in the evening breeze. In the equatorial climate, there was no need for glass windows, and so the organic houses had simple openings, allowing air to flow freely through. A hundred cooking meals overpowered the mild forest scents. Roasting fowl, rich soups and frying bread made Xia's stomach growl. It had been a long day.

Digging her claws into the coarse bark of a familiar tree, Xia scrambled up the side. The wood would wear over time, but lifeSigners would constantly check the trees, healing damage and making sure all residents had sure handholds. The branch ladders were mostly there for the non-Elf-an, whose clawless fingers struggled to find purchase on the rough wood.

Holding onto the trunk with one hand, Xia shoved aside the trapdoor entrance to their home and pulled herself up. She reached down to give Eddan a hand— her brother looked exhausted after the day's excitement, and the last thing she needed was for him to fall so close to home. Difficult as always, Rikk climbed through a nearby window, chirping as he sprawled over a bear-fur rug.

'We're home,' Xia called, reverently propping up her rifle against a wall.

Their mother's head popped around the corner. 'Great timing. Dinner's just finished.'

Hungry, Xia hurried through the kitchen-dining room, helping their mother ladle a steaming pot of soup into four ceramic bowls. Father already sat at the table, looking like an older, wiser version of Eddan. Same short hair. Same sharp jaw.

'No luck in the hunt today?' their mother asked as they all took their seats. 'I thought you were planning on finding a deer this morning.'

'It's a long story…' Xia began, unsure how to explain everything that had happened without alarming her parents.

'We saw a Daem-an!' Eddan exclaimed before Xia thought of the right words.

Both their parents gave bemused expressions. 'What?'

'A Daem-an,' Eddan repeated. 'Tall and black. Had wings and talons. Don't think it could fly. It killed this deer, ripped it in two.'

Mother and Father's expressions turned to stone, eyes locked on Xia.

'It's true.' Xia stirred her soup, apprehension growing. 'We were following some unusual tracks and… yes. A Daem-an. A real, living, Daem-an, like in some history show.'

'We were saved by a Deathless.' Words poured from Eddan's mouth, the kid oblivious to the growing dread on their parent's faces. He excitedly described the tracks, the deer, the scout, the Daem-an, the Deathless. Xia occasionally interrupted to correct his embellishments. Not that any were needed. The truth was already unbelievable.

After Eddan had described the hoverjet's departure —sound effects and all—a heavy silence hung over the room. The cooling soup had been forgotten. Xia's parents too shocked to eat, Eddan too busy to get much more than a mouthful between breathless descriptions, Xia feeling sick at the thought of her parents response.

'You tracked a Daem-an?' Father asked at last.

'Well, yes,' Xia admitted. 'But I didn't know what it was at the time.'

Father stood, pale face turning maroon. 'You tracked a Daem-an *with your little brother?*'

'I didn't know what we were following.' Xia held his gaze, indignant.

'Dragon-shet.' Her father's hands balled into fists, braced against the table. 'You're not some amateur— you hunt as well as I do. You knew those tracks weren't normal.'

'I didn't know they were from a Daem-an.'

'Then what?'

'A ogre, maybe.'

Father turned his back on her, stalking towards a window. 'So you thought you were bringing Eddan to a ogre? That's hardly an improvement.'

'So I was meant to just let an ogre run loose in the forest? Whatever happened to "wardens protect the forest against any threat"?'

'Not at the cost of your brother's life.'

'So Eddan's more important than all of Vandar Forest?'

Xia's mother tried to calm the situation. 'That's not

what your father meant, and you know it.'

'No,' Xia snarled. 'He just meant that it would be
my duty to hunt down a rogue ogre, to risk *my* life to
protect the forest. But not if it means putting Eddan in
harm's way.'

Father slammed a fist against a living-wood
kitchen counter. 'Eddan is ten. He's a child.'

'Then he shouldn't be hunting.'

'You started hunting when you were ten.' Father
turned, exasperated.

'And you and Mother would never have let an ogre
loose to keep me from harm's way.' Xia glared at her
father, daring the denial. Daring him to claim that
Eddan wasn't the favourite.

'Out,' he hissed. 'Take your meal to your room. I'll
speak to you in the morning, when you're not
throwing a tantrum.'

'Fine.' Xia snatched her bowl and stood, spilling
some of the thick soup over the wooden floor. She
stormed towards the staircase, grabbing her rifle on the
way. The stairs creaked as she flung herself up past the
first landing, which lead to her parent's room, and to
the top floor.

At the end of the fur-floored hallway, she spared a
glance right, into her brother's room. Toys littered the
floor, his room a state as always. At his age, she'd
been scolded when she left anything out. Posters lined
the walls. Characters from that Hum show he loved. A
kid's show.

Shaking her head, Xia pushed open the door
opposite Eddan's and entered her room. Here,
everything was in its place. Clothes neatly folded in
her pine dresser. Books stacked on shelves. Towel

drying on the electric radiator. Her parents would accept nothing less.

Xia dumped the bowl of soup onto her writing desk, the lukewarm broth dribbling onto the worn cedar surface, and turned to her rifle closet. She followed a familiar ritual, unloading the rifle, stripping it, cleaning every part, then reassembling.

As she worked, she calmed. Shouting at her father like that would do her no good, but she was just so sick of their unhidden favouritism. When she had been Eddan's age, there was no way her parents would have backed away from their duty for her sake. No, they'd likely have knowingly brought her directly to a Daeman. Probably got her to shoot the thing. But not precious Eddan. They hadn't even given him a rifle yet, so fearful that he might come to harm.

With a sigh, she pressed the weapon into the rifle rack, metal bars slamming shut to hold it into place. A green LED bloomed to life, confirming that the weapon was secure. A dimly glowing pad waited for her palm-print to unlock.

Tired, she sat at her desk. The soup was cold. She forced down the bland, green mush, quieting the growls from her stomach. She had planned on catching up on her reading tonight, but found she could not concentrate on the novel's words, entire pages forgotten as soon as she finished them. After half an hour, she gave up and started preparing for bed. Surely tomorrow would be better.

Xia woke to the smell of sulphur. Faint. She sighed and looked out the open window into the night-shrouded forest. Street lights flickered between branches, the electric glow illuminating the village's walkways and ladders. Through the canopy she could see the gas giant, Watcher, reflecting blue and red light down on the forest. All was still—the only ones still awake at this hour would be the Gobl-an on night duty. The smell was probably just a trick of her mind, an echo of the day's stress.

Feeling her way through the dark, she walked by Eddan's closed door and into their shared bathroom. The fur floor gave way to ceramic tiles—the Hum style was becoming ever more popular in Vandar. The brass taps reflected the weak light as she turned them, splashing cold water onto her face. It was enough to wake her, but not rid her nostrils of the sulphurous stench. She turned to the shower, wondering if the Daem-an's foulness had buried itself in her hair.

Then came the screams.

Distant, distorted, but Xia's Elf ears could still hear the guttural yell of a Gobl-an. Then another. More. A snap resounded from the forest floor and the village was plunged into darkness. Without the street lights, only planetlight and a few stars gave illumination, most of it obscured by the upper branches. Even to Elf eyes, making out anything was a struggle.

Rikk's warning screech echoed through the house, quickly joined by a dozen other vulfiks across the village. Elf voices joined the chorus, the community waking up to the disturbance.

Downstairs, Xia's parent's door slammed open. She peered down the staircase to see her parents—still in nightgowns—gripping rifles.

'Stay there,' Father ordered.

Xia shook her head as Eddan emerged from his

room, bleary eyed. 'But…'

'No.' Father's tone was final. 'Stay here. Protect your brother. Rikk, come.'

The vulfik bounded up the stairs to pause by Xia's parents. He whined, turning a questioning gaze towards her. For whatever strange reason, Rikk had long ago decided that Xia was his master, and always waited for her commands. Part of her wanted to argue, to use Rikk's loyalty to force her parents to let her come, to see what was happening on the forest floor, but she had already earned enough of her father's ire.

She nodded to Rikk. 'Go. Obey Father.'

Father gave Xia a nod of thanks and took off down the staircase, Rikk in tow.

'Stay safe.' Mother gave a calming smile before leaping down the stairs, rifle in hand.

A door opened and shut, leaving the house in an unsettling silence. Raised voices drifted through the various open windows, concerned villagers speaking over one another. Father's voice cut through them, authoritative. Technically, the police or the mayor should take command, but few could resist Father's orders. As the village's most senior warden, all trusted him to know how to deal with the dangers of the forest.

Xia started to creep down the staircase, but heard a creak on the wooden floor behind her. She turned to see Eddan following close behind.

'Go back to your room,' she commanded.

'But I want to help.'

'Help by staying out of sight.'

'But what's going on?'

'Probably just a bear. Stay in your room.'

With a childish sigh, Eddan relented, slinking back up the stairs. Xia shook her head and hurried to the lowest floor. Peering out the window, she could see the villagers clambering down the trees, their way lit by a handful of battery-powered headlamps, the unnatural white glow cutting into the pitch-black forest.

Xia stuck her head out the window, watching the lights disappear beneath the lower pine branches, knowing her parents would be leading the others.

Probably a bear, she told herself, but her fear kept growing. Some disturbance in the Gobl-an's home, after all that had happened? It could be a coincidence. It would not be the first time a bear had disturbed the powerhouse, drawn by the static energy and noise of chargeSinging. Perhaps a creature disturbed by the passing Daem-an, seeking new shelter and finding the cavernous home on the forest floor. Perhaps.

The house trembled. The vibration was weak, barely perceptible, but enough to send a chill down Xia's spine. A second thud followed, then a third. There were a hundred explanations—inexperienced climbers jumping between trees, forest creatures running from the commotion, some late-night worker slamming into office doors in the dark. No line of reasoning settled Xia's stomach.

The sulphur stench increased. She could no longer pretend it to be a figment of her imagination. The smell was overpowering, nauseating. The exact scent she had faced earlier that day.

Trembling, Xia leaned out further, hands gripping the living wood sill. In the patchy planetlight, she could see movement below. Not the steady climb of a group of 'an, not the elegant movements of a vulfik, not the agile darts of birds. The movement was lurching, uncoordinated. Something large dragged its way up the trunk. In the poor light lumbered an unmistakable silhouette. Asymmetric legs dug into the bark, flanked by two massive wings, talons at their tips slamming into the tree. A stubby, sinuous head writhed in the middle of it all.

The Daem-an.

Xia stumbled back, heart pounding. Had the monster followed her? Had she been tracked like a deer, bringing this terror to her home? She suppressed the questions. All that mattered was that the creature was here, and she and her brother were on their own.

She backed to the stairs, crouching in the darkness, listening to the approaching thud of bone into bark. The creature's misshapen eyes must give it poor eyesight. Perhaps it would be unable to make her out, wander elsewhere. She just had to be still, be silent.

The thuds shook the house, knocking free dust from forgotten recesses of the entwined wood ceiling. The falling debris caught beams of planetlight, silver spears stretching from windows to floor.

A shadow darkened the room. That black silhouette hauled itself up to the window. A stubby head peered through the opening, black orbs of eyes searching the room.

Those eyes met hers.

The Daem-an let out a piercing shriek that echoed through the village. Xia leapt up the first few steps, then slipped. Her bare knee slammed into the living wood, pain blooming through her leg.

Ineffectually, wingtips slammed into the wooden

walls. Xia looked as the creature struggled. The walls were thick, too thick for it to break through. It was far too large to fit through the window, yet too weak to dig through the walls. Even if the thing could operate doors, it was surely too large to fit through one designed for an Elf-an. With the racket it was causing, Father and the others must be alerted by now. They would be on their way back. She was safe.

That strange head twisted away, replaced by a wingtip, the vicious spine probing into the house. Even wedged up to its shoulder, the wing only reached half way to the staircase. Xia grinned at the monster's pathetic attempts at murder.

A wet crack filled the room. Then another. The sick sounds of dislocating joints, tearing tendons, ripping skin. The creature forced itself through the window, dangling limbs oozing through the opening. Bones relocated. Flesh moved or tore. Haltingly, the Daem-an forced itself into the living room.

Grin long gone, Xia fled. She ignored her knee's protests as she took the stairs two at a time. Bypassing her parent's floor, she dashed to the top. Her brother's door was still closed. Good. Let the Daem-an focus on her.

She ran into her room, flinging open her rifle closet as the racket continued downstairs. She slammed her hand against the rifle rack's release pad. It flashed red, not recognising her palms. Too much sweat.

A crash echoed from the stairway—the beast was inside.

She wiped her hands on the synthetic fibres of her sleeping shorts. This time, the panel accepted her print, glowing green. The steel catches released, freeing her weapon. She seized it, feeling the rifle's familiar weight.

More sickening slurps from downstairs. The Daem-an was forcing its dislocated joints back into their sockets. It would be here soon.

Hands shaking, she shouldered the rifle and opened the ammunition drawer, grabbing a magazine and box of rounds. The box's cardboard top stuck. She forced it, tearing the box, spilling rounds over the floor.

Thuds crashed up the stairs. No time for the magazine, she grabbed the first round she found, cramming it into the rifle's chamber.

With a screech that rattled her bones, the Daem-an slammed into her doorway, that ridiculous head opening up towards her, twisted teeth catching the light.

Safety off. No time to aim. Just fire. The sound of the shot was deafening in the confined space, the recoil of the unsteadied weapon almost knocking her from her feet, but the round hit home. A dark spray erupted behind the creature, the air filling with the smell of blood and something foul.

The Daem-an reared up, slamming its head into the ceiling, its shriek distorted, whistling—she had hit its throat. Screaming, it staggered down the stairs. She had not killed it, but clearly the beast knew terror. She heard it force its way back out the downstairs window, wet coughs echoing through the house, then silence.

She was safe.

Standing, Xia grinned. Chasing off a Daem-an, saving the village—she would be the talk of the town, the entire forest. She looked back towards her bedroom door, taking a breath to let Eddan know that he could come out from hiding. If he looked up to her before, now he would worship the ground she walked on.

Her grin faded. Eddan's door was open. Planetlight streamed through his window, outlining objects. His bed. His dresser. Discarded toys.

A body.

'Elf-az, please no…' Xia dropped her rifle and sprinted to Eddan's room, but came to a crashing halt at the doorway. She stared in open-mouth horror at the scene. Eddan lay behind the open doorway, darkness pooling around his head. There, caught by the pale light, was her brother's face, and on his forehead, the hole from a single bullet.

Chapter 3

Xia's cry of terror echoed through the night-shrouded village. The rifle slipped from her limp hands and thudded onto the fur carpet. Xia staggered to her brother, shaking as she collapsed by his side. The scent of fresh blood cut through the Daem-an's lingering stench. Gunshot wound. She'd been trained for this. All wardens knew first aid.

What was first? Stop the bleeding? No, wait, check for breath. She bent over, cheek hovering above Eddan's mouth, straining to see any faint movement of his chest, to feel any sign of life.

Nothing.

No point checking for a pulse. If he wasn't breathing, his heart would soon fail. No matter. She could handle this, just had to keep his blood moving until a lifeSinger arrived. Rescue breaths weren't used anymore. Chest compressions would keep air flowing and blood pumping.

Xia found the centre of Eddan's chest—all too easy on his frail frame. She could feel every bone under his smooth night shirt. Locking her arms, she pushed hard. Better too strong than too weak. A broken rib could be healed. A blood-starved brain could not.

In the pale planetlight, she could see a glint at Eddan's forehead. With each push, blood lazily boiled from the bullet wound. No use trying to keep his blood flowing only for it to ooze from his body. She had to stem the bleeding.

Desperately searching the room, she found a discarded towel. She seized the rough cotton material —not a perfect bandage, but it would have to suffice. Binding it tightly around his head, she tied a firm knot. Sloppy work, but she had no time for perfection.

Settling back over her brother, Xia continued rhythmically pushing his chest. What was taking the others so long? Surely they had heard the Daem-an's racket or her scream. At the very least, they must have heard the gunshot. Xia prayed to Elf-az, hoping against hope that the villagers would have the sense to come help her before setting off to hunt the wounded monster. Father might be willing to put the forest ahead of Xia, but surely he would come back for Eddan.

She considered shouting again, urging the lifeSingers to hurry, but she was using all her energy trying to keep Eddan's blood flowing. Chest compressions were exhausting, and her breath was already coming out in ragged bursts.

Sweat bled into her eyes, but she ignored the sting. Darkness blossomed over the ad-hoc bandage, the wound soaking through the cotton. With each push the darkened patch grew. By keeping his blood flowing, she was pushing it out his small body. But what choice did she have?

Downstairs, the trapdoor crashed open.

'Eddan? Xia?' Father's voice called.

'Here,' Xia croaked, not pausing for a moment. Under her hands, something grated with each push. A broken rib?

Harsh electric light illuminated the room—a torch

scanned the scene, then settled over her and Eddan.

'LifeSigner, here,' Mother shrieked, voice barely recognisable. 'Now.'

More figures flooded the room. Mud-caked boots hammered dirt into the fur carpet. Hands tugged at Xia. She resisted, but wiry arms wrapped around her, dragging her back. Xia recognised her mother's rose perfume as she was pulled into a desperate embrace.

LifeSigner Fennel knelt over Eddan's form, the lilting healing Song already on the Elf-an's lips. The holy tune faltered as Fennel's hands touched Eddan's skin. With mournful eyes, the lifeSigner turned to Xia's mother, shaking his head.

'His soul is already with Elf-az,' he whispered. 'He's dead.'

The morning sun crept through the kitchen window, rays shifting as they worked their way past the forest canopy. Shadows played with points of light as branches rocked in the breeze, casting patterns across the living wood walls, the scratched dining table and Xia's bloody hands.

Dazed, she rubbed at the blood—long dried. It flaked away easy enough, but left dark stains in the grooves of her skin. The last of her brother, refusing to leave.

Xia's mother placed a steaming cup on the table and took the neighbouring seat. Sap tea with a little lemon—the drink they had always been given when feeling unwell. Xia doubted it would help today.

Still, she leaned over, letting the sweet vapour waft over her face. Even wrapped in a fur blanket, Xia was cold—shock, lifeSigner Fennel had said, a problem of the mind, and would need a Hum mindSinger to treat. Ethelan had none, and the nearest city was an hour's flight away. Xia would just have to recover with time.

Fennel stood in the doorway, speaking quietly with Father and Kriss. The Drak police officer grimly nodded, taking occasional notes on his digital pad. Ordinarily, Xia would be able to hear a hushed conversation so close. Today, even her ears seemed blanketed in a fog.

With a hissing sigh, Kriss beckoned to the others and led them into the kitchen. Father leaned back against the brushed metal of the stove, arms folded, eyes fixed on the floor. Fennel hovered uncertainly to one side, while Kriss took a seat opposite Xia. Like all Drak-an, he was tall—a good seven foot—and even sitting he loomed over Xia. His jet-black scales scattered the morning light, making his snouted head seem all the more impressive. Stern silver eyes regarded her for a moment, then a forked tongue lashed out of his mouth to wet his lizard lips, revealing rows of serrated teeth. The race of male Drak-ans may have been far smaller than their female Dragon counterparts, but they were still imposing, especially Kriss in his pressed black police uniform.

'Xia.' His voice hissed, adding to the chilling look in those small eyes. 'If you feel ready, I need to take a statement. What happened here?'

Xia opened her mouth a few times, trying to find the words. A supportive hand fell on her shoulder, and Xia turned to see her mother leaning close. There was strength in her almond eyes. Xia took that strength and pushed out the words.

'A Daem-an broke into the house. Attacked us.'

Kriss's scaled brow furrowed. 'Are you certain it was a Daem-an?'

Xia nodded. She still saw its deformed body every time she closed her eyes. Its sulphur stench lingered over the house, tainting every breath. 'It was the same one I saw in the forest.'

Kriss made a note in his pad, the graphite stylus scratching over the glass surface. He did not seem surprised—Father must have told him of her encounter. 'I know this is hard. But how did your brother die?'

Xia blinked away tears. 'I tried to hide, but the Daem-an saw me. It forced its way through the window. I ran upstairs but… it was too fast. It attacked us.'

The forked tongue lapped over Kriss's jagged teeth. 'Xia… Eddan was killed by a bullet to the head.'

Eddan's still form flashed in Xia's mind, the glint of planetlight on blood, the stunned expression on his young face. 'I tried to stop it. Got my rifle. I hit it, in the neck I think. Wounded it. I… the bullet must have gone through.'

Kriss cast a curious glance at Fennel.

The lifeSigner nodded. 'The wound was shallow. Too shallow for a hunting rifle at that distance. It must have lost most of its energy passing through something else. I'll find more when I do the autopsy, but it would make sense if the round went through a large creature first.'

'That would match with the blackened blood stains in the hallway.' Kriss tapped idly at his pad, focused on Fennel. 'And the Gobl-ans? Do you think a Daem-an could have caused those injuries?'

'Possibly.' Fennel shrugged irritably. 'I can do some research, but most accounts of Daem wounds from Bulwark are outdated. Most lifeSigners a hundred years ago had a habit of... embellishing their reports. These days, a lot is classified. Have to apply for a permit to three separate departments to get a single medical file from them. You know Bulwark and their bureaucracy.'

Xia frowned. 'What do you mean, the Gobl-ans? Did something happen to the Greenok family?'

The others glanced around uncertainly, clearly none wanting to answer her question. Eventually, her mother spoke, words full of sympathy. 'Xia, the Greenoks were killed last night. Something attacked the powerhouse.'

'The Daem-an.' Xia closed her eyes. How much did that monster have to take?

Kriss let out a hissing sigh, then turned to Xia's father. 'I think it's clear that this was an unfortunate series of events. There's no intent here. Xia fired at the attacker. The bullet ricocheted into Eddan. There was no crime. Just a tragedy.'

Father stood motionless, eyes still downcast.

'With your permission,' Fennel said to Father. 'I'll autopsy the body. If the results confirm Xia's story, then I can then make arrangements to prepare the body for the funeral.'

Father just nodded absently, a tear rolling down his cheek.

Kriss stood. 'My condolences. This was a dark night for Ethelan.'

In the awkward silence that followed, Kriss and

Fennel left the room. Footsteps hurried up the stairs.
Minutes later, they slowly descended. Through the
doorway, Xia caught a glimpse of the two men moving
a hover-stretcher down the stairs, carrying a black
body bag. The form inside seemed desperately small.

The silence continued after the door had shut, the
investigators making their way through the village to
file reports, take measurements, examine the body.
Eddan's body.

Xia looked up. Father was staring at her. He still
leaned against the stove, shoulders hunched, arms
crossed. His expression was cold, accusing.

'What?' she asked sullenly.

'You fired the bullet that killed your brother.' His
words were quiet, void of emotion, but they cut into
her, sending a chill down her spine.

'You blame me for what happened to Eddan?' she
asked, startled.

'You fired the bullet that killed your brother.'

'I was trying to stop the Daem-an,' she objected.

'And killed Eddan,' he snarled.

Xia stared, opened mouth.

'Grotan,' Xia's mother said to Father, placating,
'now's not the time.'

'No.' He pushed off the counter to pace the room,
arms still held close, hands balled into white-knuckled
fists. 'It's not the time. It's too damn late. Eddan's
dead.'

Fresh tears blurred Xia's sight. 'And you blame
me.'

'Who else?'

'The Daem-an!'

'The Daem-an wasn't holding the rifle. The Daem-

39

an didn't pull that trigger.'

Xia came to her feet, knocking the wooden stool to clatter across the kitchen floor. 'What should I have done? Let that thing kill us both?'

Father paused, arms wide in exasperation. 'Hide. Run. Call for help. Anything but fire a rifle inside this house. What's the first thing we told you, before you even held a gun? Never let off a round inside the house, never inside the village. Never fire when someone is downrange. We've trained you for years. I thought you knew better. Yet somehow you still fired towards your brother's room. You. Killed. Eddan.'

Mother was on her feet. 'Grotan, that's enough. You heard Officer Kriss—this was an unavoidable accident.'

Father punched the wall, knocking a watercolour landscape from its hook, the glass frame cracking on the living wood floor. His face was contorted in rage, veins bulging, an angry red reaching the tips of his pointed ears. 'An accident, maybe, but unavoidable? I think not. Someone a little more concerned about her brother and a little less concerned about the glory of killing a Daem-an would have found a way through this.'

Fury overcame Xia's fear at her father's mood. She stalked across the room to glare into his eyes. 'You certainly seem to have all the answers, so I have just one question—where were you?'

'What? Father scoffed.

'You heard me. You clearly know how to handle a Daem-an in the house, so where were you?'

'You know where I was, on the forest floor.'

'Exactly. You weren't here.'

'How dare you…'

'No, how dare *you*? You're blaming me, but you weren't even here. You didn't see that thing, hear its shriek, stare down its gaping maw. You left us alone. Yes, I pulled that trigger, but I did it to save us.'

'No, you pulled the trigger so you could boast about how you killed a Daem-an.'

His words stung. How could her own father be saying this? Xia had always been closer to her mother, but this? This was something new. She wanted to explain it away, say his grief was getting the better of him, but she knew this went deeper. This wasn't just anguish. His rage was real. He hated her.

Again, Mother tried to intervene. 'Grotan, please. If Xia had not taken that shot, then we'd be burying two children. She's right. There was no way for this to end bloodlessly. We should thank Elf-az that Xia is safe.'

Silence descended, her father pausing. In his expression, Xia saw the answer, the reason for his fury.

'That's just it. He's not thankful I'm alive.' The realisation cut deep.

'Don't be stupid,' he muttered, but there was no conviction in the words.

She smirked to hide the betrayal slicing into her heart. 'If Eddan had fired the rifle and I'd been killed, you would not be acting this way. You'd be comforting him.'

'Eddan wouldn't be stupid enough to fire a weapon in the house.'

'That's not a denial.' Xia felt faint, but forced herself to glare at her father, defiant. The redness had faded from his face, angry veins settling, replaced by guilt. At least he could feel that. 'Look me in the eye. Look me in the eye and tell me that you wouldn't prefer for Eddan to be the one standing here… for me to be in that body bag.'

His eyes met hers, tear-stained and red. She could see his torment, his guilt and rage. Xia longed to be wrong. She prayed to hear him swear to her that he was glad she was alive, that he saw this was the Daem-an's fault, not hers, that he loved her.

Silence.

Xia felt sick. She shouldered her father aside and stormed up the stairs, chased by her mother's pleading. Two steps a time, she reached the top floor, pausing outside Eddan's door. The grey fur of the carpet was stained dark red with her brother's blood. This was the single worst moment of her life, and her father held her to blame.

Her eyes flicked to the door frame. The Daem-an's black blood congealed around the contoured wood, still reeking of sulphur. No, she had not killed her brother. The Daem-an had. And it was still out there.

Without thinking, she turned to her room and began to pack. Portable stove. Sleeping bag. Dried rations. Filtration kit. She packed light—a warden could survive off the land indefinitely and these were merely to make things easier, allow her to focus on her task.

Rikk padded through from Eddan's room, whining as she pulled on her grav-belt. He was intelligent enough to know what had happened to Eddan. Even if Xia was Rikk's master, Eddan was a member of his pack, and would be mourned by the vulfik. She gave him a reassuring scratch behind the ear until he settled on her bed.

Turning to the weapon rack, Xia looked up at her rifle. Kriss and his deputies had placed it back in its locker after finishing their investigation. She paused at the sight. Was her father right? Had there been another way? Had she sealed her brother's fate last night by taking her weapon?

No. The Daem-an was at fault. If it had not invaded their village, Eddan would be alive. The Daem-an had shattered her family, and Xia would make it pay.

She shoved several boxes of rounds into her pack, then placed her hand on the panel, releasing her weapon. It had wounded the monster. Now it was time to finish the job.

Her mother stood in the doorway. 'Your father just needs time—he didn't mean any of that.' She paused, taking in Xia's pack, belt and shouldered rifle. 'Where are you going?'

'I'm going to kill that thing.'

'You can't be serious.'

'That monster can't get away with this. It's still out there.'

'And you're going to take it down on your own?'

'I'm a warden. Who better? It's not like you and father are going to do anything about it.'

Mother shook her head. 'Xia. We have to bury your brother. You need to be here.'

'No, Mother, I need to be out there. I'm going to stop that thing.'

'No.' Her mother raised her voice, blocking the door. 'I've lost one child. I *won't* lose you.'

Sensing the tension, Rikk leapt from the bed, stalking alongside Xia, growling.

Xia glared at her mother. 'And how are you going to stop me?'

'I'll lock you in here if I have to. You're *not* leaving.'

At the shout, Rikk barked, snapping his needle-like teeth. Mother flinched away, backing out the doorway. Xia smirked and pushed past. 'I thought so.'

She stormed down the stairs, trailed by Rikk. Her father stood passively in the living room, not uttering a word as she flung open the door. Without glancing back, she activated her grav-belt and leapt from the house and into the forest. Eddan's true killer was out there, wounded and fleeing. Xia would track down the beast. Perhaps Eddan could rest easy once the Daeman was dead.

Chapter 4

The Daem-an's trail of destruction stretched before Xia. The beast's tracks were easy to spot—shattered underbrush, furrowed soil, and always the clinging stench of sulphur. The ugly scar extended in a straight line through the otherwise pristine forest, veering only to avoid the thickest of trunks. Even these had not survive unscathed, bark ripped aside, sap bleeding from deep gouges.

The Daem-an destroyed everything it touched.

Xia flung herself from tree to tree, well above the devastated forest floor—any closer and the monster's reek turned her stomach. Up here, the forest retained its natural scent. Morning dew. Pine bark. Spring saplings. The familiar perfection of Vandar.

Rikk followed one tree behind, having followed from Ethelan. Xia was grateful for the company. He, at least, did not blame her for what happened to Eddan. If anything, the vulfik seemed to know that the Daem-an was to blame, as eager to follow the trail of destruction as Xia. She had been tempted to send him ahead, get some idea of how far the Daem-an's lead extended, but had decided to keep him close. Safe. She had no misconceptions about Rikk's chances against that monster. A pack of vulfiks might be able to take down a Daem-an if they were lucky. One hound would barely distract the beast. Rikk was loyal, but he wasn't smart, and Xia wouldn't be surprised if he recklessly charged the Daem-an.

As she landed on the next tree, she disturbed a juvenile akken. The orange monkey scampered up the trunk, screeching a warning to its troop hiding among the thick greenery. The canopy came alive, a dozen warning calls screamed at Xia and Rikk. The cacophony startled the nearby birds, who took flight, bright forms flitting between trunks. The wildlife was on edge after the Daem-an's passing, the intruder leaving its mark on the creatures as much as it did on the forest floor.

The morning wore on. Xia's pain of betrayal had only hardened. Father may have been in grief, but so was Xia. What kind of parent turns on their child like that? She needed comfort, not condemnation. Support, not rage. Love, not hatred. The Daem-an had taken Xia's brother. Father had taken her family.

Xia paused, claws gripping the rough bark of a tree as she checked her surroundings. The Daem-an's razor-straight path continued. At first, she had assumed it had just been fleeing Ethelan, trying to put as much distance as possible between it and its attacker. Now, she was not so sure. She recognised this route—had travelled this way a hundred times. The Daem-an was headed for the village of Ekkin.

Taking a deep breath, Xia kicked off the tree, pushing herself even faster. Ekkin was Ethelan's neighbour, a quiet little farming village, famed for its apples. In many ways it matched Ethelan—its small community dominated by Elf-ans, single schoolhouse, handful of workshops and offices. One important difference separated the two: Ekkin had no wardens. Xia and her family would patrol this way regularly, maintaining the deer population, chasing off bears,

keeping baboon packs at bay. The arrangement had
served well for decades. Now, though, Ekkin faced a
far greater threat than bands of predators.

And there was no one to stand in their defence.

Xia had to reach the village before the Daem-an.

She increased her pace, kicking off trees with all
her strength. There was an art to keeping pace through
the trunks. Leap between trees too close together, and
you wasted time scrambling around the trunk to kick
off again. Jump towards a tree too far away, and you
would lose momentum before you reached your target.
Worse, you could slow to a stop, stuck in the void
between pines, forced to turn off the grav-belt to sink
to the forest floor and walk to the nearest trunk.

Xia had always considered herself fast, easily
matching her mother when tree-leaping. Now, she felt
painfully slow. Every moment circumscribing a trunk
dragged. Every leap seemed too weak, leaving her to
drift lazily between the bark towers.

Ahead, the forest opened. The Daem-an's tracks
ploughed into a mass of thorns two hundred meters
across—Drek Mire. The formation was ancient, a
twisted mound of jagged branches, stubborn ferns and
the broken stumps of pines long dead.

When her parents had first brought her here as a
child, Xia had thought the Mire an ugly blight upon
the forest, an dark tumour in the heart of Vandar's
green beauty. She quickly learned the truth. The Mire
was a sanctuary of life. Sparrows, chinnets, rabbits,
fifils—all the forest's small creatures flocked here to
raise their young, safe from predators. It had become
her favourite stop on the route to Ekkin, especially in
the spring, when you could spot newborns in the

thicket, learning to walk, screaming for food, gnawing at brambles.

Now, however, it was just an obstacle. The Mire had choked the life of the larger pines as it had formed, and no saplings could survive in its dark heart. This gave Xia no trunks to jump between. She would have to go around, wasting valuable minutes. She considered proceeding on foot, sprinting after the Daem-an down the shadowed tunnel it had forged through the thicket. Looking into that dark passage penetrating the bracken quickly forced her to abandon this plan—she had no intention of being caught in close quarters with that monster.

No, she had to go around. Gritting her teeth, she kicked off, making her way around the trees that surrounded the Mire. Her hands ached from hitting the wood with such force, the course bark grating on her calloused fingers and chipping her claws. Despite the pain, she pushed herself ever faster. The Daem-an would not get a chance to destroy another family.

Reaching the far side of the Mire, she scanned the forest floor to try to rediscover the Daem-an's tracks. Nothing. A deer trail rounded the bracken, winding towards Selis River. Bent leaves indicating where a badger had forced its way through the undergrowth. A line of droppings from a host of chinnets. The normal signs of life of the forest. None of the crude destruction left by the Daem-an.

Confused, Xia continued to make her way around the edge of the thicket. Perhaps the Daem-an had changed course, disoriented by the close-packed branches. Excitement briefly flared as she saw a line of destruction up ahead, only to realise this was where the creature hand entered the Mire—she had circumnavigated the mound of thorns.

Xia circled the Mire once more, cautious this time, checking the ground for any sign of disturbance in case the Daem-an had changed its movement pattern. Only the undisturbed serenity of the undergrowth surrounded the thicket, broken by that ugly scar the Daem-an had left in its wake. The beast was somewhere inside, lying in wait.

It could be dead, but Xia had doubts. The forest here was too quiet. No tweets, no cries, no chirps. The local wildlife was terrified of something.

More likely the creature was recovering in the relative safety of the thicket. Perhaps it knew it was being followed. Maybe its wound had made it nervous of moving during the day. Either way, this posed a problem for Xia, and an opportunity.

She had caught up to the Daem-an, and now had time to think, to plan. Going into the thicket seemed madness. The only route for her was the tunnel the Daem-an had carved out for itself. Did Daem-an's sleep? Even if they did, one noise could wake the beast, then she would be trapped, caught in a tunnel with a monster from the underworld.

Starting a fire in the dry brush would be easy, burn the beast alive, but the thought made her stomach turn. Destroying the Mire would decimate the wildlife in this area—too many species relied on the bracken's protection. Besides, forest fires could easily flare out of control. LifeSingers hardened trees near settlements against fire, but this far out the bark could easily burn. She was a warden, a protector of the forest, not its destroyer.

She could wait for it to emerge, but the Mire was too large to cover its entire perimeter, even with her rifle's scope. The Daem-an could slip through, make its way to the next village while she waited here, impotent.

No. She knew where the creature headed. She knew where she needed to lay her ambush. At Ekkin, the Daem-an would meet its end.

Xia stared into the night-shrouded forest. Planetlight filtered through the trees, dappling the underbrush. A handful of fireflies drifted between trunks, dancing to the music of a dozen crickets. Insects loved the early hours of the night, still warm but free of daytime predators. The forest would come alive for hours, settling only as the cooling temperature bled the energy from these bugs.

Plants took advantage of the boom of life, flowers opening as dusk fell. Not like the brightly coloured petals of meadows and hillsides, the plants of the underbrush relied on smell to attract pollinating insects. The result was the forest floor becoming blanketed in thick scents, some sweet, some floral, some putrid—each attracting a different form of evening creature.

Xia rested on the stump of a long-dead branch, part way up a giant oak, back braced against the smooth bark. Rikk hung to one side, claws hooked into cracks on the tree's surface. Vulfiks could happily sleep like that, clinging to a trunk, but Rikk was alert, furred ears twitching, snout sniffing the breeze. Like Xia, he knew the danger that approached.

Ekkin village hid amongst the leaves far above,

visible as a series of neon bulbs shining through the branches. Below, a dull white light filtered through the windows of the Ekkin's powerhouse. The Gobl mound was traditional, covered in turf broken by curtain-covered windows. Inside would be far more modern—the finest luxuries, high end decor, and the latest gadgets. After centuries being shunned and distrusted, the electronic revolution had allowed Gobl-ans to use their chargeSigning to become integral to modern society, filling their bank accounts.

Nearly a thousand people lived in Ekkin, all blissfully unaware of the advancing Daem-an. Xia had decided against alerting the population. Ekkin had no warden, and a mob of civilians would just get in the way. All warning them would achieve was a panic. Some would flee—scattering into the forest, easy pickings for the Daem-an. No, Xia would keep them all in one place, where she could protect them. Besides, here she had the advantage. She knew where the Daem-an would strike. Here, she set her trap.

The crickets' incessant chirps abruptly died. Fireflies scattered, green rumps dimming. Rikk uttered a low growl, reorienting his body to point sidewards, staring into the distance.

The Daem-an was here.

As before, the smell reached Xia long before the creature. The heavy scent of the forest floor was smothered by the Daem-an's sulphur stench. Next came the rumbling, the shattering bushes under the monster's unsteady gait. There, in the distance, something moved.

Xia raised her rifle, activating the low-light enhancement. Peering through the scope, the world appeared in grey monochrome, but she was easily able to pick out the features of the forest—twisted branches, ancient trunks, and the monstrosity bearing down on the village.

The Daem-an's form was familiar now, but looked no more natural. Its mismatched legs struggled to propel it forward, leathery wings slamming into the ground to keep balance. Its ludicrously small head writhed ahead of the beast, needle-teeth snapping in hunger.

It bore the scars of their last meeting. An ugly, black rend marred its sinuous neck. A black trail from the wound oozed down its body, flaked in leaves stuck into the dried blood. It had been a good hit, just left of centre. The opening was small, the bullet entering neatly, but as the monster loped through the trees, Xia could see the exit wound—a mass of broken flesh and shattered bone the size of her fist. For any normal animal, the wound would have proved lethal. The Daem-an barely seemed weakened.

Xia took a deep breath. The monster was clearly resilient. But it was not immortal. Daem-ans died in droves at Bulwark, had done so for centuries. If some peasant with a spear four hundred years ago could kill such a thing, surely Xia could manage it with one of the most advanced weapons of the modern age.

She took her time. A single shot to the brain was all she required. Nothing could survive that, not even a Daem-an. It charged towards the powerhouse, repeating its previous attack pattern. Two hundred meters. Hundred-fifty. She let it approach, let its ugly face grow in her scope. If she startled it too soon, it would surely flee. Her first shot had to find its mark.

Following its motion, she exhaled. It's jarring movement, the poor visibility even with the scope, the small target. The shot would be hard—impossible for nearly anyone else. Not for Xia.

Her finger closed over the cold metal of the trigger. Squeezed. A shot rang out into the night, recoil burying the wooden stock into her shoulder. Blood sprayed into the night air, black globules caught by planetlight.

The Daem-an collapsed.

Twigs and turf were launched ahead of the collapsing mass. Birds and small mammals scattered in terror. Warning yelps from a dozen vulfiks echoed from the houses above.

Xia peered through her scope. Her shot had flown true, entering through one of the beast's bulbous eyes. As it exited, the bullet had taken off most of the creature's head. Its open skull was exposed to the night air, a bone bowl steadily filling with tar-like blood.

Dead.

Lowering her weapon, Xia grinned. It was over. She had taken down the beast. She had saved the forest. She had avenged Eddan.

A figure emerged from the powerhouse. A Gobl-an's hunched silhouette peered out, leathery skin and wide ears illuminated by an electric lantern. Xia was about to call out, tell the villager to relax, when a wet cough drew her attention.

The Daem-an twitched, then gave another choking cough, blood spurting from its wound. One after the other, those leather wings rose and slammed their talons into the damp soil. It wrenched itself up. Skull shattered, gore pouring freely, the beast impossibly stood.

A shriek of fury filled the air, accompanied by another gout of blood. That fury seemed to find focus on the Gobl-an, the Daem-an's one remaining eye flicking towards the powerhouse.

It charged.

The Gobl-an froze with fear. Xia was quicker to act. Again, she took aim. Perhaps some of the creature's brain had survived. Maybe it was small, like the coastal lizards—creatures ten meters long with brains the size of a greennut. She moved her crosshairs over the centre of the beast's head and fired. Then again. The rounds smashed into the remains of the head, ripping off chunks. The remaining eye disappeared in a bloom of black. Teeth flew into the undergrowth. A shattered jaw hung freely. The Daem-an stumbled.

But continued its charge.

Its momentum carried it into the Gobl-an. A wing-talon lashed out, taking figure in the chest. The woman's cry echoed into the night, cut short as the Daem-an lifted its victim into the air, holding her aloft like a prize as it smashed over the powerhouse. Beams gave way, the turf roof collapsing, flashes of light and wafts of smoke rising, accompanied by muffled screams. The Daem-an waded through the wreckage and into the forest.

Xia hesitated. She couldn't fire again. The Gobl-an might still survive. No matter how much she wanted to kill the beast, she was not going to risk firing another round into an innocent.

The Daem-an seemed barely slowed. Its head was

a mess, spraying ichor, howling wetly, but the creature's loping stride continued. Xia could only watch in horror as it dragged the screaming Gobl-an into the night. Somehow, the monster still endured. Xia had failed.

And the Daem-an had claimed another victim.

Chapter 5

Exhaustion numbed Xia's mind. Her legs ached with each kick. Her head spun as she flew from trunk to trunk. Her hands burned on every landing. Xia's entire body cried to stop, but she couldn't, not until she had found the wounded Gobl-an. The Daem-an had already spilled too much blood.

Following the beast proved easy, even in her cracking mental state. Its tracks were more pronounced, a wide swathe smashed through the underbrush. Trees in its path were dented, bark shattered, black blood splattered where the Daem-an had run headfirst into the trunk. The wake of devastation indicated a blinded creature, running in panic.

But how was the monster still alive?

Xia had all but cleaved off the beast's head. Blinded it. Shattered its skull. Ripped open its jaw. Nothing should be drawing breath after such trauma, let alone sprinting through the trees. Xia had never felt so outmatched.

Rikk panted after her. A soft whine sounded each time he landed, occasionally followed by a hungry whimper. Vulfiks might be fast creatures, but they were not built for endurance. They stalked through trees, ambushed their prey, taking them down in short bursts. Even Rikk, used to their long patrols through the forest, was reaching his limit.

Desperately, Xia wanted to give in, come to a stop.

Take the weight off her aching limbs. Break open a ration pack to state her grumbling stomach. Close her drying eyes.

But surrender was not an option. Not with the Gobl-an still at the mercy of the mindless beast. Logic told Xia that the Gobl-an was long dead. That she had bled out. That the cries had ceased long before the Daem-an had escaped from earshot. In her sleep-deprived state, it was easy enough to ignore logic. She needed the Gobl-an to survive. Needed this journey to be vindicated. Needed some good to come out of this catastrophe.

Grimly, she pushed on, focusing on each individual action. Kick off tree. Drift between foliage. Stretch out hands. Take the next trunk's impact. Grip the course bark. Shuffle around. Identify next tree. Kick. Float. Grip. Shuffle. Kick.

A new scent broke the repetition. From the forest floor, almost drowned by the Daem-an's sulphurous reek, drifted a tinge of fresh blood.

Nausea replacing her hunger, Xia lowered the power on her grav-belt and descended. The sight awaiting her shocked her to the core.

In a pool on planetlight lay the Gobl-an—or what little remained. The body had been crudely ripped apart. Blood, bone and chunks of meat were scattered across the crushed bushes and driven into the soil. A hand here. A leathery ear there. Most chunks Xia could not identify. More chilling than what was left, was all that was missing. Most of the carcass was gone. It looked as if the dead woman had been eaten, but how did a headless creature eat?

Xia shook her head. She knew that Daem-ans were

strange, but even the most embellished film seemed to undersell these beasts. By Elf-az, how did Bulwark take down these things in their hundreds?

Sighing, she stalked from the remains, but travelled only a few hundred meters before she halted. The possibility of saving the villager had been all that pushed her on. With that gone, Xia's exhaustion returned anew.

Hands shaking, she clambered up the side of a tree. The Daem-an could climb, but somehow being high made her feel safe. She was Elf-an—the trees were her home, her protection, her sanctuary. Even against the minions of the underworld.

She pulled herself onto a thick branch of a particularly tall pine, feeling her muscles relax as she leaned back into the trunk's jagged bark. Worried her exhaustion would cause her to fall, even with her Elf sense of balance, Xia searched through her pack for a rope and tied herself to the branch.

Rikk struggled up the tree to settle on the branch before her, slumping onto the wood, panting. Hands like lead, Xia pulled out a ration pack from her satchel and peeled the foil wrapper. She handed a chunk of the dry block to Rikk before taking a bite. The baked bar was dry, flavourless. Grey and disappointing and dull, it matched her mood.

From such a tall tree, Xia could see over the forest. The canopy shone silver with planetlight, contrasting against the jet black of the night sky. Stars smeared the darkness, vibrant here so far from the unnatural light of settlements. High in the sky as always, Watcher looked on. At night, the multicoloured storms of the gas giant were clear, winding their way over the surface. In Vandar, Watcher was always directly overhead, day or night. Its constant vigil had been maintained since before the arrival of the Avatars, through the dragon wars, the Daem-an's invasion, the Northern Extinction, the Gobl attack on Vandar.

And it still looked on.

With a Daem-an loose for the first time in centuries, Xia wondered if she was witnessing the start of something epic. Would people a hundred years from now speak of these events? Would this pass as some minor note for history class, or was she at the start of an apocalypse?

Her mind was too weary for such heavy questions. Meal finished, Xia leaned back into the trunk, her pleated hair her only pillow, her thin warden shirt and shorts her only blanket. Nonetheless, sleep came fast.

Xia's back ached. She woke at dawn, the sun shining bright on her face as it found a path through the canopy. The breathable synthetic material of her shirt and shorts made exercise in the heat of Vandar comfortable, but served as poor padding.

Rikk chirped curiously, roused by her motion. Lifting his head from crossed paws, he gave a gaping yawn, sharp teeth catching the morning light.

Smirking at the way the vulfik started to sniff around her pack, Xia pulled out another ration bar, breaking off a chunk for her companion. Hurriedly, she chewed the rest, forcing the stale, dry material down her throat. How she longed for her mother's cooking. Even a simple fried fifil sounded wonderful, but she had no time to cook, let alone hunt. The murderous invader was still out there, lurking below the green needles of the forest. It was up to her to end its rampage.

Washing down the bar with a mouthful of water, Xia repacked her supplies, releasing the rope that secured her to the tree.

Graceful, she swung on the branch, slipping below the canopy. Beneath her, the Daem-an's tracks were still clear, its unwavering path of destruction cutting through the ferns. Activating her grav-belt, Xia kicked off the great pine, restarting her pursuit.

Her muscles ached, but it was a distant pain, ignorable. Still, she knew it would turn to agony by the day's end. How long could she maintain the chase? How long could a headless Daem-an run?

She tried to push the kernels of despair from her mind, focusing on the immediate task of travelling through the trees. Staying high up the trunks, she avoided the worst of the sulphur-stench. It meant working her way around the occasional low-lying branch, but that was a small price to pay for the clean, fresh forest air.

Above her, Rikk kept pace. The agile creature had no issues navigating the dense canopy, happily running along branches, using them as a ladder to recover the distance he lost when making his membrane-assisted leaps between pines. If he was weary from yesterday's marathon, he hid it well.

In the brief moments between trunks Xia took in her surroundings, but could spot no familiar landmarks. She was far east of Ekkin, farther than she had ever patrolled before. Sure, she had travelled greater distances—on vacations to the coast, or shopping trips to the cities—but that had always been by air travel. Surrounding her were alien trees, unfamiliar rivers, an unknown landscape.

Xia slowed as the forest brightened. A few trees further ahead, she came to an opening in the forest—a field, hundreds of meters across, without a single tree for purchase.

The Daem-an's trail crossed the field, a path where the green stalks of grass and occasional wildflower had been stamped flat.

Looking to the side, Xia's heart sank. This opening was long and thin, stretching for kilometres in either direction. Going around would take hours. She had to cross on foot.

Powering down her grav-belt, Xia descended, scents of wildflowers reaching her a moment before the Daem-an's stench.

Even having seen the tracks stretching into the distance, knowing that the beast seemed less active in the day, Xia's heart pounded as her thin climbing shoes met the soil. She stared dubiously at the field. Other than the Daem-an's tracks, the grass was undisturbed, reaching well above her head. A Hum-an might have been able to look over the blades, but to her it was an impenetrable green barrier.

The beast had cut a clear thoroughfare, a perfectly straight road of flattened grass and packed soil. The idea of following in its footsteps terrified Xia, but not as much as the thought of wading through the tall grass, blind to anything more than a arm's reach away.

Hesitant, she stalked along the Daem-an's tracks, packed grass firm under her light rubber soles. The creature's great wings had served as a bulldozer, crushing every last blade and flower.

Rikk followed close behind, hunched low to practically slither along the ground. Vulfiks hated being on the open ground, and the fact that he followed without protest was a testament to the daft animal's loyalty.

Xia's nose wrinkled. The sulphur hung heavy here, imprinted in the ruin left behind by the Daem-an. Scattered black globs littered the path—the beast was still bleeding. Good. Still, it was not frail. The deep, miss-sized claw prints were identical to those she'd seen days earlier. The talons had left clear rents to mark its passage. The beast was evidently strong enough to maintain its unnatural lope.

Xia stilled. Vibrations trembled through her shoes, a rumble filling the air. She crouched, unshouldering her rifle. The approaching sound was muffled by the grass, echoing from the surrounding trees. Even to her Elf ears it was hard to pinpoint its direction, but it grew louder. Closer. Xia frowned. It almost sounded like it came from above.

Overhead a shadow loomed.

Unthinking, Xia rolled to her side, weapon raised as a massive form cleared the tree line. Not the broken leather of the Daem-an, the surface of the object was polished silver.

A hoverjet.

The heat of its exhaust washed over her, filled with the sharp stinging odour of burnt propellant. The jet slewed over the field, coming around to hover a few meters in front of Xia. The smooth underside opened, landing skids descending just as the aircraft vanished behind the wall of grass.

Rikk growling alongside, Xia crept forward,

weapon ready. A pneumatic hiss filled the air, then heavy footsteps on metal. The footsteps softened as they met soil, headed towards Xia.

Rifle raised, she waited, listening to the footsteps, the swish of tall grass being pushed aside. A grey face peered over the greenery. Then a familiar, stony expression focused on Xia. Black orbs of eyes gazed at her, void of emotion.

The Deathless.

Almost twice her height, the woman towered over Xia. Black Kevlar armour added to her bulk, complementing her grey skin. Over her shoulder poked a worn hilt. Xia could only guess at the size of weapon such a large warrior could carry.

'Ah,' the giant woman grumbled, 'the warden. That explains much.'

Hurriedly, Xia lowered her rifle, though the Deathless had not seemed bothered by the barrel pointed at her chest. 'What are you doing here?'

'Following the Daem-an, of course.' The Deathless sniffed. 'A better question is what are *you* doing here? Last we spoke, you were adamant about staying away from the creature. You do know these are its tracks?'

'Of course.'

'Then why?'

Xia faltered, caught off guard by the question. Why *was* she here, chasing a Daem-an that she could barely wound, that could rip her apart without a second thought? To protect the forest? To avenge Eddan? To escape Father's blame? All her reasons seemed weak, foolish. 'It killed my brother.'

'Ah.' The Deathless nodded, as if her answer explained everything. 'So you were the shooter at

Ethelan and Ekkin?'

'Yes. Wait, how did you know about them?'

The woman looked towards the horizon. 'We've been following distress calls. We arrive too late to help —the Daem-an cuts power before it attacks. Takes villages time to send out signals. We arrive only to investigate the aftermath. Heard reports of a warden at Ethelan, of shots fired at Ekkin, found bullet holes. You wounded the Daem-an. Impressive.'

Xia snorted. 'Didn't do much good. It's still alive.'

'Daem-an's are resilient.'

'Even to a shot to the brain?'

Black eyes turned towards her, the woman's icy voice patronising. 'What makes you think you hit its brain?'

'I saw the wound. I took off most of its head.'

A smirk. The strongest emotion the Deathless had shown so far. 'Assuming a Daem-an's brain is in its head is like assuming it will rain tomorrow. These things are for the 'az to decide.'

Xia shook her head, not following. 'But the weather's to do with climate, heat, humidity, not 'az or their Avatars.'

The Deathless sniffed. 'My point is that Daem-ans are not like any other 'an, or any animal for that matter. I've seen a Daem-an with a stomach on the outside. Seem one with eyes on its fists. Ones with jaws on their tails. They are a broken reflection of our world, a jumble of parts trying to find a whole.'

'Can they even be killed?'

The Deathless nodded. 'Of course. But not by you, I suspect. Daem-an's die the same as any creature. Destroy the brain. Pierce the heart. Drain the blood.

Any will do. But doing so is no easy task for the untrained.'

'I'm a warden,' Xia reminded the woman. 'I've been trained for the last eight years to hunt.'

Another smirk. 'And I've practised killing Daem-ans for the past four centuries.'

Xia dropped to a crouch, caught by the realisation of her stupidity. She was a warden. Taught to manage the wilds. Hunt deer and fifils. Occasionally shoot a rogue bear disturbing the balance. Why had she thought that she could take on a Daem-an? 'You want me to go home,' she said, glum. 'Stay out of your way.'

'No. I want your help.'

'What?'

'I asked before for your aid, I still need it.'

Xia shook her head. 'You just said I was too "untrained" to kill a Daem-an.'

The Deathless nodded. 'Yes, but I do not need you to kill the monster. You track well. Are determined. Smart. You will find it again. Engage it again. On your own, you may eventually kill the Daem-an, but in that time more villages will be attacked. More will die.'

Xia shivered at the matter-of-fact delivery. 'So what good am I?'

'I can fight, but not track. On my own, I may eventually find the Daem-an, but in that time more villages will be attacked…'

'More will die,' Xia finished.

'Exactly. I asked for your help tracking the beast at our first meeting. Perhaps now you can see how vital this is. You take me to the Daem-an, and I will strike the killing blow. We need each other.'

Xia's turn to smirk. 'You can't find the Daem-an with that?' She waved in the direction of the landed hoverjet.

The Deathless turned her grey face towards the craft, clearly able to see over the tall grass. 'It cannot fly through the trees, and cameras can't see through the canopy.'

'Don't you have…' Xia struggled for the words learned in the schoolhouse, 'infrared?'

The grey head cocked to the side. 'Also blocked by the canopy. I thought one from your generation would be more familiar with modern technology.'

Xia grimaced. Eddan was more into all that tech stuff. Xia knew how to maintain her rifle and equipment, but little else. For her, nature had always held greater fascination. 'So you came to Vandar with no way to search a forest?'

'No,' the Deathless replied flatly. 'I came with a scout. You saw her die.'

'Oh.' Xia looked at her hands, palms still raw from the previous day. 'Sorry.'

'I have no need for sympathy. I have need of a scout. Will you help me? Will you stop this Daem-an?'

The answer seemed clear. This is what she should have done days ago. Perhaps if she had accepted the Deathless's first offer, Eddan would be alive. Swallowing, she knew it was too late for that now, but perhaps she could make things right. End this before it became any worse. Before the body count increased.

'I'll help.' She stood, meeting the Deathless's black eyes. 'I'll find that Daem-an for you. Just promise me that you will kill it.'

A smile twitched on the ashen face. 'That I can promise.'

Xia held out a hand. 'It's a deal. My name's Xia, by the way.'

The Deathless bent down to grasp her hand in a bone-crushing grip, shaking once. 'I'm Drekene the Deathless. Welcome to my crew, Xia the Warden. Come, meet the others.'

Drekene turned, the towering woman stomping back through the grass. With only a moment's hesitation, Xia followed. This may not have been as satisfying as bringing the creature down on her own, but that mattered little. All Xia cared about was making the Daem-an pay for its crime.

Avenging Eddan.

Chapter 6

Xia followed Drekene's trail towards the hoverjet. The Ash-an had disappeared into the tall grass, but the thud of her heavy boots on soil was clear, as was the path of bent leaves and snapped stems. Not as destructive as the Daem-an's passing, but still trivial to track.

Within a few steps, Xia came to the hoverjet. The silver craft was daunting, easily as large as a house. Its thick wings had crushed the field beneath, polished landing skids dug into the soft soil. The mirrored surface reflected the fresh green underneath and the crystal-clear blue above.

Beckoning as she reached the rear of the aircraft, Drekene strode up the boarding ramp. Xia followed, the grated metal of the ramp a sharp change from the field—hard, unnatural.

Xia stepped into surprisingly cramped cabin. The air felt heavy here, a mix of recycled air, aviation fuel and body odour. Most of the hoverjet's interior was taken up with bulky engines, fuel cells, charge stores, cargo racks and a dozen other devices that Xia could not recognise, all coated in the same polished metal. This left little more than a narrow corridor stretching the length of the craft.

Into alcoves were built four bunks—three of which contained scattered possessions. Tools, lengths of wires and dog-eared manuals littered a lower one. Above lay a bunk with various books crammed around the mattress, a poster from some aircraft movie stuck to the ceiling. Opposite this, Drekene's bunk was easy to identify, the alcove modified and lengthened to accommodate the woman's size. Below that, the last bunk was pristinely made with fine cotton sheets, but sat empty, abandoned.

'Cadden,' Drekene called down the corridor. 'Come, meet our new scout.'

At the end of the hallway, a few metal steps led to a raised cockpit, light streaming through the wide windows. A head poked around the doorway, a Human—from near the equator judging by his dark skin and mop of curly black hair. He looked Xia's age, maybe a little older. As he hurried down the stairs, Xia was caught by his piercing green eyes—must have some Southerner blood in him.

He grinned, extending a hand down to Xia. 'Great to have you onboard. I'm Cadden, Drekene's pilot.'

She shook the hand. 'I'm Xia.'

Drekene nodded. 'She's the shooter from the last two villages.'

'Really?' Cadden raised an eyebrow. 'Well, anyone who can wound a Daem-an is good in my book. Did Bulwark send you?'

'Er, no. I'm local.'

'She's volunteered to help,' Drekene explained.

'Ah.' Cadden grinned again. 'Welcome to Bulwark.'

'I'm not joining Bulwark,' Xia clarified, defensive. 'Just helping the Deathless track this Daem-an. I've signed no papers. Bulwark can't draft citizens of Vandar.' She had no intention of letting these people drag her into a lifetime of service. She wanted the

Daem-an dead, not the rest of her life wasted in some ancient fortress.

Cadden's disappointed look was quickly covered by a smile. 'No problem. Never come across temporary volunteer before is all. Still, it's good to have you on the crew. Finding this thing with no scout has been a nightmare.'

Drekene grunted. 'Where's Ket?'

Cadden opened his mouth to reply but was cut off by a hissing snarl echoing through the wall.

'Where the shet d'you think? I'm where I always am, fixing your damn jet.'

'Ket,' Drekene replied patiently, 'I have a new scout.'

'Yeah, yeah,' echoed the reply, 'I heard it all. Gimme a damn second.'

The lights on the ship flickered. As they brightened again, a hum sounded from behind a panel. Seconds later, a grill popped open near the floor, and a Greml-an clambered out. He was tiny, even compared to Xia's small frame, not even two feet tall. His scaled head poked out a grease-stained grey jumpsuit, his pointed ears almost as wide as he was tall. Wiping clawed hands on a rag just as dirty as they were, he gave Xia an appraising look with large, slitted yellow eyes. Whatever he searched for, Xia seemed to lack.

He bared a row of needle-sharp teeth. 'So you're Cattin's replacement.'

Cadden gave a mournful smile. 'Cattin was our last scout.'

'Yeah.' A thin tongue passed over the Greml-an's teeth. 'I hope you don't die quite as fast.'

Drekene frowned. 'This is Ket, my chief engineer.'

'"Chief", my arse,' Ket grumbled. 'You only have one engineer. And it's a full-time job when you treat a trans-continental transport like a damn tourist ferry. I told Bulwark that I needed another hand to keep this thing running, but no, they needed every other metalSigner they got greasing the cannons.'

Xia had no idea how to respond, but was saved as Rikk padded up the ramp, softly whining as he stepped into the cabin's artificial light.

Ket took a step back from Rikk, who stood eye-to-eye with the Greml-an. 'And what the shet do we got here? We letting the wildlife aboard now?'

'Rikk's not wild.' Xia gave the animal a reassuring scratch behind his furred ear. 'He helps me hunt.'

Cadden seemed far more enthused. 'Can I pet him?'

Xia gave a small nod, and the Hum-an knelt to tousle Rikk's forehead. The vulfik hesitated, sniffing the stranger, but seemed to calm as Xia gave no reaction.

'Great.' Ket stuffed his rag under his tool belt. 'But I ain't cleaning up after that thing.'

'He's house trained.' Xia assured the Greml-an.

'Yeah, so's Cadden, but he's still filthy.' Ket's words were void of humour.

'Hey,' Cadden replied, defensive. 'Look at my bed compared to yours and say who's neater.'

Ket sniffed. 'I don't use mine to sleep, so it's fine being a storage closet. You actually lay in that sty.'

Drekene grunted. 'We don't have time for your bickering. Cadden, get Cattin's equipment.'

The young man turned to the polished steel wall, opening a small cupboard with a metallic thud.

Fishing inside, he retrieved a small bag and handed it to Xia. She sorted through—a plastic earpiece and an electronic tablet, both recently cleaned.

'The comms unit and an uplink to the Hawk's computer,' Cadden explained.

'The Hawk?' Xia asked.

He gestured to the corridor enclosing them. 'This hoverjet. The uplink will let us send you what data we can get from above the canopy. Cattin... said she found it useful. The comms unit will let us talk, and track you.'

Xia popped the plastic piece into her ear. Cold. Uncomfortable. Unnatural. The tablet, at least, already had a carabiner and easily hooked onto her shorts. It was heavy, but shouldn't slow her too greatly.

Cadden scooped a bag from the cupboard, which jingled as he held it up. 'Cattin's grav-belt didn't survive, but I see you've got your own.'

'Every Elf-an does. Avatar's sake, everyone in Vandar has at least one.' Xia shrugged. 'So how does this work? I track the Daem-an down there, you follow above the canopy?'

Cadden nodded. 'Pretty much. We'll be sticking close, after what happened to Cattin.'

Xia grimaced. 'And when I find it? You land somewhere and let off Drekene?'

Cadden nodded and opened his mouth, but the Deathless cut him off.

'No. I'll be going down there with you,' she said, firm.

Surprised, Xia replied, 'You know how to tree-leap?'

Drekene shook her head. 'I can learn.'

'No offence,' Xia started, 'but that will take too long.'

'I learn fast.'

'Even so, you'll slow me down. The Daem-an is getting farther with every minute. Teaching you is a waste of time.'

Drekene's hairless brow furrowed. 'I disagree. I may need to learn to track this creature without you.'

'Why?'

The Deathless's unwavering black gaze fixed on Xia. 'In case you are killed.'

Xia swallowed. There was no hyperbole in Drekene's words. Even with a Bulwark team backing Xia, even with all this advanced equipment on hand, even with a Deathless alongside, the Daem-an was a threat. She had seen what it could do. It destroyed a powerhouse simply by stumbling into it. It had ripped the last scout to pieces in a heartbeat. It could dismember her with a casual flick of a taloned wing.

Ket gave a mischievous little giggle. 'Oh, don't look so scared, kid. It's not like Drekene only wants to learn how to jump between trees in case you die. Nah. You could also be maimed. Blinded. Left brain-dead. Shet, dying might be the best outcome for us—you could always come back as a Deathless.'

'Ket,' Drekene barked. 'That's enough.'

The Greml-an rolled his yellow eyes. 'Just trying to help the kid know what she's in for. Anyway, there's another problem with this plan of yours, Drekene.'

'What's that?'

With a sly grin, Ket scuttled up the wall, using vents and door cracks as handholds. A dark green claw lashed out, knocking the bag from Cadden's hand. It clattered the floor, spilling its mangled contents over the grating.

'That.' Ket hopped down, picking up two halves of a circuit from among the debris. 'Is the only grav-belt we got. Even Bulwark don't design parts to withstand being crushed by a Daem-an. So unless you're part vulfik, Drekene, we have a problem.'

Drekene stared at the Greml-an, impassive. 'Well, can you fix it?'

'You kidding?' He stooped to pick up a handful of twisted metal fragments. 'You seen this? The power core is in two. The circuit controller is shattered. The casing is… well all over the floor.'

'Can you fix it?' Drekene repeated.

The grin grew, stretching across the Greml-an's wide face until it almost touched each ear. 'Of course.'

Ket scampered over the floor, collecting the grav-belt debris into the discarded cloth sack, then climbed up the wall, settling himself onto a pile of wires in an equipment closet barely large enough to fit the diminutive engineer.

'Greml-an's like small spaces,' Cadden explained.

'That's racist,' Ket grumbled.

'But true.'

The Greml-an shot a yellow-eyed glare at Cadden, but gave no further objection. Xia couldn't help but smile at the strange pair—not at all what she expected on board a Deathless's ship, but then what *had* she expected? Daem skulls? Ancient texts? An exotic arsenal?

Her trail of thought halted as Ket began to Sing. This was nothing like the hopeful, lilting melody of

Elf lifeSigners. Greml metalSinging was deep, coarse, guttural. The otherworldly notes reverberated through the ship, through Xia's chest. She looked to her skin, expecting to see the tell-tale glow like whenever she had heard lifeSigning in the past. Instead, it was the ship that bloomed to life, a subtle glow, but obvious in the low light of the fluorescent lamps.

Ket's words were nonsense to Xia, a series of grunts, chirps and snarls, held together with a rumbling tune. Still, even her fellow Elf-ans' lifeSinging came out as gibberish to her, though far more melodic. It took years of training just to understand the Songs, and years more to get the melody to do more than annoy your neighbours. Xia had never been interested. Why spend a lifetime studying dry books and listening to professors chant the same lines over and over when you could be outside, leaping through trees, experiencing something real.

However, the Greml-an was clearly more than an amateur. The pieces of metal flew from the bag, twirling and dancing in time with his words, glowing ever brighter. Even the cracked computer chip hovered before the Greml-an, gold wires glowing brightly as they lifted their backing's green plastic.

Xia watched in fascination as the Greml-an worked. Ethelan had a couple of metalSigners, but Xia had never watched them Sing. Eddan did so often, of course, fascinated at how they could make the latest electronics or repair even the most damaged home appliance.

The metal melted and folded together. Shattered fragments met and sealed. Gold circuit lines bled and merged. The work was not fast, taking the better part of an hour as Ket commanded the pieces to move in the obscure language, never halting his constant song.

When he finally fell silent, a grav-belt sprawled over his lap, bearing not so much as a blemish to give away its previous damage.

'There.' Ket turned mischievous eyes to Xia, voice hoarse. 'I've done the easy part. Now you gotta teach an eight-foot tall, four-hundred-year-old Ash-an how to gracefully leap through trees.'

To Xia's surprise, Drekene picked up tree-leaping quickly. There had been no hesitation on the first jump. Normally it took a great deal of persuasion to make a beginner let go of the tree that first time. Every instinct screamed that letting go of a trunk thirty feet from the ground was suicide. Even Xia had been no exception, in tears on her first lesson as her parents tried to coax her to release the bark.

Drekene had required no such urging, throwing herself from the tree as soon as her grav-belt activated. The hulking woman proved unexpectedly agile. She still could not keep up with Xia's experience at rounding trees, the Deathless's fingers too large for most handholds, her lack of claws stopping her making her own. She compensated by her jump distance. Powerful legs combined with that bulk allowed Drekene to jump between distant trees, her momentum carrying her across the gulf.

Xia looked back at where the Deathless followed a few trees behind. 'Just let me know if you get tired.'

Drekene's reply came through Xia's earpiece. 'Deathless do not get tired.'

'You don't need to take breaks?'

'No.'

'Sleep?'

'No.'

Xia shook her head. So much about Deathless in films was inconsistent. She had no idea what was fact, what was embellished, and what was simply invented by the production companies in Lantus. 'Then why do you have a bed?'

'The others sleep. I need somewhere to wait for them. Laying down to read or meditate is more comfortable than doing so in a cramped cockpit.'

Cadden's voice cut in over the headset. 'Hey, my cockpit's perfectly comfortable.'

'It's my cockpit,' Drekene retorted, void of emotion.

'Eh,' Cadden replied, 'my point still stands. I sit in this chair all day and I'm fine.'

A sliver of humour entered Drekene's voice. 'Then perhaps you can sleep there. I'm sure Ket can repurpose your bunk as a storage cupboard.'

'Ha,' came Ket's grating voice. 'Or an exhaust converter. Bet I can get a few more percent on the fuel efficiency with all that room.'

'Okay, okay,' Cadden conceded. 'Everyone can keep their bunks.'

Smiling, Xia continued to follow the Daem-an's tracks. They were strewn across the landscape, obvious as ever. The flow of blood had slowed, and now the black ichor only marred the occasional branch. The swath of destruction was still just as thick, still slamming into trees, shattering low branches, scarring their bark with deep talon-wounds.

It had not deviated all day, a straight line of devastation carved from the Ekkin Village through the forest. Wherever the Daem-an was headed, it was single-minded.

'Huh,' Xia said to herself. She pushed faster to give her a greater lead ahead of Drekene. In a few leaps, she caught up to Rikk, who scouted ahead, easily following the Daem-an's trail. They had kept low to the ground, in case the inexperienced Deathless missed a tree and had to be helped to the forest floor. This meant the Daem-an's sulphur stench was clear to Xia, and must be overpowering for the vulfik.

Once she was far enough ahead of Drekene, Xia pulled herself to a stop. Hanging by her claws from the rough bark of an aged pine with one hand, she pulled the tablet from her belt. It took her some time to work the unfamiliar operating system, but soon had the map program loaded on the glowing screen.

A birds-eye view of the forest appeared before her, composited from a dozen satellite images, updated from data from the Hawk's instruments. Her location appeared as blue dot on the screen, Drekene several tree-lengths back as a black marker. The Hawk hovered overhead. The hoverjet was invisible through the canopy, but Xia had easily tracked the hum of its engines just above the treetops. Its position was indicated by a cartoon outline on the map.

Back from their position stretched a dotted line marking their route. Their paths zigzagged across each other as the need to follow the trunks led them to deviate from the Daem-an's razor-straight route, but pinching the touch screen to zoom out soon revealed the path they traced through Vandar—a direct line from Ekkin village and out to… nothing.

Drekene landed alongside Xia, the tree vibrating as the woman's mass slammed into its side. She may be more agile than Eddan, but her momentum still made its impact. Her bulk was not helped by her gear—the heavy Kevlar was designed for combat, not tree-leaping. She shifted her foothold, rubber-soled boots not giving nearly the grip of Xia's thin climbing shoes.

The Deathless turned her black eyes to Xia. 'Why stop?'

'Just trying to work something out.' Xia pointed to the screen. 'The Daem-an is heading in a straight line, just like it did from Ethelan to Ekkin. I assumed it was going towards another settlement, but…' She traced the line forward through the map.

'But there's no village in this direction,' Drekene finished.

'Exactly. Could it be confused? I did blind it—I think.'

Drekene shook her head. 'I doubt it's lost its way. This path is too straight. Besides, Daem-an's have an excellent sense of direction—helped them overrun the Dwarf holds. If they can negotiate twisting cave systems in pitch darkness, they can navigate the forest without eyes.'

'Then where could it be going?'

The Deathless paused for thought. 'How badly did you wound it?'

Xia shrugged. 'It would have been lethal for anything normal. First shot went through its throat. The others were in its head. Both eyes gone, jaw broken, most of its skull shattered.'

'I think it may be running.'

'To what?'

Drekene gave a cryptic smile. 'Not to anything, from something.'

'Fine, then *from* what?'

'You.' The smile widened, terrifying below those black eyes. 'You frightened it.'

'Those things can get scared?'

Drekene nodded. 'Of course. They hunger, they sleep, they startle. They're more like most 'an than you'd think.'

'Don't seem like any 'an that I know,' Xia scoffed. 'I've seen fifils with more intelligence.'

'I doubt that. They may seem like mindless beasts, but the Daem-an's are anything but. They're smart, vindictive, vengeful. All that separates them from us is a constant hate, a desire to destroy. Normally it rules them, dictating their every action. But they can give in to other urges. Even for these beasts, survival is a strong driver. Besides, if it's too damaged to continue its hunt, it will retreat to mend its wounds. I've seen wounded Daem-ans try to flee the field of Bulwark. Decimated creatures, with bullet wounds the size of fists, missing limbs and opened organs, all trying to drag their way back to the cave from where they emerged.'

Xia nodded slowly. 'So this thing is fleeing. But where would a monster run?'

Those black eyes held Xia's gaze, voice firm. 'Towards where it originated. To where it broke through from the underworld. It's returning to recuperate in the hell from where it came.'

Xia felt determination grow.

'Then we have to kill it before it escapes.'

Chapter 7

From a rope below the Hawk Xia dangled, treetops brushing her climbing shoes. Even with the hoverjet keeping to low speeds, the air roared past her ears. At least this high she was free of the Daem-an's stench, the air beautifully clear with just a hint of pine bark. The sun, however, scorched from the cloudless sky. Used to being protected by the forest canopy, she could already feel her pale skin burn.

Cadden's voice barked in her earpiece, 'Arriving at Position Seven.'

The hoverjet's engines slewed forward to slow the silver craft to a stop. Xia's momentum tugged on the nylon rope, sending her swinging back and forth like a pendulum. Once she came to a rest, she inspected the canopy below, spotting an opening among the thick green needles.

'Three meters east,' she directed. The Hawk smoothly drifted over the opening. Cadden certainly seemed an able pilot, but Xia would still have preferred to be tree-leaping. However Drekene was right—the Hawk moved faster. In the last few hours, they had covered a day's worth of ground.

Tightening her rip on the textured rope, Xia reached down to turn her grav-belt's power dial. 'Belt's active, release the rope.'

With a jolt the rope was slackened, now held loosely between Xia's hovering form the jet above. Xia lowered the setting on her grav-belt and began to descend into the canopy, dragging the rope along.

She passed through the pine needles, the ends of the larger branches tickling her legs. She had picked a sparse point in the forest, but the branches were never far apart in Vandar. The ancient forest left little space for light to creep through, let alone a person.

Ignoring the scratches, she peered below the branches. Running through the forest floor was the same sight she had seen at the last position—a line of shattered underbrush, trampled plants and gouged soil. They had not yet overtaken the Daem-an.

'We're still behind it.' Xia sighed. 'Winch me back.'

With a lurch, the rope pulled upwards. Xia clung tight, closing her eyes against the fronds that batted at her face. They had discovered this to be the easiest way for her to quickly peek under the canopy.

The grav-belt was enough to almost cancel out the world's pull, but could not reverse it. It had been tried, of course, but every test had led to the grav-belt—and whatever unfortunate object it was attached to—accelerating off in a random direction. Half the time they would launch into the sky, never to be found again. The rest of the tests had ended with the grav-belt burying itself into ground. Xia's teacher had tried to explain it once, that nullifying too much of gravity's influence had unexpected effects. Xia had failed that test.

She could use the belt to slow her fall, but had to rely on the old-fashioned technique of being winched on a rope to lift her back from the forest. It was slow, and her skin was growing coated in a hundred tiny grazes, but it was a damn-sight faster than locating a place for the Hawk to land.

Emerging from the branches, Xia lowered the power on her grav-belt—no point wasting the battery when she had a firm grip.

'Clear,' she said once her feet ascended above the tallest pine.

The rope shuddered to a stop and Cadden's sigh came through the earpiece. 'Heading to Position Eight. Hold tight.'

With a wash of kerosene-filled air and ozone, the hoverjet's engines flared, pushing the aircraft forward. Xia tightened her grip, her rope trailing behind and below the airship as it roared over the forest.

Cadden had suggested lowering a camera below the canopy, but Xia did not like the idea of squinting at a small, unsteady image to find what her own eyes could locate in moments. Ket had offered to rig up a harness to attached Xia to the craft's tow rope. She had quickly pointed out that she was more than capable of holding onto a line. Elf-ans had been bracing their weight on their fingers since Elf-az gave them life, and Xia's forearms were well trained.

Drekene had approved of the low-tech plan—not surprising for someone over four hundred years old. The Ash-an had been born in the days when flight was the preserve of dragons, before gunpowder had been invented, let alone electronics. Xia liked nature, but she could not imagine a world without synthetic fibres, grav-belts, deodorant.

Another wave of heat and fuel passed over Xia, the Hawk slowing to a stop again, followed by Cadden's bored voice. 'Arriving at Position Eight.'

Once again, Xia adjusted her grav-belt, gave the

call, and began to descend through yet another opening in the foliage. Branches clawed at her already-grazed body, leaving hashed cuts on her pale skin, beads of blood welling where the cuts met. Perhaps she should have accepted Drekene's offer of a thick flightsuit. It may have been stiflingly warm, but it would have given better protection. For now, she would just have to bear through the pain.

Emerging in the shade of a hundred pines, Xia looked to the ground. No shattered branches. No torn soil. No bloody trails. The underbrush was pristine, green, undisturbed. The Daem-an had not reached this far.

Yet.

The shards of light piercing the forest dimmed to a dull red. Xia shifted on her perch—the stub of a long-dead branch of an ancient oak, the trunk's smooth bark pressing into her back. Cool air blew across her exposed arms and legs, bringing sweet relief to the multitude of grazes that littered her skin.

Drekene stood imperiously on the forest floor, staring into the distance. Her weapon was still tucked into a black sheath strapped to the Deathless's back, only its hilt peaking out—a hilt as long as Xia's forearm. Even with her padded armour and towering frame, the woman looked exposed on the forest floor. When surrounded by great pines, even an Ash-an looked small. Vulnerable.

Bait.

Hopefully the Daem-an would see her as no threat. Xia asserted that the blind creature would not be able to see Drekene, let alone tell whether or not she could defend herself, but the Deathless had insisted that the Daem-an would sense her presence, be drawn to it, eager for blood.

At this point, Xia was willing to believe anything regarding these monsters. It had survived a rifle round to the throat. It endured without a head. She would not blink an eye if the 'az-damned thing started to sing Hum opera or dance a Gobl jig.

Of course, Drekene was not as exposed as she seemed. The pair had used the failing light to construct a trap, an adaptation of a simple design Xia's father had taught her to use if she ever tracked an ogre to its cave. Saplings would act as springs, far larger that any Xia had practised with, but the Deathless had no problem bending stalks as tall as a bear into position. Xia had suggested using something smaller, more predictable, but Drekene insisted that only the most massive of traps could slow a Daem-an. So Xia had carved the largest set of barbs she had ever seen and bound them tight to the springs, preparing the simple tripwire and covering it all in undergrowth. It was a crude trap, but had been used for centuries, hunting everything from fifil to ogres.

Darkness descended. Early insects began to flit between the trees, crickets sounding their incessant tune, fireflies weaving intricate trails through the low branches. The forest filled with the pungent smell of the evening plants, floral odours mixing with the sweet and the foul. After so long following in the beast's reek, the evening scents relaxed Xia. This was how Vandar was meant to be. Clean. Fresh. Tranquil.

As the night wore on, doubts began to gnaw at the edges of Xia's mind. What if the Daem-an had diverted? What if she had extrapolated the route incorrectly? Worse, what if it had reached its destination? Drekene seemed convinced that the creature had burrowed its way through the ground, and was determined to return to that hole. If it had already reached that opening, it would be gone forever, able to recuperate with the rest of its kind. Eddan's death would go unavenged. All of this would have been for nought.

They should have worked their way back towards the trail. Sure, they would have lost the opportunity to set an ambush, would not have the element of surprise as they came crashing through the forest ahead of the beast, but at least they were more likely to reach it before it escaped. For all they knew, the breach in the soil was a few hundred feet ahead.

Xia shifted, stretching aching muscles as she planned her arguments. She had to persuade Drekene to move, to go on the offensive. They could not risk the Daem-an getting away.

Then it struck her.

Sulphur.

Carried on the evening breeze, the smell was unmistakable. Nothing in Vandar came close to the Daem-an's noxious scent.

'It's here,' she whispered.

Drekene's quiet reply came through Xia's earpiece. 'I know. Get ready.'

Xia flicked the power switch on her rifle. Looking down the light-enhanced scope, she saw the forest in sharp monochrome. The black undergrowth became a series of grey branches criss-crossing the forest floor. Looming silhouettes became clear trees, their bark patterns easy to distinguish. The weak green glow of fireflies became vibrant blooms of light that bounced over the landscape.

Silence smothered the forest. As one, every cricket fell silent, the mewling cry of an infant monkey cut out, the hairs of Xia's neck bristled. Instinctively, every living creature knew something *wrong* approached.

Below, Drekene unsheathed her sword. At first, it seemed laughably small, more of a cudgel than a blade suitable for such an imposing warrior. Then the hidden mechanisms kicked into action. The blade extended until it nearly matched Drekene in height. Vicious barbs extended from the side, jutting back towards the hilt, each a slightly different shape. Even the cross-guard sprouted a set of jagged teeth. An Ash rendblade —a favourite of gory horror films the world over, Xia had seen them a hundred times in the cinema, but they had not been used in battle since the Northern Extinction. Or so Xia had been taught.

The familiar loping rumble of the Daem-an filled the air, shattering underbrush and thudding bark. This was covered by a new sound. Music?

Xia looked down, amazed, as the Deathless began to Sing. It sounded like no Song she had heard before —a low drone, every fourth note shouted to create a steady beat. Unfamiliar syllables filled the air, but the sense of power was clear. This was Ash battleSinging, a sound long lost to history.

Time seemed to slow as Xia's heart pounded in time to the notes. The world became a little brighter, every sense a little sharper. The fear of the Daem-an's pending arrival faded, replaced with clarity.

Aiming down her scope, Xia looked into the distance. Through the trees the Daem-an charged. Even in the poor light, she could see the creature clearly. Impossibly, its shattered head had begun to heal. The jaw had reattached—imperfectly. A bulbous tumour grew from where Xia's rounds had broken the skull. There, on the growth's surface, staring from a twist of scar tissue, sat an eye. The orb was misshapen, stunted, but lashed around with all the rage and hunger of the creature's previous eyes.

Desperately, Xia wanted to fire, to smash round after round into that malformed skull, to bring the monster yet more terror. But she kept her trigger finger relaxed. The Daem-an must not be alerted. She had already failed to kill it twice. Now was the time to let Drekene put their plan into action, finish this thing, make it pay for all the bloodshed.

The creature bore down on Drekene, letting loose a choking, rage-filled cry. Fear gripped Xia. What if the trap failed? What if the saplings had been tied down too long to snap shut? What if the tripwire was missed? Even Drekene was dwarfed by that monster. She would be killed.

With a twang, the Daem-an snapped the tripwire.

The trap snapped shut.

Two saplings, released from the tethers holding them down, sprang upright, slamming the serrated spears tied to their tops into either side of the monster. One impacted a wing, shredding the membrane but came free. The other hit hard into one of the Daem-an's thighs. The branch strained against the beast's momentum, groaned, then held, dragging the Daem-an to a abrupt stop. The screaming beast crashed to the ground a few paces ahead of Drekene, a waft of sulphur billowing out from the felled monster.

Drekene attacked in a flash, ducking in and expertly swinging her massive blade, cleaving the talon from one wing. Before the creature could counter with its other wing, Drekene dodged back, leaving the Daem-an to flail piteously, held at bay by barbs still dug into its side.

The saplings they has used were ricketwoods, which grew deep roots before ever extending more than a foot above ground. It was hard enough to pull out with industrial digging equipment—the Daem-an would never manage to uproot the plant. Xia grinned. With the beast pinned, Drekene could just dodge in an out, completely controlling the fight. One cut at a time, she would dismember the creature, until piercing the Daem-an's heart with her horrific blade.

A crack echoed through the forest. The creature strained against its restraint, uttering a unearthly howl. Drekene responded by Singing louder, calming the terror that the howl elicited in Xia's heart. Still the creature struggled, then with a sickeningly damp rip, managed to lunge forward. Xia stared in disbelief.

The beast had ripped off its own leg.

The bloody chunk of meat was still rooted to the trap, but the creature had simply left it behind, staggering forward on its remaining leg and its one uninjured wing.

Drekene's song paused, the Deathless startled by the creature's determination. As the notes faded, Xia felt her focus drop, felt fear begin to take hold. The Ash-an stumbled as she backed away from the advancing monstrosity, turning an ankle and sprawling to the floor, blade escaping her grip.

The Daem-an staggered on, miss-set jaw hungrily snapping at the defenceless prey. Xia was meant to observe, not to fire, to flee at the first sign of disaster, but this was no time to obey instructions. As the creature slammed its remaining wing-talon into the ground, Xia took aim, picking out the bone running through the membranous appendage.

She fired.

Black blood sprayed across the forest. The round shattered the wing's bone, which had been supporting the creature's weight as it struggled forward. The wing snapped and the beast collapsed to the ground.

It was the chance Drekene needed. Without hesitation, she leapt to her feet and snatched the sword from the bracken.

Even as she dived onto the Daem-an, the beast twisted around. Jagged blade met bone. Shredded wings wrapped around Kevlar. Two howls of rage intertwined. In an instant, the two combatants became one ball of violence writhing on the forest floor.

Then all fell still.

Through her scope, Xia stared wordlessly. All she could see was the creature's wing draped over the mass of its body, Drekene somewhere underneath. Neither moved. No screech of pain or rhythmic song reached Xia's ears, just a silence that turned her stomach.

The wing twitched. At first, Xia thought she had imagined it, but then it moved again. The great, black, broken wing unfurled.

Tears filling her eyes, Xia took aim. How many lives must this creature take? How long could it keep fighting? Killing?

The wing thudded to the ground.

Drekene stood in its place. With a wrench, she hauled her rendblade from a gaping wound in the Daem-an's body. Gore and gristle spiralled into the air, black droplets raining across the low bushes and hidden forest creatures.

Face covered in gore, Drekene looked up to Xia. 'Good shot.'

Shakily, Xia stood on her perch. 'Is… it…?'

'Dead?' The Deathless kicked the creature and nodded. 'Yes.'

Needing to see for herself, Xia dropped down the oak, falling a few feet, shoes crunching into the dried leaves below. Cautious, she picked towards the Daem-an. Its stench was thick, suffocating. The creature's skin appeared all the uglier this close, seemingly broken a thousand times, as if the creature had been charred then stretched over and over, tearing and cracking every inch of its hide.

Its bones jutted at odd angles, some shattered, others simply malformed. Blood oozed from its myriad of wounds, but mostly from the hole Drekene's sword had carved—wide enough that Xia could probably climb inside the creature. The blood, however, did not spurt. There was no pulse here, no heartbeat.

The Daem-an was dead.

It was over.

Relief robbed Xia of her remaining strength. She collapsed back, finding a lichen-coated rock to rest upon. They had succeeded. The creature was dead. Xia had expected to feel elation, pride, a sense of justice. The evil was dealt with, Eddan had been avenged. So why did she just feel empty?

'I can't believe it's over,' she whispered.

'It's not over.' Drekene wiped her blade on the creature's broken wing.

Xia shook her head. 'What do you mean? Its dead, right? It can't come back to life. Can it?'

Drekene's blade collapsed into itself, barbs retracting, teeth flattening, point shortening, until it was small enough to be slid back into its sheath. 'Yes, it's dead, and no it cannot come back to life. At least not in this body.'

'Then we're done.'

'Far from it, young Xia the Warden. This beast was fleeing back to the hole from where it came. But Bulwark is not this way.'

'So?'

'So that proves there is a new opening. This creature did not sneak through Bulwark's defences and wander into Vandar. Somewhere near here, it dug its way through from the Dwarf holds.'

Xia shrugged. 'But it's dead. Why does it matter where it came from?'

'Because if hole was large enough for one Daem-an, it is large enough for a thousand more. Bulwark is built on the site of the only known entrance to the Dwarf holds, to the underworld. Each month thousands of creatures push through, time and again, year after year. We hold them back because we know where they emerge, we kill them as they exit. But if a new opening is in Vandar Forest… well, you have seen the destruction one Daem-an can achieve. How will Vandar fare against legions?'

Xia closed her eyes, exhausted. 'We would be overrun.'

Expression grim, Drekene nodded. 'Last time, it took a unified effort from all 'an to force the Daem-an's back. Tens of thousands died. Millions were displaced. We cannot let that happen again. We cannot let a new opening be established. Only one Daem-an has come through so far, so we may have time to find the opening, set up a defence, but we have to hurry. Xia, I know you only came to avenge your brother, and I know that has been accomplished, but I need your help. I need a scout.'

Steeling herself, Xia nodded. Perhaps this was why she felt empty. Their task was only half accomplished. Eddan's murderer was dead, but he was far from avenged, not when the forest was still at risk, not when a thousand more beasts were set to spill over Vandar. Perhaps once the hole was closed, once more Daem-ans were dead, once the threat was over, then Xia would have closure.

'Alright.' She met Drekene's black eyes. 'Let's find us a hole to the underworld.'

Chapter 8

Exhausted and still stinking of the Daem-an's corpse, Xia desperately clung to the rope that hauled her through the forest canopy. In the darkness, she could not see the branches that clawed at her face and arms, so closed her eyes, accepting the fresh cuts.

As she emerged from the top branches, the glow of planetlight bathed her. It must be near midnight—the entire face of the planet glowed save for her world's shadow, a speck at the centre of the intertwining colours. The storms that raged in the endless atmosphere of the gas giant seemed to peaceful, pinks and purples melting into one another, highlighted with bands of red and orange.

The Hawk obscured her view. Overhead, its silver shell appeared speckled in grey as it reflected distorted images of the treetops. The lower engines glowed bright blue, their heat and chemical odour flowing over Xia as she was winched ever higher.

Drekene, visible only as a great black shadow against the planet and ship, held into the rope several meters above Xia. Effortlessly, she reached for a handhold at the Hawk's open rear ramp, swinging herself into the hoverjet. The motion sent the rope swaying, and Xia tightened her grip. Even on the longest of patrols into the forest, she had never struggled to support her weight, but now every buffet of wind, every jolt on the rope, every breath seemed ready to dislodge her, to send her tumbling towards the forest floor. She should have activated her grav-belt for safety, but had not been thinking straight. Now it was too late—if she released one hand, she would surely fall to her death.

Shuddering, the rope came to a stop. Xia peered into the Hawk's central corridor, the ramp hovering barely a foot to her side. Ket clung to one wall, clawed feet curled around a handhold while he dangled from a pair of levers that operated the winch. Drekene loomed in the hallway, stooped as not to hit the hoverjet's ceiling, boots on the ramp while she braced her weight on a handle along the corridor's upper edge.

The half-meter between Xia's feet and the ramp stretched before her. Normally she could leap the gap without a thought, could probably step over it with enough effort, but now the very idea made her shudder. Logic told her that it would be easy to move her legs, swing the rope back and forth until she could simply drop onto the ramp. Logic could not compete with her debilitating fatigue. Xia just clung there, hopeless, weak, useless.

Drekene saved her, the woman's thick arm stretching over the gulf. Her grey hand latched around Xia's shoulder, which looked so frail in the giant's grip. With a lurch, Xia was hauled into the corridor. It took all her strength to stay upright, back braced against the cold metal wall.

How long had it been since she had slept properly? The last few days were a blur of tree-leaping, snatching scant moments of rest between hours of patient waiting. Now, with the Daem-an finally put down, those days of constant work caught up, blurring her vision and making her head swim.

Ket threw a lever and the ramp eased up. As it sealed against the back of the airship, the roar of the engines faded into a distant drone, the fresh air replaced with the stale atmosphere of the Hawk.

Cadden's head poked around the corner from the cockpit, pearly teeth gleaming under the planetlight. 'Well? Is it done?'

Drekene nodded. 'The Daem-an is dead.'

The pilot's cheer echoed down the metal walls. Ket lifted a tiny fist, grinning madly.

'What now?' Cadden asked. 'Do we need to burn the body?'

'No.' Drekene stomped down the corridor, peeling off her armour one pad at a time. 'We only cremate them at Bulwark to clear the killing field and produce explosives. For now, just find a place to set us down for the night.'

Xia staggered after the Deathless, unslinging her rifle to unload its magazine. 'The body won't damage the forest?'

Drekene shrugged. 'No more than any other corpse. Animals instinctively know to leave well enough alone. The body will decay in time. Plants will grow over what remains. Centuries ago, Daem bodies littered the continent. Now you'd be hard-pressed to find one such grave that's not part of some museum.'

The hoverjet lurched to the side—Cadden no doubt heading towards an opening in the forest—and the jolt almost knocked Xia from her feet, only just able to steady herself on the polished walls.

Ket hopped down. 'So we done? Going back to Bulwark?'

'Not yet,' Drekene replied. 'We have to find where the Daem-an came from. Xia has volunteered to accompany us.'

'She has?' Cadden sounded strangely excited. Ket gave a sly laugh, no doubt at some in-joke, but Xia had no energy to decipher it. Instead, she slumped into the empty bed, Cattin's bed. She meant to ask if she was allowed to use the bunk, but could not find the words. She just needed a break, to take the weight off her legs, to rest her head against the firm pillow, if only for a moment.

Xia woke to the sun's glare. Groaning, she held out a hand to block the light pouring through the cockpit windows. She lay atop the sheets. Even with this extra layer, the bed was firmer than her own back in Ethelan, but after nights spent in the forest, this felt wonderful.

Muscles aching, she swung her legs over the bunk's edge to perch on its side. Still wore her climbing shoes.

'She lives.' Ket sat in what could only be described as a nest in the wall. In an open panel near his assigned bunk, the Greml-an rested in a pile of cotton, suspended by a tangle of wires running behind the bulkhead. The space was small, even for the tiny man, but he seemed perfectly comfortable, curled up in his space, gripping his leg between his leathery hands having paused chewing on a gnarled foot-claw.

Cadden strolled over, wearing a light-blue flightsuit of faux-leather and Kevlar padding. 'Morning.'

He handed her a steaming bowl. Porridge. Xia's

nose wrinkled at the Hum food, but she took the bowl, desperate for anything to quell the pain in her stomach.

'Thanks.' Using a plastic spoon, she shovelled the mush into her mouth. Like most Hum meals, the bulk of the food held no flavour, instead relying on a combination of spices for any impact. The cinnamon was clear, as was the antwort, but she could not identify the half-dozen other foreign herbs crammed into the slurry. Still, she forced down the warm slop.

The Greml-an laughed. 'Looks like someone on this craft can stomach your cooking, Cadden. Thought the Elf-an would've hated it.'

'I'm capable of eating things I don't enjoy,' Xia retorted. Seeing the dismayed look on Cadden's face, she quickly backed up. 'I didn't mean it like that. For Hum food, this is good.'

Ket laughed again, a mischievous little cackle. '"For Hum food." I like this one. Drekene, we should keep her.'

The Deathless sat cross-legged to the rear of the hallway, mostly empty bowl of porridge in her lap. 'I believe that is up to her. And Cadden's cooking is healthy, full of carbohydrates for the day ahead. It is exactly what the warden needs most.'

'Thank you,' Cadden replied. 'I'm glad someone appreciates what I do.'

Ket's giggle continued. 'Yeah, Drekene likes your cooking. But a Deathless complimenting food's like a blind man complimenting a painting. I wouldn't take it to heart.'

Cadden rolled his eyes and perched on the bunk opposite Xia, digging into his own breakfast.

'Can Deathless not taste?' Xia asked.

'We can, but it's different.' Drekene put her spoon into her bowl, black eyes staring blankly ahead. 'I can taste whether something is bitter, sour, sweet. I can tell if it's hot or cold, lumpy or smooth. But... it's hard to explain. The joy is gone, or conflicted. Everything I enjoy, I equally hate. Everything ends up feeling... grey.'

'Hence her ability to stomach the lad's cooking.' Ket grinned. 'The cost of immortality is steep indeed.'

'The cost is far greater than that,' Drekene replied, stern.

Xia frowned. 'What do you mean?'

When Drekene failed to answer, Ket gave another chortle. 'Well, girl, you see all Deathless have made a pact-'

'Enough,' Drekene snarled. 'The warden is a temporary recruit. She does not need a horror story from you.'

'But,' Ket started, only to be cut off.

'I said enough.'

Silence filled the cabin. To avoid the growing discomfort, Xia tried to change the subject. 'Sorry if I insulted you, Cadden. The food really isn't bad. Just not what I'm used to.'

His smile was full of warmth. 'None taken. We've had a few Elf meals since we started this mission, and that certainly takes some getting used to. Bulwark gets most of its food from Vandar, but seems we have different ideas on how to cook. You lot really seem to avoid your herbs and spices.'

Hesitant, Xia returned the smile. 'No need to sprinkle in additives if you keep the food's original

99

flavour strong. I've seen Hum-an's in my village make a fine soup, only to pour away the broth—that's where the taste is. Of course the solids left over need spice if you boil out their best parts.'

'She has a point.' Ket had moved to chewing his other foot, sharpening the claws. 'Greml cooking takes the best of all cultures, and you know we don't include the bland, over-boiled mush of Hum dishes.'

Xia couldn't help but smile at Cadden's baleful look. 'What did Greml-an's take from Elf cooking?'

'Hmm.' Ket paused his gnawing to think. 'Well, probably your insistence on freshness. Oh, and cooking in oil to keep in certain flavours. Me gran made a mean bilbok stew—Elf roots, Hum spices, Gobl sauce. Beautiful.'

Xia smiled at the thought. Her mother had tried making Greml meals a few times. The complicated preparation had always involved a great deal of muttering and more than a few choice expletives, but had never disappointed come mealtime. The memory was enough to get her through the rest of the porridge. Despite the satisfied smile she flashed Cadden, she was relieved when the bowl was empty. She never thought she would have preferred a ration bar.

'What about him?' Cadden nodded to Rikk, who sat to one side, sullen, staring at Xia's empty bowl. 'What does he eat?'

'Vulfiks can eat pretty much anything 'an can. Do you have more of this for him?'

'Of course.' Cadden grinned as he took her bowl. Moving to a small stove build into the far wall, he ladled a few scoops of the grey slurry into the bowl and set it in front of the vulfik. Before the Hum-an had placed it on the grated floor, Rikk already had his head in the bowl, happily lapping up the milk and oats.

'Ha.' Ket peered out his alcove to watch. 'Well, if you ever get tired of failing to impress 'an with your cooking, Cadden, I think you've got a career waiting in pet food. I hear Callum's Kibble is hiring.'

Cadden rolled his eyes again, and Xia found herself laughing. Drekene's crew were certainly nothing like the Deathless.

As if sensing her thoughts, the large woman came to a hunched stand in the corridor, her shoulders stretching the passage's entire width. 'We've wasted enough time resting. Cadden, take us back to the Daem-an's corpse.'

With a rushed salute, the pilot clambered back down the hallway to the cockpit. Moments later, the clicking of countless dials was replaced with the hum of the engines starting up, the cabin's air taking on a tinge of the jet fuel as the intakes breathed in the exhaust.

Drekene clomped close. 'Xia the Warden, get your gear ready. It is time we finish this. Take me to that Daem-an's hole.'

Determined, Xia nodded. 'Gladly. Maybe we'll get to kill another Daem-an.'

Drekene's eyes seemed to look through the bulkhead. 'For your sake, I hope we do not. But I fear you will get your chance.'

Frustration built as the morning dragged on. Xia had no idea what she was looking for—what did a breach to the underworld look like anyway? In films, they were always gaping maws spewing fire and echoing with the screams of the damned. Somehow, she doubted the real thing would be so well advertised. The opening had to be large enough for a Daem-an to fit, but she had seen the beast squeeze itself through a window. She could be looking for something no larger than a badger hole.

She had even less knowledge of the opening's location. It was safe to assume that the Daem-an had been fleeing towards where it had broken through to the surface, but that could be over the next rise, two days walk, or a hundred kilometres away. For all Xia knew, they had already passed it, missing a break in the ground beneath some patch of bracken or hidden by green fronds.

Sighing, she pushed off another tree. She kept her kicks weaker than normal, allowing her to slowly drift just above the underbrush, searching for any hints of disturbance. All she saw were the same signs she had all morning—the forest floor, decaying leaves, snapped twigs and hardy ferns, broken only by fifil holes and deer tracks.

The forest steadily darkened, the rapid midday twilight plunging the world into a dark as deep as any night.

'The noon eclipse.' Xia paused on her tree, turning to find Drekene a few trees behind. 'It'll be too easy for us to miss something. We should stop.'

The Deathless thudded into the tree alongside, shaking some of the red bark loose. 'Agreed. Good time to take lunch.' She adjusted her earpiece and spoke louder. 'Cadden, we're stopping until the eclipse passes.'

The rumble of engines above changed pitch and

began to circle, the blue glow lighting the darkened canopy. Cadden's voice came through clear. 'Confirmed. Putting the Hawk into a holding pattern. Have a nice break.'

Xia scanned the dim forest, eventually finding a boulder peaking out of a tangle of bracken. With two leaps, she reached the rock, lowering the power on her belt to bring her to a gentle landing. The stone was covered in thick moss, giving a surprisingly soft surface. As the rubber soles of her climbing shoes scuffed the moss, a wonderful green smell filled the air, like freshly cut saplings. A fine change from the days spent breathing sulphur with every lungful.

Setting her rifle to one side, Xia sat on the rock, bare calves hanging over the edge, tips of shoes rustling the fronds of a great fern. Drekene was not far behind, imitating Xia and cutting her grav-belt mid-leap to land on the rock. Her heavy boots scraped over the moss, exposing the dark shale beneath, but Xia suspected the damage was caused more by the woman's bulk than a lack of agility.

'You've picked up tree-leaping quickly.' Xia retrieved a ration bar from her pack, peeling away the foil.

Drekene lowered herself to rest next to Xia, the Deathless's long legs stretching deep into the greenery below. 'I learn most techniques fast.'

'Another Deathless trait?'

Shaking her head, Drekene tugged her own ration bar from her belt pocket, breaking the Bulwark symbol that sealed the foil. 'No. I quickly picked up skills even before I died.'

'Yet over hundreds of years, you never learned

how to tree-leap?'

'Never needed it before. Never been to Vandar.'

Xia nearly choked on her dry meal. 'Four hundred years old and you've never been to Vandar?'

Drekene shrugged. 'Deathless stay where the enemy lurk. Until recently, that has thankfully been restricted to Bulwark.'

'They don't let you take a break? A holiday?'

Drekene's hairless brow furrowed. 'The Daem-an's do not take breaks, so neither can we.'

Looking into the distance, Xia shook her head. 'No breaks. No sleep. Can't enjoy food. Seems to me that being a Deathless is a pretty poor deal—very high cost just for immortality.'

Drekene turned her black eyes to Xia, the void there sending a shiver down the Elf-an's spine. 'The cost is far more than you can imagine, Warden.'

'What do you mean?'

She was answered with silence, the Deathless chewing her grey bar, staring into the distance. Pushing down her curiosity, Xia let the woman keep her secrets—for now. The other two seemed far more open about such matters. If Xia could get a moment alone with Cadden or Ket, she would need to press them for information on how Deathless were really created. Surely two people from Bulwark would know truth from legend.

Finishing her lunch, Xia started to run her hands over the rock, enjoying the moss's soft texture, the dew's dampness, the clear fragrance released as she disturbed the surface. She had always loved the forest. Wherever she looked, she found wonder, from the diversity of life, to the tenacity of the creatures, to the resilience of the great pines. Vandar was certainly worth protecting.

Frowning, Xia paused as her hand passed over a patch of moss just under the lip of the rock. The covering was thinner than the surroundings. Curious, Xia hopped to the forest floor to get a better look, soft soil easing her fall. Even in the poor light of the eclipse, the mark was clear—a band of nearly exposed rock where the moss struggled to heal over an area that had been scraped clean. Pushing the thin moss aside, she saw bright patches of the rock. Something had ploughed into the stone, hard enough to splinter the surface.

To search the floor, Xia crouched, pushing aside ferns. Even with Elf eyes, it was hard to make out anything in the darkness, so she was forced to run her hands over the soil.

'What are you doing?' Drekene asked.

Xia ignored the question, probing the ground. Brambles pricked her hands, twigs scratched, thorns clawed, but she ignored the sting. Shuffling around in the darkness, she passed her hands over felled branches, rotting leaves and shallow roots.

Then she found it.

A furrow ran through the ground. Partially washed away by the rains, hidden below a young bush, the mark was still deep and long. Far too large to be left by a deer or badger, there was only one creature Xia knew that left such a scar in the soil.

'This is a Daem track.'

Drekene stiffened. 'There's another Daem-an?'

'I don't think so.' Xia picked her way through the thorns, and sure enough found another gouge right where she expected. 'These are not recent. Before the last rainstorm. Weeks old.' She turned to the ancient woman, excitement building. 'I think these are the Daem-an's old tracks. We follow them, and we find where it came from.'

Drekene dropped to the ground, handing Xia her rifle. 'Well then, lead on.'

Grasping the rifle's wooden stock, Xia grinned. Even aged and overgrown by Vandar's rapidly spreading foliage, the tracks were easy to follow. The beast's old talon marks would lead them to its nest, to the breach into the underworld. There, she would stop the threat to Vandar, once and for all.

Chapter 9

High-reaching thorns clawed at Xia's climbing shoes and exposed calves. She threw herself from pine to pine just above the thick bracken. Occasionally, she would misjudge her kick, or fail to notice a tall stem hidden amongst the patchy shadows of the canopy. Each error would earn her a torn sock, a grazed leg, a bruised shin.

She had little choice but to endure the pain. The Daem-an's old tracks had been well covered—the forest never rested long. Hungry saplings had sprouted in the clear path the beast had forged. They had grown rapidly, fighting for space with the neighbouring ferns, which exploded into the newly opened space. Those plants that claimed what little sunlight filtered through the pine branches would thrive, while those that grew too slow were smothered, their decaying remains falling to the floor, fertilising the soil and filling the deep gouges left by the Daem-an.

All of this gave Xia little to work with as she attempted to follow the fading trail. The holes left by the monstrous talons were either filled with decaying shoots or covered by the thick new growth. Any branches and stems snapped by the beast's passing had long since healed or withered. Even the Daem-an's sulphurous stench had faded, leaving only the fresh scents of pine bark and mouldering leaves.

Instead of the prominent tracks Xia had been following for days, she found herself peering into the underbrush, spotting the occasional shallow groove or snapped root hidden under the foliage. Mostly, she followed the colour. The new growth was more vibrant than the old underbrush, the stems still fresh, the leaves undisturbed by hungry insects or defecating birds. Through the shadowed forest, she hurled herself between trunks, following this pristine path.

Her technique was far from perfect. If an insect swarm had passed over an area, all leaves—new and old—would be decimated. Birds and monkeys alike left their droppings over the underbrush, marring the path. Deer and larger animals pushed through, forming misleading trails of their own. All too often she found herself lost, staring into the endless forest, unable to locate her route.

Ahead, Rikk chirped. Xia turned to see the vulfik clambering up the base of a tree. A second chirp confirmed that he had found the trail. Xia kicked towards the creature as he leapt to continue his pursuit. Rikk had been invaluable during the search. Although her nose could no longer pick out what little remained of the Daem-an's scent, the vulfik had no problem detecting the slightest residue. Every time she lost the path, she just had to send the daft mutt ahead and he would set her back on the right track. When this was over, she would need to give him a treat. Maybe some imported muscles from the coast—the strange animal had always loved seafood.

Drekene crashed into the tree alongside Xia, the trunk shaking at the impact. The woman had no problem keeping pace, but seemed hopeless at tracking. She may well have been able to follow the Daem-ans fresh path on her own, but now she just diligently followed Xia.

'We're still on the trail.' Xia kicked off after Rikk.

Drekene's reply came through Xia's earpiece. 'I'll take you at your word.'

'If nothing else, Rikk will keep us right.'

Drekene grunted. 'A useful creature indeed. How did you come to own him?'

'I don't own him. He's like a family member. We've had him since he was a pup. What, Deathless don't have pets?'

'Some do. I don't. Seen enough loved ones die over the centuries.'

Xia frowned. 'I don't understand. I'll probably outlive Rikk. Most people outlive their pets.'

'Most people don't outlive every single person they know. Every man, woman and child I meet will die long before me. There's enough loss in a Deathless's life without inviting more.'

Xia fell back into silence, kicking after Rikk's content chirps. The thought had never really occurred to her—being immortal spared the Deathless, but not those they loved. What must it be like, to meet a young child knowing full well they would die decades or even centuries before you? The thought sent a shiver down Xia's spine.

She tried to change the subject. 'Can I ask you about the Daem-ans, Drekene?'

'Yes.' The Deathless's response was flat. 'It would be wise for you to know what horrors we are up against.'

'Well, they're called Daem-*ans*, right? So they're 'an, like me and you and Cadden?'

'Yes.'

'But they're mindless. Rikk seems smarter than them—at least he can communicate, in his own way.'

'Daem-ans are far from mindless. They are driven by a hatred of life, wanting only to destroy and kill, but they are not some stupid creature charging through the land. No, they are cunning, adaptable, insidious. The one we killed? It purposefully went for the powerhouses before it attacked each village. That was not an accident, not for simplicity or some hatred of Gobl-ans. No, it cut the power to stop communications. This creature had been on the surface for a few weeks at most, and already discovered communications put it in danger, and that destroying power houses plunged a settlement into disarray. It's likely more intelligent than many of the "civilised" 'an that I've met.'

Losing the trail, Xia paused to let Rikk scout ahead. 'If they're so smart, then why do they throw themselves at Bulwark?'

Drekene slammed into the trunk alongside Xia, knocking bark fragments free. 'Even the most intelligent of us are still driven by our instincts. A starving man will go to great, self destructive lengths for a meal. The call of destruction drives the Daem-ans as much as hunger pushes any other 'an. They attack the defences of Bulwark because that was their only outlet from the underworld.'

'Until now,' Xia replied, grim.

'Until now,' Drekene echoed.

Letting the conversation lapse into silence, Xia followed Rikk's chirps as he rediscovered the Daem-an's trail. The morning was dragging on—the noon eclipse would come soon. Her legs cried out for the rest the darkness would bring. The stinging grazes on her calves begged for ointment. Her stomach growled for food. She pushed the thoughts aside. They had to find the entrance to the underworld before another Daem-an emerged.

Trying to distract herself, she glanced over her shoulder to the Deathless. 'If the Daem-ans are 'an, just like the rest of us, then do they have their own Avatar?'

'Yes. Though no-one has seen him. Their Avatar has not emerged from the underworld, but sends his minions to devastate the surface. It's possible their Avatar has moved into the ruins of the Dwarf holds. No one can say for sure.'

Frowning, Xia turned. 'But if nobody's ever seen him, how do you know he exists?'

Drekene's answer was distant. 'Deathless know much about the Daem-ans.'

'How?'

Silence. It was the same answer Xia had been given time and again whenever she pried into the Deathless. When Drekene did not want to answer a question, she just shut down. No evasion, no lies, no redirection, just silence. Even these few days had been enough to teach Xia that there was no point arguing. Once the Deathless made up her mind, it was impossible to convince her otherwise.

Instead, Xia again changed topic. 'What about Singing?'

Drekene sighed. 'What about it?'

'Every race of 'an have their own Song. Elf lifeSinging, Hum mindSinging, Drak fireSinging and so on. Can the Daem-ans sing?'

'Yes. They constantly Sing.'

Xia paused on the smooth bark of a young oak, the tree resolutely standing under the taller pines, its wide branches forcing enough of a space in the canopy to allow it a few hours of sunlight each day. 'I was close to that Daem-an many times, and never heard a note. Unless those screeches are Song.'

'Elf-ans are deaf to it. Daem-ans Sing too deep for most 'an. Greml-ans can make out a bit, Drak-an even better. Some say the Daem-ans waited for the Drak-an purge before they chose to strike, so that those few 'an that could hear them were being driven from the land. These days, we use microphones to detect the sound. Computers pick up low notes as easily as high ones. Gives us a minute's warning ahead of the seismic sensors or the chem detectors.'

Made sense, Xia supposed. She knew that Drak-an spoke to one another in such a low pitch that most 'an could not hear their conversations. It came as little surprise that Daem-ans could communicate outside of Elf hearing range. 'So what does their Singing do?'

Drekene shattered a low bush as she misjudged her kick, but the snapping brambles barely slowed the large woman. 'It's known as curseSinging.'

'But what does it do?'

Drekene's voice became mournful. 'Those who die while under the effects of curseSinging are given a dire choice—the possibility to become Deathless.'

Incredulous, Xia laughed. 'The Daem-ans make Deathless?'

'Yes.'

'Deathless, the people who lead the fight against

the Daem-ans?'

'Yes.'

'Why?'

'What better way to tempt those who die fighting against you than an opportunity to be resurrected and get a chance do it again? For that, some people would be willing to pay any price.'

Xia gave an irritated sigh. 'There you go again on that "price" thing. What exactly does it cost to become Deathless?'

'More than it's worth.'

Xia paused. Rikk had lowered himself into the underbrush. Leaves rattled as he forced his way beneath them, occasionally chirping.

'Come on, Drekene. You need to give me something. If we're working together, I should know everything I can, right? How can I help you fight this enemy without knowing what *you* are?'

Again, silence. Xia was tired of receiving cryptic answers or no answers at all. Her patience running out, she was about to launch into a tirade when Rikk's excited bark filled the forest. Hesitant, Xia realised the forest had changed. At first, she could not put her finger on what was amiss, then it struck her, the barest hint of a smell that was now horrendously familiar.

Sulphur.

'Drekene,' she warned.

'No, Xia,' the woman snapped. 'Enough of these questions.'

'No, Drekene, I think we're here.'

Heart pounding, Xia deactivated her grav-belt and settled her feet on the forest floor, long-dead leaves crunching beneath her shoe's thin rubber soles. She

113

picked her way through the underbrush, forcing aside brambles and ferns.

Drekene smashed through the forest just behind, her bulk making short work of the fragile plants that endured down here.

Following Rikk's chirps, Xia entered a sunbathed clearing. Small, only a few meters across, the clearing abounded with life—ferns, ivy, grakken, thistles, vilflower, all growing around the rotting stump of a pine. Judging by the scarring on the side, the tree had been toppled by storm a year or two ago. Cut off from the sunlight, the roots had rotted, creating a clearing of green, crossed with deep rifts where the decaying roots had collapsed.

An excitedly wagging tail marked Rikk's position at the centre of the clearing. The vulfik leapt atop the stump as Xia approached, canine head peering down. Xia found what held the mutt's attention—a deep gorge, barely wide enough to squeeze a person through and only a couple of meters long. The sunlight pouring into the clearing revealed the gorge's true splendour was not its length or its width, but its depth.

The hole stretched down, dozens, hundreds of meters. Underbrush gave way to soil, then finally to bedrock. Xia could not see the bottom, just a shadow stretching endlessly. Wafting from the hole was the familiar sulphur stench.

This was where the Daem-an had broken through.

As Drekene stomped to the cleft, the light rapidly died. Xia glanced up just in time to see the last edge of the sun disappear behind Watcher, plunging the world into its noon twilight.

Drekene adjusted her earpiece. 'Hawk, this is the

landing party. We have found the breach to the underworld. Mark our position.'

Cadden's whistle came in reply. 'Just what we feared then? There's really another opening?'

'Yes,' Drekene replied, emotionless.

A litany of curses flowed from the pilot, but Xia's attention was elsewhere—a sound she could not quite make out, just on the edge of her hearing. She pulled out her earpiece, wanting to quiet the conversation flowing from the Hawk's excited crew. The sound was faint, even to Elf ears, but she was sure she was not imagining it. Something scraped, cracked, groaned. With growing dread, Xia unslung her rifle and activated its night vision. On the scope in artificial grey and white, barely two meters down, she saw what she most feared.

Another Daem-an.

This was smaller than the last, pudgier. A ball of misshapen flesh, an eye glaring from a tumorous head, thin claws poking out of tufted fists.

At Xia's warning cry, Drekene looked down. Realising it had been spotted, the Daem-an abandoned stealth, lunging out the hole. Xia stumbled back in terror.

The Deathless kept her head. In a smooth motion she drew her sword, its barbed blade unfolding as she lifted it above her head before bringing it down in a bloody arc. The beast squealed like a fifil caught underfoot, most of its body still caught in the fissure. Drekene showed no hesitation, bringing her blade down again and again, splattering black ichor and sulphurous globs of flesh over the clearing. Finally, the Daem-an fell still, dead.

Without a pause, Drekene wrenched the beast clear of the fissure, flinging its battered corpse to the side. 'Check for more.'

Nodding at the order, Xia stumbled to her feet and shoved her earpiece back into place. Through her scope, Xia peered into the cleft. With its light-enhancement, she could see those shadows that had moments ago appeared black. The fissure stretched down impossibly far, a rent in the ground delving as far as the electronic scope could see.

And wedged between the rough walls were a dozen more writhing shapes. Leathery creatures no larger than a fox dragged their way up the gap. Others, more massive than Drekene, climbed with talons and hooves and tentacles. All of them sported thick skin coated in a thousand cuts, jagged rends in their flesh stretching from limb to limb.

'There are so many,' she whispered.

'Well?' Drekene prodded. 'What are you waiting for? Shoot them. Brain's probably in the head or centre of mass. Either way, keep firing until they fall still. Now.'

Shaking with adrenalin, Xia shifted her stance, reaching out a foot to stand astride the cleft in the ground, weapon pointed down. Taking a breath, Xia moved the scope's crosshairs over the closest of the Daem-ans, a scraggly thing with tufts of feathers sticking out from a snake-like head. She pulled the trigger. Her rifle recoiled. The Daem-an's head shattered.

She fired another round into its remains. The creature's strength failed, its grip loosened, and it tumbled, taking down a piggish Daem-an just below.

'I killed one!'

'Good. Keep at it.' Drekene glanced upwards. 'Hawk, we're going to need to seal this. Ket, do you still have your explosives?'

The Greml-an's cackle filled Xia's earpiece. 'You betcha. Want me to set 'em up?'

Xia lost track of the conversation as she continued to let loose round after round into the hole. Asymmetric beaks splintered. Armoured heads shattered. Exposed bones snapped.

A soft beep alerted Xia to reload. Feeling detached, she released the magazine and replaced it mechanically. Then the killing continued. Five dead. Eight. Eleven. The monsters, caught in the chasm made easy targets. They could barely move, let alone dodge. Firing straight down meant that Xia did not even have to account for bullet drop. This was easier than the shooting range. The brass casings flung into the air with each round. Some settled on the forest floor, others rolled free and toppled into the chasm. There they joined the falling corpses and dismembered limbs as Xia's vengeance continued.

Sulphur melded with gunpowder and sweat. Still, Xia did not hesitate. Each shot was payback for Eddan. Every dead Daem-an was justice.

So why did she still feel empty?

A blue glow illuminated the clearing. Then, suspended by the Hawk hovering overhead, a rope slapped onto the floor. With a childlike shout of glee, Ket slid down the rope, a pack almost his size strapped to his back.

'Hoo ho.' He grinned as he landed. 'Seems someone's having fun.'

Xia ignored him. Maybe one more Daem-an corpse would rest her brothers soul, would settle the gnawing pain in the pit of her stomach. One way to find out. She fired again.

Drekene turned to the Greml-an. 'The blast must be as large as possible, but put it on a delay—best if it went off in the bedrock layer. The more mass we can pour into this gap, the more time it will take for the Daem-ans to dig their way out.'

Ket chuckled as he ducked a spent shell casing from Xia's rifle. 'One giant delayed boom coming right up.'

As the gunshots continued, the little engineer tugged something from his bag—a black metal cylinder, glowing controls at the end. After a few adjustments, he looked up to Xia. 'Might want to step back, lass. Unless you want to be cut in two by shrapnel.'

Dejected, Xia stopped firing. Almost twenty Daem-ans had just died by her hand, but she felt like she had achieved nothing. She stepped to the side. Perhaps watching this hole be blown to dust would settle her heart.

Ket tottered to the cleft's edge, holding the cylinder over the void. 'And... fire in the hole.' In the blue glow of the hoverjet's engines, his wide grin sparkled, then he flicked a switch and released the cylinder.

As the little man scurried back, clawed hands shielding his wide ears, Xia moved further from the opening. Rikk, sensing danger, whimpered and followed close.

The ground shook.

With a sharp roar, dust and pebbles were launched out the hole. Monkeys screeched overhead. Birds took flight. The tallest of great pines shuddered. The soil slumped towards the hole, vibrations shaking through Xia's boots long after the blast's echo had faded.

Through the raining debris, Xia picked her way back towards the breach, or where it had been. All that remained was a depression in the soil.

'It's sealed?' she asked.

Ket grinned. 'Buried under a hundred tonnes of rock fragments. And there I thought I wasn't gonna get to blow nothing up on this trip.'

Drekene grunted. 'This is the best we can do for now. But the Daem-ans will be back.'

Xia sank to her knees, comforting the startled Rikk. 'They will dig through a pile of rocks that deep?'

Drekene nodded, grim. 'Yes. The blast fractured the rockface, filled in the hole, but only with loose fragments. Worse, we've weakened the bedrock all around here. When they come back, the opening will be larger. They will come through faster. At best, this was a delaying act. It will buy us time. A couple of weeks. Maybe a month. Then this forest will be filled with their kind.'

'You're sure they're that determined?'

'You have no idea.' Drekene's black eyes bored into Xia's. 'We tried filling the first breach, near Bulwark. They dug back out. So we filled it with molten metal. They broke through a short distance away. Once the Daem-an's find a way to the surface, there is no stopping them.'

Hopeless, Xia closed her eyes. 'Then what's next?'

Drekene sniffed. 'We do what we did at Bulwark. We defend the opening. We slaughter them as they emerge. For that we're going to need help. A lot of help. But that is not your concern, young Xia. I have asked much of you already. I no longer need a scout. You may return home. Your duty is done.'

Xia paused. How could she go home feeling like this? Something still gnawed at her. Killing the Daeman had not helped. Sealing this opening had done nothing to ease her ache.

She shook her head. Eddan's memory could not rest until she saw this through to the end. Standing, she held Drekene's black gaze. 'No. I'm coming with you.'

PART II

Chapter 10

Sunlight had just started to peek around Watcher as the Hawk's ramp descended, the midday twilight giving way to a dazzling afternoon. Xia stepped down the grated metal and into the sunbaked grass. Short blades bent under her climbing shoes, the field kept in check by the herd of thannin hurrying to the tree line. She waved to a tired herder who desperately tried to settle his flock.

Xia collapsed onto the soft ground, the greenery becoming a mattress. The sharp smell of grass filled her, relaxing a dozen overworked muscles.

Rikk snuffed as he padded over, nuzzling into her plaited hair with a curious chirp. She laughed, ruffling the thick fur behind his ears.

'Not a bad place for lunch.' Cadden hopped down the ramp, plastic box in hand.

Ket clambered after him on all fours. 'Eh, bit exposed.'

'We'll be fine,' Drekene assured him. 'The Hawk's sensor will alert us if anything approaches.'

Ket settled onto the grass alongside Xia, pushing the blades down to form a small nest. 'Still open. Thought in Vandar of all places, we'd be enclosed.'

Pushing herself up, Xia smiled down on the Greml-an. 'There are fields in Vandar too, believe it or not.'

'Yeah.' Cadden sat down. 'And no matter how much you want to have lunch in the forest, the Hawk doesn't like to be wedged into trees.'

'Don't see why we can't eat on the jet,' Ket grumbled.

'The fresh air makes you less cranky.' Drekene sat alongside Cadden, opposite Xia. 'And the sun is good for you.'

'Great.' Ket picked at his teeth. 'Health advice from an immortal.'

'Health advice from an elder,' Drekene corrected.

Cadden peeled the lid from his box, releasing a fragrant mist that made Xia's stomach growl. The young pilot proceeded to ladle out four steaming bowls of an orange-red stew. Taking her bowl, Xia sniffed the meat-filled concoction, the scent of a dozen overlapping spices filling her nose.

'Genuine royal steak mandar,' Cadden explained, enthusiastic. 'That's beef from the Adrous Farm, finest in the world. Had this frozen in storage for a special occasion. I'd say sealing a tunnel to the underworld counts.'

Ket grinned, spoon in hand. 'Not to mention our new recruit here slaughtering a dozen Daem-ans.'

'Nineteen,' Xia corrected.

The Greml-an cackled. 'Oh-ho. All the more reason to celebrate.'

'Our task is far from done,' Drekene interjected, stern.

Ket rolled his eyes. 'Oh, you just have to suck the fun outa everything. Can't you let us have this win? The girl did good.'

'She did.' Drekene spoke with a mouthful of stew. 'We have made much progress, but we mustn't forget our task. Vandar is far from safe.'

Cadden ran a hand over his black mop of hair. 'So what's next? We returning to Bulwark?'

Drekene shook her head. 'I've already messaged command. They don't have anyone to spare. We should try to raise a local militia to guard the breach until we can get more forces here. Xia, what sort of army is available in this region?'

Swallowing the bitter stew, Xia shrugged. 'Army? None really. Vandar's been at peace for so long, there's no need. We rely on the Bulwark for protection against Daem-ans—guess you know that. There is the Forest Guard at the capital but...'

'But?' Drekene pressed.

'But I doubt the prime minister will consider leaving the capital undefended. The Forest Guard are sworn to protect the Avatar, and she's not left the capital for centuries.'

Cadden slurped his stew. 'But Avatars are immortal. More so than Deathless, they can't even be harmed. What's the point of guarding them?'

Xia shrugged again. 'Respect to Elf-az, I suppose? You might be able to persuade the Avatar to move, but I don't know how you'd go about convincing a messenger of the 'az to do anything.'

'What about the wardens?' Drekene asked.

'What about us?'

The Deathless had drained the last of her lunch. 'The wardens protect the forest. They are armed. Trained. You've certainly shown your ability. A band of wardens should be able to hold the breach, for a while at least.'

Xia slowly nodded. She swallowed, forcing the words out. 'We should go back to Ethelan. Speak to my parents. They have contact with all wardens.'

The idea filled Xia with anxiety. Throughout this excursion, she had pushed thoughts of home from her mind. She did not want to think of Father, let alone confront him. Still, what other option was there?

'We have a plan then,' Drekene announced. 'Cadden, after we finish here, take us back to Xia's village.'

The others brightened, content to have a plan. Xia, though, found herself fixated on the coming meeting. Would Father be proud of what she had accomplished? Would he apologise for his attitude when they last parted? Or would he still blame her for failing to save Eddan?

Sighing, Xia forced down the rest of her lukewarm meal. She had known that she would have to face her parents again sometime, but had not expected it to be so soon. Why did the thought fill her with more dread than she had felt standing over a pit filled with Daemans?

Illuminated by silver planetlight, Xia slid down the rope, plunging into the night-shrouded canopy. The electric glow of a hundred bulbs shone below her feet, marking the walkways and houses of Ethelan Village —the powerhouse must be back online.

Xia lithely swung onto a branch and descended a pine, the rough bark providing excellent grip. She was glad to be back in civilisation, the trees carefully manicured by lifeSingers. The bark's edges were sharp enough to provide traction, but did not rub her claws blunt like those trees in the wild. Any loose sections were quickly replaced with firm holds, and descending this tree was a dream compared to the past days in the deep forest.

While Xia moved silently, Drekene was far less subtle. Ignoring the trunk, she came crashing through the canopy, weight braced on the rope. Branches were shoved out of her path or simply snapped, a rain of debris and green needles falling over Xia. When he saw the destruction, LifeSinger Fennel would throw a fit—it would take him hours to repair the damage.

Xia hopped onto a walkway, sending the wooden boards held on interlocked branches swaying, the attached bulbs throwing erratic shadows over the neighbouring trunks. She reached out for the rope, hauling it to the side to guide Drekene's descend. As the Deathless landed on the living platform, the branches supporting them groaned.

'My home's this way,' Xia urged, not wanting to delay and put the strength of the walkway to the test. Kriss, the Drak police officer, managed to navigate the hanging paths without issue, but even he was not as large as Drekene.

Xia hurried along, running a hand along a railing made of woven vines, still green and vibrant. She rarely used these walkways, preferring tree-leaping and climbing trunks. For today, she walked the path for Drekene's sake—and that of the villagers. They had enough reasons to be on edge without an eight-foot Deathless slamming between their trunks.

Few villagers were out this late in the evening. Most were teenage Elf-an, maybe a couple of years younger than Xia. All faces she recognised from Ethelan's single school, though none were in her year. They shot her curious gazes as she passed, then wide-eyed stares at the Deathless in her wake. Caught between fear of another behemoth intruding on their town, and intrigue at such an unusual stranger, the groups of kids froze. Behind, Xia could hear a few following, their passage marked by the creak of wood and rustle of leaves.

Most families were indoors. The scents of the evening meals lingered in the air—roast roots, fried venison, pakapie. The smells of home.

No one expected visitors. Even though power was back, communication still was not. The Hawk hovered overhead—the village's one landing platform currently occupied by a grain hauler from the Greendip Corporation, no doubt loading the village's supplies to take to city markets. Besides, the idea of turning up at her parents' door unannounced appealed. She wanted to see their unrehearsed reaction to her homecoming.

As she stepped onto an adjoining walkway, her heart sank. Up ahead lay her family home, a fat growth midway up a pine trunk. In the darkness, its living bark exterior appeared only as a black shadow against the village lights behind. A steady yellow glow streamed from the oval windows. Her parents were still awake.

Taking a deep breath, Xia crossed the path and tried the round door—locked. Strange, Father never barred the door. Hesitantly, she knocked. To the side, mutters flowed through the open windows, the wooden floor creaking as the occupants paced to the door.

Two latches were dragged on the wooden door's far side, then it creaked open. A face tentatively peered around the edge, eyes red from tears.

Mother.

Without pausing, Mother threw her arms around Xia, pulling her into a tight embrace. Stunned at the passion, Xia hesitantly returned the hug. Rose perfume. Xia was home.

The door swung fully open to reveal the living room. Familiar sofas and tables stood in their normal places, but the walls were bedecked with far more pictures than before. Photos of the family, of Xia and Eddan at the beach, of her brother eating a birthday meal, littered the walls. Some Xia had never seen before.

And there, standing in the centre of it all, dour faced and holding a glass of sapwine, stood her father. His expression was as expected, staring blankly at her as if she were a leaf that just blew through the window, neither unwelcome nor wanted.

'You're home,' he said, distant.

Mother tightened her arms. 'I was so worried. We thought we wouldn't see you again. I'm so glad you're back.'

Xia managed to extricate herself from her mother's grip, meeting her tear-filled gaze. 'Only briefly. We've come to ask for your help.'

'We?' Then her mother finally noticed Drekene's hulking form on the walkway. She took a step away, mouth open.

'Don't be scared,' Xia said. 'This is Drekene. She's-'

'A Deathless,' Father barked.

Following Xia's beckoning hand, Drekene stooped to enter the living room. The fearsome warrior looked ridiculous in the space designed for Elf-ans, shoulders hunched, knees bent. 'Greetings, parents of Xia the Warden.'

Mother gave a shaky nod. 'Did... thank you for keeping our daughter safe.'

Drekene sniffed. 'I did no such thing. She assisted me in taking down the Daem-an.'

'It's dead then?' Father blinked.

Drekene nodded. 'As are nineteen others by Xia's hand, perhaps more.'

Xia turned to her father, looking for the pride her actions deserved, acknowledgement that she was right to seek out the monster, joy that his firstborn was safe.

He smirked. 'So what? You skipped your brother's funeral to go play Bulwark soldier?'

His tone was enough to make Xia feel that she'd been slapped. She stepped back, angry at the tears stinging her eyes. 'I went to protect the forest from the worst threat it's ever faced.'

'And she did a fine job,' Drekene insisted. Of course a Deathless would show more compassion than her own father. 'Without her aid, the beast would likely still be out there. The death toll would certainly be far higher.'

Father drained his sapwine cup, then slapped it onto a side table with such force that Xia was surprised the glass stem did not shatter. 'Wonderful. Well, Xia, you got to kill a Daem-an after all. I hope your accomplishment is worth the price—your brother's life.'

'Grotan!' Xia's mother shouted. 'That's enough. We have our daughter back. We should be thanking Elf-az, not dwelling on what's happened. Don't chase our daughter away again.'

'It's fine,' Xia muttered. 'I won't be staying long.'

Mother stiffened. 'Oh, Xia, please say you've not signed up to the Bulwark.'

'She's not sworn any oath.' Drekene lowered herself to a kneel, giving her room to raise her head without hitting the living wood ceiling. 'She has simply volunteered to aid me during this task. Given her skills, I am grateful to accept.'

Mother shook her head, fresh tears. 'No, Xia, you can't. I forbid it. Bulwark has no right to enlist service from Vandar citizens.'

Trying to comfort her mother, Xia reached out for her weathered hands, only to have them flinch away. 'Mother, this was my choice. Drekene did not coerce me in any way.'

'No,' Mother repeated. 'I forbid it.'

Heart sinking, Xia shook her head. 'You can't. It's my choice.'

'I'm your mother.'

'And I'm an adult.'

'You're eighteen.'

'An adult,' Xia insisted. 'We can call the lawreader here to verify, but you know I have the right to make my own choices.'

Xia's father wrapped an arm around Mother as she sobbed. 'Fine,' he spat. 'If you did not come here to ask our permission, why *are* you here?'

'Xia brought me here to speak with you,' Drekene explained.

'For what?' Father snarled. 'You want to apologise for stealing away our daughter? For letting a Daem-an through the defences to terrorise our forest, to kill my son?'

Drekene shook her ash-grey head. 'No. I require your help. I must enlist the aid of the wardens.'

Disbelieving, Father guffawed. 'You must be joking.'

'I have no time for jests, Warden. The Daem-an that attacked your village was merely an advanced scout. It did not bypass the defences at Bulwark, but broke through the ground in the deep forest. We've sealed the hole it burrowed from, but it will not be long before its fellows tunnel through again.'

Father shrugged. 'Sounds like a problem for the Deathless, not wardens.'

Drekene's black eyes were piercing. 'The Deathless are few in number. Right now, Bulwark cannot spare enough defenders. We need trained fighters to hold the new route to the underworld until proper defences can be constructed. We need the wardens.'

'The wardens do not fight wars against the Daem-ans.' Father's voice was cold.

Xia sneered. 'The wardens protect the forest.'

'Against overpopulation,' he retorted. 'Against ogres. Against forest fires. Not against monsters from the underworld.'

Xia shook her head in disgust, hearing her old arguments in Father's words. Had she really been this naive, not able to see the threat the Daem-ans posed to the forest? The world?

'I must insist,' Drekene urged, voice hard.

'No,' Father yelled. 'You do not get to insist. Your kind are meant to protect the world, yet you let a beast loose amongst us, let it slaughter our people... my son. Your failure took my boy away. Your talk of great things has brainwashed my daughter, taking her on this deadly fool's errand. And what? You want me to fight for you? You want my kin to set aside their duty and die for you? No. Enough blood has been spilled because of the Bulwarks failings, because of *your* failings. Clean up your own damned mess.'

'Father,' Xia pleaded.

'No! Get out of here. I don't want to see you again, Deathless. And Xia… only return when this nonsense is out of you, when you start to care about your family more than your own glory. Go.'

Xia staggered back, stunned. Her hurt quickly turned to rage, her neck bulging, cheeks burning. She turned her back on the pair who had raised her.

'Come on, Drekene. There's nothing for us here. Let's see if we can find someone in this 'az-forsaken Forest who can see the doom awaiting us all.'

Chapter 11

Xia woke to the smell of Cadden's cooking. Leaning forward in her bunk to avoid hitting her head, she pushed herself up—the Hawk was cramped even for an Elf-an. Beside her, Rikk whimpered and rolled over, determined to remain asleep.

'Eggs?' she guessed, groggy.

Ket laughed. 'Well, the dried yellow powder Bulwark calls eggs. Pretty sure it's some sorta plastic.'

'You'll not be wanting any then?' Cadden joked.

'I never said that.' Ket replied, defensive.

Walking over, Cadden handed Xia a plate of something that resembled scrambled eggs, littered with pepper. To Ket, he handed a portion in a ramekin. 'Alright. It's not like your rations drain much of our supplies.'

Grinning, Ket dug at his food with a teaspoon. 'Eh, I do what I can to make up for the mountain that Drekene eats every day.'

The Deathless grunted as Cadden handed her a heavily piled plate. 'I eat precisely as much as required to keep up my energy reserves.'

'Aye.' Ket rubbed his mouth with the back of a clawed hand. 'And that's enough to feed a Greml family for a week. I'm telling you, if we were an all-Greml crew, we could run with a fraction of our supplies.'

Cadden sat opposite Xia, digging into his own breakfast. 'Yeah, and I'd like to see a handful of

Greml-ans trying to take down a Daem-an.'

'Hey,' Ket objected. 'If you count the guns, Greml-ans are responsible for more kills at Bulwark than the rest of the 'an put together. '

'Yes,' Cadden replied slowly, 'if you count the two-hundred tonne guns. You see any out here?'

Xia couldn't help but laugh at Ket's grumbling response, and took a spoonful of her own meal. The yellow mush wasn't too bad. The flavour came from its generous helping of ground pepper and salt, the rehydrated slurry having little taste of its own, certainly nothing remotely resembling eggs. Still, it filled a hole.

'I suppose a Deathless Greml-an might be able to take on a Daem-an.' She chewed her breakfast thoughtfully. 'Wait, are there any Greml Deathless?'

'Two.' Drekene nodded. 'Ikkan and Thet. Ikkan was killed by a stray bullet two centuries ago. Thet died in a cannon malfunction. Unfortunately, they were both within earshot of the Daem-ans' Song. They came back.'

'Both great engineers,' Ket piped up, proud. 'Half the weapon systems at Bulwark were developed by them. Take the brain of a Greml-an, give it an endless life to work, and they can make wonders. Far more useful than you big hulking Deathless who can do no more than swing a sword.'

Drekene stared flatly at Ket. 'The Deathless do far more than swing swords.'

'Aye,' he replied. 'Some of you've learned to use guns too.' His gleeful laugh echoed in the cabin. Drekene gave no reaction.

'I always imagined the Deathless holding the line

at Bulwark.' Xia set her empty plate to the side. 'Hard to picture a Deathless in a workshop inventing weapons.'

Drekene shrugged. 'We do what is needed to defeat the Daem-ans.'

'Speaking of which,' Cadden said, unusually dour. 'Looks like the wardens aren't going to help us.'

'No.' Xia sighed. 'At least, my parents won't. I don't know where the other wardens are based—never seemed important 'til now—but we could stop in the larger settlements and ask around.'

Drekene turned to her. 'Is there any reason to think they will be any more cooperative?'

Glum, Xia shook her head. 'No. They'll probably take Father's lead. He's respected among the wardens, for whatever reason. Some might think differently, but I've no idea who would be best to ask.'

'We don't have time to flit across the forest searching down every last warden.' The Deathless paused to think. 'Is there a command structure for the wardens? A leader?'

Xia shrugged. 'Sort of. There are is a council of retired wardens in Enall, the capital, who organise the wardens, make sure every area is covered. They answer directly to the prime minister though. And he answers to the Avatar.'

Cadden frowned. 'Thought you said you had no idea how to convince the Avatar to do anything?'

'I did.' Xia sighed. 'But I doubt the wardens or the Forest Guard will help us without her order.'

'Our course seems clear then,' Drekene stated. 'We travel to Enall and persuade the Avatar to help us.'

'You make it sound easy,' Xia replied dryly.

Drekene shrugged. 'The flight will not take more than a day.'

Xia rolled her eyes. 'I meant convincing an Avatar.'

'We will do what we must.' Drekene rose, plate empty. 'The Avatars put aside their wars and signed the Concordant after the last Daem outbreak. Surely she will see the need to act.'

'If you say so,' Xia replied, unconvinced. The Avatar of Elf-az had barely moved for over a century. For most, she was a symbolic symbol of Vandar, an ideal for all Elf-an, the spiritual heart of the forest, not a leader. It was hard to imagine her speaking, let alone ordering a new campaign against the Daem-ans. But Drekene was right—what other option did they have?

'Then we have a plan,' Drekene announced, voice filled with authority. 'Clear up here and get the Hawk ready. Cadden, I want to arrive at Enall by sundown.'

'Aye, sir,' he replied, gathering the scattered plates to take to a sink built into the silver bulkhead.

Xia hopped up alongside him. 'Let me deal with that.'

He beamed. 'You sure?'

'Of course. I'm no use right now. Best have the pilot doing piloty stuff.'

Chuckling, he backed off and headed for the cockpit. Xia set to work cleaning the plates, warm water and soap flowing from hidden nozzles. The action eased the awkward feelings that gripped her. Until now, she had been at the centre of their operation, the group relying her scouting ability or local knowledge. Now? She was a passenger. She had no idea how to help in the capital, let alone be useful on such a technical ship. The least she could do was to lessen the others' busywork.

Once the cutlery was cleaned and stored in a neighbouring cupboard, Xia took the opportunity to clean herself. The sink did not have a mirror, but even in the poor reflection of the brushed metal backing, Xia could see the muck that covered her face. The Hawk had no shower—much to her alarm—and the toilet was little more than a cupboard with a hole in the floor. Washing in the sink was difficult, set a little too high for Elf-ans yet too narrow to fit her arms into. Still, it felt great to wash some of the dirt and caked-on sweat from her hands, face, shoulders.

Her clothes still felt uncomfortably stiff, and smelled worse, but that could not be helped. She had not brought a change of attire and so had been working and sleeping in the same synthetic shorts and vest she had worn since leaving home. The Hawk had little privacy, and she did not relish the idea of standing in full view of Cadden and Ket while washing her clothes. For now, she would just have to be a little grim. Besides, the others had to deal with the same level of hygiene, as was made clear with the general stale odour that filled the cabin.

The starting of the engines was announced by a high-pitched whine echoing through the jet. So far, Xia had spent the flights in her bunk, catching up on sleep or maintaining her rifle. This morning, however, she was well rested and her rifle hung on the cabin's weapon rack, clean and ready to use.

Legs crossed near the jet's ramp, Drekene meditated. Ket crouched in his bunk-come-workshop, tinkering with some wire-coated device that Xia had no idea how to identify. Neither would want to be disturbed.

Curiosity drew her towards the cockpit. She scaled the short staircase—steps a little too large for an Elf-an to comfortably use—and poked her head into the switch-filled room. Above and below the curving window lay panels coated in dials, levers and digital displays. Two plush leather seats lay side by side, one occupied by Cadden.

'Can I join you?' she asked, hesitant.

Cadden's face lit up. 'Of course. Please, sit.'

Following his nod, Xia climbed into the empty chair. It was far too large for her, its black surface enveloping her small frame. With some adjustment, she managed to work the seat until she could see out the curved windows and across the nearby tree line. They had set down in the same field where Xia had first met Drekene, the field in which Xia's predecessor had been killed. Her final resting place now lay at the clearing's edge, a lone sapling marking her grave.

'Strap yourself in,' Cadden commanded, 'in case we hit turbulence.'

Reluctant, Xia pulled the straps over her chest and waist, buckling them together. It felt strange, being so restricted, surrounded by metal and plastic.

Xia's anxiety only grew as Cadden slipped a hand into a bulky, glove-like contraption and the jet lurched into the air. They rapidly ascended above the trees, Xia gripping her armrests as the craft swung through the air. Her heart pounded as they throttled forward, treetops flicking by just below the jet's metal belly.

'You alright?' Cadden asked.

Xia gave a weak smile. 'Didn't seem this fast when

I was in the bunk.'

Cadden laughed. 'Quite a rush, hey? I've loved this feeling since my mum first took me up. Knew then that I'd be a pilot.'

His confidence infectious, Xia felt herself relax—a little. 'That why you joined Bulwark?'

'Know another place that will train you to fly for free? Was meant to be just temporary—wanted to go into civil aviation after this. But now? Hard step down to flying passenger liners after piloting the Hawk.'

'I prefer passenger liners,' Xia mumbled. 'Safety in size.'

He laughed again, flashing a grin. 'Ah, that's just novice nerves. You'll grow out of it in no time. The Hawk's a breeze to fly. Has never let me down.'

'I'll take your word for it.' Xia peered from the window, trying to get her bearings. The forest looked so strange from above. Gone were the endless trunks, shadows pierced with rays of light, constant calls of wildlife. Now an infinite, uneven green stretched as far as the eye could see, broken by the occasional clearing or river. Only by the light of the sun could Xia judge that they flew north.

'Do you want to give it a go?'

'Huh?' Xia turned her attention back to Cadden, who looked far too lively for this time of morning.

'Do you want to fly?'

'You can't be serious.'

'I'm always serious.' His grin seemed to prove otherwise. 'It's not that hard. Here, I'll give you some height.'

Xia's stomach lurched as the jet ascended, trees disappearing form view. 'I don't know about this. I've never driven anything before.'

'First time for everything. Take hold of your control pad. You'll be fine—I'll be right here.'

As much as Xia wanted to argue, Cadden's enthusiasm was hard to resist. She had never been one for machinery, but this journey had been nothing if not filled with the new and unexpected. Besides, Drekene —an Ash Deathless four hundred years old—had embraced tree-leaping without hesitation. Xia could not let herself be outdone.

Laughing with nerves, Xia followed Cadden's gaze towards a contraption beside her, matching the one his hand was tucked into. She reached towards the opening in the black oval. It was held by a lever extending from the dashboard and resembled a swollen glove. Felt cold to the touch, hard.

She eased her hand inside, feeling the opening break into individual finger holes—far too large.

'I don't think it's designed for Elf-an,' she said, partially relieved, partially disappointed.

With a snap, the device shut around her hand, making her jump. The finger holes shifted, closing together and shrinking, wrapping her hand perfectly. She tried to jerk her arm back, only to feel the Hawk shudder to a stop.

'Easy.' Cadden couldn't keep all the panic from his voice. 'It's just adjusting to you, keep your hand still.'

She froze, heart hammering. The jet steadied itself, much to her relief.

'The controls are straightforward,' Cadden explained. 'Here, I'll show you. Our pads are linked— as I move mine, yours will move too. Just let your arm relax. The Hawk copies your hand. Tilt your hand, and the Hawk tilts.' She felt the device turn around her hand. As it did, the view twisted as the Hawk rolled to the side. 'Lift your hand up, and the Hawk goes up. Push it forward, and we go forward.' He demonstrated, the craft responding to his inputs. 'Now you try.'

Licking her lips, Xia nodded. Hesitant, she dipped her fingers down. Instantly, the Hawk's nose dropped, the windows filling with a view of trees. Yelping, Xia pulled her fingers back until the Hawk levelled out. Despite her pounding heart, Xia could not help but grin.

'Fun, hey?' Cadden laughed. 'Push your hand forward, away from you.'

She obeyed and the Hawk accelerated. She stretched her hand further forward and their speed increased, the roar of the engines growing as they ripped over the treetops.

Ket's shout ended the fun. 'Would you two quit it. I'm trying to work for Avatars' sake.'

'Sorry.' Xia called back, but could not help laughing. She relaxed her arm and the device returned to its original position, the Hawk slowing to a stop.

'Splay your fingers to release it.' Cadden matched her broad smile. 'Told you it was fun.'

'Alright, I'll give you this one.' She rubbed her hand as it came free from the device. 'Though I'll leave the flying to you. Don't want to annoy Ket.'

The Hum-an laughed. 'Probably for the best. Never know when he'll mess with the lighting above your bunk, or tweak the pressure in the toilet. Never pays to annoy a Greml-an.'

'I heard that,' Ket grumbled, only eliciting laugher

from the two in the cockpit.

Taking back control, Cadden pushed the Hawk into motion, far steadier than Xia's efforts. Summoned by the laughter, Rikk padded up the steps to settle between the two chairs. For a time, Xia relaxed, scratching the vulfik between the ears, actually enjoying the flight.

As the adrenalin faded, Xia turned to Cadden. 'Can I ask you something?'

'Of course.'

Xia kept her voice low. 'I'm still wondering about the Deathless. I've asked Drekene about what it costs to become one, but she never answers.'

'Probably doesn't want to tempt you. Everyone at Bulwark has it drummed into them how terrible a choice it is to become Deathless.'

'So it *is* a choice?'

Cadden nodded. 'Supposedly. Anyone who dies near a Daem-an is shown two futures and given the option of which to follow. The first is what priests will have droned at you since you could speak. Lavish paradise by the side of your patron 'az, surrounded by family and friends, the whole malarkey.'

'And the other?'

The Hum-an sighed. 'The other future is them coming back as Deathless, the ageless, tireless warriors that are our final line against the Daem-ans. But even Deathless do not last forever. They can be killed, and when they do, there is that dark price.'

'Which is?' Xia prompted, impatient.

He scratched at his freshly-shaven chin. 'Their immortal soul.'

Xia shook her head. 'What? Like after they die,

they disappear?'

Drekene's voice cut through the conversation. 'Worse.' She stood just behind Xia, black eyes boring into her. 'We are brought back again, but this time in service of Daem-az, the god of those beasts. We turn into the very monsters we fight.'

'How is that worse than not existing?'

'In that vision of the future we see what it is to be a Daem-an. They are born in agony, hatched from the darkness. Constant pain wracks them, the only relief arriving when they kill, when they destroy. Then, there are granted a fleeting pause in their misery, but in a heartbeat they return to their torture. They are driven ever onward, wanting to destroy anything that was not created by their 'az. And when they die? It starts again. Over and over, a cycle of pain and death until the end of time. That is what awaits Deathless. That is what awaits me.'

Xia opened and closed her mouth, trying for words. 'I didn't know.'

'And I pray you never will, Xia the Warden. The Deathless are grateful for all who stand by us to help protect the world from the Daem scourge, but we pray that none follow us into this sacrifice.' There was a yearning in those black eyes, a desperate plea. 'Xia, by everything you hold dear, never make that deal. If by some cruel twist of fate you fall in the presence of a Daem-an, never, ever, accept that offer. You will regret doing so for the rest of your existence.'

Seeing her face, hearing the emotion in her voice, Xia believed the Deathless.

Chapter 12

Xia's breath caught. The landscape bathed in the setting's sun orange as Enall came into view. In the twilight, the metropolis was illuminated by the glow of a million neon lights. She had never seen such a large settlement. Even the coastal tourist cities her family frequented in the summer seemed tiny in comparison.

A composite of a dozen architectural schools, Enall grew out of the dense forest. Trees morphed by lifeSinging into vast organic dwellings grew alongside Hum towers of brick. Gobl mounds hunkered below Drak spires. Modern glass skyscrapers fought for space with manicured parks.

The lights seemed to stretch endlessly onwards, meeting somewhere to the north with the calm waters of Winter Bay. To the east and west, the lights melded with those of Enall's countless suburbs. Here, surrounded by the world's largest forest on three sides, stood the centre of Elf civilisation.

Cadden did not seemed phased, tapping his communication panel. 'Enall Control, this is Hawk, Bulwark transport T-876, requesting landing clearance at the parliament's hub.'

The static filled response blared out from the cockpit's speakers, the Elf-an's accent distinctly northern. 'T-876, this is Enall control. Follow inbound traffic route Twenty-Seven Left. We have you cleared for landing on Pad-Thirty.'

'Confirmed, Enall Control. Twenty-Seven Left to Thirty.'

Cadden's attention shifted to the myriad of buttons and switches that coated the cockpit. Xia left him to it, peering out the window. Streets—both on ground level and strung between trees and skyscrapers—criss-crossed the city in an elaborate web.

Following a stream of other jets and rotorwings, the Hawk flew through the city, passing between gigantic trees and towers. Some of the skyscrapers gave a nod towards Elf traditions, their brick-and-metal structures bound in climbing vines, glass windows bedecked in flowers. Other structures stayed determinedly modern, all sharp edges, polished glass and neon lights.

Ket clambered onto Xia's headrest, peeked over her shoulder and whistled. 'Phew. What a mess. Wouldn't find such a mismatch in a Greml city.'

'That's because Greml-ans don't have cities,' Xia retorted.

'Aye,' he replied. 'Well, if we did, it would be a shet-sight neater than all this.'

'Yeah,' Cadden interjected. 'Your bunk just screams neatness.'

Xia laughed at Ket's scowl.

Drekene trudged up the stairs, causing the startled Rikk to jump onto Xia's lap. Together the crew stared at the passing city, flight paths marked by streams of aircraft flying above and below one another. A thousand vehicles, all traversing the evening sky along invisible highways.

Up ahead, a colossal oak sat at the city's heart. The trunk alone was wider than the entirety of Ethelan, its branches stretching out hundreds of meters in all directions. Xia had seen enough pictures to recognise Vandar's parliament, the home of the Avatar.

They turned out of the river of aircraft to approach a cylindrical tower. Its edge was divided into a hundred alcoves—docking platforms packed around the tower's perimeter. Many already contained vehicles, from small personal 'copters to hoverjets larger than the Hawk.

Cadden guided the aircraft into one of the alcoves, the sun's red replaced with the harsh white glare of fluorescent lamps. With a grating noise, the landing skids settled onto the structure's bare concrete.

'And we're here.' The pilot began a byzantine sequence of button presses and switch flicking, warning lights flaring to life and fading away until finally the engines droned into silence.

'Great.' Ket yawned. 'What's next?'

Drekene sniffed. 'Next? We go to the Avatar and get an army.'

The short walk to the parliament building astonished Xia. She had always thought that Ethelan was cosmopolitan, but she had never seen such diversity. Under the looming branches of the massive oak, they passed countless variations of 'an. The expected pale skinned central Elf-ans, like herself, were joined by their tanned cousins from Sulsine. Drak men towered over Gobl-ans, whose wrinkled skin was so pale as to remind Xia of a shaved cat. Dark-skinned continental Hum-ans like Cadden walked alongside the paler offshoot from the Stalton Archipelago. Greml-ans scuttled around the edges of the vine walkway, cackling to each other as they set to their evening excursion.

On this single walkway stood more people than lived in Xia's home town. This was but one street in one section of this colossal city. What really sent a shiver down Xia's spine was the recollection that Enall was half the size of the Hum capital. Never before had Xia felt so insignificant.

'Well there it is.' Cadden nodded to a set of arching stained-glass doors built into the oak's trunk.

'Can't believe we're going to meet the prime minister,' Xia breathed. 'And the Avatar.'

'Big day huh, kid?' Ket scrambled on all fours. Side by side with Rikk, he looked like a small, bald vulfik. He had not appreciated the comparison.

'Yeah well, I'm not used to all this,' Xia pointed out. 'Two weeks ago, the worst I had to worry about was the possibility of an ogre running loose in the forest. Not practised in all this end-of-Vandar shet.'

Ket gave a rueful cackle. 'Aye. Well if it helps, when I signed up to Drekene's crew, we were meant to be doing recruitment drives around the continent. Here we are, just over a year later, and I'm throwing explosives into bottomless pits.'

'Don't pretend you didn't love that,' Cadden laughed.

'Aye well, my point was we've all been thrown into the deep end... 'cept for Drekene, I suppose.'

The Deathless grunted. 'This is the first time I've tried to set up a defence at a breach from the underworld. I was born after Bulwark was constructed.'

Ket huffed. 'Aye, well, all this killing Daem-ans

shet? That's what you Deathless have always done.'

Drekene shrugged. 'All Bulwark forces are trained to fight the Daem-ans. Yourself included.'

'Dragon-shet,' Ket retorted. 'I was trained to keep big cannons firing. The kid was taught to fly supply craft. Girly here knows how to jump between trees. A couple of weeks ago, the only one of us that'd been within spitting distance of a Daem-an was you.'

Drekene just sighed. Any further argument was forestalled as they approached the double doors. A functionary hurried down the living-wood stairs leading to the doorway. The man, tall for an Elf-an and bald, could not hide his disgust at the sight of the group. Xia suddenly realised how they stood out among the capital's finery. Their clothes were stained —either with oil or mud—nails and claws ground short, numerous scratches highlighting any exposed skin. Even Xia's plaited hair must be a sight, having barely been cleaned for a week.

'Can I help you?' The man somehow turned the words into a threat.

'I am Drekene the Deathless, here on behalf of Bulwark with urgent news for the prime minister.'

The functionary ponderously scrolled through an electronic tablet. 'I'm afraid I don't have a record of your appointment.'

Drekene sighed with impatience. 'We don't have an appointment.'

'Then I cannot help you.'

Drekene cocked her head to the side. 'Did you not hear that I am from Bulwark?'

At the intensity of her voice, the man took a step back. Behind him, the door was flanked by six Elf-ans wearing the vibrant green cloaks of the Forest Guard, beautiful white ceremonial bows peeking over their shoulders. All six were watching Drekene with unnerving focus.

The functionary recovered, raising his nose to stare down at Drekene from the steps, imperious. 'I did hear you, and the parliament of Vandar would be glad to grant you an audience… with an appointment.'

Drekene's glare could have frozen the sea. 'This matter must be dealt with *now*.'

'Then perhaps you should have alerted us in advance.'

'This is an emergency.' The Deathless's hands closed into fists.

Slowly nodding, the functionary returned his attention to his tablet. 'In that case, I can grant you an emergency session… three days from now, in the afternoon.'

'Not good enough,' Drekene snarled.

The functionary met her gaze, impassive. 'It's the best I can do.'

Xia couldn't believe what she was hearing. 'This is serious,' she blurted. 'It's about Daem-ans.'

The man's gaze turned to her and looked her up and down, not attempting to hide his disgust. 'Of course it is. Bulwark discusses nothing else.'

She shook her head. 'You don't understand. This isn't about attacks at Bulwark. There were Daem-ans right here, in Vandar.'

'Of course.' His voice dripped with condescension. 'We've heard such threats before, many times.'

'These are not threats,' Xia pressed. 'They are real. I've seen them causing havoc in the deep forest.'

'Then it is a good thing that I have granted you an emergency audience.'

'We don't have time for this nonsense.' Drekene pushed past the man, nearly knocking him down.

In an instant, the six Forest Guard reacted. Their ceremonial bows forgotten, they ripped ivory pistols from holsters, levelling them at the Deathless. Drekene froze, hand halfway to her sword. Xia took a step back, the air buzzing with tension as the Deathless stared down six armed soldiers.

'Enough,' the functionary sneered. 'No one is permitted into the parliament without authorisation. Not envoys from Bulwark, not even Deathless. You are a guest in our land, and you will act like it. Now, we are happy to provide you with accommodation until your appointed meeting. Or, if you prefer, you can push further and end up in a prison cell. Or worse.'

Xia could only watch in terror. She saw the tensing of Drekene's muscles, heard the creak of her armoured suit. Her Kevlar could stop pistol rounds without issue, but she had no helmet. The Forest Guard were known as the finest marksmen in the world—most being ex-wardens—but would they be able to stop a Deathless? Would they even try? Would Drekene force their hand?

Drekene's arm dropped to her side and she took a step back. Relief washed over everyone, the Forest Guard and Drekene's crew alike. Even the functionary seemed to relax, though he quickly hid his reaction. It was only then that Xia noticed the crowd they had attracted, members of every 'an staring in curiosity and fear at the standoff.

'Fine,' Drekene barked. 'If you are so insistent, we will delay. I pray none die because of your stubbornness.'

The functionary went back to that condescending smile. 'Oh, I highly doubt that is a real risk. Please, let me organise lodging for you nearby.'

Xia could hardly comprehend the man's blithe attitude. Sure, living in a small village, she had not been prepared for Daem-ans wandering the forest, but this was the government. Was the whole world blind to the Daem threat?

At Xia's feet, water the colour of rosewood flowed down the shower drain. A week of sweat, mud, ichor and blood trickled from her skin. She teased out tangles in her hair, freeing the occasional twig or pine needle. The warm water eased the aches in her limbs, the sharp apple scent of the hotel's shower gel leaving her skin tingling, her mind refreshed.

Grudgingly, she turned off the water and stepped out onto the ceramic tiles of the bathroom. The hotel was a strange hybrid of Elf and Hum design. The exterior could not have been more at home in Vandar, an ancient pine morphed by lifeSingers into a bulbous tower, capped with the evergreen needles of the living building. Inside, the decor was clearly inspired by the Avatarium of Hum—all ceramic tiles, nylon carpets, plastic walls.

As the wafts of steam faded, Xia saw her reflection in the floor-to-ceiling mirror. Bruises, grazes and cuts littered her pale skin. Her whole life had been spent outdoors, and she had received her fair share of knocks and bumps, but had never seen herself so battered. She looked as if she had fallen out of a tree, hitting every branch on the way down.

Turning from the mirror, she dried herself with the hotel's wonderfully soft towel, then pulled on the jumpsuit Drekene had given her. Xia no longer needed her breathable vest and shorts, and so had given in and put them in the laundry, accepting a Bulwark flight uniform. The material was coarse, and the jumpsuit was a tad large, but it was wonderful to wear something clean. She still pulled on her climbing shoes—none of the Hawk's boots had come close to fitting.

The white panelled door creaked gently as Xia pushed it aside and entered the main room. Drekene and Cadden sat on two of the three single beds, the fine mattress looking little more than a stool beneath the Deathless. Ket had taken up residence in the cupboard, having arranged the spare towel shelf into a nest. Out the large window—curved glass framed with living wood—Enall's lights glittered.

Cadden lit up at the sight of her. 'Better?'

'Much.' Xia walked to the dresser and began to tame her hair, drawing it into a pleated ring that crowned her head.

'So what's for dinner?' Ket called from his perch.

Looking to Drekene, Cadden shrugged. 'We've got supplies on the Hawk. I could reheat something.'

In the mirror, Xia stared at him. 'You kidding me? We're in the Elf capital, all expenses paid by Parliament, and you want to eat that packaged food?'

Cackling came from Ket's cupboard. 'Have I mentioned I like the new girl?'

Cadden glanced at Xia, awkward. 'What would

you suggest?'

'Well, we passed that fancy restaurant in the lobby. I think it's time I showed you some real Elf cooking.'

Standing, Drekene nodded. 'I concur with Xia's plan. We should avoid using the Hawk's food stores if we can—we don't know when we'll next be able to resupply at Bulwark.'

Ket laughed, clambering down from his nest. 'Whatever your reasons, I'm happy for anything that gives us a break from Cadden's slop.'

Cadden simply rolled his eyes.

Grinning, Xia led the others to the door. 'Come on then.'

The corridor was more of the same amalgamation of Hum and Elf tastes. The living wood floor was flanked by white plastic walls. Neon lights were suspended by vines. Holographic paintings sat encased in carved oak frames.

The elevator was completely modern, mirrored walls and a floor-length window looking out into the city beyond. The four crowded into the space, Drekene's bulk taking up as much room as the other three put together. In eerie silence they descended, the expertly crafted mechanisms not giving the slightest noise. Xia could only wonder how much power this one building required—probably had its own team of Gobl chargeSingers tucked away in the basement.

The doors slid open to reveal a palatial restaurant. Located just off the main lobby, the room took up half of the vast trunk's width. Gone were the Hum affectations, this room was traditional Elf-an, moss carpet, living wood tables, bone cutlery.

An Elf woman wearing an elegant robe strolled

over to the group. 'Welcome to Vassin's Lounge. Table for four?'

Drekene nodded. 'Please.'

The head waitress nodded and lead them across the soft floor. 'Our meal today is a root salad with a side of crushed summer fruit.'

'No choice?' Cadden whispered.

Xia smiled. 'Not in Elf restaurants. Choosing your own meal is a very Hum thing. Here we trust the chefs.'

'What if you don't like what they offer?'

'Well, you go to a different restaurant.' Xia shrugged. 'You wouldn't visit a friend's house and dictate what they should serve you, right? Well, this is the same thing.'

Cadden shook his head as they sat around a table coated in a green cotton sheet. 'Elf customs are confusing.'

'See what I mean? "All other 'an are mad."' Ket laughed as he pulled himself onto a Greml highchair that the waiter pulled over. 'Told you Cadden's racist.'

'That's not what I meant.' Cadden stammered.

Xia eyed him wryly. 'No, you just meant we should be more like Hum-ans.'

'That's... No I...'

Laughing, Xia patted the poor pilot's arm. 'I'm just teasing. I can imagine how strange it is to be half a world from home.'

Cadden gave an uncertain laugh. 'Well, we'll just need to take you to Hum at some point. Show you not all Hum cooking is that bad. My mum makes a fantastic soup.'

Mischievously grinning, Ket cackled. 'Already

asking her home to meet your parents? Shet, Cadden, you do move fast.'

Xia couldn't help but laugh as Cadden spluttered, struggling for words. His misery was ended as the waitress returned, laying out four plates onto the table, Drekene's serving massive, Ket's smaller than a child's.

'See, Cadden? Xia grinned. 'The other advantage of the Elf way—if they know what everyone's having, there's no need to wait while they prepare it from scratch.'

Sharp smells drifted over the table. Xia hungrily dug into her dish, the finely-shredded carrots, vettan, parsnips and shadet calling out to her. After a week eating prepackaged and dehydrated meals, the fresh vegetables tasted wonderful, the crushed fruit drink deliciously sweet.

'Good hey?' she asked.

'Good,' Cadden replied, uncertain.

'You don't sound convinced.'

He shrugged. 'I dunno. It's missing something.'

Ket giggled. 'Well, to make it like yours, it's missing about two hours in boiling water. Look, even Drekene's packing it away.'

'That's not saying much,' Cadden replied. 'I've actually seen her eat a bag of dried rice.'

Drekene grunted. 'Ket was repairing the stove.'

The table broke out into laughter, save for the Deathless.

Cadden turned to Xia. 'Alright, I'll admit this is a nice change. If you like, I'm sure I can make something similar. Will just have to get some fresh ingredients onto the Hawk.'

155

'Be careful, Girl,' Ket warned. 'You've seen what does to Hum cooking. You really want him to butcher your favourite dishes?'

Xia smiled. 'Now, I think I would like that. If you're serious, Cadden, I'd be grateful to have to Elf cooking on board. I can even give you a hand.'

The young pilot beamed at her. 'I'd love that.'

'Someone else cooking?' Ket giggled. 'That gets my vote too.'

Cadden swatted at Ket, almost getting himself bitten for his efforts. Again the table broke into an easy laugh. Even Drekene looked amused, some life entering her black eyes. In the company of these three, all the fears of Daem-ans and frustrations at bureaucrats faded. She smiled to herself. Perhaps together, they would actually manage this, end the threat to Vandar once and for all.

Chapter 13

'You sure about this?' Xia asked.

Nervously, Cadden nodded, face inches from hers, close enough to smell his aftershave. 'Yes.'

Grinning, Xia shoved him. With a yelp, the Human was flung backwards, spiralling as he drifted into the void between trunks, suspended by his grav-belt.

They were at the outskirts of Enall, where the mismatched buildings finally gave way to the scattered trunks of the forest. Homes and offices were still incorporated into the lifeSung trees, but the lower levels were free of the obstacles that littered the main city. As a place to learn to tree-leap, this would suffice.

Laughing at Cadden's flailing attempts to steady himself, Xia kicked off the trunk. Midway between the trees, she caught him by the collar, her momentum carrying them both to a nearby tree. She sunk her claws into the rough pine bark, holding the pilot tight as he rebounded, steadying him until his hands latched onto the trunk.

'Not too bad, hey?' Xia grinned.

Cadden struggled for breath. 'Think I shet myself.'

'Now, where's the confident pilot gone? You fly much higher than this for a living.'

'Yeah, but that's in the Hawk. It's different when you're encased in a few tonnes of steel.'

'A few tonnes of steel that's going to come crashing down on top of you when you fall.'

'A few tonnes of steel that will crush whatever I

land on,' Cadden corrected. 'I assure you that far more people die from falls than from air crashes. Probably.'

Rikk landed on the tree just above the pair. Face-down, he sniffed at Cadden.

'Inquisitive little fellow.' The pilot squirmed away from Rikk's attempts to lick his face.

'Can probably just smell your terror-sweat.'

Cadden smirked. 'I'll blame that on my instructor.'

'Hey,' Xia objected. 'Learning to tree-leap was your idea.'

'Learning to leap, yeah. Seemed like a good way to pass the day. I never agreed to be thrown from trees.'

Xia shrugged. 'The easiest way to make someone have faith in a grav-belt is to suspend them by one. It's like tossing kids into the deep end when training them to swim.'

'Pretty sure I learned to swim in a kiddie pool,' he grumbled.

She couldn't help but laugh at how defensive the young man had become. 'Here, maybe this isn't a good idea after all. Tree-leaping's not for everyone. You want to head back to the others?'

Cadden held her gaze. She could see his internal debate, but the doubts fled from his face. Xia had no idea what suddenly motivated him, but the pilot seemed convinced. 'No. I'd prefer to stay here.'

Unable but to smile at his newfound confidence, Xia pointed to a nearby trunk. 'Right, so you know how to swim, right? Kicking off a tree is just like kicking off the edge of a pool. Just keep your eyes on the trunk and push off.'

To demonstrate, she kicked the tree, easily passing

the few meters to its neighbour. Chirping excitedly, Rikk scampered up his tree and jumped after Xia, landing beside her.

'Now you try,' Xia urged.

With a deep breath, Cadden kicked after Xia. He misjudged the leap, erring slightly too far to the side. Without help, he would miss the trunk all together, drifting onwards to stop high above the forest floor. Luckily for him, this was far from the first time Xia had instructed a beginner.

Sinking her claws into a scar where the tree once held a branch, she stretched out her free hand. In desperation, he reached for her. With a slap, his dark hand wrapped around her jumpsuit's wrist. She clamped down on his forearm and swung him into the tree. Not expecting the change in motion, he couldn't stop himself rebounding off the bark, and would have spiralled away had she not quickly grabbed his waist, pulling him safely close.

Face to face, they paused, Cadden staring into her eyes, almost too close to focus. For a moment, the forest stilled, the chirps of birds became distant, even Rikk's panting quietened.

Face reddening, Cadden twisted to the side, coughing awkwardly.

Xia frowned at his reaction, confused. 'Come on, don't be embarrassed. Everyone misses trees at first. Well, except for Drekene, but she does have a few centuries on most beginners.'

Cadden turned back to her, words caught in his throat. He shook his head, blushing, and looked away. 'Yeah. Guess I just need more practice.'

'Well, there's a whole forest here.' Xia held out her

hand.

Cadden forced an awkward laugh, then turned to kick off towards the next tree. They continued for the rest of the day, and Cadden rapidly improved, but his nerves did not calm. She kept catching him staring furtively at her, stammering at praise and blushing whenever he made a mistake and needed rescuing. Xia was taken aback, unable to explain the shift in his mood from the confident pilot he had been the previous day. It seemed even hardened Bulwark soldiers could be complicated. Despite this, Xia found herself far more relaxed than she had for the past week, something remarkably freeing about simply spending time with Cadden, away from all the stress and fear of the doomed world.

Smoothing the coarse fabric of her flightsuit, Xia followed Drekene towards the stain-glass doors of parliament. There were a few rips on the blue material —teaching Cadden to tree-leap was almost as exhausting as pursuing the Daem-an. He seemed hard to put off, and had been all too happy to go out again the previous day for another session. At least when she had taught others to leap, they were normally children, or at least only Elf-an. Cadden was a good half-foot taller than her, and weighed a lot more. Her shoulder ached from having to repeatedly catch his weight to direct him to a narrowly missed tree. She thanked Elf-az that Drekene had taken to tree-leaping like a natural —having to grab the Deathless would probably have dislocated Xia's arm.

All four of the Hawk's crew had washed and ironed their clothes this meeting—anything to make the right impression—and they still smelled of the hotel's washing powder. Their efforts went unappreciated by the functionary, who looked immensely tired at the sight of their approach.

'You are prompt, at least,' he murmured.

'Now you will let us speak to the parliament,' Drekene stated, threat clear in her tone.

'Now that you have an appointment, of course.' The man turned and led the way up the steps. The Forest Guard stood rigid at their posts, eyes ahead, though Xia could see how their hands tensed over their pistols as Drekene neared.

The functionary forced aside the doors, leading into a surreal hallway. Grass carpeted the floor, neatly trimmed. The walls were bedecked with runner vines and bright flowers, climbing their way over the oak's curved interior. Air as fresh as any meadow drifted on an impossible breeze. The corridor was brightly lit, though Xia could not locate the origin of the light, which seemingly came from all directions at once. A shiver ran down her spine when she realised that the group cast no shadow as they paced the hall.

'At all times, you will show respect in the presence of Parliament.' The functionary glanced over his shoulder, levelling a stern gaze at Drekene as he talked. 'You will bow once to the Avatar when you enter, and once as you leave. Do not look directly at the Avatar. Do not speak to the Avatar unless addressed—and don't expect to be addressed. All your questions should be directed towards the prime minister.' He glanced over his shoulder again. 'I see you have brought your weapons?'

Drekene grunted. 'Is that going to be a problem?'

Xia had argued against it, but the Deathless had insisted that the group should look the part of envoys from the warriors of Bulwark. At least Xia had managed to persuade the ancient woman that Rikk should stay behind. He may look imposing when riled, but Xia dreaded the idea of the daft mutt being in the presence of the Avatar. He wouldn't do anything malicious, but she would not put it past the creature to relieve himself in the holy room. Then chirp for praise.

The functionary smirked. 'Hardly. I do not care how armed you are. Forest Guard will have weapons trained on you the entire time. They are ordered to shoot to kill at the first sight of threat, so don't try throwing your weight around as you did the other day.'

'The Deathless are allies of Vandar. I am no threat to the Avatar.'

Another smirk from the smug man. 'I know that, otherwise you would not be in this building. I would just like to avoid you doing anything foolish and leaving us to clean up the mess… literally. Remember, although you may have authority at that little fort of yours, here you are guests. You will do as you are told or you will be removed. You will show deference to the sovereignty of Vandar, or you will be removed. You will not make us regret giving you this audience.'

Xia rolled her eyes. If this was how her government behaved towards its allies, Xia could only imagine how they would treat an enemy.

Ahead, a round door styled as a series of overlapping petals peeled open to reveal a dazzling chamber. Following the functionary, the group stepped into a vaulted hall formed from glowing amber. The

162

entire space—floors, walls, pillars and furniture—was hewn from a single solid block of the dried sap. The orange stone was highlighted with climbing vines and mounds of flowers that had never seen the sun.

Striding over the translucent surface seemed unnatural, Xia's feet passing over an orange haze as she saw the smoky imperfections in the amber fade well below the surface, backlit by some hidden light source. Each step echoed sharply, the circular walls reflecting back every sound with eerie clarity.

The far side of the room was flanked with two galleries of benches—also amber—seating over a hundred Elf-ans: the ministers of Parliament. Between them, sat on a glowing bed of pillows and flowers, was the most beautiful woman Xia had ever seen. Fair brown hair draped down an olive dress, face immaculate, eyes the colour of cut emeralds.

The Avatar of Elf-az. The living conduit to the creator of all Elf-ans.

Xia averted her gaze, but was overtaken by the irresistible urge to drop to her knees, pressing her head against the cold floor.

'You may rise,' came a clear, male voice. Xia looked up to see the speaker standing before the Avatar. The Elf-an wore a dark green suit, embroidered with flowers encircling amber. Xia had seen enough news reports to identify the prime minister.

Quickly rising to her feet, Xia blushed at the realisation that she was the only one to have crouched, the others merely bowing. Had they not looked at the Avatar, or did the influence of Elf-az only cover Elf-ans? She had no time to dwell on the question as she hurried to keep pace with Drekene.

The functionary bowed to the audience, then called in a clear voice, 'Your honour. I present Drekene of Bulwark. Drekene, be honoured to meet Prime Minister Zeand Grell.'

The Deathless stopped a few paces from the prime minister. 'I am Drekene the Deathless, and we have already wasted too much time waiting for this meeting.'

Prime Minister Grell gave a thin-lipped smile. 'And what does Bulwark ask of Vandar today?'

'To defend itself against annihilation.'

Grell raised an eyebrow. 'I see Bulwark is dramatic as ever. Care to explain?'

'There is a new breach from the underworld, right in the heart of the forest.' Drekene proceeded to recount the story, describing her assignment to chase down rumours of a Daem-an in Vandar, the attacks on villages, killing the Daem-an and finally sealing the breach.

'It's true.' Xia stepped forward. 'All of it. I saw the beast with my own eyes.'

Grell tore his gaze from Drekene to face Xia. 'And you are?'

'Xia Redseed, a warden from the village of Ethelan.'

'She has been vital in my efforts to track the Daem-ans,' Drekene explained. 'Without her skills, the damage would have been much greater.'

Appraisingly, Grell looked Xia up and down. 'I am glad our wardens continue to provide such unwavering service, even if on unauthorised missions.' The criticism in his tone was clear. 'But I fail to see why this required an emergency meeting today. We are well aware of the reports of attacks in the south, and the presence of a Deathless in Vandar. While we are relieved to hear of your success, such news could have been delivered via message. You hardly need an audience for this. You have our gratitude, but I fail to see what else you could require.'

Drekene cocked her head to the side. 'The threat is not over.'

The prime minister opened his arms in confusion. 'I thought you said that the Daem-an was dead, that you sealed the breach to the underworld.'

'We did,' pressed Drekene, 'but that is temporary at best. Before long, the Daem-ans will dig through the crumbled rock and emerge once again, this time with far more than a single scout. When they do, fortifications must already be prepared, manned by soldiers ready to face the attack.'

'And you've come before us because…?'

Drekene blinked, confused into a moment's silence. 'Because we need personnel to construct the new fort. We need materials for its construction. Moreover, we need trained soldiers to hold the site. The wardens or the Forest Guard.'

Grell barked a laugh. 'The wardens maintain the natural balance. The Forest Guard protect the capital.'

The Deathless shook her head. 'Xia has demonstrated the warden's ability has not diminished over the centuries. What we need are trained marksmen, like the wardens.'

Another disbelieving laugh. 'No, what you need are soldiers, like the thousands you have at Bulwark.'

'Bulwark has no one available right now. We need

Vandar to protect itself until reinforcements can be raised.'

'And there we have it.' The prime minister turned to the galleries, proudly calling to his fellow ministers. 'Just as I predicted. Just as Vandar has feared for decades. This is merely an excuse to draft Vandar citizens to complete the task that Bulwark is charged to handle.'

'This is not an excuse,' Drekene insisted. 'The threat is real.'

'Of course it is,' Grell snapped. 'And you would hold this threat to our throats until we renegotiate our treaty. Long has Bulwark increased its demands for supplies. We have accommodated, our farmers bled dry to feed foreign soldiers, but it is never enough.'

Drekene shook her head. 'The supplies have increased as our manpower has increased. The Daem attacks are stronger than ever, yet we have kept you safe.'

'And Vandar has fed you for centuries. We supply the entirety of Bulwark's food use, all of its medical supplies. But every year we receive your demands to do more, to send our young to die on the front line so the other 'an can take a back seat. And now you finally have the threat you need to compel us into action. Well, Deathless, you have underestimated Vandar's resolve. We will not be bullied by you soulless monsters or your pawns.'

Frustration erupted in Drekene's shout. 'This is not the time for posturing. This is about a danger to the entire world.'

'A danger that Bulwark is tasked to contain,' retorted Grell. 'The Concordant was clear, the treaties are clear. Bulwark protects the world from the Daemans. Vandar feed Bulwark. If your soldiers want to keep eating, you will do your duty and defend Vandar. By all means, if Bulwark sends an army to protect Vandar, we will feed them too. We will honour our end of the Concordant, but you best honour yours. If you are incapable of protecting us, then perhaps it is time that Bulwark be replaced with a modern force, one that can do the task without draining the rest of the continent. But I will be damned if we're going to strip our economy for nothing. Either Bulwark protects the world—all the world—or Vandar's supply shipments stop.'

Xia could not believe her ears. 'You would risk all of Vandar to avoid deploying a few wardens?'

She felt sick at the pitying look Grell gave her. 'Oh, Warden, I appreciate your efforts, I honestly do. I know how easy it is for those so young to be swept up by the words of these fearmongers, but you have no reason to be afraid. Bulwark is not going to let Vandar fall—they won't dare allow the world to see them for the greedy charlatans they are. No, they are just taking this opportunity to press us further. The bounty of the forest is not enough, they also want our children's blood. I will not let that happen.'

Murmurs of agreement rippled over the assembled audience. Xia's face flushed. Were the Elf leaders, those sworn to serve Vandar, really going to risk the safety of the forest for some political ploy? She had heard the arguments on the news, of how Grell had been elected for his pro-Vandar policies, not wanting Elf-ans to die at Bulwark. Sending a hundred wardens to defend the breach might lose him some credibility, maybe cost him the next election, but surely that was a small price compared to the devastation that would follow if they refused to act.

Disgusted, Xia turned her attention to that glowing mattress at the room's centre. The Avatar was beyond such frivolous concerns. The 'az who create the Elf race would not allow them to be destroyed.

Forcing down nerves, Xia turned her eyes back to the wondrous woman. 'Avatar. Elf-az. You have to stop this.'

The functionary, who had been meekly standing to the side, glared at Xia. 'Silence, girl. No one addresses the Avatar.'

'No.' Xia strode forward, a wave of dismay flowing over the gallery. 'Avatar, you must listen. We have to stop this breach before it is too late, before the Daem-ans destroy everything we love. Before-'

Cold and clammy, the functionary's hand clamped over her mouth as Forest Guards seized her from behind.

Grell's face was stone. 'You are a fool, Warden. The Avatar only speaks when absolutely necessary. She certainly is not going to overrule her government on behalf of a Deathless—one who has turned her back on her own 'az. Enough of this. Remove them.'

Xia tried to scream through the functionaries hand, rage and desperation boiling over as she stared at the Avatar. The immaculate woman was motionless, not blinking, not glancing around, not even breathing. She just stared into the middle distance, a statue of impossible accuracy, frozen in time.

Then the emerald eyes snapped to Xia.

Hope flared in her heart at she met the Avatar's

gaze, seeing the wisdom there, the agelessness, the authority. Unable to speak, Xia pleaded with her expression, desperate for the conduit to the gods to speak, to move, to do something.

The Avatar's gaze flicked away.

The doors to the chamber swung shut as Xia and the others were dragged back.

In Xia's heart, her last faith in Elf kind died.

Chapter 14

Fury giving way to exhaustion, Xia collapsed onto a cable spool. The setting sun crept into the Hawk's hangar bay, catching the multitude of tools, pipes and fuel drums left by the maintenance crews. The Hawk itself stood beautifully polished against the oil and grime of the well-used parking alcove. The smell of jet fuel and solder hung heavy despite the open wall facing the city.

'I'll call Bulwark.' Drekene stormed onto the Hawk, boots hammering on the metal ramp.

Ket clambered onto a tool rack. 'Well she sounds pissed.'

'You blame her?' asked Cadden. 'The Elf-ans just said they'd rather risk their entire country than help us defend this place. Er, no offence, Xia.'

'None taken,' she muttered. 'I can't believe they just stood there. Can't believe they'd use this emergency like some publicity stunt. Don't they realise that people have already died?'

Ket sucked his teeth. 'People die at Bulwark all the time. Most folk in the world couldn't give a damn.'

'I suppose.' Xia sighed. 'I just thought they would care when it came to their own people.'

Cadden shrugged. 'They probably do, in their own way. They think giving in now will lead to Elf-ans being stationed on the front full-time. They just don't take this threat seriously, or they'd see there's far more at stake than a few recruits manning Bulwark's walls.'

'At least we got something,' Ket pointed out. 'They did agree to supply an army sent to defend Vandar. Feeding hundreds—or thousands—of soldiers ain't a small task.'

'Great,' Xia muttered. 'Now all we need is what we actually came here for. An army.'

Silence followed her words. The silence dragged into painful minutes. Out of frustration, she picked up a discarded bolt, turning the cold metal over in her hand before tossing it across the hangar. The echo of the bolt against concrete rang clear. 'I sort of get the politicians being like this, but the Avatar? She was here when the Daem-ans first broke through. Elf-az sees all in Vandar. She knew exactly what is at stake and she did… nothing.'

'Eh, Avatars're all the same.' Ket spoke between chewing his foot claws. 'They've been here too long. The 'az have existed since time began, and part of them has been stuck in their Avatars for twelve hundred years. I've been in this body for thirty-two years, and already am sick of it. A millennium dealing with the shet of this world? It's no wonder the Avatars barely move.'

'What about the Glac-an and Ash-an Avatars?' Xia asked. 'They're active.'

Ket snorted. 'Active beating the shet outa each other, sure. They don't care about the world's problems anymore than that ancient lass you shouted at. Face it, Girl, the gods are bored of this world. We're on our own.'

A shadow falling over her heart, Xia stared out of the open hangar. Lights flickered on all over the city, illuminating colossal trees, granite towers and glass skyscrapers. Millions called Enall home, scattered between those buildings, shutting up shop for the day, heading back from the office, collecting kids from school, starting the evening meal. How many knew the games their leaders were playing? How many would care?

Judging by Drekene's raised voice, her discussion with Bulwark was not going well. To Xia, it seemed madness that finding people to help fight the potential apocalypse was somehow more of a challenge than killing that 'az-forsaken Daem-an.

'Are all the governments so thick-headed when it comes to dealing with Bulwark?' Xia muttered.

Ket cackled. 'Oh no, Girl. The others're much worse.'

She snorted. 'I find that hard to believe.'

'It's true.' Cadden leaned back on a set of partially rusted fuel barrels. 'Think about it—this is Vandar's attitude towards us, and all they have to give is food and supplies. Every other country has to provide their annual quota of troops to serve at Bulwark. If there's a shortfall, then they're forced to implement drafts. If you think the Elf-ans are cold, consider how it goes for governments whose citizens are dragged to the front against their will.'

'That still actually happens?'

Cadden nodded. 'It's rare, but still takes place. Two years ago, Sulsine failed to meet their quota of volunteers so one and a half thousand were drafted. Ket and I volunteered, but we both know a dozen draftees.'

'Aye,' Ket agreed. 'And with Greml-ans incorporated into every society across the world, always the minority, who'd you think gets first on the list of those "randomly" selected?'

Thankfully, Xia was born in Vandar. Her involvement with Bulwark was purely voluntary, and would end the moment she chose. 'Wouldn't have thought Greml-ans would be overly useful on the front line.'

Ket snorted. 'Shows what you know, Girl. These days, on the front they want metalSingers more than any other 'an. Tech is where it's at now. We're a long way from spears and bows.'

'Yeah.' Cadden gave a dark chuckle. 'Even bad metalSingers, like Ket, are valuable.'

The Greml-an hissed. 'Quiet. I'm a damn fine Singer and you know it. All you do is drive the Hawk. I keep her alive.'

Xia gave a weak smile, but she could hear the tension behind their friendly jibes. They were worried. If this pair who had seen Daem attacks at Bulwark were concerned, what by every 'az was she doing here? Hopelessness began to settle in her heart.

Her dark thoughts were interrupted by heavy footfalls clanking down the ramp. Xia looked up to see Drekene stalk forward, every muscle tense, jaw held tight.

In front of the three others, the Deathless halted. 'Command has refused my renewed request for reinforcements.'

'What?' Cadden scoffed. 'How can they do that?'

Drekene shrugged. 'They still claim not to have enough forces to spare—apparently the Daem-ans have increased the frequency of attacks. There've been losses.'

Ket swore. 'Daem-ans ain't stupid. This is a ploy. They want to keep our focus at Bulwark, give 'em a chance to get a foothold in Vandar.'

'Agreed.' Drekene snarled. 'I told Command as much, but they still refused, said Vandar must look after its own security.'

'And if the Elf-ans won't?' Cadden asked.

Drekene looked grim. 'Then they will die.'

'Dragon-shet,' exclaimed Xia. 'We can't stand by while the forest burns.'

'No, we can't.' Drekene shook her head sadly. 'But it seems no one wishes to take this threat seriously.'

'So what do we do?' Xia asked. 'Go to another country? See if the Avatarium of Hum will help? Sulsine?'

The Deathless shook her grey head. 'No. If we cannot get the Elf government to raise an army in its own defence, we will have no luck with its neighbours.'

'Then what?'

Drekene sighed. 'The only people trained to handle this can be found at Bulwark. We will go in person, *make* them see what is at stake.'

'And if they won't listen?' Cadden asked quietly.

Drekene turned her soulless stare to the young pilot. 'Then pray to every 'az to help Vandar. Without aid, this forest is doomed.'

Silently, Xia gasped. Out the Hawk's windows she saw an alien world. The endless green of Vandar Forest—the green she had known her entire life— finally ended. Stenlis River marked the border between Vandar and the Avatarium of Hum, along with the limit of the land maintained by Elf lifeSigners. Although trees still grew on the river's far bank, without the Song to help them thrive, keep them healthy, mould their shapes, the pines and oaks in the Hum land looked sickly, stunted. Barely reaching a third of their potential height, the trees were misshapen, bent by winds and scarred by storms. No Symmetry. No Design.

The withered 'natural' trees thinned and rapidly gave way to grassland. Kilometre after kilometre of fields, pastures and meadows—divided by hedgerows—stretched over rolling hills as far as the eye could see. Sprinkled onto the countryside were villages and hamlets, quaint brick cottages huddled around modern mansions and the occasional corrugated iron warehouse.

Without the covering of trees, the land looked exposed, vulnerable. Xia could see every settlement from here to the horizon. Each hill, valley and stream sharply stood out against the barren background.

'First time outside of Vandar?' asked Cadden, cheerful.

Mute, Xia nodded.

'Must be quite something.'

She marvelled at a delicate town that passed off the Hawk's wing, buildings seeming like mere toys. 'I've seen plenty of films and shows set out here.'

'But it's something else to be here it in person.'

'It is,' she agreed.

Softly, he laughed. 'Yeah. I remember the first trip I took out to the Ghost Cities up north. Frozen planes of the purest white, littered with the decaying Glac settlements. That was quite an experience.'

'I used to think going down to Vandar's coast counted as sightseeing. I feel like such a shut-in.'

Cadden's laugh was so free, it brought a smile to her face. 'Hey, we're all born shut into our little worlds, until we make the effort to see what's out there. Part of why I love this job. I've seen more of the world in the last couple of years than most people manage in their entire lives.'

Xia smiled softly, staring out the window, every rise concealing new wonders. 'I didn't realise Bulwark pilots went so far.'

'Oh, yeah. As a transport pilot, I went to all corners, picking up supplies and new recruits. Gallat Hold, Drossen Camp, Sulsine, Shaleridge—every member of the Concordant. Since I was assigned to Drekene's crew, I've even been to Thator Lair when she was sent to meet with the Drak-ans. Been all over the continent.'

'Sounds like you must have seen just about everything.'

'Nearly. Someday I'd love to visit Obsidian Isle, or the Archipelago, but the Hawk doesn't have that kind of range. Still, who knows? Stopping the first new breach from the underworld in five hundred years... now that qualifies for a promotion. Should be able to get assigned to one of the big birds after this.'

Xia shook her head. 'A couple of weeks ago, I had no interest in anything outside of Vandar. Never thought I'd want to leave the forest.'

'And now?'

She turned to give a shy smile. 'Now, I feel like I've been missing out.'

He laughed, then hesitated, a mischievous twinkle

in his eyes.

'What are you thinking?' she asked, hesitant. 'You look like Ket before he pulls a prank on you.'

'Just had an idea. Here, let's take a detour.'

'Why? Won't Drekene mind?'

'It's only a little out of our way. I'm sure you'll love to see this.'

Unable to argue with the enthusiasm that had taken over the pilot, Xia shrugged and turned back to the window. As Cadden sent out a series of cryptic communications to the region's flight control, she watched cities pass on the horizon. They were a strange sight, not a single park or tree to be seen, all brick and glass structures. Shorter, fatter buildings huddled around cores of skyscrapers. The Hum architecture glittered in the midday sun, countless windows casting haphazard reflections over the landscape.

They turned north, skimming a hundred meters over the ground, passing fields of sheep and wheat. Here and there, she saw figures of men and women tending the fields, tiny, even to her Elf eyes. Fragile looking from this distance, various vehicles cut the crops into neat lines.

Cities and towns became less common as they pushed on. Villages, hamlets, then eventually even farms disappeared, the landscape turning over to a wilderness of bushes, trees and birds.

Xia started to feel uncomfortable as even this rough wildlife began to die away, the land turning to bare dirt or sand save for a few stubborn patches of bracken clinging to depressions in the ground. 'Where are we?'

'You'll see.' Cadden flicked a series of switches around the cockpit. A screen in front of Xia flickered to life, mirroring one before Cadden. It took her a moment to realise what she was looking at—a camera feed from the Hawk's hull.

Cadden manipulated a small stick to his side, slewing and zooming the camera's view over the landscape. He scanned back and forth, attention focused on his displays.

'There,' he announced at last. 'Now *there* is a sight.'

She stared at the screen, two small figures moving in the centre of the wasteland. The image zoomed further, resolving to a bizarre sight. Two people, one naked, the other clothed in a silver suit of armour, bitterly wrestled. The bare figure towered over his opponent, his skin grey as Drekene's and just as hairless. His foe's skin was paler than Xia's, her hair pure white.

The two combatants' mouths moved, though the camera had no microphone to pick up their words. Xia gasped as a sword crystallised out of the air into the short woman's hand—a beautiful weapon as clear as glass. She swung the blade, catching her taller adversary in the neck, sending the man spiralling.

Around the fallen warrior, the spray of dust settled. Impossibly, the tall man pushed himself to his feet, unharmed, ripping a branch from a long-dead tree to meet his opponent's attack. The force of his blow shattered her silver armour. As the fragments fell to the ground, Xia realised the armour was not metal, but made of an intricate weaving of ice.

Without pause, the woman continued her attack.

The fragments of her armour melted, then rose to incorporate themselves back into her coating, repairing her protective shell.

'The Endless War,' Cadden explained.

Xia nodded, having already realised what she was witnessing—the Ash and Glac Avatars fighting their centuries-old duel. Two immortals, continuing the battle that had wiped out their races.

'Documentaries on the Northern Extinction do not do this justice,' she whispered.

'No,' he agreed. 'Nothing does.'

'It's mad. Why do they do it? They can't kill each other.'

Cadden shrugged, turning the jet back to its original course. 'What else do they have? The Extinction wiped out their 'an. The 'az controlling those Avatars have lost everything. All they hold onto is their hate of one another.'

Xia frowned. 'What about Deathless? Drekene can't be the only Ash-an left.'

'Well no, but the remaining handful of Ash-an are all Deathless, and the Ash-az doesn't care about them.'

'Why?'

Drekene's voice cut through the conversation. 'Because I turned my back on Ash-az the day I died.'

Xia shivered. It was unnerving how quiet the giant woman could be when she tried. 'What? But surely the 'az see the sacrifice you've made.'

'Hardly,' Drekene snorted. 'I turned down eternity at Ash-az's side for this. I'm now doomed to serve Daem-az, the rival of all other gods. I am dead to Ash-az. Don't look so surprised. Becoming Deathless is a betrayal to everyone who loved you.'

'Everyone?' Xia frowned. 'Even your family didn't support you?'

'Of course not. I gave them up too. Think about it, Xia—I will never see them again. I could have gone to the afterlife, seen my grandparents again, waited for my parents to arrive. We could have been together, watching new generations build a better world, but I made this choice. They never spoke to me again.'

Xia turned back to the screen, staring at the image of the two battling Avatars. They faded from view, covered by a hill as the Hawk turned back east. Drekene's words chilled Xia. For as long as she could remember, she had taken it for granted that someday she would be reunited with lost loved ones. It had been all that had comforted her when her grandmother had passed—knowing that they would meet again. The thought had kept her going during the long nights of this past week. When she died, she would reunite with Eddan, tell him how sorry she was for not saving him, see the look on his face when she explained how she avenged his death.

To give that up seemed a greater insanity than the Avatar's eternal battle. She could not comprehend making such a decision, all for the sake of some borrowed time suffering on this world, fighting an enemy as endless as the stars in the sky. She would be glad to be done with this, to get away from Drekene and the implications of her twisted pact.

'Why did you do it?' she whispered. 'Why give up so much?'

Drekene turned to her, black eyes stern. 'Because I was a fool.'

Chapter 15

On the third day since leaving Enall, Xia sat in the cockpit alongside Cadden, bare feet propped up on the plastic dashboard. The pilot had objected to her having her climbing shoes on his cockpit's panels, but had just rolled his eyes when she took them off.

The morning sun shone on her toes, a luxury in the cramped cabin. After days stuck breathing the filtered air, heavy with the musk of her three crewmates, Xia longed to be outside again. Last night, she had opted to sleep on the grassy field where they had landed rather than remain in her bunk—much to Ket's amusement.

In the footwell below, Rikk whimpered and rolled over. He too was having difficulty with their new living conditions. Like her, the poor mutt itched to run free, bounding between the trees. The novelty of air travel had faded into claustrophobia, Xia feeling like a caged bird.

In the rear cabin, she had tried to exercise, but could do little more than stretch in the enclosed hallway. Her attempts at using the bulkheads as a climbing frame had quickly been shut down by Ket's grumbling about her huge body damaging his ship. Xia had never been called huge.

At least Cadden had proved decent company. He had clearly picked up on her souring mood, and frequently attempted to cheer her, letting her fly the Hawk, telling her stories of his youth, pointing out sights.

And what sights there had been. Ancient forts, dragon skeletons, canals, highways. The highlight had been Caldron, the Hum capital. With the Hawk skirting the outer edge, Xia had not even been able to see the far side. Glittering canals had cut between impossibly tall skyscrapers. The light scattering from the thousands of windows made looking at the city as painful as staring at the sun. She still had not come to terms with the teeming life, a million hoverjets and 'copters swarming over the metropolis in an organised chaos.

At an insistent alarm from the dashboard, Cadden leaned forward to adjust the communications panel. 'Bulwark Control, this is T-876 Hawk, inbound, now crossing into Bulwark jurisdiction.'

After a short delay the gruff, distorted reply barked back, 'T-876, we have you on radar. No Daem activity. You are cleared to approach.'

Xia peered out the window. 'We're at Bulwark?'

Cadden nodded. 'Over the restricted zone, yes.'

The land outside looked no different from what she had seen for the past few days—rolling hills and small copse of trees linked by streams. The network of fields had faded, given over to an unmanaged wilderness, but Xia could not hide her disappointment. 'I was expecting something a little more… impressive.'

Cadden chuckled. 'This is just the outskirts. Bulwark's exclusion zone has always stretched out as far as our weapons can reach. These days, that's a good couple of kilometres. Look, up ahead.'

Squinting, Xia could just make out a dark smudge at the foot of the mountains lining the eastern horizon.

The mountains themselves were impressive, seeming to get ever taller as the Hawk approached, great steeples of rock, capped in snow.

The smudge gradually resolved into a pillar of black smoke drifting from a mountain. No, not a mountain.

A city.

Sprawling from the cliff side in two great wedges lay a hundred factories, silos, watchtowers and bunkhouses, most belching thick black smoke. The city was cleaved in two by a clear path that stretched to a dark opening in the cliff.

'That's the Gauntlet,' Cadden said, nodding to the strange thoroughfare. It was flanked by ten-meter tall concrete walls bearing cranes, floodlights, and strange, house-sized blocks that Xia could not identify.

'What are those?' she asked, pointing to the blocks and their strange protruding fingers.

'Bulwark's main guns.'

Xia blinked, finally seeing the cannons for what they were. The barrels of the guns must be large enough for her to easily fit inside, held by turrets larger than the Hawk. Their barrels were directed up the Gauntlet, towards the opening in the cliff face.

As they closed, Xia could see countless smaller turrets filling the gaps between their larger siblings. Hundreds of barrels were trained down the cleared path. Near enough now to distinguish details, Xia spotted heaps of scrap piled behind the defences, along with yards filled with boxes. Inside some open containers she could see cannon shells larger than Drekene, waiting patiently to be loaded into those massive weapons.

They descended over the surrounding buildings, activity buzzing below. Mechanical lifters carried bull-sized crates along roads. Members of every 'an scuttled back and forth, shouting, hauling and running between concrete factories. None bothered to look up —not surprising as the Hawk blended into line of a dozen hoverjets, most far larger, all drifting to the edge of the strange complex.

Following some logic that Xia could not comprehend, Cadden peeled away from the line and flew in a grid over a great dark grey field littered with hoverjets of all designs. Stunned, Xia realised this was not a field, but a flat platform of concrete, hundreds of meters wide. A parking pad large enough to fit Ethelan a hundred times over.

The Hawk descended, coming to a gentle stop in the centre of a white-painted square on the concrete. No sooner had Cadden flicked switches to allow the Hawk's engines to wind down, than a dozen figures came running. Hum-ans, Greml-ans and Gobl-ans alike dragged supply crates, toolboxes and fuel lines towards the Hawk, moving with practice precision.

'Welcome to Bulwark.' Cadden flashed Xia an ecstatic grin. 'Home sweet home.'

Dodging forklifts, wheelbarrows and sprinting technicians, Xia trailed Drekene through the chaos of Bulwark. Although this was the oldest front line in the world, Xia had not expected the fortification to be so frantic. A palpable tension hung in the air, as evident as the acrid fumes and hammering of machinery. Urgency was carved onto every exhausted face they passed, dread in every pair of bloodshot eyes.

'Is there an incoming attack?' Xia whispered to Cadden.

He grimaced. 'Always. When it will hit? Who knows. Might be next week. Might be in half an hour.'

'It can't be predicted?'

'No such luck. They seem random. I've seen three in one day. Sometimes we have weeks without an attack. Think the Daem-ans change the timings to unnerve us, keep us off-guard. These days we have chemical sensors, microphones and seismology, but that gives us a few minutes' warning at best. Only general trend seems that they prefer to attack at night, but that's far from guaranteed.'

'Why attack at night?' Xia asked.

Drekene glanced over her shoulder, her bulk parting the crowds. 'Same reason we'd prefer them to attack during the day. They live their short lives underground. Darkness is all they've ever known.'

Xia shuddered, once more wondering what could have possessed Drekene to promise to become one of those monsters after death.

At the foot of the cliffs, Drekene led the group to a concrete tower. It stood to one side of the fortification's wall, the opening in the cliff hidden behind the array off cranes and guns that lined this side of the Gauntlet. The tower's twin stood on the far side, another utilitarian cylinder of concrete, broken only by narrow windows.

The guards at the door—Hum-ans wearing Kevlar —saluted as Drekene passed. Inside, the auditorium was no less drab than the exterior. Bare concrete walls, floor and ceiling, lit with the bright glare of fluorescent lamps. Men and women of all 'an hurried to and from the offices lining the outside of the round room, clutching folders, datasticks and electronic tablets. In the centre of the hive of activity sat a circular reception desk, staffed by half a dozen clerks.

Drekene pushed her way through a queue and planted her hands on the desk in front of a gnarled Gobl-an. The man peered at her over half-rim spectacles, his dark uniform contrasting his skin's sickly white.

'Back of the line,' he muttered.

Drekene ignored the demand. 'I must speak to Command at once. It is a matter of the utmost urgency.'

The Gobl-an spoke slowly, as if to a child. 'Well, I would be happy to make arrangements… when it is your turn. Back of the line.'

'I'm a Deathless.'

'I'm not blind.' The Gobl-an sighed. 'And unless I am mistaken, even Deathless are capable of queueing. The line ensures all are dealt with in the most expedient way. You are causing delays. Back. Of. The. Line.'

The towering woman caught herself, stopping her fist from slamming into the desk. With a snarl, she on a heel and walked back down the length of the queue, glaring at every person she passed.

Xia followed in her wake, flashing an apologetic smile at the unnerved men and women. At least half took Drekene's hint and left the line to join another. Only a few stubborn, hurried or oblivious people remained between Drekene and the clerk, all of whom must have been able to feel the Deathless's glare piercing the backs of their heads.

'I can't believe they'd turn away a Deathless,' Xia muttered as they waited.

Ket laughed. 'Welcome to Bulwark, Girl.'

'Yeah,' Cadden agreed. 'The only thing we love here more than killing Daem-ans, is rules. Procedures.'

Xia scratched Rikk behind his ear, the poor creature clearly unsettled in the artificial surrounds. 'Would have thought Bulwark would have been a bit more... efficient.'

'This is all about efficiency,' Cadden explained. 'Supposedly. We're on such a tight budget. Procedures are here to make sure nothing is wasted.'

''Cept time.' Ket cackled.

'It's ridiculous,' Drekene muttered.

Xia couldn't argue. The woman in front of them got served by the clerk, getting some no-doubt critical form triple stamped before being dispatched to one of the surrounding offices.

Finally, Drekene returned the front of the queue.

The Gobl-an smiled as if nothing had happened. 'What can I do for you?'

Drekene spoke through clenched teeth. 'I need to meet with Command at once.'

'Well, you need to bring form M-12 signed by a senior officer.'

'I'm a Deathless.'

'Of course. In which case, your own fingerprint will suffice to ratify the form. Would you like me to fetch you one?'

'No, I need a meeting, now. There is another breach to the underworld. The Daem-ans are going to launch fresh attacks *outside* of Bulwark.'

The clerk paused, fear clear on his wrinkled face. Over his shoulder, a grey-haired woman approached. From the Hum-an's immaculate uniform and demeanour, Xia guessed that she was the clerk's supervisor.

'Is there a problem?' the supervisor asked, curt.

'Perhaps.' The clerk proceeded to repeat Drekene's request. The supervisor nodded, then turned and stalked away. Xia watched, intrigued, as the woman had a hurried conversation into an earpiece. Perhaps there actually was some sanity left in this world.

After painful minutes of waiting, the supervisor returned, a bright red sheet in her hand. 'I have the urgent audience form. I need you thumbprint here, Deathless, and your enlistment number.'

Drekene scrawled on the paper, pen tiny in her hand. She pressed her thumb onto a small square of plastic, leaving behind a black print.

'Thank you.' The supervisor tucked the sheet into a card folder. 'I will get this processed at once. You will be contacted on your com-channel as soon as Command has time to spare for a meeting.'

Drekene drummed her fingers on the desk. 'When will that be?'

'It's hard to say.' The supervisor gave an apologetic smile. 'Command has been very busy, as always. They are fully booked today, and tomorrow's not looking good. Don't worry though—we should be able to fit you in by the end of the week.'

'The end of the week?' Xia blurted. 'You have got to be kidding.'

'I will get you the first possible appointment, I assure you. Please direct any further requests to my colleague.'

The woman tapped the Gobl-an on the shoulder and strode away. Xia could only stare, dumbfounded. Vandar would be overrun long before they found a single person who comprehended the Daem threat. Even here, on the front line of the perpetual war against those monsters, no one seemed to care if the world burned.

'That is so weird,' Xia breathed. Sky orange, darkness flooded the landscape, a full hour before sunset. The sun dipped behind Watcher, an event Xia had experienced every day of her life, but this far east the gas giant hovered just above the horizon, the eclipse hastening night instead of darkening noon.

Standing beside her, Cadden laughed. 'No. That's far more normal than Vandar's dark midday. Even where I grew up, Watcher was closer to the horizon than the centre of the sky.'

Xia smirked. 'Hey, it's not my fault that my ancestors settled on the side of the world that faced Watcher. Just means the ancient Elf-ans were more sensible than your forefathers.'

'And yet your people made sure to block their view of the sky with trees.'

She laughed. 'Fair point.'

'It could be worse. Out in the Archipelago, they never see Watcher.'

Xia shook her head, wondering how such an empty sky would look. Night must be so dark.

'Here, you should see this.' Cadden touched her shoulder to get her attention, then snapped his hand away. 'Sorry.'

'Sorry for what?' Xia asked. The pilot had been acting strange all afternoon. After their pleas and demands for a meeting with Command had fallen on deaf ears, Cadden had insisted on taking Xia on a tour of the fortifications. Wanted to show her his world in return for her guidance in Vandar, he'd claimed. She had happily accepted, needing a distraction, and his company settled her nerves. He, on the other hand, seemed more on edge than ever.

He shrugged, turning as he blushed. 'Nothing. Look over there.'

She followed his hand. The pair stood on a raised metal walkway running over the numerous buildings that made Bulwark. Constructed from brick, concrete and sheet iron, the structures ranged from cramped barracks to barren food halls to humming factories. All of it hung under a black haze, choking on the chemical stench that seemed to billow from every other building.

The structure he pointed at was a broad metal building, ringed in silos of corrugated iron. Thick black smoke poured from chimneys, adding more darkness to the sky.

'That's the largest ammunition factory in the world,' he explained. 'Spews out hundreds of rounds an hour. Feeds half the guns on the wall.'

'What's with the smoke?' Xia asked. Most factories were powered by Gobl electricity, nice and clean. Even those that used Drak fireSingers as a heat source released few pollutants.

'The Daem-ans. When they're processed, that soot is the byproduct.'

'Processed?'

Cadden nodded, strolling calmly down the walkway. 'With so many corpses, we have to find a way to dispose of the mess or we'd drown in them. They get burned in stages, the smoke is mostly what's left behind.'

Wrinkling her nose, Xia took this in. The air was not heavy with some industrial runoff or woodsmoke, but with the remains of countless Daem-ans. With every breath she drew in fragments of those monsters. She felt sick. 'Why not just dig graves?'

His laugh was too merry for their topic of conversation. 'Oh, if we did that, we'd have filled the entire exclusion zone a hundred times over. Besides, even with modern digging equipment, we don't have the manpower. Anyway, the Daem corpses are useful.'

Xia frowned, moving aside for a squad of soldiers hurrying in the other direction. 'I was always told Daem-ans were poisonous.'

'We don't eat them.' He grimaced. 'But they burn well. Cheap heating for the long nights. Their main use, though, is for munitions. Burn them at just the right temperature, in just the right atmosphere, and they make a great accelerant. Far better—and cheaper—gunpowder than any other kind you'll find. It's Bulwark's one export, though most gets used right here, in those.'

He nodded to the great cannons looming ahead. The behemoths glittered under the glare of the floodlights, their grey-painted frames looking more like abstract sculptures than weapons of war. Each of the monstrosities proudly displayed its spray-painted name. Ironside. Unshakable. Reii's Vengeance. Conquerer. Little Watcher. Hand of Hum-az.

Next to each name was an image, from photo-real art to crude drawings to indecipherable symbols. Under the names, written in red, were numbers, ranging from three to three hundred.

'Those their kill count?' Xia guessed.

'Oh, no.' Cadden chuckled. His green eyes met hers, lingered for a second, then snapped away. 'We'd run out of paint. Besides, it's hard to gauge how many little Daem-ans the big guns take down in their blast. No, those numbers are the weight of the largest Daem-an confirmed killed by a given gun crew. Kind of a running competition. Eases tensions from accidents and casualties.'

'Weight? In kilograms?'

'Tonnes.'

His face lit up at her shock. He looked ecstatic as he stared at her, vibrant emerald eyes full of life. Again, the moment ended as he blushed, turning away. 'If you think that's something, then you'll need to see this.'

He beckoned to her and hurried up a set of steps to the wall between the large cannons. Grinning at his enthusiasm, she followed, the metal steps clanking under her climbing shoes. She would need to get better footwear before Bulwark's rough edges ground the thin soles to dust.

Reaching the top, she blinked at the scene. Below her, sandwiched between two massive walls, stood a kilometre-long stretch of dirt. A hundred meters across, the path was rough, crossed with countless gouges. The source of the marks became apparent as a crane swung over the trench to dump a load of soil. Other mechanical arms moved over the pile, spreading the mud and ploughing deep furrows.

'It's a hard balance.' Cadden stood close to her side. 'We don't want to make it too easy for the Daem-ans, but we can't make the terrain impassable. This starts to look too much like a blocked path, and they'll dig a new one. We learned that lesson long ago. Look.'

She followed his gesture to the cliffs stretching away in the distance. Half way to the horizon, the cliff glittered, something reflective catching the first light of the ending eclipse.

'That's the first breach,' Cadden explained. 'The one that was filled with molten steel. It only made the Daem-ans dig through here, where we were not prepared. Since then, we've been careful. Tried to keep their focus here.' He sighed. 'I guess we failed.'

Xia turned to Cadden, finding a guilty expression below his discordant hair. Perhaps that explained his strange behaviour—the pilot felt Bulwark had failed to keep the Daem-ans bottled up, and now Vandar was under threat.

She reached over to give his hand a supportive squeeze. His face lit up, but she could still see the pain in his eyes, the Hum-an seeming torn between joy and agony. Xia couldn't blame him. The last few days had been a lot for all of them to deal with. She felt less sure than ever whether the world was going to be saved, or about to face the apocalypse.

Chapter 16

Xia followed Cadden into the humid hall, Rikk padding behind. Beyond rows of polished metal tables, steam rose from great vats. Men and women in blue and green Bulwark uniforms queued before the vats, where servers slopped the evening meal onto out-held trays. Cadden had been hesitant to take Xia to these canteens, and now she understood.

Reluctant, she picked up an almost-clean tray from a stack and trailed after Cadden. The queue shuffled ever onwards, taking her up to the cauldrons of simmering liquids. Signs promised steak stew, vegetable soup, chaltet casserole. The varying shades of beige bubbling away bore no resemblance to their labels.

Hunger beating out her distaste, she pointed to the vat of vegetable soup, getting rewarded with a dollop of congealing stew in the centre of her aluminium tray.

Propping her rifle against the table, she took a seat opposite Cadden, the metal bench digging into her flightsuit. He handed her a spoon—battered steel— and nodded encouragingly.

'Remind me why I insisted on coming here.' She probed the food with her spoon. Soup was not meant to hold its shape.

Cadden grinned. 'You said you wanted to see what people at Bulwark eat.'

'Yeah.' She smeared out some of the soup, trying in vain to detect any recognisable vegetable in the slurry. 'Ket insisted this would be better than what we had on the Hawk.'

His green eyes glittered playfully. 'Ket being untruthful? Never.'

Xia rolled her eyes and scooped a spoonful. The mush stank of herbs. Tasted of salt. 'Never thought I'd miss your cooking.' She gulped as she heard her own words. 'I didn't meant it like that.'

Thankfully, Cadden laughed. 'No, I get it. I do my best with what Hawk has, but it's never going to be great. I'd love to take you to a real Hum restaurant, but you're not going to get anything like that in Bulwark.'

'Well, maybe once this is all over we can take a trip out to the Avatarium.'

He beamed. 'Sounds like a plan.'

The joy in his smile warmed her heart. It had been an infuriating two days, waiting impotently for an appointment with Bulwark's leaders. Ket and Drekene had not been pleasant company, the Greml-an constantly erupting in curses at the slightest provocation, the Deathless simply glowering at all who approached.

Being near Cadden, on the other hand, always brought calm. He was clearly as stressed as the rest of the Hawk's crew, but seemed to brighten up when she was around. His playfulness in turn helped distract her from the world's madness. Without the pilot, she'd probably have started to claw out her hair in frustration.

Though even he could not make this slop palatable. She forced it down—spoonful after lukewarm spoonful—to quieten her stomach, but would be glad if she never saw the inside of one of these canteens again. Even Rikk, nestled by her feet, made no attempt at stealing the so-called food.

She was saved from one more mouthful by a shrill siren that pierced the air. Painfully loud, the alarm was at least short-lived. As it faded, she could hear other horns echoing throughout the city. The room froze, spoons falling still, uniformed soldiers stopping in their tracks.

Then chaos broke loose.

Meals forgotten, the 'an filling the room piled out the canteen. The ground rumbled with a thousand footsteps slamming over the metal and concrete paths. Machinery whined as generators powered up, the din of grinding gears filling the air.

She knew what was happening before Cadden opened his mouth.

'A Daem attack.'

Snatching her rifle, Xia jumped to her feet, eyes locked on Cadden. She commanded Rikk to stay put, glaring the vulfik into submission before turning to the pilot. 'Where do we go?'

'The wall.' He checked the pistol at his hip and started to dash for the door.

Xia struggled to keep up with his longer stride. 'Won't we get in the way?'

He shook his head. 'Every member of Bulwark must be on station during assaults. Auxiliaries— mechanics, couriers, clerks… pilots—we all man the rear section of the wall.' Kicking up a spray of gravel, he ground to a stop and turned to her, eyes intense. 'You should go back to the Hawk. It's not safe.'

Holding his gaze, Xia smirked. 'I've killed more

Daem-ans than you. I'm coming.'

He looked like he wanted to argue, but quickly folded. 'Hurry.'

New boots clattering on the metal grates over mud that served as streets, Xia kept pace with the pilot. The boots were heavy—steel toed with reinforced soles—but on the sharp grilled streets her climbing shoes would not have survived.

Thousands of personnel rushed back and forth, Greml-ans dodging between the legs of Hum-ans and Drak-ans. Gobl-ans hurried to powerhouses, while tanned Sulsine Elf-ans leapt up stairs to the battlements.

Cadden led the way up a zigzagging stairway bolted into the side of the wall. The metal frame creaked and rattled under the weight of the two-dozen bodies hurling their way to the fortifications. Xia cast concerned glances at the rusted bolts where the staircase met the wall, the concrete marred with partially-sealed cracks. The construction seemed solid, heavy rivets and painted steel, but clearly had gone too long with only minimal repairs, and now looked as if the structure could collapse at any moment.

Thankful, she stepped off the top of the stairway and onto the firm concrete. Following Cadden through the sea of uniforms, Xia pushed to a low railing at the edge of the wall. Unlike the deserted scene she had been greeted with when Cadden had first brought her here, the wall now swarmed with people. Men and women bearing pistols and rifles stood or knelt near the wall's edge, a good ten meter sheer drop only inches away, barred by a rusted steel barrier. They stood far from the cliff face, in the final third of the wall. The heavier guns were all ahead, great barrels angled towards the crack in the cliff.

As the stragglers arrived the wall fell still, a kilometre long line of defence, mirrored on the far side of the killing field by a second barrier. At the end of the corridor of land stood less than a hundred figures. Xia could see Drekene's hulking form among them, and guessed the others were Deathless. A thin final line of defence. Behind them stretched the open landscape, a tempting target to draw in the Daem-ans time and again.

'I thought you said the alarms only gave five minutes of warning,' Xia said. It had been nearly ten.

Cadden spoke quietly, worried. 'Must have been an early warning today.'

'Isn't that a good thing?'

The Hum-an shook his head, eyes fixed on the cliff. 'No. Early warning means a lot of seismic activity. Means a lot of mass coming our way.'

Xia turned to the cliff. The low rumble that had been building for the past few minutes sharpened into an echo reverberating from the great rent in the cliff. It sounded like rushing water, combined with a high-pitch ring.

The sound grew into a din, dust knocked free of the walls at the vibrations. A heavy stench of sulphur washed over the battlements, building in intensity as the ringing resolved into a thousand overlapping screams.

Then they arrived.

In a burst of twisted flesh, the cliff opening disgorged dozens of Daem-ans. Hundreds. A few smaller creatures, the size of a deer, poured out first.

Some ran on two legs, some on four, some on twelve.

These were quickly dwarfed as a colossal beast erupted into view. Thirty feet tall and almost as wide, the black-skinned monster could barely fit out the cave. With a roar like a jet engine, the creature swung a shield in front of its body, completely blocking itself from view.

Xia blinked. The building-sized grey mass that the creature hid behind was not a shield.

It was an arm.

A single tumorous bone formed an impossibly large barrier. It seemed as if a gigantic turtle had ripped off its own shell and now cowered behind it. Only it was not cowering, Xia realised, but advancing. One ground-shaking step at a time, the leviathan approached.

Bulwark's great cannons answered. In a deafening staccato they fired into the Daem-an. While trails from the smaller guns—which fired at amazing speeds—trickled over the lesser creatures, the shells from the largest guns pounded the leviathan. Some shells exploded into clouds of orange fire and black soot, scattering ripples of shrapnel into the air. Others slammed straight through the bone sheet, cleaving holes or leaving smouldering welts on the surface.

Relentless, the creature continued. Its footsteps sent tremors through the ground. That massive armoured wall it used as a shield pushed forward, ploughing through the bodies of its fallen comrades. The buzzing of the small guns, useless against the heavy armour, fell silent. A painful delay dragged on, the roar of guns replaced with a distant grinding as the cannons reloaded.

A second volley echoed down the Gauntlet. This time there were no explosions. Every shell smashed through the armoured shield. The great lumpy mass of bone shattered, fragments as large as hoverjets tumbling to the ground, leaving the Daem-an with an ugly, misshapen wreck of a limb.

Even this did not slow the monster's progress. If anything, the loss of weight only sped its advance. It lunged forward, lumbering with far more speed than Xia would have thought possible for such a giant.

A blast filled the air. One last cannon shot brought the beast down, pulverising its vulture-like head into a mist of gristle. In a shower of dirt and debris, its massive frame came crashing down.

Xia let out a yell of exhilaration. All it earned her was withering glares from those 'an surrounding her. It did not take her long to realise why no one else celebrated. Before the dust had settled, the creature's body writhed as hundreds more Daem-ans clambered over its corpse.

Once more the small turrets on the walls opened up, their fire rate so high as to sound more like a harsh rasp than a series of gunshots. Glimmering tracers ploughed into the wall of flesh, but nothing could contain so many Daem-ans. The survivors leapt over the dead, a sea of black and broken skin flowing down the Gauntlet.

While most Daem-ans sprinted down the clear path, some launched themselves at the walls. Beasts as large as ogres piled onto those smaller than a Greml-an. Spindly beasts formed climbing frames for rotund nightmares. Hands, claws and tentacles writhed up the sides, ploughing through the constant hail of bullets that flowed from the far wall. Still the Daem-ans pressed on, crawling over the shattered corpses of their dead, using them as grisly shields, pushing ever higher up the walls.

Inevitably, some broke through. Forcing misshapen bodies onto the wall, the Daem-ans launched into an attack. As nearby soldiers ran to confront the assault, the party of beasts slammed into one of the smaller guns, crushing its metal shell beneath claws, talons, stinging barbs. Bulwark soldiers rushed to retake the section, rifles firing. The desperate battle fell into flashes of light, sprays of blood, screams of agony.

The bulk of the Daem horde pushed straight down the Gauntlet. Small guns raked back and forth, felling Daem-ans by the hundreds, but the task seemed like trying to harvest a field with a pair of scissors. The Daem-ans just pushed on, ignoring the casualties, the stench of their sulphurous blood in the air, the cries of their wounded.

The mass of bodies were thrown apart as an explosion ripped into the horde—a shell from one of the great cannons. The explosions spread shrapnel over the area slicing down the invaders in a wave of blood and ichor.

In seconds, the gap was filled.

Effective as the large weapons were, most were trained on the cliff face, where two more gigantic Daem-ans had emerged, one similar to the first, but with an armoured shield on both arms. The other looked like a fifty-foot tall armoured rhinoceros, its obsidian horn glittering in the evening light as it dug chunks out the concrete wall.

A pillar of smoke caught Xia's attention. It

billowed from one of the great cannons, flames flickering from the end of the barrel. Then the cannon's walls cracked, steam and fire leaping out from numerous breaches that appeared in its side. From a doorway figures fled, coated in flame. They did not survive long.

Xia squinted as the landscape darkened. The sun slipped behind Watcher, plunging the Gauntlet into an eerie black. Tracer lines cut across the scene, explosions illuminating the slaughter in momentary flashes of blood red.

With an audible crack, the floodlights activated. Xia blinked against their harsh glow. Bathed in the artificial white glare, the scene became otherworldly. Greyscale monsters threw themselves across the mud, up walls, over their dead. Some took flight, membranous wings highlighted by searchlights for an instant before flak fire broke them into bloody chunks. The colossal centrepieces of the attack pushed ever onwards, shrugging off cannon fire as if it was nothing more than hail, paving the way for a thousand smaller creatures flocking in their shadow.

As the assault continued, the flow of Daem-ans refused to cease, their sheer mass forcing the river of claws and teeth and fangs down the gauntlet. Before long they had passed the last of the cannons. The wall lit up with small arms fire, a thousand clerks, pilots and chefs firing sidearms and submachine guns into the black mass.

Belatedly, Xia remembered the rifle hanging from her shoulder. At first, Cadden's insistence that she be armed at all times seemed strange, a needless formality. Now she saw the all-too-dire necessity. This was not some strange factory, not a landmark or a hermit kingdom.

This was a battle.

A endless conflict. And she now stood in its heart.

The line of Deathless, minutes ago looking so imposing, now appeared too thin. Over a metre stood between each of the figures, their custom swords, rifles, rocket launchers and plasma torches all seeming so fragile. Even Drekene, stood in the centre of the line, looked like a mere ant facing down a tsunami.

Determined not to let the Daem swarm reach Drekene, Xia raised her rifle, flicking on her scope's power. The air around her resounded with a hundred shots. Pistols, assault rifles, handcannons, shotguns, all unleashing an endless barrage into the unstoppable mass.

The sound seemed to fade as she focused down her scope. From of the writhing mass, she picked out a creature. Taller than Drekene, the beast tottered on three legs, which met at the base of an enormous scorpion tail. The barbed end was long enough to skewer three men at once. Xia would not allow it the opportunity.

Her first shot obliterated its twisted knee, toppling the creature. The second round slammed into the base of the tail, severing its weapon. Whether the beast survived or not, Xia would never know, as it was quickly overtaken by its dreadful brethren.

Emptying her clip, she brought down two more. Reloading was mechanical. Every action seeming as distant as the muffled din around her. She picked out the larger targets, her rifle's heavy rounds making quick work of armoured beasts, while the pistols of those around her sprayed haphazardly into the smaller creatures.

Something was shoved into her hand. She looked down to see a Greml-an, satchel of magazines strapped to his back.

'12.5 millimetre rounds.' He nodded to her, handing her a box of bullets, before taking off through the legs of the combatants.

She crammed the extra ammunition into her rifle and continued to fire, bringing down one monstrosity after another.

The flood slowed, then stopped. As Xia and those around her piled round after round into the mass of flesh and bone, the surviving creatures struggled to climb over the mound of dead. Xia took Cadden's lead, firing at any sign of movement. Many of the fallen beasts were still alive. Broken creatures with one arm, gaping wounds or cracked skulls crawled forward. Driven by some determination Xia could not fathom, they pushed on with mortal wounds. It was all Xia could do to put them out of their misery.

The movement softened. Died. Slowly, guns fell silent down the length of the line. A single siren note sounded, bringing a sense of finality to the battlefield.

'It's over,' Cadden panted.

Dumbly, Xia nodded, staring into the carnage. The corpses were piled several bodies thick down the length of the Gauntlet. The bodies of the larger creatures had become mountains, capped with the mangled corpses of those that had come after.

Cranes came to life around the walls. Claws larger than some trucks were lowered into the mass of remains, digging into them like soft soil, swinging their morbid cargo behind the walls into sorting yards. Other cranes were capped in bulbous magnets, rattling as they pulled shells—small and large—from the killing field. Here and there, Daem-ans slammed into the magnets, suspended by the mass of bullets that riddled their corpses.

Catching the floodlights, smoke rose from the walls where turrets had been destroyed by Daem-ans or malfunctions. In the relative quiet, the screams of the wounded rang clear. Dying pleas fighting for attention in the evening sky. Agonised calls for help from choking voices. Cries of anguish from those who clutched fallen friends.

Xia collapsed onto the concrete, exhausted. She could only stare at the scene, shaking gently. This was a true Daem attack. Not the lone monster she had tracked across Vandar. Not the dozens she had shot in the cleft in the ground. But hundreds. Thousands. A wall of evil. A tide of death.

And here at Bulwark, these attacks happened several times a week. She swallowed bile. If they failed to find help, if Bulwark Command refused to listen, if the Daem-ans managed to break through at Vandar, *this* would be unleashed into the forest. Her home, everything she knew, would be washed away in a tide of sulphur and bone and blood.

Her world would die.

Chapter 17

The crunch of footsteps over fragmented concrete alerted Xia to Cadden's approach. She looked up as he handed her a plastic bottle of water. Gratefully taking it, she turned back to watch the aftermath of carnage. Since the attack she had sat on the wall, legs dangling over the killing field, head braced against the rough surface of the railing. The rusted metal had been blessedly cool at first, but had steadily warmed over the last hour.

Below, under the glare of the floodlights, the cranes toiled away. Load after load of broken monstrosities were dug from the mounds of carcases. After a full hour, the industrial operation had barely dented the sheer bulk of Daem-ans.

Rikk snoozed to one side, having come so quickly when she called that he must have ignored her command and stayed close. She did not have the energy to reprimand the mutt.

'How are you doing?' Cadden sat alongside her, voice full of compassion.

Xia shrugged, taking a swig from the bottle. Tainted by the lingering stench of sulphur, the water tasted bitter. 'I wasn't injured.'

'You know that's not what I meant.'

She sighed. 'I know. Honestly? I have no idea how I'm doing. I don't know how to think about *this*.' She jabbed a hand towards the macabre field. In the distance, sparks flew as a circular saw three times the

206

height of Drekene ripped into one of the leviathans, cutting it into pieces small enough for the colossal cranes to lift.

'I understand. Seeing an attack for the first time is… hard. At least my first was relatively small. Eased me in, so to speak.'

'Are attacks this big common?'

He grimaced. 'No, but they're not exactly rare. When they're done with the cleanup we'll get confirmation of the total mass, but estimates say that this wasn't even the worst attack this year.'

'I never imagined this scale. The historical films always make them seem much smaller.'

'They used to be. Daem-ans adapt, just as we do. Gone are the days of 'an-sized beasts that exclusively walk up and bite. Nowadays some fly, some are massive, some vomit poison, some fling bones like javelins.'

Bitter as it tasted, the water at least soothed Xia's dry throat. 'Surely there's a better way to hold them back.'

Cadden shrugged. 'Oh, sure. But the defences don't just have to be effective, they have to be affordable. So far, bullets have proven to be the most cost-efficient weapon we have.'

'What about fire? Jet-fuel sprayed at the cliff, ignited as they come through.'

The pilot's laugh was unnervingly dark. 'Oh, fire just pisses Daem-ans off. They're from the underworld remember? Magma flows are their rivers.'

'Poison?'

A smirk. 'You find something that's poisonous to Daem-ans, and I'll make sure they build you a statue.'

Xia felt sick. 'So there's no hope of ending this?'

He wrapped a supportive arm around her shoulders. His touch was uncertain, but still brought comfort. 'I wouldn't say that. We have whole departments working on new weapons, or perfecting those we have. We test their inventions all the time. Some work out, like those small phoenix turrets. Others, not so much, like weaponised hoverjets—just ended up being weaker cannons that ran out of ammunition faster. If you're volunteering, I'm sure they'd love a smart person like you helping in the labs. But you'd have to put up with a lot of Greml-ans far more grumpy than Ket.'

Closing the bottle, Xia groaned at the thought. 'I find that hard to believe.'

'Oh, believe it. Greml-ans tend to mellow with age, and Ket's over thirty—basically a pensioner for his kind. He's the Greml equivalent of a kindly old granny.'

Despite her mood, Xia laughed.

'There you go.' He squeezed her shoulder. 'See? No matter how dark the world, poking fun of Ket makes it better.'

She smiled, leaning into him playfully. 'Good advice. Strange for you.'

'Hey!' he objected. 'I'm a font of wisdom. Why do you think Drekene has me on her crew?'

With a smirk, she turned to him. 'Pretty sure it's because she can't fly a hoverjet.'

'Oh, right.' He grinned. 'That makes more sense.'

Shaking her head, Xia chuckled. Sat next to each other, their height difference was less noticeable. She rested her head against his shoulder, glad for the companionship. At a times like this, she needed a friend. For a heartbeat, his presence was enough to push her worries away, but the calm quickly died. The rock in the pit of her stomach grew heavy once more.

Cadden seemed to sense her worsening mood. 'It's a lot to deal with. I know.'

She grimaced. 'It's just looking at this, thinking of what would happen if so many attacked Vandar.'

Slowly, he nodded. 'I get it. There's so much we need to do before they reopen that breach. We need all this set up. The guns, the factories, the cranes. At least here at Bulwark we've had time, the Daem-ans slowly building in their intensity. If the attacks at Vandar start with assaults this strong, it's going to be a struggle.'

Closing her eyes, Xia tried to shut out the familiar, taunting image from her mind. Mounds of corpses, pillars of smoke, muddy fields. Vandar would become a reflection of Bulwark. Only the corpses would not be Daem-ans, but Elf-ans. The smoke would not come from factories, but burning villages. The muddy fields would be all that was left of the ancient forest.

Cadden squeezed her shoulder. 'Hey, despite all that, I'm not worried. We'll find a way to stop this.'

She gave a bitter laugh. 'You sound so sure.'

'I am.'

'Why? How?'

Another squeeze. 'Because we have you. The Elf ranger who instead of fleeing from a Daem-an, charged it, tracked it through the forest. With dedication like yours on our side, what could stand in our way?'

His words sounded so heart-felt that they actually calmed her—a little. At least here, facing the end of the world, she had the support of such a friend.

Xia woke to the pounding of Drekene's feet against the Hawk's metal floor. Bleary-eyed, still smelling the stench of sulphur from the previous day's assault, she peered out her bunk.

'It's time.' The Deathless hurriedly strapped her sword to her back. 'Command has finally accepted our request for an audience.'

Cadden rolled out his bunk, rubbing his face. 'When?'

'Now.' Drekene threw him his sidearm. 'We have to hurry. Ket…'

'Yeah, yeah,' the Greml-an grumbled as he emerged from his alcove in the wall. 'You're in a rush, I know the drill.' He hopped out and clambered up to perch on Drekene's shoulder. Squinting down at Xia, he asked, 'Hey, how come she doesn't need to get carried? She's short.'

'She's faster than you.' Cadden fastened his holster around his waist and smoothed his thick flightsuit.

'Debatable,' Ket retorted. 'We haven't had a ground race, far as I can recall.'

Xia zipped up her own flightsuit, the material rough against her skin. Still, the fact she had a change of clothes meant she could wash it from time to time. The chemical smell of the washing powder was a dramatic improvement over the stagnant body odour she had to endure in the forest. 'Well, I do have more endurance than you. Do you really want to run all the way to the command building?'

Grumbling, Ket turned away. Cadden just laughed.

'We'll need to keep up a good pace.' Drekene was

already heading down the rear ramp, Greml-an on her shoulder. 'Command's bureaucracy does not allow for tardiness, and I will not let this chance pass us by.'

Xia followed at a run. Despite her confident words, she found it hard to keep up with the Deathless. She was fit, probably more so than Cadden, but she was used to tree-leaping. Her muscles had little practice with running across open ground, and what little experience she had always involved undergrowth and grass underfoot, not the metal grilles that clattered under her boots.

Rikk had no such issues, happily running alongside the group, or hopping onto buildings to scurry over their corrugated-iron roofs. The vulfik seemed to enjoy the excitement.

In the morning's first light, they ran through the warren of factories and warehouses and barracks. Even at the early hour, and on the morning after such a large attack, the streets teemed with activity. Gobl chargeSingers exchanged shifts at the numerous powerhouses dotted through the fortress-city. Factory workers toiled away, recycling recovered casings and crumpled bullets to form new rounds for the next assault. Teams of Greml-ans worked on damaged components, metalSinging shattered motors back into place. Every 'an moved with an urgency, all knowing what Xia was coming to realise.

That it would not be long before the next attack.

Xia was not sure how they coped. Their task was endless, hopeless. The Daem-ans would come again, and again. Somehow, the men and women of Bulwark found the strength to hold the line, week after week, month after month, year after year. This is what

Vandar needed. These people had the fortitude to do what was necessary, to hold back the Daem-ans at all costs. Drekene should have come here first, not wasting time with the foolish Elf leaders.

Now Xia could only hope that Bulwark Command were more sane than her own government.

By the time they reached the great tower where the wall met the cliff, Xia and Cadden were both panting and dripping with sweat. Even Ket seemed out of breath, having exerted so much effort holding onto the galloping Deathless. Drekene, of course, breathed easily, acting as if their sprint through Bulwark had been a pleasant stroll.

Drekene hurried straight to the circular reception desk. An unfamiliar clerk turned his eyes towards her, ready to launch into his rehearsed script, but the same Hum supervisor they had previously met cut him off.

'Deathless,' she said. 'Command is waiting for you. Please take the elevator to the top floor.'

The towering woman nodded once and led the way across the room, boarding one of a pair of glass elevators tucked into the rounded wall. The four 'an crowded in, Ket hopping down from Drekene to stand alongside Rikk, who panted contentedly in the group's centre.

Far more violent than necessary, Drekene jabbed the controls, sending the room hurtling upwards. Level after level whipped past the glass doors. In flashes, Xia glimpsed offices, barracks, planning rooms, libraries and halls full of computer servers. The ticking brain of Bulwark, a bureaucratic mind focused on orchestrating the constant slaughter in the Gauntlet.

With a jolt, the elevator reached its destination and

the passengers disgorged into a circular room, which took up the entire top floor of the tower. Circumscribed by thick window panels, the room was dominated by a single curved table, seating a dozen men and women from every 'an, all in pressed Bulwark uniforms of dark green and covered in medals. Surrounding the table were countless smaller desks, cabinets, and electronic screens detailing lists of data: attack dates, munition inventories, casualty counts—the minutiae of war, all described in the same efficient font.

Her crew in tow, Drekene strode to the centre of the room, footfalls echoing heavily. The murmured conversations fell silent as every eye in the room fell onto the group, studying them with a mix of concern and scorn.

From behind a computer desk tucked to the room's side, an officious Gobl clerk spoke. 'This is meeting D-E-5-7-9-1-2-8. Drekene the Deathless has requested an urgent audience to discuss... Vandar.'

A grey-haired Hum-an nodded to Drekene. Bedecked in an immaculate black uniform stiff with medals, sitting at the table's centre with such an air of authority, it was clear the man commanded this room, and therefore all of Bulwark.

'Greetings, Deathless,' he said in a deep baritone. 'You have the floor.'

Drekene cut straight to the point. 'There is a breach to the underworld in Vandar Forest. We have sealed it by explosion, but the Daem-ans will dig through before long. When they do, all of Vandar will be under threat.'

A silver-haired Gobl-an, with a deep scar mangling

her face, sniffed. 'You're certain this breach led to the underworld?'

Drekene nodded. 'Daem-ans came through it. One caused significant damage to Vandar, many more were in the process of climbing out when we sealed the breach. I suspect it actually leads down to part of the old Dwarf holds, and from there to the underworld. Either way, it poses as much of a threat as the breach here at Bulwark.'

A woman missing her left eye asked, 'And what would you have us do?'

Drekene ignored the speaker, directly addressing the man at the centre of the table. 'High Commander Terrethson, we must send personnel and equipment to the site, establish a new defensive line, before it is too late.

Terrethson drummed his fingers on the desk. 'You delivered this request to us already via communication. I fail to see why we required a meeting in person to repeat what we have already told you. We turned down your petition twice before, and must turn it down again. We simply do not have the resources for a second defensive site.'

'Commander, please reconsider.'

'We have considered,' he barked. 'The fact remains that we are stretched thin. The attacks are getting more intense, yet our funding falls, year after year.'

Drekene's grey hands curled into fists. 'We will need far more resources if the Daem-ans get a foothold in Vandar.'

The commander nodded, eerily calm. 'That may well be, but someone else will have to foot the bill. If we strip our defences here to protect Vandar, then we will lose Bulwark. The world will face two unhindered Daem incursions, not one. Better Bulwark does what Bulwark does best, hold the Daem-ans here, as we have done for centuries. If there is a new breach, then it requires a new cadre of defenders.'

Drekene shook her head. 'Who else will come? Vandar have already denied our request, demanding that you honour the Concordant to protect all the world.'

'And we will protect it, from attacks here at Bulwark. It is not our failing if the world turns a blind eye to this new disaster. I'm sure if the Daem-ans do come through from a new breach, the governments will respond, just like our ancestors did here so long ago.'

Xia could take no more. She stormed forward, ducking past Drekene. 'And how many will die before then? Do you even care?'

Commander Terrethson turned his brown-eyed glare to her. Veins bulged on his forehead as he shouted, 'You would speak to a superior officer like this?'

'I'm not part of Bulwark,' Xia snarled, 'just borrowing the uniform.'

'Then by Hum-az, what are you doing in my fortress?'

Drekene put a hand on Xia's shoulder to forestall another outburst. 'This is Xia. She's been assisting me. She's a warden from Vandar.'

Terrethson snorted. 'That explains it.'

'What's that supposed to mean?' Xia shrugged out of Drekene's grasp.

The commander gave her a patronising smile. 'A

Vandar Elf-an, a Wood Elf-ans, here demanding that Bulwark fight the forest's battle so Wood Elf-ans can continue to sit back while others die.'

Xia shook her head. 'Vandar contributes as much as any country.'

Another snort from the commander. 'Dragon-shet you do. Long have we asked for Elf troops from the forest. Sulsine gives us our finest marksmen, and our main source of lifeSingers. We desperately need more, but no, because of a centuries-old treaty Vandar only provides food, while the rest of the nations pay in blood. Look around you, Elf-an, see how many of my brothers and sisters here bear scars—scars that could have been healed if we had enough lifeSingers. If Vandar actually did its part.

'Go to any other country in the world, and you'll find war veterans, scarred and torn. You can't throw a stone in the Avatarium or Drossen Camp or the Hold without hitting someone who has lost a relative at Bulwark. In Vandar? We're nothing but an inconvenient tax. For so long, you have lived in the luxury of being protected without sacrifice.

'No, Elf-an, for centuries your countrymen have let others die in your stead. Now you want us to risk the world to save your precious forest?' He smirked, grimly shaking his head. 'No. You brought this fate on your own heads. Perhaps now you will see what it's like to fight while others turn their backs on you. I tell you what, we'll be as generous to you as you are to us. All these years, you've given us only what you have in abundance—food. So we'll give you the one thing we have in abundance—ammunition. Same terms that you give us. Transport it yourself. Use it yourself.

Fight yourself. We'll throw you our leftovers, and now it's your turn to act grateful.' Terrethson gave a bitter laugh. 'Perhaps the 'az have a sense of justice after all.'

Face flushing, Xia took a step forward, ready to punch that grin off his callous face. Hands gripped her. She spun, expecting to see Drekene, but came face-to-face with Cadden. His green eyes bored into her, imploring. Gently, he shook his head.

'Soldier or not,' he whispered, 'they'll hang you if you attack the commander.'

'But we can't give up,' Xia said, eyes tearing. 'We can't let the forest fall.'

'We're done here,' Drekene said, resolute. 'We'll find no more sane heads here than we found in Enall.

'But we're not giving up.'

Chapter 18

The elevator's glass doors swung open, disgorging the Hawk's crew into the lobby. Xia stormed through the early morning crowd, much taller 'an jumping out her way. As she passed the reception desk, it took all her restraint not to punch the clerk's patronising smile.

Outside, she released her frustration on the tower's concrete wall—and immediately regretted the decision, the rough material cutting into her knuckles. She glared at the red stain left on the wall's grey, furious at her stupidity, furious at Bulwark Command's pettiness, furious at the whole 'az-forsaken world.

Without pause, Drekene shot by. 'I need to make a call.'

Cadden and Ket exited behind, watching the Deathless as she stomped along the metal-grilled street. At Rikk's whimpering, they turned, noticing the mark Xia had left on the tower's side.

'Urgh, shet,' muttered Ket. 'I'll leave this one to you, Cadden. I'll go... anywhere else.'

The Greml-an scuttled off, leaving Cadden to stare at Xia, stunned.

'I'm fine,' she barked, turning and storming down a side street. She had no idea where she was going, could barely navigate this concrete-and-metal hive, but did not care. In that instant, she just had to get away, far from the tower filled with moronic bureaucrats and heartless leaders, far from the masses who only pretended to care about innocent lives, far from reminders of the death that would soon plague her home. But where could she go? The entire world was filled with callousness, short-sighted men and women all too happy to pass their burdens onto anyone else.

Frustrated, she realised she used to be one of those people. Only a couple of weeks ago, she had turned down Drekene's plea for assistance because it had not been her problem. Not her duty. Deathless hunted Daem-ans. Wardens protected the forest. Simple.

Eddan's death had changed that, shattered her naivety. How many more deaths would be required before world leaders made the same realisation? Did Enall have to burn before Vandar acted to defend itself? Did the world have to be overrun by nightmares before Bulwark appreciated this new threat? Did every living creature have to die before the 'az turned their divine eyes to this unfolding tragedy?

Alongside her, Rikk's claws clattered on the grilled road. He whined, hating the sharp metal against his paws. Normally, he would clamber along walls and leap from electricity pylons, but sensing her mood he stayed down, ears back, subdued. Another long awaited meeting. Another useless gift. Food from Vandar, ammunition from Bulwark, but no soldiers to use either. Worse, they were expected to transport the ammunition themselves. With what? The Hawk? No. They had supplies to feed a non-existent legion, and ammunition stuck half a world from the breach. Vandar would fall. Not because of an insurmountable threat, but because of apathy.

The hammer of boots on metal behind her alerted her to Cadden's pursuit. She increased her pace, but he caught up easily. Times like this, she hated how much shorter Elf-ans were compared to Hum-ans.

'I'm fine,' she muttered.

'Heard that one before.' He gave a compassionate smile.

Xia replied with a glare. 'Well, what do you expect? That bastard is going to sacrifice thousands of Elf-ans, and for what? To make a point? Out of spite that Vandar hasn't helped enough?'

'I get it.' He easily matched her speed, even though she moved as fast as she could without breaking into a run. 'To think that the head of Bulwark would play political games when the stakes were this high, it makes me sick.'

'Then why did you hold me back?'

Cadden grimaced. 'Because you getting hanged would not have helped Vandar.'

'I suppose.' She smirked. 'But beating that grin off his face would have felt good.'

His laugh was so free it brought a smile to her face. 'True. Maybe not quite worth the price.'

'Maybe.' She came to a stop, wrinkling her nose at the stench. 'Urgh. What is that?'

'Sewage treatment plant.' He pointed to a gap between two blockhouses, a brown-yellow ooze being slowly stirred by massive paddles. 'Bulwark has the infrastructure of any city. Some sights are just less… impressive than others.'

Of course she picked the one direction that led to the outlet for the fortress's toilets. This was just turning into a perfect day.

'Here, I'll get us to some fresher air.'

Cadden reached out a hand for hers, only to snatch

it away in revulsion. Confused, she looked down to see her hand dripping with blood. Her knuckles had been cut worse than she realised, and blood trickled down to form a sticky mess gathering at her fingertips.

Taking her by the wrist, he tugged her along. 'Come on. Let's get somewhere cleaner, and I'll take a look at that.'

He led her down a series of alleys and side streets —dodging forklifts, messengers and soldiers—then up a rusted staircase on the side of a warehouse. Away from the treatment plant, the air had lost the sewage stench and was now thick with a burning, but more bearable, chemical tang.

Striding across the tarmac roof, he indicated for her to sit on an air-conditioning vent. Cold to the touch, it vibrated softly from the motion of its fans, matching her hands' quiver. With the weight off her legs her adrenalin faded, leaving her exhausted.

From one of the many pockets on his flightsuit, Cadden pulled out a hand-sized pack that bore the trigonal symbol synonymous with medicine. He unzipped it, revealing a surprisingly complete first-aid kit nestled in the compact packaging. 'Let me see that.' He reached for her hand. Taking a cloth from the pack, he carefully wiped the blood from her fingers, the white linen quickly turning bright red.

Wincing as he scrubbed the gravel from her torn knuckles, she tried to distract herself with the view. Pillars of black smoke rose over the skyline, yesterday's mound of corpses being rendered into new munitions. The cranes still toiled at the wall, some lifting loads of body-filled mud, others dumping fresh soil into the Gauntlet. Distant figures swarmed over the turrets, no doubt making hasty repairs. On the roads below, carts loaded with empty cartridges trailed away from the wall, passing those with fresh rounds headed in the other direction. The whole city-fortress was hurriedly preparing for the next assault.

'This will sting.' Cadden pulled out a small bottle, spraying a neon-green liquid onto her hand.

She focused on the burning, trying to drive the pain into her memory. Losing her temper like that had been pointless, childish. Had the punch been a little harder, she'd have broken a bone. Judging by the concerned look on Cadden's face, he was thinking the same, but did not say anything. For that, she was immensely thankful.

'Where did a pilot learn first aid?' she asked.

'Bulwark basic training.' He leaned in to inspect the wound. Satisfied, he fished around in his pack. 'Doesn't matter whether you're a clerk, a pilot, or a soldier, everyone here is trained in the two most important skills at the front line—how to shoot, and how to heal. You'd be amazed at how many lives can be saved if everyone is taught how to tie a tourniquet, identify a concussion, or deal with someone going into shock.'

Reverently holding her hand, he wrapped her knuckles in a bandage. His touch was so gentle, so hesitant. There was no pain, just relief as the gauze encased her wound. He took care over every fold, smoothing out any wrinkle that might irritate.

Suddenly, Xia felt embarrassed. 'You're really too kind to me.'

'What? For stopping you bleeding all over Bulwark?'

She laughed. 'No, well yes, but not just that. Teaching me to fly, trying tree-leaping, taking me on tours… every time I need distraction, you seem to be there. Even when you're stressed, you make time for me. More than Ket, more than Drekene—shet, you've been kinder than my parents. Why?'

His emerald eyes fixed on hers, voice quiet. 'Do you really not know?'

The longing in his voice struck her, the compassion in his eyes. No, not just compassion… love.

She looked at him, as if for the first time. Those hurt expressions of his when she spoke without thinking, those blushes when Ket teased him in front of her, his constant doting attitude, she now saw it all in a new light.

And in that new light, she saw him. His tanned skin beautiful. His messy hair wonderfully carefree. His green eyes so intense. In all her life, no one had picked up on her mood as well as he had. No one had managed to cheer her so fast in her darkest moments.

Crouching in front of where she sat, his eyes were level with hers. She stared into them, overwhelmed by the depth of feeling there—a feeling she found reflected in her own heart.

She leaned forward for a kiss.

He hesitated, then leaned into her, unshaven chin rough, but lips so warm. She relaxed, her worries fading fast. For a few seconds, all seemed right in the world.

Then the buzz of a communicator shattered the moment. With an awkward laugh, Cadden pulled away, popping in his earpiece as Xia did the same.

Drekene's voice came through, stern. 'Cadden,

Xia, do you read me?'

'Yes,' they chorused.

'I have convinced the Deathless to meet with us. It is our last hope for assistance in Vandar. I need Xia there, with her local knowledge. Cadden, guide her to the Sanctuary.'

The call cut out. Cadden gave an apologetic smile. 'Duty calls.'

Xia laughed. 'At the worst time.'

'As always.' He reached for her.

Beaming, she reached out with her unbandaged hand. Side-by-side, they walked through Bulwark's industrious warrens. The world was still in peril, but somehow she now had hope.

Hand in hand, Xia and Cadden strode towards the outskirts of Bulwark. The factories and warehouses became fewer and further between, replaced with single-storey barracks and offices. Through wall-length windows, Xia glimpsed clerks hurry about with ledgers and folders, working at computer terminals, validating documents. The lesser-known lifeblood of Bulwark—paperwork, as endless as the conflict it tracked.

These buildings gave way to the training fields. Young men and women Xia's age sat in classrooms, staring at whiteboards depicting everything from schematics of rifles to trigonometry. Behind the schoolhouses lay firing ranges, running tracks, assault courses—everything the latest batch of Bulwark draftees needed to learn how to face down the countless assaults from the underworld.

'There it is.' Cadden nodded to a squat dome at the

very edge of the settlement. Nestled against the end of the wall, the decrepit building looked as if it would collapse under a slight breeze. Stone pillars were overgrown with dark grey vines. So little of the roof remained that the structure would likely have caved in if not for the interwoven branches holding up every row of tiles. Despite the mass of plants, Xia could see not a single leaf. The vines and branches, like the stones they swamped, were old, dead.

'Not what I pictured when I heard "Sanctuary,"' Xia muttered, looking up at the structure. The only signs of life were the crows nesting between dead stems and crumbling tiles.

Cadden laughed. 'It's the home of the Deathless. They don't really do cheery.'

'Yeah, but they didn't have to try to make it look so morbid.'

'Just wait until you see the inside. Drekene brought me here before, when she selected me as her pilot.'

Growing more unnerved, Xia let Cadden lead her to the building's entrance—half a door frame alongside a pile of rubble. To her surprise, there were no guards, but then Xia supposed nobody in their right mind would head into the den of the soulless protectors of the world.

True to Cadden's words, the inside was stark. Little light broke through the fragmented ceiling, falling in twisted patterns across the stone floor. Each step kicked up a cloud of dust, heavy with a mildew. Ahead, stood or sat on the floor in a wide circle, were a hundred figures. Drak-ans and Greml-ans, Hum-ans and Gobl-ans, Elf-ans and Ash-ans. All were heavily scarred, looked middle-aged, and had eyes of pure black.

The only furniture were the hundred pedestals, which ringed the room. Atop each sat a skull, from Greml bones no larger than an apple, to hulking heads of extinct Glac-ans. Each was dribbled in wax, as if a candle had been burned down over them but never replaced. Xia was not sure what she expected from the home of the world's undying defenders, but it was not *this*.

Drekene waited at the circle's centre. Her eyes flicked down. Belatedly, Xia realised she still held Cadden's hand, and quickly snatched it away. If Drekene cared, she made no indication.

'Here she is,' Drekene announced to the room, voice echoing unevenly from the domed roof. 'This is Xia the Warden. My pilot, Cadden Creakson, you have already met.'

A ripple of response spread through the crowd—nods, smirks, greetings and cackles. Xia's neck prickled at the sight of so many featureless eyes fixed on her.

From one side, a particularly scarred Hum-an spoke. 'I'm Assen the Deathless. You have come a long way, Xia. Drekene has told us the details of your experience, but we have questions.'

Unsure how to address a room of ageless warriors, Xia nodded.

Assen continued, 'It has been a long time since most of us have spoken to one from Vandar, and we need a updated opinion. Do you believe Vandar can fight this threat itself?'

Xia looked at Drekene and Cadden, who both

nodded supportively. Swallowing, she stepped forward, trying to make her voice loud enough for the cavernous room. 'Honestly? No. A few weeks ago, I would have said yes. But now it's a firm no.'

'What changed?' Assen asked.

'I now understand who Vandar's leaders are, and what they will face. I've seen the Avatar of Elf-az. I've spoken to the Prime Ministry of Vandar. And… I've witnessed the attacks here.'

Assen nodded sagely. 'Always a sobering experience.'

Xia shivered at the memory. 'Yeah, you could say that. Vandar isn't ready to face such an assault. The government seems set on waiting for Bulwark Command to help, and Bulwark Command have refused.'

To one side, a Gobl-an shouted, 'Surely Vandar will defend itself once the Daem threat is seen, and Bulwark troops are nowhere to be found.'

'Sure.' Xia turned to the gnarled woman. 'But by that time, half the forest will be overrun. And then? What can Vandar do? We have no army. Just the Forest Guard, and they are too few. Maybe if the Forest Guard and wardens together gathered at the breach, maybe they could hold. But once the Daem-ans are out, flooding the forest?' She shook her head bitterly. 'No. Vandar will not stand.'

'It's as I said,' Drekene announced. 'If the Deathless do not go to Vandar in force, the forest will be lost.'

Silence descended over the room, a hundred ancient soldiers mulling over the threat, debating the fate of the world. Xia felt scared to even breathe, lest she distract them, somehow cause the downfall of her homeland.

A Greml-an missing an ear ended the quiet. 'Pity. I always liked the forest.'

Another voice chimed in, sombre. 'First the Dwarf holds fell. I've always wondered who the Daem-ans would claim next.'

'Five hundred years we've held them here.' A black-haired Hum-an woman gave a grim smile. 'Not bad.'

Cackling darkly, the Greml-an replied, 'Yeah. At this rate, civilisation might last a few millennia before we're overrun.'

Drekene frowned. 'There's no need for such loss of hope. With all of us together, we can stop this attack. Or at least hold it.'

Assen frowned. 'And abandon Bulwark?'

'We'd hardly be abandoning it,' Drekene countered. 'Bulwark's defenders are skilled, even without us. When was the last time the Daem-ans reached our line? A year ago? And then only one.'

'And if we were not there, that one would have been unleashed into the wilderness, into the Avatarium.' Assen grimaced.

Drekene nodded. 'Better one here than a thousand in Vandar.'

'We don't have the numbers to protect the world, not anymore. Look at us, Drekene.' Assen waved his hands over the circle. 'This is all that's left.'

'Besides,' the gnarled Gobl-an added, smug. 'I quite like not being on the front line. I don't know about you, but I don't fancy hastening the day when I join Daem-az's minions.'

Drekene sniffed. 'Deathless are not so selfish.'

'It's not selfishness,' Assen explained. 'Gretta has a valid point. If we're on the front, we will fall, the Deathless will be wiped out.'

'That's our role,' snapped Drekene. 'Deathless fight to protect others, or have you forgotten why we took that forsaken pact?'

Assen sighed. 'And when we die, who will replace us? Our youngest members took the pact two hundred years ago. Yet every decade we lose a brother or sister. We're a dying breed.'

Xia frowned, confused at what she was hearing. 'I was told that the lack of new Deathless was a good thing. That it's a horrendous price.'

'It is,' Assen replied, patient. 'But it is a price that is sometimes required. A price the world is no longer willing to pay. If we're gone, then who will advise Bulwark? Who will teach of the inner workings of Daem-ans, explain their tactics, their mentality? The Deathless are needed. No, Drekene, I have not forgotten our duty, but the world has.'

Shaking her head, Xia snarled, 'So what? You're going to let Vandar fall? All those people die?'

Assen shrugged. 'All 'an die. Live as long as we have, and you learn that. Death is unavoidable. We stand here not to stop death, but to make sure some still live, that civilisation endures.'

Drekene stepped alongside Xia. 'And when the Daem-ans are done with Vandar? They will not stay in the forest. The whole world will fall. Civilisation will end. The only creatures alive will be Daem-ans.'

'Oh, I don't believe it will come to that,' Assen replied, flippant. 'The world beat back a Daem invasion once before, when we were armed with spears and bows. We can do it again.'

Drekene's voice cut through the air, the most intense Xia had ever heard the woman. 'And how many will fall before then? How much damage will be done before the world's armies manage to contain the horde? It could be decades until they are beaten back. Cities will burn. Entire countries will be erased from the map. The world will be shaken to its core.'

Quiet blanketed the room once more. Weathered faces exchanged glances, empty eyes studying one another. Xia could see the hesitation there. Some wanted to help. Some knew what must be done. Some gave her hope.

'Perhaps a shock is exactly what the world needs.' The audience turned to a Drak-an sat cross-legged on the dirt floor. A pink scar ran down his face, bright against his black scales. 'Assen is right—the world has forgotten why they need us, why they need Bulwark. We are a legend to them, an entertaining tale, nothing more. They have forgotten the siege of Calidren. The Red Fields. The Displacement. That is why there are no new Deathless. That is why Bulwark continues to suffer budget cuts even as Daem attacks rise. The 'an of the world have forgotten what threat we truly face.

'As much as we may hate to admit it, maybe another breach is a gift, not a curse. Let Vandar burn. Let the world remember what is at stake. Maybe then they will take the threat from the underworld seriously once more. Maybe then, our numbers will swell. Maybe then, we might stop the Daem-ans efforts to slowly bleed us dry.'

Nods spread over the room. One by one, the scarred, weathered faces seemed convinced.

Xia shook her head. This was their last chance. Everyone else had turned their backs on Vandar, even its own government. If the Deathless would not fight the Daem-ans, all hope was lost.

'You can't do this,' she pleaded. 'If you do not act, millions will die. Vandar will fall.'

Assen took a step forward, tone full of compassion even as his words cut into her heart. 'I understand, Xia the Warden, but a few million casualties is a small price to pay in order to ensure the survival of the Deathless, to ensure the survival of the world.'

And with the man's kindly smile, the last trace of hope in Xia's heart died.

Chapter 19

Xia staggered after Drekene, forcing herself to move. After meeting with Vandar's government, she had felt disgusted. Their short-lived discussions with Bulwark Command had left her filled with rage. Now, walking away from the Deathless at Sanctuary, she simply felt empty. Hollow.

Padding in the mud to the side of the metal road, Rikk kept pace, head down. Cadden walked alongside her, shoulders slumped. Even Drekene appeared broken—the woman had never looked so *frail*.

None spoke. No need. They all knew the truth. They had failed.

Vandar was doomed.

Despite the lack of a noon eclipse this far east, the city was still plunged into a gloom. Clouds spilled down from the mountain range beyond Bulwark, blanketing the land in a low, grey layer.

'Drekene,' a woman croaked from behind. Xia stopped to see Gobl-an approach from the Deathless Sanctuary, or part of a Gobl-an. The woman limped on a metal spring that replaced her right leg below the knee. Her left hand ended in another prosthetic, a claw of a hand constructed of black, jagged metal. No attempt had been made to replace her right arm, which was missing, no doubt from the same injury that had left her face horrendously scarred. One eye the black of the Deathless, the other burned into a white orb. If not for the voice, Xia would not have been able to tell the Deathless' gender.

'Kyor,' Drekene nodded.

'Quite a shet-show in there, hey?' Kyor grimaced, the act contorting her scars horrifically. 'Never thought I'd live to see the day the Deathless became as petty as the rest.'

'Then why didn't you speak up?' Drekene snapped.

Kyor barked a laugh. 'As if they care about me. You know how it goes. The day I lost my arm, they all but gave me retirement. No one's listened to a word I've said in over a century. Well, except maybe you.'

'I didn't think Deathless could retire.' Xia muttered.

'We can't.' The woman's mismatched eyes looked amused. 'Well, not without dying, but I didn't have the grace to do that. So they put me in charge of the Deathless logistics corps.'

'Never heard of them.'

'Not surprised. We don't do anything. Oh, back in the day, before we pinned the Daem-ans back here, we kept Deathless supplied all over the continent. Quite an effort with only carts and canal barges. Now? Drekene's the only Deathless operating outside the shadow of the Wall. And all she needed was one transport. No, my post is just an order to stay out of their way.' The woman paused, a devilish glint in her eyes. 'But you know what? To Daem-az with the lot of 'em. They turned their backs on you, like they turned their backs on me. So let's use this empty title they thrust on me.'

'How?' Drekene asked.

'I still have a hundred transports under my

command. Right now Bulwark's logistics corps uses them, on loan from me, but they're mine to do with what I want. You need them? You call.'

Cadden turned to Drekene. 'It would let us ship the ammunition Bulwark promised. Arm the defence of Vandar.'

The hope in his voice filled Xia, but died a moment later. What good would it do without an army? They did not travel to Vandar's capital for food. They did not fly across the continent for bullets. They came to seek help, real help. Men and women who would stand and fight for what was right. Instead they had supplies. Supplies would not stop the forest from burning. Looking at the faces around her, Xia saw her companions felt the same. Even this one well-meaning person was not enough. After everything, they had truly failed.

Drekene thanked the Gobl-an anyway. Promised to be in touch, then set back off down the path away from Sanctuary. Walking back through the city, every building, every passing soldier, every pillar of smoke filled Xia with dread. All of this was required to hold back the Daem-ans. Thousands of personnel, hundreds of turrets, kilometres of wall, all to contain the tide of otherworldly invaders.

What did Vandar have? A handful of wardens. Scattered trees. Ineffective Forest Guard. And countless defenceless civilians.

Drizzle began to fall. Not the heavy beads that would descend from the forest canopy, but a fine mist that soaked into Xia's flightsuit, saturating her short hair. It weighed her down, made every step difficult.

Rikk whimpered, his feet sticking in the

dampening mud. Still unwilling to bound as normal between buildings, he instead took to running along the base of the neighbouring wall. Barely a foot from the ground, he scuttled along, claws finding purchase in cracks in the concrete. Reluctantly, he hopped down as they passed between structures, scurrying over the road with sodden fur, only to cling to the bottom of the next warehouse. The poor creature could not comprehend what was happening, but clearly knew something was wrong. Desperately, hopelessly wrong.

As they staggered closer to the heart of Bulwark, the crowds became more dense. Scarred soldiers filled the roads. Beside the path, factory technicians sat on crates to snatch a short lunch break before resuming their shifts, not even bothering to wipe the grease from their faces. Even administrators, holding clipboards and directing forklift convoys, seemed grizzled, bags under their eyes, hair too grey for their years.

Bulwark was awash with these dedicated men and women, trained and drilled for this endless conflict. Back home barely anyone who wasn't a warden knew how to fire a rifle. None knew how to deal with a Daem-an. Few could even bandage a wound.

Drekene turned a corner, and the group passed into the landing field at the edge of the fortress-city. Hoverjets and rotorwings of all sizes were scattered over the mass of tarmac. Neatly arranged in a grid pattern, the parked aircraft swarmed with workers. Mechanics replaced landing skids and attached fuel lines. Labourers dragged crates from larger aircraft. Sergeants directed newly arrived draftees towards enrolment centres. Greml metalSingers repaired ageing turbines.

Overhead, a constant stream of aircraft flowed. One by one, they peeled away, following complex patterns between the grid of parked craft, before descending onto vacant slots. Freshly refuelled hoverjets lifted off, rising to join the lines of outgoing traffic. The air hummed with a hundred engines, stank of jet fuel and solder. This was a constant operation. All day and night the landing continued, bringing vital supplies to a city that grew none of its own food, mined none of its own metal.

Again, Xia could not help but compare this to her home. Vandar had plenty of food, at least. But arms factories? Mines? Training camps? Bulwark drank men and materiel thirstily. Vandar did not even have enough landing sites for the volume of traffic required, even if they could convince the other countries to donate supplies.

Everywhere she looked she saw one simple, inescapable fact. Vandar was outmatched. The forest could barely cope with a single Daem-an. It would never stand against what approached. They needed an army. They had nothing.

Ahead, Xia heard the guttural rhythm of Ket metalSinging. She looked forward to see the Hawk, silver skin drab as it reflected the darkening sky, one of its engines on the floor before the Greml-an. As he chanted, glowing pipes and wires arranged themselves in its exposed workings. His beat increased, and the entire engine—larger than Drekene—started to glow, then took to the air. Noiselessly, it blended into an opening under the right wing, rivets flying into place. Reflective panels leapt from a storage rack, melding themselves onto the surface, covering the engine.

With a satisfied grunt, Ket let his Song die, and turned to glance at the others. 'Thought that was your clomping steps, Drekene.' The Greml-an saw their expressions and his face fell. 'Y'all look cheery. That good, hey?'

Drekene replied in a flat tone, 'The Deathless have refused our requests.'

'Well, shet.' Ket sucked his teeth, thoughtful. 'What now?'

Sitting on an empty fuel barrel, Drekene shrugged. Xia collapsed to the hard tarmac. Whimpering, Rikk padded over. He was far too large to fit fully on her lap, but that did not stop the daft mutt from trying. Xia ran her hands through his fur. The drizzle had eased a little, but he was already soaked, as they all were, somehow the fine mist drenching clothing and fur more than a downpour.

The underside of Rikk's chin was at least relatively dry, and Xia scratched away, the familiar feeling of his fur, his warmth, settling her heart. His content chirps brought her some comfort, reminding her of a better life, the one she had but weeks earlier.

'Well, I'm not sure what we do next,' Cadden announced, forcing joviality, 'but I do know that I'm hungry. Who'd like me to cook up some lunch?'

He was answered by shrugs, but apparently took that as agreement and disappeared into the Hawk. Metallic thuds and the sound of a blender echoed from the open ramp, shortly followed by the hearty aroma of sliced vegetables.

'Well, the Hawk's ready for whatever we do,' Ket said. 'Repaired that shetting number-two engine. Should take us anywhere. That includes over the sea, if you want to book it.'

Drekene simply nodded, staring into the distance. Xia followed the woman's gaze, but could only see the wilderness beyond the landing area. Her eyes struggled to pick out shrubs and low trees out in Bulwark's exclusion zone. The barren landscape, off-limits to all civilians, was meant to protect the citizens of the neighbouring Avatarium of Hum from stray shells, so that no innocent found themselves caught in the crossfire.

Vandar would have nothing like that. When the time came for its desperate defence, there would be no separation between the Daem-ans and the unarmed masses. How many would share Eddan's fate, killed by stray bullets fired in their defence?

Grim, she realised that even if Bulwark's entire force was deployed to Vandar today, collateral damage would be unavoidable. The region around the new breach had countless small villages, scattered through the forest's heart. Vandar's population was dispersed across the land. Other than a handful of large cities, most Elf-ans there lived in small communities, low in population but numerous. Those isolated towns would be the new front line, their citizens nothing but targets for the rampaging monsters.

Cadden returned with a tray bearing five bowls of varying size, and handed them out. Taking hers, Xia was surprised to find not the heavily spiced stew she had expected, but a pile of shredded vegetables.

'Thought I'd try my hand at Elf dishes.' Cadden smiled as he sat next to her. He took one bowl himself, leaving the other on the tray for Rikk, who dug in noisily.

Xia took a forkful of the colourful meal. The vegetables were nowhere near as fresh as back home, and the blender had shredded the material a little more than she was used to, but after so long eating the same spiced slop day after day, none of that mattered. 'It's delicious,' she said honestly.

He beamed and started on his own. Drekene shovelled her serving into her mouth mechanically, eyes not wavering from the horizon.

'I'll give you this.' Ket picked at a string of carrot caught in his teeth. 'You didn't completely butcher the meal this time. Makes a nice change.'

Shaking his head, Cadden just smiled. The silence continued as they ate, but it was a companionable silence. Something about sharing a meal together chased away the darkness, even the drizzle not ruining the mood. Shards of light broke through the clouds, giving moments of warmth. It was enough for no one to suggest moving into the dry but cramped Hawk.

All too soon, Xia found her bowl empty. The others finished theirs just as fast, Rikk sniffing around for any missed scraps before licking already-clean bowls. With a jaw-stretching yawn, the vulfik returned to Xia, laying his head on her lap and starting to snooze.

'So.' Ket set his bowl to the side. 'Hate to be that guy, but I gotta ask—what's next?'

Xia closed her eyes. 'Next, Vandar is destroyed.'

An arm wrapped around her shoulders. She opened her eyes—vision blurred with tears—to find Cadden leaning against her. He kissed her softly on her damp hair as she rested against his shoulder.

'This is new.' Ket cackled. 'Was sure you two'd

stay in denial for a bit longer.'

'Yeah, yeah,' Cadden replied, playful. 'Let's get it all over with.'

The Greml-an grinned. 'Oh, shet-no. I'm going to drag this out for a good long time. The kids make an adorable couple, don't they, Drekene?'

The Deathless tore her gaze from the horizon to regard the younger two. She merely grunted.

Xia pulled away a little, face flushing. 'Um. Is this... allowed?'

'A Hum-an and an Elf-an?' Ket giggled. 'Oh, I'm sure logistically you'll have problems—size mismatch 'n' all. Not as much as a Greml-an and a Drak-an, but stranger coupling have happened. This is the thirteenth century. I hear a Dragon matriarch took a Gobl-an lover the other year.'

Face warming, Xia shook her head. 'No... that's... Not.' She sighed. 'I mean, relationships. In Bulwark.'

Cadden tensed. 'It's not banned... but I guess it's frowned upon.'

'To maintain discipline,' Drekene replied, stern eyes fixed on Xia. 'To make sure one considers one's duty in the heat of combat.' Her face softened. 'But, of course, you are not a member of Bulwark, Xia. And relationships with outsiders are encouraged. After all, it helps to keep in mind those we fight for. Reminds us why we man this fortress.'

'Yup.' Ket's grin was far too wide, reaching from ear to ear. 'Besides, it's not like regular Bulwark soldiers don't pair off. You take people, put them in strenuous situations all day, then bunk them together and... well bunks get shared. Every career-officer's done it at some point.'

Cadden laughed. 'Even you?'

'Of course.' Ket scowled. 'Shet, I'm sure Drekene here has a few stories. Can't live five centuries without breaking a few hearts.'

The Deathless sighed. 'Not for three hundred years.'

Ket whistled. 'And I thought I was having a dry spell.'

Drekene's black eyes finally turned from Xia, focusing on the Greml-an. 'When you know that everyone you meet will die long before you, it pays to avoid attachment.'

'What about other Deathless?' Xia asked. 'Surely some have... paired off.'

'Some do.' Drekene shrugged. 'I don't see the point. There is no happy ever after for Deathless. No eternity in the verdant forest of Elf-az, or the endless plains of Hum-az, or Greml-az's glittering caverns. When I die, I know what awaits me, and it will not be reuniting with those I care about. Love is precious, but it is a thing for mortals.'

Xia grimaced, leaning back into Cadden for comfort. 'I didn't think of it like that.'

'Course not,' Ket replied. 'You two're kids. Probably don't think further ahead than tomorrow's breakfast.'

'This, from the man who gets impatient waiting five minutes during a landing approach,' Cadden teased.

The Greml-an scowled, earning a laugh from Xia and Cadden. The cheer quickly faded. Talk of death brought Xia's thoughts back to her brother.

She met the Deathless's gaze. 'Drekene, I... I need

to ask you something.'

The woman nodded calmly. 'Go ahead.'

'You spoke about when you… when you died.'

'Yes.'

'You said you saw the afterlife. The normal afterlife, I mean. Your friends, your family waiting.'

Drekene's face turned a darker grey. 'Yes.'

'Is. Did.' Xia sighed. 'Did you mean that? Did you really see them?'

'I would not lie about such things.' Drekene frowned. 'Why do you ask?'

Xia struggled, trying to make sense of her chaotic thoughts. 'I just wanted to make sure. I want to know that Eddan's in a good place.'

Drekene gave an uncharacteristically kind smile. 'Yes. If he did not immediately rise as a Deathless, then he is with Elf-az, or whichever 'az was closest to his heart.'

Fresh tears stung Xia's eyes. 'So I really will see him someday?'

The smile broadened. 'Yes, child. Hopefully someday far from now, but you will be with him again.'

Xia nodded, latching onto the strange sense of hope. 'Thank you.'

The Deathless shook her head. 'For what?'

'For some confidence. I don't know why, but knowing he's out there helps. Even if the worst happens, even if Vandar falls, my family will be whole again.'

Cadden squeezed her shoulder. 'It's a beautiful thought. But let's hope it doesn't come to that.'

'Aye,' Ket grumbled. 'But that brings us back to

what the shet do we do now?'

Rubbing her face, Xia tried to calm her tears, focus on the problem at hand. 'We still need help, but who else can we turn to? The Avatarium?'

Cadden grunted. 'I doubt they'll help. Bulwark might be pissed that Vandar doesn't contribute soldiers to the front, but it's Hum-ans that bear the brunt of the strain. If Vandar hasn't sent troops to defend the Avatarium, why would the Avatarium send troops to help the forest now?'

'What about our other neighbours? Sulsine, Drossen Camp, or Gallat Hold?'

'Nah.' Ket sucked his teeth, the slurping sound rousing Rikk. 'Sulsine has no love for Vandar, I'm afraid. They did flee the forest for a reason. Drossen's too small to be much use. And Gallat? They're happy hiding behind Nesken Ridge—even Bulwark has trouble getting them to send their share of recruits.'

'What about the countries that don't contribute to Bulwark?' Cadden offered. 'The Archipelago must have troops to spare.'

Ket laughed. 'The Archipelago would be glad to watch the mainland burn. They're still worried that the Avatarium will invade, reclaim the lost colonies. They'll take all this as a blessing. Besides, they probably think Daem-ans can't swim.'

'Can they?' Xia asked, tired.

'Eh.' The Greml-an shrugged. 'They've not had much reason to here, but I wouldn't put anything past them. If they can't, then they'll learn.'

Cadden sighed. 'That leaves the Drak lands.'

'We'll find no help there.' Drekene stood to begin pacing. 'Some Matriarchs are still alive from the days before the Daem-an's invasion. The purges are burned into their memories. More Dragons were felled by Elf archers than by the rest of the 'an put together. The matriarchs won't shed a tear over Vandar's fate.'

'So it's hopeless,' Xia whispered. 'We're alone.'

The silence that followed cut into her chest. She wanted to scream, to run, to do something—anything —but felt too weary. This was how her homeland's fate would be sealed. Not with a final stand. Not with some clever argument. But with their small band running out of places to turn for aid. Alone, having apparently alienated the rest of the world, Vandar Forest would face the Daem onslaught.

And would be utterly destroyed.

Xia scratched Rikk's chin. How many of his kind would fall? Vulfiks went hand-in-hand with Vandar culture, the animals in almost every household. Rikk had showed he was willing to face down a Daem-an to protect his masters, and Xia doubted that other vulfiks would have any better instincts for self-preservation. It was not just the Elf-ans in Vandar that would suffer, but the entire forest. Animals and plants, wild and domesticated, would all feel the Daem-ans' wrath.

'No.' Drekene stopped her pacing, turning to the group. 'We will not give up.'

Ket scoffed. 'You know of a country we've not considered?'

'No,' Drekene said, firm. 'You were right when you said we were alone, but alone or not, we know what must be done. Even if it is only the four of us...' She was interrupted as Rikk gave an excited yip. 'Even with the five of us, we will return to Vandar, to the breach.'

Cadden shook his head. 'But what will we do? One Deathless, one jet—it's nothing.'

'Far from nothing.' Drekene's tone was forceful, hopeful. 'It is the best Bulwark has to offer. We will go and do what we have always done. We will protect the world against the Daem threat.

'Whatever the cost.'

PART III

Chapter 20

At the flick of a switch the windows darkened, dimming the orange sunset that glared into the Hawk's cockpit. They had flown all day, passing over wonders that would have amazed Xia a week earlier. Sprawling cities, enormous canals, industrial farmlands. Now all Xia could think about was the people who lived there. Were they aware of the stance their leaders were taking? Would they object to the slaughter that awaited Vandar's Elf-ans? Or would they agree with Bulwark, believing that the forest should pay for its misdeeds?

'It's getting late,' Cadden called to the rear of the hoverjet.

Preceded by heavy footsteps, Drekene arrived. 'Very well. Best not fly if you're tired. Find us a place to set down.'

Banking the jet, Cadden looked over his displays. 'Looks like there's a fallow field near a farmhouse nearby. Seems a good spot to set down.'

'Won't the farmer mind?' Xia asked.

Cadden shrugged. 'Bulwark has rights to set craft down in any open land. The farmer will just be happy that we're not crushing his crops.'

Turning back to the window, Xia nodded. The sprawling farmlands of the Avatarium stretched to the horizon. With few lifeSigners, the farmers had to use mundane methods to produce enough food to feed their population. Even with irrigation, tractors and industrial fertilisers, feeding the densely populated Hum cities required huge expanses of land. Despite its vast fields, the Avatarium still imported much of its food from Vandar, where lifeSingers could make plants bloom with fruit all year round, where vegetables could thrive even without sunlight.

Xia wondered what would become of the world with Vandar crippled. Bulwark may have condemned the Elf-an's refusal to commit troops, but the forest still fed millions outside its borders. Even if by some miracle Drekene succeeded in holding back the Daemans, how much damage would be done before their havoc was halted? How many Elf farmers and lifeSigners would fall? How many orchards would be torn apart? How many would starve?

Almost clipping a tree line bordering two fields, the Hawk sailed towards its landing spot, hovering in midair briefly before settling onto the unkempt grass. A shudder ran through the ship as the engines powered off, Cadden running through the complex shutdown procedure. Rikk, who had been sleeping in the footwell below Xia's chair, chirped, excited. The vulfik hated being cooped up on the Hawk, but would probably be even more stressed if he knew they headed to war.

'Come on,' Xia said to the mutt. 'Let's get you outside.' Might as well let him enjoy himself while he still could. While they still lived.

Rikk took off down the hallway, earning himself a curse from Ket as he hurdled the Greml-an and jumped onto the still-closed ramp. He scratched at the metal surface until Xia caught up and hit the control panel. The ramp had barely begun to descend when

Rikk clambered up, squeezing himself out the opening and into the field beyond.

Waiting for the ramp to fully descend, Xia followed. As her boots met the wild grass, a brisk breeze swept over the field. Xia deeply breathed the scents of greenery and wildflowers, smiling. At the far end of the field stood the farmer's cottage, its traditional stone walls well weathered.

Running her hands over the tops of the taller grass tufts, she strolled towards Rikk. He sprinted across the field, chittering gleefully, bounding up the side of the a tree and leaping off. Furred membrane flaring, he caught the breeze, gliding through the evening air to land just short of Xia.

She ruffled his head as he clicked, content. He then turned and sprinted back to the field's edge to repeat the process.

'At least one of us is happy,' Drekene said. Xia turned to see the imposing woman stomp over, leaving a clear trail in the grass.

'Yes.' Xia smiled. 'I don't think Bulwark is good for vulfiks.'

'I don't think Bulwark is good for anyone. But I understand your point. Even after five hundred years living there, it is still oppressive to me. For a wild creature like him, it must be awful.'

'He's only at home in the forest, like me.' A sigh shook Xia's body. 'And now that forest is doomed.'

'It is not doomed. Hope is not lost.'

'Isn't it? How can the four of us stop a Daem invasion?'

Drekene's silence felt like a kick to the gut. She was trying to keep a brave face, but clearly had no idea how to save Vandar. The woman had five hundred years of experience fighting the Daem-ans, had been on the front line centuries before Xia's great grandparents were born. If she had no plan, perhaps this was hopeless. Perhaps this was just a strange funeral procession, leading the four of them to their pointless deaths.

Would that be so bad? No matter what happened, the world would never be the same again. Vandar Forest, the beacon of tranquillity in this modern world, would be forever scarred. Instead of orchard keepers and wardens, children would be raised as warriors. Countless families would be ripped apart, the soil fertilised with Elf blood.

Dying before she witnessed that new torment seemed a blessing of sorts. She would go to her brother. Wait in the pristine woods of Elf-az, luxuriating in the shade of a million trees until their parents arrived. Their family would be together, far from this world of pain.

Footsteps hurrying down the Hawk's ramp silenced Xia's morbid thoughts. Cadden carried a steaming pot, his grin broad as his eyes met hers. The joy on his face twisted her heart. Not everything in this world revolved around suffering. Her relationship with Cadden was so new, the pair having not even found time to be alone since that first kiss, but already Xia felt her soul drawn to him. Just sitting with him in the cockpit, talking of childhood memories or future dreams, filled her with a calmness, a contentment that kept her going through these hopeless times.

Somehow, more than anything, the thought of losing him made her fear death. They had only just met each other, only had a few moments of one another's company. It seemed horribly unfair for that to be ripped away so soon. He was Hum-an, she Elf-an. They had different patron gods, would go to different afterlives. Interracial married couples agreed on which afterlife to go to, so that they could be together for eternity. Her relationship with Cadden was too young for either to consider turning their back on their 'az. When they died, they were likely never to see each other again.

Xia blinked away tears, annoyed at herself. How could she dwell on such simple matters when the world hung in the balance? She had never been the type to pine after a boy she fancied, so why did this upset her so?

'Dinner's ready,' Cadden called.

The Hawk's crew gathered around the pilot as he ladled out their meal. Ket trooped down the ramp, muttering to himself, but took the bowl. Even Rikk leapt from the tree and sprinted through the grass for his serving.

'Afraid it's back to Hum stew.' Cadden handed Xia a bowl, apologetic. 'All I could do with the supplies we have. Hopefully we can restock when we reach Vandar.'

She sat next to him, the tufts of grass offering a surprisingly soft mat. 'I'm sure it'll be great.'

'Greml-az,' Ket muttered. 'I think Cadden's toxic. Barely a day with him and the poor girl's already delirious.'

Cadden swatted at the small man. 'Shut up and eat your food.'

'Gladly,' Ket retorted with a grin. 'Once you hand

me something that qualifies as food.'

Smiling, Xia took a spoonful of stew. Tasted like the normal Hum fare, heavy with spice, light on any real flavour. But it sated her stomach, and the warmth was pleasant against the evening breeze.

The group ate in silence—or as much silence as they could with Rikk lapping at his bowl. It seemed to be their new unwritten rule: mealtimes were free of talk of their dire situation, free of worries and despair. Meals were an opportunity to relax, to experience the moment, taste the broth, smell the air, feel the wind. A time to centre themselves, to simple be.

By the time Xia's spoon fell into her empty bowl, her worries had not evaporated, but at least seemed distant. Rikk was the first to leave the circle, chirping as he bounded into the grass. Ket was not far behind.

'Need to do some work on the Hawk,' the Gremlan announced.

'What are you doing to my ship?' asked Cadden, wary.

Ket giggled mischievously. 'Oh, you'll see.'

Staring at the retreating mechanic, Cadden sighed. 'Well, that's ominous.'

'I'm sure his improvements will be valuable,' replied Drekene.

'Yeah.' Cadden chuckled mirthlessly. 'Or he'll remove the landing legs for fuel efficiency. He had all that time at Bulwark to catch up on maintenance. That means he's now... *tinkering*.'

'It'll be fine,' Xia assured him. 'Ket loves the Hawk as much as you.'

'If he loved her, he wouldn't keep changing her. I swear she flies nothing like she did when she rolled off the assembly line.'

'Yes, but she flies better now, right?'

Cadden smiled. 'Yes, I suppose. Still, you don't have to wonder what's happened to the centre of gravity every time the Hawk takes off.'

Xia laughed, settling her head against his shoulder. 'Fair enough.' At the screech of metal against metal inside the Hawk, Xia also felt herself doubt Ket's plot.

Drekene spoke in a stern voice. 'We have far more pressing issues than Ket's inventions.'

'Ah, yes.' Cadden sighed. 'The whole doomed forest thing.'

'Yes, that.' Drekene ran her hands over her bald head.

'So what's our plan?' Xia lifted her head from Cadden. 'I agree we have to help, but what can the four of us do? Just keep dropping explosives down the chasm as they dig back through?'

'That may work in the short term, but it's a delaying tactic at best.' Drekene looked towards the orange sky. 'Each blast damages the ground, fragmenting the bedrock. Makes it easier for them to dig through, and widens the area from which they could emerge.'

Cadden grimaced. 'Not to mention that we may already be too late. Who knows how many Daem-ans will be loose by the time we get there to seal the breach?'

A hopeless silence smothered the group. Xia turned at the sound of Ket's voice and saw the Greml-an walk down the ramp, two large Bulwark rifles—the kind held by Drak-ans—glowing behind him, held aloft by his metalSinging. Keeping up his Song, he walked around the Hawk, floating rifles in tow.

'So we seal the breach and then go hunt down the Daem-ans,' Xia suggested.

Drekene shrugged. 'It took us a week to hunt one Daem-an. Who knows how many will have escaped? By the time we find them all, others will surely have reached the surface, and probably in greater numbers.'

Headache growing, Xia rubbed her brow. 'So it'll be a hopeless cycle. We put down one pack of them, just for another to appear. Another Bulwark.'

'Almost.' Cadden squeezed her hand. 'Only that Bulwark has the strength to hold back the increasing assaults. I can see us quickly being overwhelmed. As the hole is widened by each blast, the Daem-ans will come through faster. It'll be like trying to reverse a waterfall one bucket at a time.'

From the far side of the Hawk, Ket's metalSinging increased in intensity. Xia could only catch glimpses of activity, her view obstructed by the hoverjet. Glowing panels came free to lower themselves to the grass. Flashes of arcing electricity lit the evening sky. Ket paced back and forth, pointed ears poking over the wildflowers.

'Perhaps that is all we need.' Drekene levelled her empty gaze at the couple. 'If it has reopened, we detonate explosives into the breach. We track any Daem-ans that have surfaced, hunt them down and then repeat the process. If we're lucky, the Daem-ans may still be digging their way out, in which case we hold the breach for as long as we can.'

'And when they eventually overwhelm us?' Xia asked.

Drekene opened her palms. 'They will, certainly.

Even if the breach is still sealed, they will eventually dig through where we are not expecting, or emerge in a wave so large that they cannot be contained. Sooner or later, they will get through, but that isn't the point.'

Xia grimaced. 'Then what is?'

'The point is not to defeat the Daem-ans, but delay them. The four of us cannot halt an invasion, no, but we can slow it until sane heads prevail. Once Vandar sees the threat is real, once Bulwark sees its food supplies are truly in danger, once the world realises that they face an uncontrolled outbreak, then soldiers will come. Whether from within Vandar or without, troops will be sent. We only have to hold out until they do, until a real defence can be erected.

'We cannot stop the tide ourselves, but maybe we can delay it long enough for others to arrive, others who can hold the line.'

The three looked between one another, faces growing in determination. This might be a suicide mission, but it was not without purpose. They had a goal, a difficult, insane, but achievable goal. The forest may yet survive.

A whistle cut across the field. All three looked over to see Ket beckoning them onward.

'Alright,' Cadden sighed. 'Well we have a plan. Let's see what our mechanic has done to hinder us.'

Strolling through the thigh-high grass—or knee-high in Drekene's case—the three rounded the Hawk's silver frame. Ket waited at the front, arms folded, smug. Next to him, the Hawk's smoothly curved nose was broken with two protrusions. It did not take Xia long to identify the rifles she had seen earlier, now mounted into the Hawk, barrels pointing forward like

255

angry antennae.

'Take a gander at the new and improve *war-*hoverjet.' Ket's grin widened.

'What have you done to my ship?' Cadden exclaimed.

'It's my ship,' Drekene corrected. 'But yes, what is this?'

Ket cackled. 'This is two DR-22s mounted to the Hawk. Had the idea the other day, back at Bulwark. Years ago, we abandoned trying to weaponise aircraft there because what was the point? Wall-mounted cannons can put out heavier rounds and have far larger magazines. No point sticking small weapons on a hoverjet. But out here? We've got no cannons, no wall. What we do have is the Hawk, and now the Hawk has teeth.

'I'll get it linked up to the systems tonight, have them all controlled from the cockpit. I wanted to make them flush with the hull, but they're too long, and I guessed that you didn't want a gun stock in your foot well, Cadden.'

'How very considerate,' the pilot grumbled.

'I like it,' Xia said. At the sight of Cadden's bewildered expression, she clarified. 'We're fighting a war unlike any that's been fought for half a millennium. The Daem-ans have certainly developed their tactics in that time. Makes sense for us to have some surprises of our own.'

Slowly, Cadden nodded. 'You're right. These look like they can cut a Daem-an in half.' He ran a hand over the joints were gun met hull, then turned with a grin. 'Alright, Ket, I'll give you this one. With these, we'll rack up a few extra kills before reinforcements show up to hog the glory.'

Xia couldn't help but smile at his sudden positivity. He was forcing it, she could tell. Putting on a smile for the others, for her, but even forced his confidence lifted her spirits.

Looking into his green eyes, her mind drifted back to her earlier question of why she felt so afraid to lose him. Now standing here, she knew the answer. She had never met anyone quite like Cadden, someone who could take the worst in the world and give it a positive spin, someone who was ready to cheer when she needed it most, no matter how he felt inside. She wanted to get to know this person, wanted months, years getting closer, learning how he managed to keep up that grin.

With him by her side, their plight did not feel quite so hopeless.

The cockpit was still a mess, Xia's seat uncomfortably cramped. Ket had been playing around with the jet every day during their journey across the Avatarium, finding places to store the new rifles' ammunition supplies, the controls for the weapons, the access panels for maintenance. He kept rearranging the consoles, only for Cadden to snap at him and insist he replace control panels and displays that the Greml-an had decided were unnecessary.

In the end, they had settled for the extras to be placed around the co-pilot's seat. Sharp edges of Ket's prototype designs jabbed into Xia, her foot well filled by a nest of wires coated in all colours of the rainbow.

Xia rested her feet on a large crate of ammunition. The Greml-an had made quite a few acquisitions at

Bulwark, getting a hold of numerous parts to bring his invention to life. Those parts he had not been able to source, he made—the days filled with the rhythm of his Song as he shaped intricate components.

'There's the forest,' Cadden announced. They still had found no time for real privacy, only stolen kisses in the evening, occasional held hands. It was enough for her. She enjoyed the flights, the days sat next to him, talking about nothing and everything.

She turned her attention out the window. Far ahead the endless grassland and rolling hills of the Avatarium gave way to a wall of trees, the edge of Vandar Forest. It felt good to see home again, the landscape blanketed in pines and oaks.

Frowning, Xia pointed to a dark smudge on the horizon. 'What's that?'

'I don't see anything.' Cadden squinted. Of course, Hum eyes were not as sharp as an Elf-an's.

'It's there. Some dark cloud.'

Cadden fiddled with a series of controls. The Hawk's camera flickered to life, one of the dashboard's screens taken up with the panning view. Xia took over, guiding the camera over to the darkness, zooming in.

The smudge resolved itself into three black columns rising in the morning light. Smoke. Too isolated to be from a wildfire, too thick to be from cooking. Those columns rose from burning villages.

The Daem-ans had returned.

Chapter 21

'Ready,' Xia shouted.

The Hawk's rear ramp descended, the forest canopy stretching below. The wind brought the familiar odours of pine bark, tainted with the reek of sulphur.

After checking her grav-belt one last time, Xia nodded to Drekene.

The ancient woman nodded back once. 'We don't know what's down there. Be ready.'

Pulling her rifle's shoulder straps tight, Xia nodded. 'Let's get this over with.'

Together they leapt off the ramp and plummeted towards the green fronds, slack ropes unfurling from the Hawk, attached to harnesses at their waists. Just before reaching the tips of the trees Xia activated her grav-belt, slowing her descent. The needles still scratched at her, branches tearing her jumpsuit, but her fall was controlled enough that she managed to catch a limb of a tree, swinging herself to a stop just below the canopy. Not pausing, she scuttled down the trunk, manoeuvring around the unevenly spaced branches, finally gaining a clear view of the forest floor. She saw exactly what she expected.

And she was still terrified.

At the centre of the crater that remained from the first breach, a fresh cleft now rent across the forest floor. At this new gaping maw struggled a fat Daeman, three arms trying to force its bulbous belly from the opening. Xia would not give it the chance.

She unshouldered her rifle, taking aim down its sight, calm.

'Eddan,' she whispered, pulling the trigger. The first round shattered its skull, a too-large jaw flying free. The next two shots punched into its torso, black ichor slopping over the trampled saplings that surrounded the cleft. With a gurgle, the monster fell limp. Another dead Daem-an. Another step closer to justice for her brother.

The thought brought little comfort. The signs were clear. Shattered underbrush. Crumpled leaves. Prints from feet and hooves and claws. Other Daem-ans were already through. Dozens. Monstrosities that now spread over the forest, bringing death and ruin.

The pillars of smoke had faded before the Hawk could reach them, but it mattered little. They were too late to help those villages. Their priority had to be sealing this breach. Then they could deal with whatever terrors stalked the trees.

A black shadow hurtled past—Drekene. The Deathless balanced the power on her grav-belt, falling as fast as she could, landing on the forest floor with a resounding crunch of shattered branches.

In three quick paces, the woman closed the distance to the Daem-an's corpse. Neatly dissecting it with sword strokes, she sent the monster tumbling back down the pit.

At Drekene's signal, Xia kicked away from the tree, lowering the power on her belt to bring her to a gentle landing next to the breach. She was met with a suffocating stench of sulphur, both from the hole and the black blood scattered over the shrubbery. Between her shots and Drekene's sword, they had made a mess. Intrepid vines had sprouted over the damaged floor, green needles that would one day grow into mighty pines, now coated in a syrupy blackness. Elsewhere, similar tendrils had been stamped flat, or simply ripped from the ground by impossibly large claws.

'Check it.' Drekene stepped to the side.

Xia hurried over, twigs and leaves crunching under her thin climbing shoes. She straddled the cleft, aiming down as she activated her scope. In the monochrome of its digital display, she saw the new tunnel the Daem-ans had carved. Shattered rock was packed to the sides of a winding corridor, claw marks clear on the shaft's walls.

Down in the dark, two lizard heads struggled around a corner. One was stunted, cruelly fused to the cheek of its larger sibling. Xia felt no remorse as she pulled the trigger, smashing the vile heads, sending the creature tumbling back to the underworld.

'It's clear down to fifty metres.' She nodded to Drekene. 'Beyond that, the tunnel curves, I can't see.'

'That should give us enough time. Release your rope.' Drekene paused long enough for Xia to obey, then did the same, unattaching the rope from her harness. She reached up to her earpiece. 'Hawk, the site is secure. Ket, get down here with the package.'

A cackle answered. 'Oh I do like when you let me destroy stuff. On me way.'

One of the ropes dangling from the Hawk began to writhe. Xia looked up to see Ket descending, one clawed hand on a metal contraption that gripped the rope, the other clutching a steel cylinder.

Landing on the exposed soil, Ket gave Drekene a

mocking salute with the pipe bomb. 'Explosive delivery service reporting in, on time as always.'

Drekene grunted. 'Just seal the breach.'

'Wait.' Xia held up a hand, something on the edge of her hearing. 'What's that?'

Drekene frowned. 'I hear nothing.'

'Neither do...' Ket's words faltered. His ears—almost as long as Xia's despite his short stature—twitched. 'Wait, sounds like...'

The scratching echoed from below, bone scraping against rock. It was quiet, but rapid, almost like Rikk scampering across stone. Xia aimed her rifle back into the cleft, peering down the scope.

Before she could react, something flew out. From the hole, a ball the size of Ket shot into Xia. It collided with her rifle, sending it spiralling from her hand. Pain flashed across her head as the ball continued on, something sharp ripping up from her eyebrow.

With a cry of pain, she fell back. Pandemonium erupted around her, Ket's curses competing with Drekene's warning shout and an otherworldly screech. Xia clung to her forehead, blood oozing through her fingers as she whimpered.

'What's going on down there?' Cadden's voice yelled through her earpiece. His tone was panicked, startling enough to shock her into action. She sat up, peering through a torrent of crimson flowing over one eye. Ket cowered near a trunk, shielding the bomb in his hands. Drekene swung her sword wildly, her battleSong punctuating her movements.

Xia finally caught a good glimpse of her attacker, a Daem-an the size and shape of a Greml-an, taught muscles bound in black skin and crossed with bloody rips. The thing looked as if it should be dead, its hide torn in a hundred places, but seemed not to notice its wounds as it sprang back and forth, flaring claws at Drekene.

The Daem-an moved impossibly fast, but Drekene was faster. She bent sharply to avoid its pounce, her blade lashing out to clip the creature, eliciting a squeal. The wound just made the beast more angry, the squeal turning into a snarl as it leapt back, oversized hands reaching for the bald woman's throat.

With unshakable calm, Drekene sidestepped, swinging her blade into the thing's path, cleaving it in two. Blood showered the underbrush, the crumbled chunks of Daem-an rolling over the soil, stinking of sulphur.

'What's going on?' Cadden repeated.

Xia sunk to the dry ground, head throbbing. Blood flowed freely in front of her right eye, dousing dried leaves and filling cracks in the soil.

'Ambushed. Xia's hurt.' Drekene sprinted over the bloodied ground. 'Ket, get the charge ready. Cadden, put the Hawk into auto-hover and prepare to winch us up.' As the others barked acknowledgements, Drekene dropped to a knee, grabbing Xia's wrist to slap her palm tight over her forehead. Blood still trickled through Xia's fingers, but pressing on the wound eased the pain.

Scooping up Xia, Drekene turned and attached one rope to both their harnesses. Holding the Elf-an close, maternally, the Deathless tugged at the rope, signalling Cadden. With a lurch, they were hauled up, Xia clutching her forehead while being cradled by

Drekene.

The stench of blood was so strong, the throbbing in her head so great, that Xia was barely aware of the blast of Ket's explosive sealing the cleft.

With a clank, the rope stopped. Xia prized her eyes open to see Cadden standing in the Hawk's corridor. Effortlessly, Drekene tossed Xia to the pilot, who staggered as he caught her, his face twisted with worry.

Footsteps sounding distant even as he held her, the pilot hurried down the corridor and set her on her bunk. She lay back, feeling warm blood trickle around her fingers and across her face.

Rikk ran over, whining at her side, but having the sense to stay out the way.

Cadden grabbed a first-aid kit. 'Let me see.'

She peeled her hand from her wound, trying not to dwell on the squelch it made, or the shock on his face. He pressed a gauze pad over the wound, frowning as he rummaged.

'It's not that bad.' He smiled weakly.

In reply, Xia turned her palm towards him, drenched red.

'Head wounds always bleed profusely,' he assured her. 'Even small ones. I'm sorry but this is going to sting.'

He pulled the pad back to spray a green fluid onto her forehead. She whimpered as it burned, her sinuses filling with its acetic tang.

'How's she doing?' Ket jumped onto the ramp, tossing Xia's rifle to the deck, and climbed up the wall to slap the ramp controls.

'Needs stitches.' Cadden replaced the disinfectant bottle, searching for something else out of Xia's sight. 'But will be alright. It'll scar.'

'War marks.' Drekene crouched beside Xia. 'You're starting young.'

'Would have been worse if not for you.' Xia winced at the pain that her own words brought. 'How'd you move that fast?'

Drekene shrugged. 'In sleepless centuries practising combat, you learn a thing or two. Besides, battleSinging helps.'

'Hold still.' Cadden drew a object from his pack, the thing looking worryingly like a taser.

'What's that?' Xia asked, hesitant.

'Autosuture.' He grimaced. 'Afraid those of us without lifeSingers have to rely on more crude methods.'

He pressed the cold metal device onto her wound. A burning sensation snapped through her forehead, then another. Cadden pulled back, nodding.

'All done.'

Xia lifted her hand to her forehead, feeling the plastic strips holding her skin together. The wound ached to at the touch, but felt strangely small. Gently, Cadden pulled her hand to the side, then fixed a soft square bandage to her head.

'You might want to wash your face.' He smiled encouragingly. 'But you're going to be fine.'

With Cadden's help, Xia rose to her feet and staggered to the sink. The mirror held a gruesome reflection, tracks of blood winding their way from the white pad on her forehead, soaking into her hairline, pooling at her chin.

'You should take it easy.' Cadden laid a supportive hand on her shoulder. 'Don't want to reopen those stitches.'

'I'll try,' Xia offered. 'But it's going to be hard to gently tree-leap.'

'Tree-leap? No. You need real rest. In the bunk.'

'No,' Xia replied, firm. 'Those tracks are from at least a dozen Daem-ans. We have to chase them down. There's no time to waste.'

Cadden turned to Drekene beseechingly.

The Deathless shrugged. 'Are you sure you're up to this, Xia?'

She nodded. 'Of course. My head is killing me, but that's nothing compared to what the Daem-ans will do to the people of Vandar. I think we all know what our priority is here.'

Looking to his feet, Cadden relented. Drekene fetched Xia's rifle and held it out.

'You'll need this, and I'm going with you. Ket, Cadden, you keep the Hawk overhead. If we get overwhelmed, we'll need a quick extraction.'

As the others nodded and headed to the cockpit, Xia grasped her rifle. Its familiar weight felt good in her hands, enough to distract her from her throbbing head.

She gave a wry smile. 'Let's go hunt some Daem-ans.'

Rikk two trees ahead, Xia flung herself from trunk to trunk. Her head still ached, pain wracking her with each impact, but a sense of urgency pushed her onward. The tracks running through the underbrush were clear. Three Daem-ans came this way, each as large as the first she had faced. She needed to reach the beasts before they caused more damage.

The smoke they had seen earlier told her that it was too late, that villages had already fallen, that lives had already been lost. She smothered the sense of hopeless, holding onto the slim chance that they could make a different today. There had been four sets of tracks leading away from the breach, but only three fires. Maybe this pack had yet not reached its target. Maybe lives could still be saved.

With an almighty thud, Drekene crashed into a tree alongside Xia, shaking bark loose. The woman kept pace, throwing her bulk between distant trees. As much as Xia hated to admit it, Drekene could probably manage this pursuit on her own. Still, the woman respected Xia's decision to be here, her need to defend her home.

The low drone of the Hawk's engines followed above, their blue glow occasionally visible through gaps in the canopy. It felt good to have the others overhead, close at hand. Even if the Hawk could not descend into the trees, even if its weapons had not been tested, Xia felt safe knowing that Cadden was nearby, knowing that he would not hesitate to give her whatever aid she needed.

Chirping, Rikk took off into the forest. He had picked up the scent of something new, though whether that was a Daem-an or a fifil was anyone's guess. All Xia could smell was pine bark and sulphur.

'Rikk might have something,' she said into her earpiece. 'Be ready.'

A minute later, the vulfik returned, lithely bounding from tree to tree. He scrambled up the trunk she clung to, ears back, whimpering. Something had upset him. Terrified him. Daem-ans?

Cautious, Xia kicked ahead. The weak breeze brought new scents. Charcoal. Roasting meat. Blood. With a sick heart, she forced herself onward, one tree at a time. Trunks darkened, sprinkled with soot. Stains of fire blackened the underbrush, the surrounding leaves bright green—the heat must have been intense to burn fresh growth like this. And then, as she rounded a large oak, she saw what she dreaded.

The charred remains of a village.

Blackened trunks littered the area, some tumbled to the ground, most defiantly standing upright despite their damage. Fragmented lumps clung midway up the trees—the remains of burned-out homes, offices, schools. The source of the fire was clear. At the heart of the village, a broken mound marked what remained of powerhouse, its roof crumbled, its walls burned to obsidian. The Daem-ans had struck there first, and the resulting fire engulfed the village. Carpets, doors, furniture, all of the decor within the homes providing fuel, the flames intense enough to roast the living wood.

It was a small miracle that the fire had not spread further, but clearly the lifeSigners' efforts to protect trees against wildfires had paid off. Without their decades of toil, the heart of the forest may have already been lost to hungry orange flames.

Not trusting the integrity of the scorched trunks ahead, Xia lowered the power on her grav-belt and dropped to the ground. Readying her rifle, she picked her way into the ruins, kicking up ash with every step. Drekene crashed to the ground alongside, Rikk following behind, ears back.

Dark lumps littered the ash-coated ground. Xia approached one, hesitant, half expecting the blackened mound to reveal itself as a Daem-an, leaping up to rend her in two. The truth was far darker—they were corpses. Broken by claws, cracked by the fall from the trees, then melted by fire, the bodies were strewn over what remained of the underbrush, some crushed by falling trees and debris, some merely mangled by their fall.

Xia scanned the area, trying to pick out some movement, some sign of life, anything. All she saw was death. Not so much as a sparrow flitted through the remains, wildlife knowing to stay far from the site of such devastation. Nothing moved. No one had survived.

Pausing to check her digital map, Xia realised she knew this village. It looked so different now, but this was Relass. The orchards would be nearby, the sweetest apples in the region. Xia had been here before, accompanying a family of grocers on a supply run during an ogre scare.

Tears strung her eyes. Tears of frustration. Of anger.

'They'll pay for this,' she whispered.

'They will.' Drekene crouched by a small body. It was so blackened, so damaged, that Xia could not tell whether it was a vulfik—or a child. 'It's been centuries since civilians have needed to fear Daem-ans. We *will* put a stop to this.'

Xia nodded, resolute. She walked through the monochrome landscape, images flashing in her mind of all the people she had met when last here. She could not remember their faces, but could not forget their kind attitude, ready smiles, cheerful accents.

Drekene rose, looking around the desolation. 'I don't mean to sound callous, but we need to move. The Daem-ans are gone, heading to their next target. We must find their tracks.'

'I understand.' Xia strode through the disturbingly soft ash, trying not to focus on the sweet smell lingering over each burned corpse, and headed to the nearest intact trunk. She scaled it easily—this close to a settlement, lifeSigners had worked the rough bark into clear handholds.

It did not take long to spot the abominable tracks left by the Daem-ans. Claw marks as large a man's torso were sunk into soil under crushed bushes and trampled saplings. Xia kicked towards the path, ready to continue the hunt.

Two jumps later she paused, struck by déjà vu. Looking around her, she tried to get her bearings in the scarred region. It had been over a year since she had visited, but she recognised the area through which the tracks led, the stream to the south, the mound where soil had built around a fallen spruce.

Feeling sick, she pulled out the map again, confirming what in her heart she already knew.

'These tracks,' she whispered. 'They are heading towards Ethelan. The Daem-ans are going to attack my home.'

Chapter 22

Xia gripped the arms of her chair. Outside the Hawk's cockpit, the hoverjet's lights cut into the noon eclipse, illuminating treetops as silver fingers that blurred as they ripped past.

'Anything?' Xia asked.

Stood at a communications panel to the rear of the cockpit, Ket grunted. 'Nothing yet. I keep sending out our warning, but I'm not getting anything back. Not even the town's nav beacon.'

'Could just be a power failure. Or their comms down for maintenance,' Cadden offered. Even he did not sound convinced.

Drekene, hands braced against the backs of their chairs, leaned forward. 'The Daem-ans would try to attack with the eclipse. We're running out of time.'

Wordlessly, Cadden pushed the throttle fully forward, flicking several switches to cut out the blaring alarms this triggered. The Hawk began to vibrate, the ghostly forest tearing by ever faster.

'Whatcha doing to my ship?' Ket barked.

'Full afterburners,' Cadden replied. 'We've enough fuel to reach Ethelan, can top up there.'

The Greml-an swore, jumping back from his console. 'Aye, if the engines hold together that long. Hawk's not meant for sprinting, kid.'

Cadden's expression was resolute. 'We don't have a choice.'

'Aye,' Ket snarled, 'I know. I'll see if I can hold

this together until we get there. Just don't bitch about how she handles after this.'

Muttering under his breath, Ket scampered back to the hallway and climbed into the bulkhead. Drekene turned to the console he had been manning, repeating the constant warning signal, a futile plea for the village to evacuate. The whole crew knew it was too late. The Daem-ans had surely reached Ethelan by now. The time for evacuation had passed.

'Thank you.' Xia squeezed Cadden's shoulder.

He shrugged. 'Defending civilians is what we do. I just hope…'

Xia nodded. He hoped what they all did, that they were not too late. That someone still survived. That they were not heading towards another crematorium.

Cadden glanced at a display showing the Hawk's current position. 'Five minutes. Drekene, you better get ready.'

'I'm going too.' Xia climbed to her feet, bracing herself against the shaking cockpit.

Cadden glanced at her, eyes pleading. 'There are three Daem-ans down there. You're still injured.'

'I'm going,' she repeated. 'I have to.'

Blinking back tears, he nodded, eyes fixed ahead. 'Be careful. Please.'

She kissed his scraggly hair. 'I will.'

Sparing one last look, she hurried down the corridor. Drekene stood at the rear ramp, grav-belt fastened, folded sword in hand. Ket was nowhere to be seen, but his voice echoed from the metal-panelled walls, alternating between metalSinging and cursing.

Xia hurriedly retrieved her rifle, checking the magazine. Rikk padded to her, claws clattering on the metal floor. She ruffled his head.

'You'll have to stay here. Stay with Cadden.'

There was little Rikk could accomplish. She had seen the tracks—these Daem-ans were larger than Drekene. Vulfiks were fast, had sharp claws but nowhere near the strength to threaten such beasts. Rikk's hollow bones would be shattered by one swipe from a Daem-an's claw, his membrane torn. No, he was a fine tracker, a loyal friend, but not a warrior.

Through the earpiece, Cadden yelled, 'One minute.'

Checking her grav-belt, Xia made her way towards Drekene, steadying herself against the cold walls as the ship continued to shake violently. The Deathless slapped the ramp's controls. With a pneumatic whine, the ramp lowered, the roar of air flooding the cabin. Turbulence sucked air out of the Hawk and spat it back in, dragging strands of Xia's hair free of her plait. The smell of jet fuel and ozone was different from normal—sharper, hotter. The jets even sounded strange, struggling as Cadden pushed them past their limits.

'This is your best tool.' Drekene tapped Xia's rifle. 'And this is your greatest asset.' Tapped her head. 'Use them both. Keep your distance. Pick the Daem-ans off.'

'Gladly.'

The sky brightened, the forest turning from black and silver to a glorious green. The eclipse was ending, illuminating the landscape. Xia felt conflicted. The light would make it easier to see the Daem-ans, easier to shoot them dead. At the same time, it indicated how long the Hawk had taken to reach Ethelan, how much time they had already given the Daem-ans to wreck havoc.

'Hold on,' Cadden commanded.

Xia stumbled as the Hawk slowed to a stop, its engines blaring, the deceleration pushing her towards the cockpit. While Xia still struggled—before the craft had come to a complete halt—Drekene leapt off the ramp. The instant the ship stopped, the force holding Xia back evaporated and she was launched forward. Using her sudden momentum, she sprinted ahead to throw herself into the air.

The fresh wind hit her along with the bone-chilling sound of half a dozen overlapping screams. It was a horrid, hopeful din. It assured her that below someone still lived, whilst also confirming that the survivors were in terror, pain.

Even from above, Xia recognised her home village. Out the canopy peaked the upper floors of homes, shops, the village library. The latter's roof was partially collapsed, its broken walls stained with blood.

She adjusted her grav-belt, plummeting towards the familiar pines, watching figures sprinting along walkways as she tried not to dwell on the smell of sulphur and blood.

Falling through the branches, Xia closed her eyes against the scratching needles. She let herself fall too fast, too eager to face the monsters below, and collided with an unseen branch. She bounced off, two more impacting her ribs before she crashed onto the roof of a bulbous house formed from the living trunk—the Brownroot's place. The mother owned a general store, while her husband worked at the landing pad. Did either still live? Or were their corpses below Xia's feet?

Unslinging her rifle, she crept to the edge, peering over the curved lip of the bark roof. The sight below was revolting. The walkways of her village were littered with bodies, some she recognised, some would require forensic experts to identify. Walls of tree homes were ripped open, claw and tooth marks gouged into the splintered bark. Bedrooms, kitchens, nurseries, all were exposed to the elements. Too many were stained red.

On the forest floor the powerhouse's roof was cleaved open once again, the corpse of a Gobl-an just barely visible. Sparks flew from a damaged capacitor, but thankfully failed to find any flammable material in the newly-constructed mound. There was no raging fire like the one that destroyed Relass. Even so, the devastation was widespread. Walkways swung free in the breeze. Damaged trunks threatened to topple. And always echoed that din, those screams of terror.

Following the petrified yells, Xia saw one of the architects of this desolation. A twisted Daem-an threw itself between the trees. Oversized hands at the end of long arms gripped trunks with ease. Its fat torso between the arms was little more than a giant mouth, serrated teeth gnashing as it pursued two children through the village. The pair had grav-belts, the only thing keeping them alive, buying them precious time as the Daem-an lost height with each lunge. Their efforts could only last so long, eventually they would slip—or simply become exhausted—and that hungry maw would feed.

Xia had to stop it, but looking through her scope,

she had no idea where to aim. The heart or the brain, Drekene had instructed her, but where would either be? There seemed little room for organs in its torso, taken up as it was by that giant mouth, which was large enough to fit an entire Drak-an inside in a single bite—Xia could let off twenty rounds and not come close to hitting anything vital.

Moving her scope to the side, she aimed at its shoulder, or whatever the technical term was for where its muscled arm met its midriff. Xia might not know how to kill the beast, but she could guess how to cripple it.

As it leapt, arms stretched, she fired. The round impacted midair, bone and black blood spraying out the exit wound. It struggled as it collided with the tree, almost falling when its arm failed to find purchase. That second great hand swept madly, a claw finally piercing the window of the schoolhouse. There it held on by a finger, damaged arm limp.

The children fled, using the chance to escape to the village edge. They were safe, but Xia was not finished. The blood on that thing's claws, in its mouth, was Elf-an. It had to pay for its sins, and dangling like a bauble, it made far too tempting a target.

She planned her attack. It would have been simple to shoot off its finger, let it drop to the forest floor, but that seemed far too quick. Besides, the fall might not kill the thing, and she wanted to make sure it would threaten Vandar no more.

It had no legs, only vestigial feet on the underside of its torso, and its wounded arm was clearly nonfunctional—probably had a severed nerve—but even one-armed, the monster could cause chaos. So she just had to remove the remaining limb.

Xia fired into the intact shoulder, the force of the blast spraying fragments into the trunk beyond. Again and again she fired, bullet after bullet slamming into the joint, rending fist-sized holes into the bloody black flesh. The skin became taught, ligaments straining to hold the Daem-an's mass despite the damage. She targeted the exposed tendons, weakening it further, until at last the remaining strip of flesh came free. With a damp tear, audible even at this range, the ruined shoulder tore, the creature tumbling to the ground, its arm still in the schoolhouse's window.

In a spray of dirt, the monster hit the ground, the thick bushes puncturing its skin, pinning it in place. It still lived, squirming against the barbs that pieced its remaining flesh, but it was helpless. Useless.

Good, Xia thought. Let it suffer. She would save her bullets for its comrades.

One of those fellow Daem-ans scuttled across the forest floor. Ten spider legs, capped in hooves, pounded across the soil, overtaking a limping Hum-an and trampling her. Before Xia could aim, the spider-thing darted behind a tree, it's barbed tail lashing against the bark.

Flitting from tree to tree, body pressed low, it scampered after a new target. Unlike its last, this figure stood her ground. Drekene waited for the beast, legs bent, serrated sword extended.

Through her scope, Xia tracked the Daem-an's progress, but its movement was too erratic to get off a shot. It lunged at Drekene, tail and legs flailing towards her from all angles. Her sword swung. Metal impacted chitin. Flesh tore. The combatants separated,

Drekene bearing a fresh gash across her cheek, the Daem-an missing two legs.

Undeterred, the monster rounded on Drekene. Xia cursed, trunks blocking her sight until the two were once more intertwined in combat, too close for her to risk opening fire. Screams of rage, both Ash and Daem, rose from the forest floor.

Overhead, the Hawk's engines whined. Xia glanced up, catching a glimpse of its silver skin hovering impotently above the treetops. No matter the size of its guns, without a clear view Cadden could not fire. Ket's idea of arming the Hawk had seemed useful at the time, but now Xia doubted that it would be any assistance in the forest.

In their struggle, Drekene came off second best. The beast booted her with three hoofed legs, launching the woman across the forest. With a thud, her back slammed into an oak, splintering its bark.

The Daem-an advanced, stalking towards its stunned prey. It's tail writhed in rage, remaining legs stamping into the soft soil, shattering bushes. As it emerged from behind a tree, Xia fired, her shell smashing into the centre of its black body. The creature stumbled, wavered, then launched itself into cover, nipping from tree to tree, always sheltered from Xia. She fired two more rounds, trying to catch it during the heartbeat it took to pass between trunks, but both shots harmlessly impacted soil. The creature knew where its attacker was, and moved with uncanny speed, keeping to cover as it bore down on the Deathless.

Drekene rose to her feet, one hand on her side, the other gripping her weapon. The Daem-an was not cowed. Through gaps in the trees, Xia could see it rear up, ready to bring its hooves down in a killing blow.

In rapid succession, three shots rang out, none of them from Xia. One fell short, fragmenting pine bark, but the other two hit home, shattering two of the Daem-an's knees, bringing the monster crashing to the ground. Before it had a chance to recover, Drekene darted in, her blade a blur, black blood flying. In seconds, she had reduced the Daem-an to a pile of broken limbs and oozing chunks.

Xia looked up, heart soaring as she identified the shooters. From the window of her family home leaned her parents, rifles ready. Her complex feeling from their last meeting faded, and Xia grinned at the sight. She stood to wave, overcome with relief at being home, at knowing her family still lived.

Then she saw it.

Writhing up her parent's tree on a hundred black legs was a centipede-like Daem-an, canine jaws gnashing, barbed tail whipping against the bark. Shouting a warning cry, Xia raised her rifle and fired. The thing's head caved in, black-and-red skin ripping open, but the creature continued, quickly scuttling to the far side of the tree, out of sight.

Alerted by her shout, her parents recognised the danger and disappeared into the house. It was a hopeless move—facing a Daem-an in such close quarters. Drekene was already climbing the tree, but it would take her too long.

Xia's parents had no experience fighting Daem-ans, but she did. With all her strength she kicked from her perch, shouldering her rifle midair so that she could grasp the branches of the next tree. As fast as she could manage, she leapt through the village, passing over snapped walkways, climbing around broken buildings, hurtling by the morbid sight of a headless man slowly descending towards the forest floor on a grav-belt. She had to reach her home, had to save her parents.

As she landed on her porch, shots rang out. Two rifles fired in volleys, her parent's screams of desperation meeting a wet hiss from the Daem-an. Squeezing through the open window, living bark scraping her arms, Xia rolled into her living room. The monster was on the stairs, its long body disappearing up the landing.

She readied her rifle, sprinting to the base of the stairs to get a better shot. Before she could aim, a blood-curdling scream echoed from above, crimson spraying down the thing's back, its legs moving with vicious determination..

Determined not to let the Daem-ans take any more of her family, she raised her rifle. As her finger moved towards the trigger, the beast's back exploded. Pain splintered over Xia's face, her arm burning in agony. She fell back in a spray of bone, arm aching intensely. Prizing her fingers from her bicep, she saw a metal glint buried in her flesh—a bullet. One of her parents' shots had passed through the Daem-an and hit her. They probably did not even realise she was in the house.

Her father's shouts of dismay spurred her into action. She caught a glimpse of him at the top of the stairs, dragging her mother towards Xia's room. The Daem-an pursued, barely slowed by its multiple wounds.

Parents out of the firing line, this was her chance. Gritting her teeth against the pain, she crouched on the foot of the stairs. From this angle, her shots would travel down the length of the creature's body. Didn't matter where it kept its brain, she would destroy it.

With a cry of rage, she emptied her magazine. Round after round smashed into the Daem-an's rear as it tried to climb the stairs, black gore slopping onto the walls, soaking into the fur carpet.

The monster fell limp, gently sliding back down before becoming wedged on the first landing. The third Daem-an was dead. Ethelan was safe. Or what little remained.

Following Father's mournful cries, Xia struggled over the perforated corpse. Her face stung, something warm flowing down her neck. Her arm was on fire, but she pushed on. She had to see what was up there, had to know that her parents were well.

At the top landing, the black blood gave way to vibrant red. A lot of red. Too much.

Staggering around the corner, Xia peered into her room, a cry escaping her lips.

Caressed by her Father's weeping form, lay Mother. Her face was peaceful, eyes open, pure white skin barely marred by a few splotches of blood.

The rest of her body was horrific. From her neck down, deep gouges crossed her flesh. A hundred wounds, tearing through her clothes and skin and organs. Her legs were merely strips of meat, a tangled mess surrounding shattered bone. Blood oozed from the myriad of wounds. No pulse. No life.

Ethelan was saved.

But Mother was dead.

Xia winced as Cadden picked out fragments of Daem bone from her cheeks. He had managed to set the Hawk down on the landing pad, scraping the paint from the Greendip Corporation hauler already there. He had claimed that the Hawk needed to land for Ket to work on the overtaxed engines, but Xia knew he had forced it down to come to her aid. LifeSinger Fennel had died trying to save the wounded, leaving Drekene and Cadden to put their first aid skills to the test.

'I can't believe I shot you,' Father whispered, head in hands.

'You shot the Daem-an.' Xia's voice was void of emotion. Along with the rest of the fifty-something survivors, they sat in the village library, the largest building still mostly intact. Light poured through its burst ceiling, claw marks still evident from where one Daem-an had broken in to kill those who sheltered inside. Now air drifted through, but the cold afternoon breeze could not remove the stench that saturated the room—sulphur, vomit, blood.

'That's my bullet your friend dug from your arm,' Father countered.

Xia shrugged, another piece of the Daem-an being pulled from her jaw. The shower of shrapnel had caused widespread damage, but it was all shallow, most of the bullet's energy spent destroying the beast.

'Blame the Daem-an,' she insisted. 'It was at fault for my injuries. Just like Daem-ans caused Eddan's death. And… Mother's.'

She wanted to cry, but no tears came. Mother's death was not a surprise, just another in an endless list of crimes for which the Daem-ans must atone. Her father had no such issues, tears flowing freely, washing away the blood and ichor that coated his face.

Yadeen, the Hum schoolmaster, approached Drekene, who stood to one side. 'Deathless, what do we do now?'

'We bury our dead,' Father announced.

Yadeen blinked back tears. 'Of course. I meant after. Do we stay here?'

'No.' Drekene replied. 'There are more Daem-ans. This whole region should have already been evacuated.'

'But where do we go?'

Xia met the schoolmaster's gaze. 'To the capital. Show our wounded to the prime minister. Make the government see that they must act. That Elf-ans are dying while they call Bulwark's bluff.'

'It's a good plan.' Kriss replied, a fresh wound crossing the police officer's scaled face. 'Get the children, the families to safety. But you said there are more of these things out there?'

Drekene nodded, tending to a woman so wounded that Xia could not tell if it was Yasha, or her big sister Isha. 'Many more out there already. Even more on the way.'

Kriss hissed. 'Then other villages are in danger.'

'That's why we're here,' Xia stated.

The police officer turned to her, reptilian eyes intense. 'And we owe you our lives. But I for one pay my debts. If other villages are in danger, then you'll need all the help you can get. You have my assistance, Xia, Deathless.'

'And mine.' Rettin, the grocer, stepped forward.

It started a flood, men and women flocking over to pledge service, to decry the Daem-ans. Thirty clustered around, nodding with conviction. Xia recognised the look in their eyes, the determination to bring justice to those that harmed their loved ones. This was a village where everyone knew everyone else. Even those whose families had escaped intact had still lost friends, colleagues, neighbours.

Drekene grunted. 'Your aid is appreciated, but we aim to move fast. To respond to Daem attacks, we must be mobile. The Hawk cannot fit many more than we already have.'

'I'll help there.' An Elf woman in a Greendip Corporation jumpsuit strode from the crowd. 'Name's Cynda. I don't care what management says, I owe you my life. My hauler's designed for crops, but can carry at least twenty in the back. More if you don't mind being squeezed. I'll start by helping the others get to Enall, but I'll be back.'

'The hauler is company property,' Rettin pointed out. 'Won't you be fired? Arrested?'

'Think losing a job matters after this?' Cynda waved her hands towards the injured masses. 'And being arrested? Well, Officer, you going to cuff me for transporting refugees?'

Kriss gave a grim smile. 'Drak-az'll take me before I do.'

Cynda grinned. 'Then it's settled. I'll help the injured to Enall, then we're joining you, Deathless.'

The crowd nodded, determination clear. Slowly, that resolve faltered, eyes drawn to the one man who had not spoken.

Father looked around the crowd, then met Xia's

gaze, eyes red with tears. 'You don't need one more rifle. You need a thousand.'

Was he running away? Xia shook her head. 'Every rifle helps.'

He sighed. 'It does. But it is time I do what I should have done when you first came to me. I'm going to gather the wardens. It'll take some doing, but I will convince them. I promise you. I will return, and when I do, it will be with every last warden in Vandar.'

Xia let herself smile, pride at the force in her father's eyes. 'And until you do, we'll protect the forest.'

Chapter 23

Xia stabbed her shovel into the damp soil. Rain beat down, fat beads from the canopy, soaking into her jumpsuit, making the ground turn to mud. Her muscles ached, but she forced herself to continue. To dig her mother's grave.

Next to her in the small pit, Father toiled in silence. Further out, the remaining survivors did the same, shovelling mounds of soil from the forest floor. Families worked to bury their loved ones, their friends, their neighbours. Drekene and Cadden worked on a larger ditch for those who could not be identified —the grim jumble of body parts, flesh and bone that the Daem-ans had left in their wake.

Out of nearly a thousand people who had called Ethelan home, only a hundred had returned. At least twice that many lay in neat rows amongst the trees, waiting for their graves to be complete. No one knew what happened to the hundreds of missing. Many had fled as the attack started, scattering into the forest. Few had come back. Whether the remainder were still out there, fleeing in panic, or whether they had been run down by the Daem-ans, Xia had no idea. There was likely more of the latter than she wanted to believe.

The rain had started shortly after the battle ended, and continued all afternoon. Familiar scents of damp greenery could not chase away the stench of death. The trunks around them bled, gore washing from the village above. Blood ran from Xia's fingers—her own, and her mother's.

Father threw his shovel out the hole. 'It's deep enough.'

Weak, Xia nodded, climbing out the grave after him, fingers sinking into the mud. She slipped, shoes sliding over the slick pit wall. Her arms flailed, struggling to keep her from falling back into the hole. A hand caught her wrist. Father. Nodding, he helped her to her feet.

'It's time,' he said, voice flat.

'I know.' Sullen, Xia followed him to where her mother waited. Neatly arranged with a hundred others, the woman who had always been there for Xia lay wrapped in bedsheets, placid face exposed. There wasn't anywhere near enough funeral shrouds to go around, so the dead had been bound in whatever was at hand. Shower curtains. Robes. Quilts. Nothing managed to keep in the blood, and the hundred figures were soaked red, the crimson driven by the rain to melt into the soil.

Nodding to her father, she crouched and helped him pick up Mother, silently thankful that he took the red and sodden end where Mother's mangled legs were bound. Gripping the body by the shoulders, Xia looked into her mother's face. Even with the tight binding, Mother's head rolled back as she was lifted. Her skin was too pale, lips still caked in blood, eyes open a crack. There had been no lifeSinger to tend the wounds, no priest to clean the body. Like all the fallen, Mother received a rushed burial, a soldier's burial.

Xia shivered. Straddling the grave, she and her father lowered the body. Fingers shaking from cold and exhaustion, Xia lost her grip and her mother's head fell the last foot. Thankfully, the mud cushioned the impact, more of a squelch than a thud, but it proved the one leaf too heavy to bear. A sob escaped Xia's mouth, and she staggered back. Tears streamed from her eyes, lost in the deluge. Her cries were drowned out by a hundred other mourners.

Wordlessly, Father took up his shovel and began to fill the grave. Stunned, she realised his eyes were as red as hers. Her father stood as a broken reflection of his old strength, shoulders slumped, hands shaking. He needed to do this, she realised, to bury Mother, to set her on her way to Elf-az. Father did not want this. He wanted to cry over the grave, sit in the mud like Xia and keen. Instead, he did what was necessary.

She would do the same.

Staggering to her feet, Xia forced herself into action. She retrieved her shovel—the wooden handle rough, cold—and began to dig. Gently, she scattered the mound of soil into the hole, steadily covering Mother's body, hiding the bloody sheets, her lifeless face, her breathless chest.

The act seemed distant, Xia too exhausted to take in the meaning of the moment. The survivors had debated postponing the funeral, but had soon realised they had no choice. There were simply too many bodies, all torn apart. If left, the village would be overrun with flies by morning. Better to get it over with, to place the bodies in the ground where they could rejoin the soil, rather than be picked apart by carrion birds.

No need to smooth the soil as the rain evened out the ground. Father headed away, returning moments later with a sapling. It was a stunted thing—bent stem, too few leaves. Normally, burial saplings were the finest that could be found, lifeSung beauties imbued with health and vitality, perfect to cover a grave. Like so many things in Ethelan, too few saplings had been located. The survivors decided that the lifeSinger and his family should be buried with the saplings he had kept on hand. For the rest, they scrounged what they could. Wild growths from the surrounding areas, houseplants, even ungerminated seeds, anything that could grow. It would make for a strange graveyard, so dense in trees, so poor in health.

Father crouched by the grave, digging out a small hole by hand for the plant—not that the sickly thing needed much room for its weak roots. He went to plant it, then paused, looked at Xia.

'She'd want you to mark her grave.' He held out the sapling.

Xia stepped forward, reverently taking the plant. 'Thank you.'

She gave a quivering smile as she knelt in the mud, caressing the sapling. Carefully arranging its roots, she lay it in the hole, directly above her mother. In time, it would stretch down, taking up the nutrients from Mother and incorporating them into its bark. There it would hold her forever, her mortal remains a part of the forest, while her soul joined Elf-az.

Even bent, weak, fragile, the sapling brought a smile to Xia. 'It's beautiful.'

'It is,' Father agreed.

For a time, the two simply knelt either side of the grave, knees deep in the mud. Around them, similar scenes played out. Families mourned, wailed, or simply sat telling stories. In the centre of the this heartfelt outpouring, Drekene led a few out-of-towners to conduct the thankless task of filling the mass grave. Grim faced they worked, industriously carrying misshapen lumps to the large pit.

Alongside them, Cadden strode, eyes stained red as he cradled a child-sized shroud and lowered it reverently into the pit. Across the forest their eyes met, the pair sharing a weak smile of support.

'I need to go.' Father stood, not bothering to wipe the filth from his knees.

'So soon? It's already getting dark.'

He sighed. 'All power's out here. Even the emergency transmitter was smashed. I'll need to get to the nearest town to send out a call to the wardens.'

'Be careful,' Xia warned. 'We don't know where the other Daem-ans are, but I doubt they're far.'

Father smirked. 'You're the one going to hunt those things.'

She pushed herself to her feet. 'You know why I have to.'

'I know.' He walked around the grave to stand before her. 'And you know that I have to find you help.'

Xia sighed. 'Yes. Just be careful.'

His hands gripped her shoulders, eyes boring into hers. 'I will. Please, Xia, take care of yourself. We parted badly, I know. Your mother and I regretted how we spoke as soon as you left. I don't want us to leave things like that again. You're my daughter. What you've done for the Ethelan, for the forest, for the world—you must know how proud I am of you. I love you, Xia.'

'I love you too.' Her voice caught.

With one last firm embrace, Father stepped back. He nodded at her, fresh tears in his eyes, then turned. He stalked into the forest. She watched as he climbed a nearby tree, activating his grav-belt and leaping away. With a heavy heart, Xia realised that he was all that remained of her family.

She could only pray she would not lose him too.

'Fire,' Xia commanded.

She was answered by a volley of rifle shots. All hit their target—a long-dead stump overgrown with vines. Chunks of ancient bark leapt free, arcing through the air, a mouldering odour mixing with the gunpowder rising from the line of volunteers.

The sight of those dozen men and women made Xia's heart sink. Sat on branches well outside of Ethelan, they had managed to hit their mark, but few coped with the recoil. Several rifles were now pointing skyward, two had fallen to the floor, and Xia's own weapon had left a gash on the forehead of young Hum shopkeeper.

With a sigh, Xia kicked off her tree, landing beside the injured woman. The cut was shallow. It would leave a nasty bruise, but did not need stitched.

'Always be ready for the recoil,' she reminded the group. 'These weapons are powerful enough to punch a hole through any animal in the forest, even Daem hide. That same force goes into your shoulder... or your head if you're not careful. Let's try again. Get ready.'

She waited while two men climbed down to fetch their dropped rifles. Twelve guns—some so rusted they'd been more at home in a museum—was all that they had managed to salvage from Ethelan's ruins. Father had donated his weapon, but the town had never been overly armed, had always relied on the wardens for protection. The rest of the weapons were sports pieces or heirlooms.

They had already contacted Bulwark, and the first load of ammunition was on its way, but ammunition was all that would be supplied. No guns. Not even body armour.

Hopefully more would be waiting when they returned. Ket had taken the village's two surviving metalSingers to collect all the scrap they could locate. The three Greml-ans would work throughout the day, crafting whatever weapons they could devise.

For now, twelve was all Xia could train at a time. This was the second group she had taken out, while the rest of the volunteers trained with Drekene and Cadden back at the village. To their credit, the survivors worked feverishly. It would take a few days for the Greendip transport to ferry the refugees to Enall and return. During that time Drekene was determined to drill these civilians into a useful force. They were getting a crash course in how to fight, to scout, to heal, to survive.

Once the men and women around her had climbed back to their trees and readied their weapons, Xia nodded.

'Fire,' she shouted.

Another bark of rifle fire. Another burst of broken wood and waft of gunpowder. Another weapon dropped.

This was going to be a long afternoon.

'That's enough,' Xia called to the group, voice hoarse. 'Safeties on.'

The volunteers breathed a collective sigh of relief, lowering the rifles. They had progressed well, at least an hour passing with none dropping rifles, being hit by recoiling barrels or falling from trees. There might yet be hope.

At least they had no issues hitting their target at this range, the stump now little more than a series of splinters rising from the soil. Xia had purposefully given the older weapons to the Elf-ans, while the other 'an got to use the modern rifles. Advanced scopes, balance gyros and recoil dampeners helped even novices get their rounds on target. For the Elf-ans, their natural marksmanship made up for the archaic weapons they wielded. Elf-az had blessed his creation with an intuitive sense of ballistics, understanding of wind effects, and ability to predict projectile drop and accurately judge distance, all without conscious effort. In ancient times, this had allowed Elf-ans to become world-renowned archers, felling prey and invaders alike. Now, it helped these survivors adapt to unfamiliar rifles in record time.

Xia looked up, spotting the reddening sky through the canopy. 'It's time we get back. Secure weapons and activate belts.'

The group obeyed, tightening their rifles' straps to fix them against their backs, then powering up grav-belts. Rikk sensed the change in attitude and chirped, excited.

'Right,' Xia shouted. 'Let's see if you can keep up with me. Remember—don't follow the person in front of you. Judge the tree spacing yourself. Don't leap for a tree your momentum can't reach. If you fall behind, call out.'

Grinning as they nodded, Xia kicked off her tree, heading towards Ethelan. Two trees later, she paused to check on the others—all followed her well. Even the non-Elf-ans had tree-leapt from time to time. Most Hum-ans preferred using walkways to navigate the village, but that didn't help them go further afield.

Impressed, Xia found herself needing to push herself ever faster to keep the leading volunteers from catching up. She rapidly scuttled around trees, digging fingers into the coarse bark, pushing off with her rubber-soled climbing shoes. Rikk bounded a few trees ahead, occasionally turning his furred head to check if she still followed.

She had decided to lead the group a fair distance from the village. Partially, this was to give them additional practice in movement and tracking, but mostly she was driven by a desire to keep the noise of their rifle fire away from the others. More Daem-ans were loose in the forest, and while she longed to hunt them down, she wanted to do so on her terms. Having the unprepared civilians ambushed would be a disaster. The thirty men and women who had opted to stay and help were all the backup the Hawk's crew had. They could not afford to lose the handful that were willing to face this threat.

Tracking her pursuers by the sound of their tree impacts, Xia kept pushing onward. Behind her the group had spread out, the light patter of Elf claws close, the other 'an falling back. Still, the group retained some cohesion. Judging by the sound, the rearmost Hum-an remained in sight.

Hands scrabbled somewhere behind, the thud of a foot against bark, followed by a shout. 'Shet. Need to stop.'

Xia turned to see the young shopkeeper drifting thirty meters back, spiralling slowly away from the tree she had missed. Face flushed, she lowered the power on her belt to drop to the ground, then hurried through the undergrowth to the nearest trunk. The cut on her head had dried over, now a black line against her pale skin.

'That was good.' Xia steadied herself on a trunk, the bark rough under her claws. 'You all kept pace well. This is a good place to stop. We're about halfway back, and it's time to put those tracking skills from earlier to the test. Who can spot the deer path?'

The others turned their eyes to the forest floor, scanning over leaves and mud. The rains had washed away many of the minor tracks. Even Rikk would have trouble following any scents above the smell of rainwater and fresh growth.

'I think so?' An Elf boy raised his hand. Xia's heart twisted in recognition—Kreddin, from two year's below hers in school. His parents had both given their lives to protect him during the attack, and he had insisted on staying with the volunteers. No one had the heart to turn him away.

Xia nodded. 'Where?'

Kreddin pointed at the ground. 'There. Two broken stems. And more to the north. Bent leaves. Leading that way.'   '

'Well done.' Xia grinned. 'That's the trail we followed to get out here. It leads back to Ethelan.'

Work together. Follow the deer path back. I'll let you know if you're getting too off-track.'

The dozen took to their task, leaping from tree to tree, just off the ground, eyes studying the underbrush for signs of disturbance.

Smiling, Xia followed. Any one of them alone probably would have missed the key signs and ended up wandering into the wilderness. Together, they compensated for each other's lapses. The school's chef spotted a scratch in the moss of a rock. The manager of the metalworks found some droppings. Kreddin saw a hoof print preserved from the rains by the thick covering of ferns. They would have no issues following the tracks of most Daem-ans. In such a group, they could likely follow even the smaller beasts.

As sunset darkened the sky, they reached the outskirts of Ethelan, eerie without lights highlighting walkways. They climbed the trees, making their way towards the few intact houses.

Under the light of a flaming torch at the library— the unofficial gathering point for the volunteers—they found Drekene working with her squad. Each held a spear, practising thrusts in time with Drekene's call.

The spears were crude things, sharpened sticks or recovered lengths of plumbing, but they would soon be replaced with Ket's creations. For now, the volunteers needed to know how to defend themselves if a Daem-an got too close. Xia was not sure what they could achieve other than wounding a beast before it killed them, but Drekene insisted that spears had served Bulwark for a century before the invention of gunpowder.

'Enough.' Drekene raised a hand. 'Take a rest. Get a meal. Tomorrow you will rotate to be trained by Xia.'

The volunteers put down their makeshift weapons and staggered towards the piled food stores taken from houses. The village had plenty of supplies, but without power they were enduring raw meals.

Perching on a bench, Xia took a tin of beans and pulled open the top to eat the meal cold, using her fingers in lieu of a fork. She alternated her mouthfuls with a bite from a fresh carrot for flavour. Everyone else made do with what they could find. Cold soup. Raw roots. Uncleaned fruits. It was hardly sophisticated, but no one complained.

The library's trap door flung open and Cadden emerged at the head of a group of tired villagers. Smiling at the sight of Xia, he took a handful of fruit and made his way across the hall to greet her with a kiss.

'How'd that go?' she asked as he sat next to her on the bench.

'Oh, you know.' He shrugged. 'Trying to remember how to actually instruct first-aid is a different beast from just patching wounds. Don't think I'm cut out to be a teacher, but at least they know how to put pressure on a wound and get someone into the recovery position.'

Xia laughed. 'Well, my lot can get off a few volleys before they drop their weapons. Might have a chance if we can actually arm them.'

On cue, Ket kicked open the door. He and his two Greml assistants tugged a wheelbarrow across the walkway behind them. With a flourish, he pulled off the tarp covering, revealing row after row of glistening rifles.

'You wanted guns.' He flashed a sharp-toothed grin. 'I gotcha guns.'

Xia joined Drekene in walking over to inspect the weapons. Not any design Xia recognised, but they looked capable. Some even had electronic scopes.

'All use standard 12.5 millimetre rifle rounds.' Ket patted the pile as one would a favoured pet. 'The scoped ones'll need batteries. Don't have many bullets to go around—can't make 'em without gunpowder—but we've enough for a few shots each. Should help us in the next fight. If that shipment from Bulwark arrives soon, we'll be golden.'

Xia took up one of the rifles. Unlike her own with its blend of metal and wood, this was entirely steel and so was terribly heavy. Despite its weight, the workmanship was fantastic, the metalSung weapon neatly assembled, the only joints to allow for dismantling of the moving parts.

'I'll get some spears done tomorrow for your old fashioned tactics.' Ket winked at Drekene. 'All in all, we'll have an armed force.'

'And a trained one.' Drekene nodded. 'It may not be Bulwark, but this is a true Daem-an-fighting militia.'

Following the Deathless's gaze, Xia turned to look at the volunteers. Below the mud that caked faces, beyond the exhaustion, she saw determination. The world had turned its back on the people of Vandar, but these few refused to abandon hope. Together, they would make the Daem-ans pay for daring to set foot in this forest.

Chapter 24

Beneath Xia's feet, the walkway groaned. It strained under the weight of so many people, all hauling crates like the one she and Cadden carried between them. The plastic container was an old cooler, found in the back of the grocer, handles well worn. They had filled it with dried food, stripped to the bare minimal packaging. The crates, boxes and carrier bags held by the others were loaded with everything from food to medicines to bullets. Anything of use was taken to the edge of Ethelan.

Reaching the village's one landing pad, they approached the Hawk. The silver vessel was precariously balanced to one side of the platform in order to make enough room for the Greendip Corporation's craft. The latter had been heavily modified by Ket's Greml assistants, the oblong aircraft now bearing storage cages along its olive-painted sides. The cargo vessel, previously only known by a tracking number, had been christened the Albatross, though Ket preferred Fat-Hawk.

The Hawk would remain as their lead vessel, a fast Bulwark jet to get the most experienced fighters to the front as quick as possible. The Albatross would follow behind, its interior stripped to offer standing room to the bulk of the volunteers. There was nowhere near enough room to sit, let alone sleep, so nights would be spent in the open, but this setup would let them rapidly deploy to meet the Daem threat.

Xia backed up the Hawk's ramp, the heavy crate making her footfalls clang on the metal. Cadden grunted as he hefted the other end. Once on board, they dropped the crate and slid it over the ship's floor, eliciting a piercing screech.

'Whatcha doing to my ship?' Ket growled, hanging from a panel.

Cadden rolled his eyes. 'Shut up and help us get this stored away.'

Grumbling, Ket hopped down and started packing the dried food into storage cupboards buried in the bulkheads. There had been some suggestions of adding more storage boxes to the Hawk's exterior, but Cadden had quickly shot those down, pointing out the advantages of keeping the Hawk lean.

'Not sure if you're going to be able to make anything good out of this.' Xia looked suspiciously at the various packets of dried fruit and vegetables. They had prioritised items that would last long and weigh little. Who knew when they would have a chance to restock? Vandar had promised food, and one of the Bulwark transports was heading to the capital, but only time would tell if the prime minister would keep his word.

Cadden laughed. 'Oh, there's a number of real chefs who volunteered, so making this into meal's going to be their problem. You're free from the burden of enduring my food.'

'Pity,' Xia said truthfully. He had made a real effort to adapt his cooking to suit her. She would have to let him know how much she appreciated it, sometime Ket wasn't hovering overhead with a sarcastic comment at hand.

'Quiet, Girl.' The Greml-an threw a pack of dried peas at her head. 'We should be thankful—real food for a change.'

She threw the pack back, almost knocking the diminutive man off his feet. His retort was cut off as an alarm blared from the cockpit.

All three ran, but Cadden reached the flashing communication panel first. 'It's on the emergency frequency.' He flicked a switch to return the signal. 'This is the Bulwark ship Hawk, we hear you.'

The reply came back filled with static. 'Bulwark? Thank Elf-az. This is Rennin Village. There're… Daem-ans. We're under attack. I repeat, we're…' The voice faded into white noise.

'Shet.' Cadden tapped furiously at the controls, twisting dials and calling into the microphone, all in vain. 'I've lost the signal.'

Clanging footsteps announced Drekene. 'Do you have a location?'

Cadden nodded. 'Half an hour out for the Hawk. Maybe fifteen minutes more for the Albatross.'

'Get the ship ready,' Drekene shouted over her shoulder as she vaulted the food crate. 'We take off in two minutes.'

Cadden and Ket leapt to the controls, flicking switches to start spooling up the Hawk's engines. Drekene's voice bellowed outside, giving crisp orders to the volunteers. The steady flow of materiel became a stampede.

Xia whistled for Rikk as she rushed to a half-empty food crate. No time to sort through, she upended it towards her bunk. Some of the packages fell to the ground and she kicked them to the side before hurrying to the ramp. Sidestepping an excited Rikk as he leapt into the Hawk, Xia flung the container. It skidded before tumbling off the platform's edge. There was no room for it on board, and leaving it on the landing pad seemed a worse idea.

Herded by Drekene, five men and women ran to the Hawk. They had proved the most skilled at combat, either with rifles or spears. Kriss ran at their head, freshly metalSung spear in hand, its tip razor sharp. The others held Ket's new rifles. Ceci, the leather worker, had added padded grips to the new weapons, though Xia still preferred the smooth wood of her own rifle.

To make way for the others, Xia hurried back down the Hawk to the cockpit, crushing a pack of dried beans underfoot. Pausing at the weapon locker to retrieve her rifle, she pushed past Ket and climbed up the steps to the co-pilot seat. Rikk waited for her on the back of the chair. His fur smelled damp—he'd been playing in the sodden canopy.

At the rear of the hoverjet, Drekene slapped the ramp's controls. 'Go, now.'

Cadden gave no delay, flaring the jets and lifting off as the ramp was still closing. Xia was pushed back into her seat as the Hawk accelerated and skimmed the treetops. Xia took a moment to ready her rifle, checking its scope, its magazine. She had only two clips, the rest of her rounds having been divided between the volunteers. Even with an abundance of Daem corpses, they had no way to manufacture gunpowder in Ethelan. Rendering the Daem flesh to useful explosives required precise temperatures, needing specialist equipment or—ideally—a flameSinger. Kriss was the only Drak-an in the village, and he could Sing no better than Xia.

For now, they had to make every round count. Xia could only hope that the delivery of bullets arrived before they all had to resort to spears.

'Albatross has lifted off.' Ket was bent over the communication console. 'Two minutes behind. Closer to twenty by the time we get there.'

'Should we wait for them before landing?' Cadden suggested. 'We don't know what's down there.'

Drekene's reply came through Xia's earpiece. 'Yes we do—Daem-ans. And we know what they're doing to the population. We will not delay.'

Glancing at Cadden, Xia could tell he wanted to argue, wanted to protect his friends—her—from harm. But he kept silent. There was no avoiding danger in Vandar anymore. Like it or not, they were all on a new front line in this ancient war, and both sides would spill blood.

Cadden peered at the map on one of his displays. 'Looks like there's a clearing at the village's edge. We could set the Hawk down there instead of dropping you overhead. Help keep you together.'

'Good idea,' Drekene replied. 'The jet can mark an evac zone. Use the Hawk's guns to hold the perimeter while the rest of us push into the settlement.'

'Yeah,' Cadden muttered, uncertain. 'The Hawk's guns.'

'They'll work,' Ket assured him.

'Easy for you to say. You don't have to fly the ship and aim it all at the same time.'

'Yeah, yeah.' Ket sucked his teeth. 'Just remember to stick to short bursts. Don't want the recoil to throw you off and make you crash my ship.'

Cadden rolled his eyes. 'Oh, that's encouraging.'

'No blind firing,' Drekene reminded them. 'There will be hundreds of civilians down there.'

'Not to mention us,' muttered Xia.

'Oh, don't worry, Girl.' Ket turned with an impish grin. 'With you down there, the lad's gonna be triple checking every shot.'

Again, Cadden rolled his eyes.

'There.' Xia pointed ahead. A dark plume rose over the tree line.

Cadden panned the camera to confirm. 'Guessing that's another powerhouse in flames. No wonder communications failed.'

'How far?' Xia shifted in her seat.

'Five minutes.'

Drekene called from the rear. 'Landing party, be ready. Ket, Cadden, give us cover. We need to protect the civilians. When the Albatross gets here, direct them to establish a perimeter at the clearing. We'll lead the survivors away and hunt the Daem-ans.'

A chorus of acknowledgements echoed down the hoverjet. Xia stood, shouldered her rifle, and kissed Cadden's hair.

'Be safe,' he whispered.

'You too.'

Ket laughed as she passed. 'What? No kiss for me?'

Despite his grin, she could hear the worry in his voice. She patted his scaled head. 'Take care.'

'Oh, don't worry about me, Girl. I'm staying in this metal-plated aircraft. You're the one going to wrestle with monsters.'

Shaking her head, she clambered to the back of the jet where the others waited, weapons ready, poised to leap into combat. Rikk nuzzled into her leg, whining.

Xia knelt. 'No, Rikk. You need to stay here again. Stay with Cadden.'

Ears back, Rikk obeyed, slinking to the cockpit. Xia knew the mutt just wanted to help, but she could not afford to be keeping an eye on him too. At least he seemed to be warming to Cadden's company, tolerating being left with the pilot more and more.

'One minute,' Cadden warned. 'I'll land with the nose towards the village. Will give you cover as you land, but get clear of the jets as soon as you're out.'

Firmly, Xia gripped her rifle, its polished wood handle so smooth to the touch, its weight so familiar. She had debated giving the weapon to one of the recruits, using Ket's newer but harder-to-use inventions. In the end, she had dismissed the idea. Mother had given her this rifle. Trained her to use it. She would never part with this last piece of her old life.

Drekene hit the ramp controls, the pneumatic whine of the mechanism sounding over the engines' roar. The opening door revealed the field outside, grass blown by the outwash of the jets as the Hawk descended.

A metre before the Hawk landed, Drekene leapt from the ramp. As the craft shuddered with the landing skid's contact, the rest poured out, Xia trailing.

Outside, Xia was overcome with the din. Hot air heavy with jet fuel rushed past, flattening grass stalks and sending wildflowers flying. Following Cadden's earlier instructions, Xia did not pause, but sprinted from the hoverjet.

The group fanned out, peeling away in either direction to flank the Hawk. Xia knelt beside Kriss, the wind from the hoverjet ripping hair from her braid, loose locks whipping her face. She had never stayed close to the active engines for this long—either jumping clear of the flying hoverjet or exiting only once the Hawk was powered down. The chemical stench of the engines was suffocating, the heat enough to sting her eyes.

Ahead, the village burned. Flames licked out of the powerhouse, scorching a neighbouring trunk. An office, constructed from the living wood like so many Elf structures, already belched white smoke from its open windows. The building was being roasted, its interior already catching alight. The tree would not be far behind.

Movement caught Xia's attention. The underbrush moved, shook, shattered. The torn black hide of a Daem-an charged through. It was a pathetic, terrifying specimen. Four articulated legs supported an upright beetle's body. Its canine head hung to the side, though Xia could not tell whether this was from a horrific injury or cruel design. Even with the handicap, the thing could easily kill just by trampling its victims. Probably had the strength to crack the Hawk's shell.

Raising her rifle, Xia activated her scope. Before she could line up her shot, she was thrown off balance by a wash of burning air. The Hawk's engines became deafening as it pushed off, rising to hover barely two meters above the ground.

The silver vessel yawed to the side, its nose dipping slightly. In a rasp of gunfire, the Hawk's weapons opened up. Clods of dirt sprayed around the Daem-an, then chunks of flesh. What the guns lacked in accuracy, they made up for in calibre, each shot slamming a hole the size of Xia's head into the black hide.

The spray of fire halted, the Hawk wavering. The Daem-an had come to a stop, two of its legs now mere stumps, its beetle body a shredded mess. It still lived, remaining limbs dragging it on with desperation, its strangely oriented head letting forth a scream drowned out by the hoverjet.

A second burst from the Hawk finished its dismal existence, pulverising its remains into oozing lumps.

'Ha!' Cadden laughed through the earpiece. 'My first confirmed Daem-an kill.'

'See?' Ket replied, smug. 'I told you the guns would work. You'll catch up to Xia's tally in no time.'

'Brilliant.' Xia rose to her feet. 'Now if only you could fly through trees, we'd be set.'

'Yeah, yeah,' Ket replied. 'One improvement at a time. You'll have to do the rest the hard way.'

Drekene waved onwards, drawing her sword. 'Hawk, hold this position. Everyone else, with me.'

While the jet hovered overhead, the seven on the ground charged. Caution would have been sensible, but they were well beyond caution. Every passing second could cost another life.

Entering the forest, away from the Hawk's engines, Xia could make out the sounds coming from the city, and they made her sick. Screams of pain, of terror, of grief. Roars of rage. The crash of a crumbling walkway.

Dropping to a crouch, mud and leaves cushioning

her knee, Xia scanned the trunks above.

'There.' Sella, formerly an accountant, pointed. 'On the white oak.'

Xia followed the Elf-an's finger, quickly spotting the dark monstrosity stalking the village. The Daem-an looked like a large, bald vulfik, its membranous wing riddled with bloody rips, canine jaws dripping with gore. It pursued a family of three, two parents trying to hurry their young daughter.

But they were outpaced. With every leap, the Daem-an closed the distance. Muscles knotted, ready to pounce.

No delay. No hesitation. Xia raised her rifle and fired. Midair, the bullet took the creature in the shoulder, throwing it off balance. Instead of landing on the hapless family, it slammed into a trunk. Its shrill scream pierced the air as it tumbled, black claws flailing uselessly to find purchase on a tree. With a crash of shattering undergrowth, the beast came down.

But it was far from finished.

Scream turning to rage, it jumped from the bush that had broken its fall. Ichor poured from its shoulder, its back covered in a hundred fragmented thorns jutting into its wounds, but none of this stopped its advance. Limping on three legs, it barrelled towards its new target—Xia.

Beside her the other rifle-armed volunteers knelt, weapons raised. Together they fired volley after volley at the weaving creature. Despite its best attempts at dodging from trunk to trunk, several rounds hit home. Blood sprayed from its chest. The membrane between its legs tore in multiple places. White bone glinted from a head wound.

The Daem-an did not even slow.

Kriss and Drekene sprinted to intercept it, but they were too late. As the rifle-bearers jumped and cowered, the beast pounced. Xia shielded her head as the thing's shadow descended. Sulphur and blood filled the air, accompanied by the sound of shattering bone.

As the crunch of claws retreated, Xia opened her eyes. To her side, blood smeared the ferns. A leg lay in the mud. A bent rifle. A hand. All that remained of Sella.

Coated in fresh blood, the Daem-an turned, bearing down on the group once more. This time, Kriss and Drekene were faster. Kriss dived into the thing's path, spear braced against the soil. The steel tip took the Daem-an in the neck, black gore drenching the Drak-an.

Screaming, the Daem-an tried to swipe at the ex-policeman, but he backed away, leaving it pinned to the muck by the spear. Its struggles only drove the spear deeper. Drekene was upon it in a heartbeat, serrated sword hacking at the monster until it finally fell still.

The six survivors stared at their fallen comrade. Sella's torso had been dragged several meters away by the impact. If Xia had not seen the woman crouched beside her moments before, she would never have been able to identify that crushed skull. It barely looked like an Elf-an anymore, just meat strewn across the forest floor.

Panicked screams drew the group's attention. The family had been joined by a dozen more villagers leaping haphazardly through the trees.

'Here,' Drekene bellowed. 'Make for the clearing. Run!'

The towering woman's voice carried well, and her authority snapped the villagers into action. Their movements were still panicked, but now had direction, the families rushing towards the edge of the trees.

And behind them, another Daem-an gave chase. Far too agile for its bulk, the thing threw its bone-covered body through the trees.

Xia and the others took aim. As one, the rifles spat forth death. Bone protrusions shattered. Limbs dislocated. Bulbous skull cracked. The monster crashed to the ground, spraying dirt and twigs.

A scream ripped through the forest. Elf-an. Xia turned to see yet another beast—a shark on three spiked legs—pounce on a fleeing Drak-an. Before Xia could raise her rifle, the monster disappeared beyond the tree line. Towards the fleeing villagers. Towards Cadden.

A warning shout escaping her lips, she sprinted for the trees. Yells echoed from the clearing beyond. Screams of fear, of anger.

A volley of rifle fire tore into the trees. Not the heavy guns of the Hawk, but a dozen small arms. The volley was answered by a cheer.

Xia plunged through a fern at the edge of the forest and stumbled into the clearing. Twenty meters away lay the broken body of the Daem-an, black tar oozing from its punctured hide. Beyond it, advancing to protect the fleeing citizens, stood twenty men and women. The volunteers. Survivors of one village, here to save another.

Xia beamed with pride.

As evening fell, Xia set down her shovel, exhausted. A hundred fresh saplings now littered the clearing, each marking a freshly dug grave. The volunteers were relieved that so few had been killed. Xia grimaced. When had a hundred dead civilians counted as low casualties?

Spotting Cadden, Xia walked towards the Hawk and Albatross, both landed in the knee-length grass. An acrid stench filled the air. At the clearing's edge, Rennin's flameSinger was immolating the Daem corpse, rendering it into the key chemicals that could form explosives.

She kissed Cadden, smelling the sweat on his skin. Even after spending the battle struggling to hover the Hawk just off the ground, Cadden had been the first in line to help the village bury their dead. He just did not know how to stop, how to rest.

'You alright?' she asked.

'Can't complain.' He grimaced. 'Unlike everyone else, I was safe in the Hawk.'

'You've been on the front line of combat before,' she pointed out.

'Yes. But I was trained. These people should never have to face Daem-ans up close.'

'No one should.' Xia turned to the gathering crowd. Most of the village had survived, but none without loss. Just like Ethelan, this was a town where every death would be felt. She could see the relief on the faces, mixed with survivor's guilt.

An ageing Elf-an led a small contingent towards Drekene. Curious, Xia caught Cadden's hand and led him towards the Deathless.

'You are in charge of our rescuers, yes?' the man asked.

Drekene nodded.

'I'm Tallic. As mayor of Rennin, I want to give you our heartfelt thanks. We all owe you our lives.'

The Deathless grunted. 'Fighting the Daem-ans is what Bulwark does.'

Tallic smirked. 'I see many saviours here, but only four in Bulwark uniforms.'

Kriss strolled over. 'The rest of us are from Ethelan. Drekene needs all the help she can get.'

'That is precisely why I'm here.' Tallic glanced at the crowd. 'We know there is more fighting to be done. While many want to get to safety, we all know you paid in blood to save us. At least half my people wish to join you. We have a few hoverjets here, enough to transport us and our supplies. We've a lifeSigner. A flameSinger. We can pull our weight.'

Drekene sized up the man. 'We'd be glad for any assistance. This fight is just getting started.'

'It's settled then.' Tallic smiled. 'Just one question. We've asked around, but no one could give a straight answer. What do we call your group?'

Kriss shared a look with Drekene, then shrugged. 'Never thought of that. We're not Bulwark, but we're not Vandar military either.'

'Guess it would be good to be able to refer to ourselves as something,' Xia said.

Cadden nodded. 'Can't have the ships named, but not our little band. But what? We're not like Bulwark, not really holding the line here, just slowing the Daem-ans.'

Xia smiled. 'We're like bracken. Thorns. Dragging

the invaders back. So how about that? Vandar's Thorns.'

Tallic made a face. 'Vandar's the government that turned its back on its own people. I'd rather leave their name out of it.'

'Then we name ourselves after a leader who acts.' Kriss slapped Drekene's arm. 'Drekene's Thorns. Has a nice ring to it.'

The others nodded, smiling with determination. Drekene grunted, as much consent as she was going to give.

'Sounds good.' Xia grinned at the Deathless. 'Well then. Long live Drekene's Thorns.'

Chapter 25

Boots sinking into the mud, Xia wound her way through the maze of hoverjets. Rikk followed, scampering over wings and leaping from cockpit windows. She was surrounded by everything from single-seater sports aircraft to colossal tankers the size of a giant redwood. Some were rusted, metalSigners barely able to keep them together. Others were fresh from the assembly line, purchased days before Daem-ans killed their owners.

A month had passed since the Hawk had returned to Vandar. A month of fighting Daem-ans, recruiting survivors, burying the dead. In that month Drekene's Thorns had grown from a militia to an army of thousands, each settlement saved offering a new batch of volunteers. Vandar's government had allowed the band to collect food from the capital but nothing more. Father and the wardens had not materialised. Bulwark did not arrive to save the day, grudgingly permitting the logistics ships to haul second-rate ammunition to Vandar. Alone, the Thorns fought on, held the Daem-ans at bay.

Smiling faces and waves greeted her as she passed. Most were Elf-ans, but they were joined by every other race in Vandar. Hum-ans shared meals with Greml-ans. Drak-ans traded stories with Gobl-ans. Some had been friends before the Daem-ans had arrived. Others only recently met, still learning the names of their new comrades. No one hesitated to help the next 'an, be they stranger or lifelong friend. They were all Thorns.

Even with the glut of lifeSinger volunteers, no one here was without scars. Some injuries were too minor to use Song to cure, others too deep for the most skilled lifeSinger to fully mend. However, no injury had caused a single volunteer to doubt the cause. If limbs were lost to Daem-ans, the Thorns adapted. Here, a one-armed woman served soup to a group of pilots. There, a Drak-an walked on a prosthetic leg—a metalSung contraption of Ket's making.

Xia recognised the conviction that drove them. Each town evacuated, every person saved, every smiling child, it made any strife worthwhile. All these 'an knew the pain of loss, and were determined to safeguard the forest, the world. It didn't matter if you were a sharpshooter or a cook, the Thorns had become a banner for Vandar's defence. While world governments bickered and passed off responsibility, these men and women fought and bled.

Stepping around aircraft crews sharing dinner, over mechanics patching fatigued hulls, past soldiers cleaning their weapons, Xia made her way through the mobile city. Drekene's Thorns travelled wherever they were required. As the Daem-ans moved, the Thorns followed. Scouting teams scoured the forest constantly, looking for sign of Daem-ans. For minor groups, a response force would be sent. For major packs, the entire fleet would go on the offensive. The thousand hoverjets could take to the skies with only a few minutes' notice, ready to drop grav-belt equipped soldiers onto Daem heads.

Often, they had to land separately, small groups of

aircraft nestling along riverbanks, in meadows, on abandoned landing pads. Occasionally, the fight would take them near enough to a clearing wide enough to fit every hoverjet. As their numbers swelled, the space they required had grown. Soon even vast fields like this had become too small, and the Thorns had been forced to cut down trees to make enough room. Even now she stepped over the hard wood of an exposed stump, cut level with the ground. The destruction of the forest made her nauseous, but she had always known that this was not going to be a clean war. The forest would bear scars as lasting as those on these warriors.

The wandering city was a strange place to live, layout shifting each night depending on where they set down. No matter how fresh the air may have been at first, an hour after landing the city always smelled the same. Jet fuel blended with the stink of emptying sewage tanks. The sound of Song fought over shouted commands and the crackle of wood fire.

Xia rounded an old camper jet, and came into view of the Hawk. It stood as polished as ever, partially due to the recent downpour, partially due to Cadden's tireless efforts. He had poured hours into cleaning the hull, as if protecting that vessel erased a little of the destruction they saw each day. Perhaps it was also the reason he doted on her so—keeping something of life intact amongst the carnage.

Other than the hull, little of the Hawk remained from its original form. After several iterations, Ket's front-mounted guns were now suspended on a turret. Controlled by the co-pilot, it could track freely and had saved countless lives by clearing landing zones.

Under the broad wings, ramshackle barrels were mounted—fragmentation bombs. Based on the shells from Bulwark, the weapons were frighteningly effective. If the Daem-ans made the mistake of clumping together in the open, half the jets in the fleet carried these, and would soon make the beasts pay. Shrapnel now littered the inner forest, iron blades buried in trunks, mud and ruined homes.

The other leaders of the Thorns waited for Xia. The Hawk's crew was joined by Kriss and Mayor Tallic. Xia always felt out of place, not experienced as the elders, not trained like Cadden and Ket, but Drekene insisted on hearing her opinion. As long as they kept killing Daem-ans, Xia was content.

'What's the emergency?' Xia took a folding chair alongside Cadden, sheltered by the Hawk's wing.

He handed her dinner—a flask of soup—and put an arm around her shoulders. 'Drekene thinks we need to change tactics.'

Settling in front of Cadden, Rikk whined until he was handed a bowl of broth.

Xia turned the Deathless. 'Why? Our efforts have been working. We're killing Daem-ans by the hundreds out there. Even without help, we can hold them.'

'I disagree,' Drekene replied. 'The attacks are increasing in frequency and intensity. The packs are getting larger. Soon, the assaults here will match the severity of those at Bulwark.'

'Our numbers are increasing too.' Xia took a sip of her soup. Mushroom.

Drekene nodded. 'Yes, but it's a losing battle. The Daem-ans are getting farther and farther from the

317

breach with each new wave.'

Kriss nodded. 'It's true. Cities that we were sending refugees to just a couple of weeks ago are now under attack.'

'Besides,' Tallic added, 'if this drags out, supplies are going to be a problem. So far Enall has condescended to give us food and even fuel, but as we're evacuating more of the forest, there are fewer orchards being tended, fewer farms being staffed. It's going to start to be a question of feeding the evacuees or feeding us.'

Xia sighed. 'But what else can we do? We drop explosives on the breach every time it opens. That's almost daily now.'

'And the area those breaches are appearing over is getting wider.' Cadden grimaced. 'Yesterday's breach was three hundred meters away from the one the day before.'

'That is why I called you all here.' Drekene stood, staring into the city. The sky had steadily darkened from orange to purple, the hoverjets now lit with the harsh glow of their electric lights and the flicker of campfires. 'We need a new plan. We must bring this to an end, before we are overrun.'

'Only one way to end this.' Ket looked up. 'We need a permanent defence around the breach. Kill the Daem-ans as they come out. We need a new Bulwark.'

'Thought you said we needed more resources for that,' Xia pointed out. 'Construction teams, architects, weapon manufacturers.'

Drekene glanced over her shoulder to Xia. 'And we have those now.' She turned, nodding towards the city. Electric lamps caught woodsmoke. The sound of a hundred conversations overlapped on the evening wind. 'We've trained the Thorns as soldiers, but we have plenty of engineers out there. Every metalSinger has been trained to make weapons. Every flameSigner knows how to render Daem corpses into gunpowder. We have the numbers, the skill, the equipment. If we recycle the older aircraft, we'd have plenty of material for construction. We can establish a new defensive line outside the breach.'

Ket sucked his teeth. 'Just one problem—or about a hundred at last count—the forest is crawling with Daem-ans. I don't fancy trying to build walls and turrets while under attack from all sides.'

'Perhaps we could form a wide perimeter,' Kriss suggested. 'Send teams out to the edge of the area the Daem-ans currently occupy. Work our way in. Clear the Daem-ans on the way, until we've drawn the net closed around the breach. Then we only have to worry about attack from one direction.'

Xia shook her head. 'According to my latest scout reports, the Daem-ans are reaching a hundred kilometres from the breach in multiple directions. We have an army, but not one large enough to contain an area that large.'

No one spoke. The group stared out across the meadow. The Hawk sat at the centre of the city. The hoverjet always led the formations in transit, was the first on the ground, whether they were going into combat or just to bed down for the night. Other Thorn vehicles clustered around, filling the available space from tree line to tree line. Vehicles from the same village tended to cluster together, forming little neighbourhoods that rearranged with each new night, each new field.

Looking up from chewing his foot claws, Ket broke the silence. 'Well, if we want to choke off the supply of new Daem-ans, then why don't we just go straight to breach? We are a flying army, after all. Build fortifications to protect us from attacks from the breach and the outside.'

'What about the Daem-ans already in the forest?' Cadden asked, gloomy. 'They might ignore our defences and continue raiding.'

Ket shrugged. 'Let Vandar take care of them.'

'And how many die before the government actually starts to act?' Cadden asked.

Another shrug from the Greml-an. 'Well it ain't a perfect plan. This's triage here. If it's a choice of the outlying cities or the entire shetting forest, I think we all know what has to be sacrificed.'

'Seems a little callous.' Kriss grimaced, his scaled lips peeling back to reveal teeth as sharp as Ket's.

'Just practical,' countered the Greml-an.

'No.' Drekene insisted. 'We've seen the world make the cold decisions, the practical choices. "Leave the war for Bulwark." "Let the forest to burn." That's why we're here alone. We're not going to become *that*. We're not going to sacrifice civilians.'

Xia stared towards the sky. The sun had fully set, and stars now sparkled across the heavens. Watcher would be overhead, obscured by the Hawk's wing. The other stars were faint, partially drowned out by the light pollution of the mobile city. Coming back from scouting expeditions, Xia had seen how their settlement looked from above. Always settled in clearings the lights shone brightly, a beacon in the forest. Thankfully, few flying Daem-ans had emerged from Vandar's breach, or they'd be drawn to the city like moths to a flame.

Kriss scratched at his scales. He would need to molt soon, had been putting it off—this was not the time to be bedridden for a few days. 'So we can't keep sending out patrols to defend the civilians or we lose the war. We can't turn our backs on them to hold the breach or we lose our soul.'

Sealing her empty soup flask, Xia frowned. 'Why does it have to be a choice? We rarely use the entire fleet in a single attack. This is more of a mobile base, a place to gather at night for protection, for supplies. Follow Ket's idea and make the new fortification our base. We can still send out hoverjets to scout and hunt Daem-ans. We recycle some of our jets for the defences, but keep half. Yes, our response time will slow if we're always heading out from a single point —we lose mobility—but we can hold the breach and defend the forest. Right now we use our downtime in meadows like this. Why not park ourselves where we can guard the breach between heading off?'

Cadden nodded. 'Makes sense. It will be hard at first—dividing our forces between the forest and the new fortification, but over time we'll kill off the roaming Daem-ans. We finally have the numbers we needed a month ago, so let's use them before it's too late.'

'Just one problem,' muttered Tallic. 'The defences we erect at night are only strong enough to protect against the odd wandering Daem-an. If we just land near the breach, we'd be overrun by morning.'

'So we build proper defences,' Xia suggested.

'Real walls, turrets, towers, defending from attacks from the breach.'

'And if the Daem-ans already in the forest return to attack us from behind?'

Xia shrugged. 'So make the defences face both ways. Two layers of walls, us in the middle.'

'Easy for you to say,' Ket scoffed. 'You ever tried to construct a fortification while under attack... from two sides? My construction crews are good, but we are just mortals.'

Drekene turned. 'So we guard your workers. Two concentric rings of troops around the breach. We land the fleet inside the lines, and convert half the metal into a strong fort ringing the breach, with a gap like in Bulwark to lure the Daem-ans. Once done, our troops fall back. We can then use the remaining transports to patrol the forest.'

One by one, the leaders nodded. It was a desperate plan, holding a line in the forest with nothing but rifles, waiting for a Daem assault. They had spent the last month picking off groups—some admittedly large —but never a concentrated army like those that would emerge from the breach. The memory of the assault at Bulwark flashed through Xia's mind. That had been terrifying enough on the relative safety of a battlement. The thought of standing in the path of that rushing mass of evil send a shiver through her body.

Noisily, Key sucked his teeth. 'Seems we're agreed. I'm gonna need every construction worker, mechanic and metalSigner we got. And a shet-tonne of metal. I'm talking every tanker, every junker, every rusty barge. We'll save the armed craft for after, but to make a fort that big, I need a lot.'

Drekene nodded. 'We divide the rest of the ground forces. I'll lead the half facing the breach. Cadden, you command the armed aircraft. Give air support where needed. Kriss, Tallic, Xia, you will be in charge out the outer line of defence. You'll have to stop any Daem-ans from the forest from reaching the construction site. Thoughts?'

'I can only see one problem,' Cadden replied. 'What if the Daem-ans in the forest concentrate their attack at one point on the outer defence? We won't know where they're going to hit until they're upon us. My guys are good, but we'll struggle to attack targets in the dense forest, and once we're out of ammo, we're useless.'

'You're right.' Drekene sighed. 'And we'll be spread out, particularly on the outer ring. We need reserves, ready to drop from the air to reinforce the line wherever the Daem-ans strike. Best if we have as many troops on board as we can, so we can react quickly to the Daem attacks, if they come. I'd say at least a quarter of the ground troops should wait on Cadden's transports.'

Xia blinked. 'This is our final showdown and you want to keep a quarter of our force out of the fight, just in case the Daem-ans mass an attack at one point on the line?'

'It's the only way to ensure Ket can get the fort built in time.'

'If you say so,' Xia grumbled. 'So who gets the honour of leading that lot? Of sitting out this last fight?'

Drekene stared flatly at Xia. The others nodded.

Looking around, Xia shook her head. 'Me? You

can't be serious.'

'You are our chief scout,' Drekene stated. 'You've led our most mobile forces.'

'No.' Xia stood, glaring at the woman. 'You're not keeping me on the sidelines. I've lost as much as anyone. I have a right to be on the front, to face those murderers.'

Drekene laid placating hands on Xia's shoulders, staring at her with black eyes. 'This is not about who deserves revenge, Xia. This is about putting down this threat to the world. You know how to move rapidly, are used to being dropped into the forest, and are a crack shot. I can think of no one better to lead our rearguard.'

Xia turned to the others, disbelieving as she saw nothing but sympathy. With a grim heart, she nodded, realising this was an argument she would not win. After all this time, after being the first to spill Daem blood in Vandar, after crossing the continent and back, she was being left out of the final battle.

She would be denied her final retribution.

Chapter 26

Out the cockpit window, Xia stared at the gathering army. The Hawk swung in a lazy arc around the clearing where the thousand hoverjets of the Thorn fleet lifted off. In the morning's early rays, tankers, personal jets, campers, and delivery haulers all rose into the sky. Far from the ordered landing field of Bulwark, there was no structure here, just a mass of aircraft lifting off as and when their crews were ready, drifting to join the circling formation led by the Hawk. It was a testament to the skill of the pilots that there were not any collisions.

Xia checked the controls on her console. Little was left of the Hawk's original co-pilot station, now converted into the gunner's seat. Screens showed views from cameras mounted to the turrets, the reserve flight stick converted to aim the guns. Ket normally manned this position, but he was with the engineers on the larger vessels, leaving Xia to operate the Hawk's weaponry.

At least it made her feel somewhat useful.

'How are we looking?' Drekene asked through the earpiece. She was at the rear of the Hawk, on the far side of a dozen men and women packed into the corridor.

'Just the last few craft taking off now,' Cadden replied. 'Two minutes.'

Xia turned to inspect the various 'an packing the Hawk. Half were Xia's scouts, condemned like her to sit out this final battle. Behind them stood Drekene's handpicked guard. Kriss was not with them but on the Albatross, ready to lead half the outer perimeter. All here were older, Xia realised. Grey haired and scarred. Perhaps Drekene had chosen them to have only veterans with her around the breach, where they expected the heaviest combat. Perhaps these elders were simply more disposable.

'That's the last jet off the ground.' Cadden twisted a dial to transmit to the entire air fleet. 'All Thorn craft, fall in behind the Hawk. Pilots, you all know your objectives. It's time to end this.'

A few of the cockier pilots rocked their aircraft or did rolls in response. Cadden just grinned.

'You're enjoying this,' Xia teased.

He turned off his earpiece. 'Of course. Never thought I'd be leading the largest air formation in history.'

'The largest in history? That can't be true.'

Cadden shrugged. 'You better believe it. Bulwark's fleet is larger, but never gathers. It's always scattered, transporting supplies and reinforcements.'

'Huh.' Xia glanced at the radar display, the bottom half of the screen littered with green dots. 'I hadn't thought of it like that before.'

'Exciting times.'

'Yeah.' She grimaced. 'And I'll just be watching it from here.'

'Spending the battle with me is that bad?'

'You know that's not what I meant.'

Cadden glanced at her, his smile sympathetic. 'We all have our part to play. I won't see combat either. I fly people around. It's all I've ever done.'

'But at least that's useful. You and your pilots transport the entire army. Without you, this attack would be impossible. But what good am I, sat here? Would it be any different if stayed in bed today?'

'If the Daem-ans mass an attack on the outer perimeter, you and your scouts might be all that keeps this from turning into a rout.'

'And if they don't mass an attack? If I spend this day letting others bleed while I sit twiddling my thumbs in this cockpit?'

His silence was all the answer she needed. Grim, she looked out the window. To the side, a hauler kept pace. Pale blue paint clung to the rusted frame, the words *Fury Dawn* scrawled in white. Once it had been a delivery transport, bringing crates of supplies from the farming villages to the cities. Now it would hold a hundred soldiers, its cargo containers reworked into troop bays.

Xia frowned. Sparks flew from the fat engine bolted to its side. The sparks were short-lived, and for a while Xia wondered if she had imagined the flash— perhaps the glint of morning sun off a new vent. But then came the smoke. And flames.

As she opened her mouth to warn Cadden, the engine exploded, a ball of orange, black and steel flaring into the air.

'Shet,' barked a voice over the earpiece, panicked. 'This is Fury's Dawn. We've just lost our number two engine. Shet, I can't hold it.'

Cadden craned his neck as the hauler dropped away. 'Can you land?'

'I think… I hope so. Brace. Brace.'

A loud bang reverberated from the cockpit's

speakers, the sound of metal scraping against metal, poorly filtered through a microphone.

'They're down in a clearing,' another voice called. 'Looks like hard landing.'

Cadden spoke rapidly. 'Fury's Dawn, do you read? Fury's Dawn? Please respond.'

Silence.

Then static.

'Just our shetting luck,' a garbled voice replied. 'We're down. Got injured, but looks like we're alive. No way we can take this back off.'

'Just glad you made it.' Cadden grinned with relief. 'Drekene, do we send jets to pick them up?'

'No,' the Deathless replied. 'We can't waste the time. If the Daem-ans realise what we're up to, it just increases the chances of them focusing an attack or laying an ambush. We push on. Fury's Dawn, hold on for now. Once the defences are up, we'll send crews to retrieve you.'

'Understood.' The voice was so distorted as to be barely audible. Clearly had damaged their antenna on impact. 'We'll dig in here. Damn, looks like we'll miss this one. Elf-az be with you, Thorns.'

Xia grimaced. 'That's a hundred fewer troops on the ground.'

'And tonnes of metal that Ket won't be able to put into the new fortification.' Seeing Xia's dark look, Cadden's tone shifted. Upbeat, if forced. 'Don't worry. We have more than enough ground forces. The Fury's Dawn was mostly carrying engineers. This is going to work.'

All Xia could do was nod. She appreciated his efforts, even if she could not believe him. It was going to be a nightmare on the forest floor, and she had a prime view to watch the carnage unfold.

As they headed closer to the breach, the forest's scars became clear. Black stains littered the canopy, scorched trees marking the position of lost villages.

The Daem attacks had followed the same pattern with each settlement, hitting the powerhouse first then moving up to slaughter the populace. Either at night or during an eclipse, the loss of the powerhouse would plunge the settlement into darkness. Often the complex Gobl equipment would ignite, starting a fire that would spread to the village. Even hardened against forest fires, the village trees would be overwhelmed by the intensity of a chemical fire, rendering homes into ash and bare trunks.

Only the 'az knew how beasts from the underworld had developed such an effective tactic.

Ahead, Vandar's greatest scar marred the canopy. A huge clearing, stained with ash, surrounded by splintered trunks. This was neither natural, nor a result of Daem attack, but was caused by the Thorn's bombing campaign. The site of the breach had been hit almost daily for the past month, at first with hand-placed explosives, later bombed from hoverjets.

Each blast resealed the breach, but also devastated the surrounding greenery. Trunks splintered, roots shattered, and eventually trees gave way. Cracked and dead, they would dry out, perfect tinder to catch alight with the next blast.

As the breaches opened over a wider areas, the trees had changed from collateral damage to targeted sacrifices. Monitoring the forest floor from the air was vital to detect breaches, and so the region had started to be purposefully deforested. Treecutters, Ket called them, explosives that detonated just above the ground, sending a disk of shrapnel to shatter the base of trunks. In order to protect the forest, Elf-ans had started to cut it apart.

Cadden brought the hoverjet to a stop above the centre of the field of ash and craters. 'Hawk to all Thorn aircraft, take up pre-planned positions and arm clearing charges. Signal when ready by setting transponders to emergency mode.'

The sky filled with hundreds of hoverjets as half the formation overtook the Hawk. Ships great and small proceeded in chaotic order to arrange themselves into a circle a kilometre across, centred on the breach.

At Cadden's nudge, Xia turned to the console at her side, flicking a series of heavy switches to bring the Hawk's bomb racks online.

Across the fleet, crews did likewise, their progress marked on Cadden's radar display, the scattered green dots of the other hoverjets turning an angry red. Emergency mode was designed to be used only by crashing vessels, there to call for rescue, but it had proved vital to coordinate so many jets without a thousand voices overloading the communication channels. Besides, Vandar's government was ignoring all signals from the deep forest, whether mundane or panicked.

As the last dot turned red, Cadden called back to Drekene. 'All set. Any last words for the troops?'

'Yes, put me on speaker to all Thorns.' The Deathless waited for the pilot to obey. 'Thorns, I will make this brief. You all know your role. You all know what is at stake. Do your duty today, and we can contain this threat. Fail, and Vandar—then the world —will be destroyed.'

'No pressure then,' Cadden whispered to Xia, then turned his own microphone to transmit to all pilots. 'Hawk to all Thorn ships, let's glass this area. Drop ordinance.'

Xia yanked a lever, its satisfying clunk answered by a vibration through the hoverjet's frame. From the thousand ships of the Thorn fleet, small black barrels dropped.

Then the forest burned.

A flash of light shone from below. In the downward-pointed turret camera, a white blast was all that Xia could see as the Hawk's bombs were joined by those from the surrounding craft. In the ensuing fireball, any fresh hole the Daem-ans had dug was buried, the heat hardening the already-scorched soil.

The blasts from the outer ships were shielded by the trees, but it was not long before their effect was all too clear. In a great circle, the canopy shook, wavered, then fell. A hundred trees, a thousand, ten thousand, toppled. Dust and birds launched into the air. In their wake appeared a new clearing, a perfect circle of death in the heart of the forest. A construction zone, ready to be turned into a metal bastion.

'Bombs dropped,' Cadden called. 'All ships, begin landing operations.'

Answering Cadden's call, the mass of ships began to descend. The Hawk rocketed ahead, burning towards the edge of the new clearing. Among countless other hoverjets, the aircraft lowered itself towards the splintered wood and felled trunks.

'Take care,' Xia shouted back as the Hawk's ramp

opened. The smell of ash and sap blew through the cabin.

Drekene turned, easily seeing over the heads of those behind her, and nodded. 'And you. I'll see you when this is over. Thorns, with me.'

And with a single wave, Drekene leapt out to the desolate forest floor. As soon as the last of her party had jumped from the ramp, Cadden pushed the Hawk back into the air. All around, thousands poured over the craters and splinters. Soldiers followed their sergeants to gather at the inner or outer ring, while Ket's engineering teams worked feverishly to turn five hundred decrepit hoverjets into a fortification. The Hawk joined the remaining vessels, protectively circling the ground troops.

An entire army, raised from volunteers, here to defend the world. And all Xia could do was watch.

Hours passed.

Xia stared through the turret's camera at the eerie calm below. Ket's workers toiled at the skeletons of a hundred hoverjets, the frame of a kilometre-wide ring of steel taking shape. Either side of this ring knelt the ground troops, weapons raised, waiting for a Daem assault.

An assault that simply never came.

Hoverjets circled. Soldiers crouched. The sun rose. Bored tension hung over the army. Evident in the impatient communications, the uncomfortable shifting of Xia's scouts in the cabin, and the fidgeting of the kneeling figures on her screen, nerves were wearing ever more raw. Waiting for something to happen. Anything. Dealing with a brutal assault would be preferable to waiting for it, expectant, fearful.

The monotony was broken, but not from below. A red flare lit the horizon, stretching into the midmorning sky.

Cadden saw it too. 'A distress flare. Must be from the Fury's Dawn.'

Xia watched as the pilot sent out multiple calls, trying to signal the downed ship. He would have no luck. Poor communication had plagued the Thorns for the past month. As relay towers in settlements were overrun, the fleet had to rely on the weak transmitters on the hoverjets. They could send signals over a long range, but could not cut through the forest.

'We know what's happening.' Xia stared flatly at him. 'They're under attack.'

Sighing, he nodded, changing his broadcast channel. 'Drekene, this is Hawk. Come in.'

'I read you.' Drekene's call was clear, coming from the now-levelled forest below.

'Fury's Dawn is under attack. They've sent up a flare.'

Drekene paused. 'They have numbers with them.'

'They're mostly engineers,' Xia objected. 'If they didn't need help, they wouldn't have sent the flare.'

A sigh came through from the Deathless. 'True, but we cannot afford to send anyone.'

'Dragon-shet,' Xia retorted. 'Send us. My scouts are just sitting up here, doing nothing.'

'We need you up there to counter the Daem attack.'

Xia had anticipated this answer. 'And that Daem attack is hitting the Fury's Dawn. Let us go. We cut off the Daem pack there, slaughter them, stop them ever reaching the perimeter.'

Drekene's reply was hesitant. 'If you leave, we're vulnerable to a Daem offensive down here.'

'And if we stay, everyone on the Fury's Dawn will die. For all we know, that could be the entire massed Daem horde, finishing the downed craft before turning on you. Please, Drekene, let us do this. We'll rescue the crew, kill the Daem-ans and be back before you know it.'

Another long pause from Drekene. 'Cadden, you're in charge of the air forces. Do you think you can make the pickup and get back without inordinate risk?'

Cadden's turn to hesitate. Xia met his eyes, pleading.

With a grimace, he nodded. 'Yes, Drekene. If we move now, we should get back with minimal losses. The more aircraft we take, the better our odds for dealing with a major attack. But even with all our mobile units, I can't make promises.'

'Fine,' Drekene grunted. 'Go. Take all air units. Be quick. Be safe.'

'And you.' Again, Cadden switched broadcast channels. 'Hawk to all air units. We're responding to the Fury's distress signal. Make best speed to the crash site and prepare a recovery.'

Followed by a swarm of aircraft, the Hawk ripped over the canopy.

'Thank you,' Xia whispered.

Weakly, he nodded. 'Just be safe. Don't make me regret this.'

She stood, kissed his head, and clambered down the cockpit steps. From its rack, she hefted her rifle, snapping a magazine into place.

Turning to the concerned faces in the cabin, Xia flicked the controls on her earpiece to transmit to the surrounding area. 'Thorn Scouts, we're going in to pick up the Fury's Dawn survivors. This is just like we've done a dozen times already, only we're picking up refugees from a hoverjet, not a city. Expect threats on landing.'

The wave of nods from the cabin, and the barked acknowledgements from other hoverjets, filled her with pride. Men and women twice her age deferred to her, obeyed without question. It was a heavy responsibility, but one she was proud to bear. She had never dreamed of having the loyalty of so many, or their respect.

From her bunk, Rikk chirped. He had finally learned to stay on board the Hawk when she dropped, but insisted on nuzzling her hand before her departures, and always got a cuddle when she returned. The small piece of routine seemed to settle them both.

'One minute.' Cadden warned.

Xia pushed her way to the rear, checked her grav-belt, and lowered the ramp. Air hot with jet fuel flooded the cabin, stinging Xia's eyes. Bracing against the wind, she attached one of the Hawk's ropes to her harness, the well-used nylon still smooth to the touch. She did not need the rope on the way down, but it would be useful for a speedy evacuation.

Cadden's voice filled her ear. 'Over the crash site. Go.'

Feet clanging over the metal, she leapt from the ramp, fresh air greeting her. In a clearing below, a long muddy trench led to the wreck of the Fury's Dawn. Engines, winglets, and cargo racks were all scattered over the meadow, but the craft's main compartment was remarkably intact. It swarmed with figures, some with bandaged arms or splinted legs, some kneeling with rifles and pistols. Surrounding them were broken creatures, the destroyed remains of the first wave of Daem-ans.

And approaching them from the forest's edge were five fresh monstrosities. Over the last month, she had become numb to their twisted forms. A horse's head on a snake's body. Insect pincers on a beast the size of a bear. Something that looked like a Gobl-an's torso atop the legs of an eagle. None of it startled her anymore. Horror was now her everyday.

Waiting for the last moment to activate her grav-belt, Xia landed hard, climbing shoes puncturing the soil. She recovered quickly, raising her weapon as a hundred of her cohort landed alongside.

They met the Daem-an's charge with rifle fire. Chitin splintered. Bone flew. Ichor poured. Xia felt a grim satisfaction as a twisted beast collapsed before her, far from the wrecked ship. This may not have been the task she had wanted, but at least she had a role to play in this last battle.

Xia's determination began to falter as the rescue proceeded easily. Too easily. At first, the hoverjets stayed safely overhead, turrets searching for prey as ropes winched the Fury's survivors. But as no more Daem-ans emerged, a few ships landed, rapidly packing in the downed crew and Xia's scouts.

As the sky darkened with the noon eclipse, Xia tensed. If the Daem-ans were going to strike, it would be now. Flares were thrown. Searchlights and turrets from hoverjets hungrily scoured the tree line, waiting for Daem-ans to charge.

Nothing.

With a heavy heart, Xia gripped her rope to be hauled back to the Hawk. They had committed all of the Thorn's reserve for this—at her insistence. They had saved the Fury's crew, but this was far from the full assault that she had expected, that she had hoped to face. There were still countless Daem-ans stalking the forest. Somewhere.

Unsettled, she pushed down the cramped cabin, giving Rikk a quick scratch of reassurance, and climbed into the cockpit.

'Take us back,' she ordered, unable to keep the worry from her voice. 'And get us high. See if we can re-establish communications with the construction site.'

Wordless, Cadden nodded, the Hawk leading the rescue party high above the canopy. It would burn more fuel, but gave them a better shot at getting a signal through the dense forest.

It did not take long for Cadden's calls for an update to receive a garbled response. He struggled to work through the static and overlapping signals, but at last a clear voice came through. Barked in panic, Drekene's voice blared through the cockpit speakers, sending a shiver down Xia's spine.

'Fall back. The line is overrun. Regroup at the southern rally point. Fall back!'

Chapter 27

Drekene watched the glowing trails of the hoverjets recede behind the tree line. She doubted her decision to let the reserves go after the Fury, but Xia had been right—sacrificing those hundred men and women for the 'greater good' was the exact line of thinking that had led the world to this situation. Bulwark was willing to let Vandar burn in order to hold their base. The Deathless Council were willing to sacrifice millions to make them relevant once more. Drekene's Thorns would be better.

She could only hope that the soldiers knelt beside her would not have to pay for her conscience.

Around her, the Thorns shifted uncomfortably. She knew the look on their faces, had seen it so many times over the centuries—the anticipation of battle. The Daem-ans would attack, these soldiers knew it as well as she, but none knew when.

They had made use of the morning, transforming the debris into a defensible position. Trunks were rolled into barricades. Splintered wood was cleared from the firing line. The steel barbs sprayed out by the treecutters had been retrieved from the mangled stumps and repurposed as barbs to impede the Daem advance.

Behind, Ket's crews were making good progress. The ring fortification took shape, old tankers steadily morphed into a long wall, broken with towers. It would be weak at first, and lacking in facilities, but those could be improved with time. It just had to hold this first assault.

To distract herself, and those around her, she broke into a sword kata. Her rendblade swung in arcs, whipping through the ash-filled air. Some of the younger Deathless had remarked on her dedication to the ancient weapon, but she had always been a reluctant learner—took nearly a century to learn to battleSing. When she tried, she picked up skills fast, but had always found it hard to motivate herself to learn something new. The idea of trying to keep up with the constant shifting weapons technology held no appeal. Spears had given way to matchlocks, then flintlocks, then breach-loaded rifles, semi-automatics, full automatics. Each required its own set of skills to use, only to become irrelevant a generation later. Her blade served her well over centuries, constantly repaired by generation after generation of metalSigners. It would serve her today.

She did not really need the practice—each step, each strike, having long become second nature. These days, she went through the motions to centre herself, a form of meditation. Her thoughts stilled, her worries quietened. The world she had been born into was long gone. She had forgotten more faces than most people ever saw. Even Bulwark, her home, was barely recognisable. But this blade never changed. The firmness of its handle, the weight of its shaft, the sound of it whipping through the air, gave consistency in an alien world.

A shadow crept over the construction site, stilling Drekene. The noon eclipse. In the darkness, a low rumble reverberated. A sweet stench Drekene had first smelled half a millennium ago reached her nose once more.

Sulphur.

Rifle-mounted torches cut into the dark. Soldiers hurled flares, filling the centre of the circular perimeter with a burning red light. But Drekene already knew what approached.

Daem-ans.

Dozens of them.

Claws and talons and gnashing jaws broke through the ground, the entire area around the first breach swarming with black and broken Daem flesh, horrific and beautiful. This was a coordinated strike. The Daem-ans had been just below the surface, waiting for the dark to descend.

'Hold nothing back,' she yelled. 'Open fire.'

As misshapen hunks of flesh lurched from the soil, they were met with a hail of bullets. Tracers scoured coloured lines into the night. Torches highlighted the emerging Daem-ans as they were pounded by the Thorn's rifle shots. Some beasts fell. Others struggled on, limping on shattered legs and dragging themselves on the stubs of arms. All were quickly replaced by the endless ranks of reinforcements that emerged from the ground.

Drekene began her battleSong. Words memorised centuries before came easily, the rhythm as natural as her pulse. Once, Ash battleSinging could be heard across the continent, in warbands, mercenary units and the halls of lords the land over. A migratory people, the Ash-ans simply moved where they could find the fiercest fight.

Now, the Song of Ash-az was all but lost. His

people reduced to a handful of Deathless, a mortally wounded race, drawing its last shuddering breaths.

Despite the destruction of Ash-az's people, the battleSong still carried power. Drekene could feel it inspire those around, feel time seem to slow as her reflexes increased. It would have the opposite effect in those who threatened her, dulling their minds, slowing their reactions. An invaluable tool in conflict, having turned the tide of a thousand battles throughout history, squandered in the Northern Extinction as the Avatars lead the Glac and Ash races to their demise, robbing the world of warriors it sorely needed.

No Daem-ans reached her. She stood, impassive, as those around her fired round after round into the charging horde. She dared not run into the fire to engage the beasts directly. Deathless or not, she could be killed by a single bullet, and this time she would not return—at least not in this form. Her soul would be dragged into the underworld, forever serving Daem-az as one of these beasts. It had been a foolish sacrifice, one every Deathless came to regret, but one that had seemed so vital at the time. Now, she would give anything to take back that decision, take back her soul.

But there was nothing to be done. The choice made long ago, all she could do now was deny Daem-az his prize for as long as possible—stay alive, and try to do some good with her stolen time.

Today, that simply involved standing here, Singing to her comrades. She wished she could Sing to the entire army, but her voice could not carry over the kilometres of this battlefield. Her earpiece would not work—Song could not be transmitted. It had been tried a hundred different ways, all without success. It was not the sound that carried the divine power, but the voice itself. No electronic gadget could replicate that perfection.

Turning north, Drekene frowned. That part of the perimeter was lit with far more intense rifle fire. Mangled silhouettes lumbered towards the line, many more than were heading for her position. The Daem-ans here in the centre were focusing their efforts north, only sending enough attacks to the rest of the line to keep the forces bogged down.

Letting her Song falter, Drekene touched her earpiece. 'Outer perimeter, any contact?'

'No,' Kriss responded. 'The south is clear.'

'Nothing in the north either,' Tallic said. 'Looks like… wait… by Elf-az, they're here. Dozens of them. Fire. Everyone open fire!'

His voice was drowned out by the snap of gunshots, then a piercing scream followed by silence.

'Tallic?' Drekene called. 'Tallic, respond.'

Her worst fears were confirmed as the wall to the north tumbled. The fragile metal framework, still unfinished, collapsed. Black figures swarmed over the twisted remains, caught in the glare of toppled floodlights.

As the inner perimeter defenders faltered at the din behind them, the Daem-ans surged. From inside and out, the monsters crashed through the line, meeting at the wall where they flung engineers like toys. The line had been breached. The Daem-ans poured into the construction site, slaughtering Ket's crews. With the air units still away, they had no way to retake the overrun wall, no way to hold their positions. The

Daem-ans would flood through the poorly-guarded engineering units, cutting them apart. The two perimeters would be cut off from one another, surrounded, doomed. By the time Xia returned, the damage would be done.

The battle was lost.

Now, all Drekene could do was mitigate this disaster. She had to save as much of the Thorn army as possible, else today was the day the world died.

She keyed her earpiece. 'Fall back. The line is overrun. Regroup at the southern rally point. Fall back!'

The soldiers around her paused, meeting her gaze with dismay, then broke into action. In teams they peeled away, half providing covering fire while the others sprinted back several paces before exchanging roles. Drekene could not help but smile with pride. These farmers, clerks and schoolteachers had become true warriors. In just a month, they had turned from a well-meaning militia into a cohesive army.

If even a few of them survived, perhaps this world was not doomed.

Cadden's voice crackled through her earpiece. 'This is the Hawk. We're on our way. Ten minutes out.'

'Begin evacuation immediately on arrival,' Drekene ordered. Ten minutes had never seemed such a long stretch of time.

Once more taking up her Song, Drekene backed away from the onrush of Daem-ans. She wanted to stay close to her soldiers so that her Song could inspire them, but made sure to put herself between the monsters and her retreating comrades.

Sensing blood, the Daem-ans rushed in all directions, charging the withdrawing army. A foot-tall monster was the first to reach her, a pig suspended from arachnid legs. So small, it weaved between the broken trees, staying sheltered from the constant fire.

It hesitated before leaping, her battleSong filling the creature with dread as it came within earshot. The delay was short, quickly overcome by the Daem-an's hunger for death, but it was all Drekene needed to fall into the required stance. As it leapt, she swung her blade. Serrated metal tore through its blackened flesh, cleaving it in two. The chunks passed either side, her face covered in hot blood that stank of sulphur.

Screams echoed through the darkness. As the army fell back in what order they could manage, the Daem-ans ran them down. Focusing their efforts from the north where they had broken through, the monsters were spreading down the building site. The partially-constructed wall became a climbing frame from which hideous creatures could launch their clawed attacks.

Pockets of soldiers were cut off by the sprinting Daem-ans. With rifle and pistol and wrench they fought, a hundred defiant last stands, ending the only way last stands ever did—slaughter.

As the surviving soldiers reached the rally point, some semblance of order was restored. A new perimeter was established on and around the half-built wall, thousands clustering in the lights of what was meant to become a tower. Sergeants hurried to regroup their squads, directing covering fire to support those soldiers still fleeing from the Daem line.

Rifle shots could be heard from the far side of the wall. They were surrounded. Looking around,

Drekene could only see a fraction of her army. How many had fallen? How many would still die?

She positioned herself ahead of the line once more, voice beginning to tire from the bellowed Song. Every Daem-an that managed to weave across the debris-filled landscape, she cut down. Her blade spun, severing limbs, claws, heads.

Bodies piled. The flow of retreating soldiers bled off, few still left on the field. Unending, the Daem-ans continued to charge.

A white glare broke over the distant tree line. The Thorn fleet. Searchlights flooded into the darkness, revealing a field that swarmed with twisted bodies, most still writhing.

Into the mass of Daem flesh, the hoverjets opened fire. A hundred turrets tore into the battlefield, rasping as tracer rounds riddled the horde. Daem bodies crumbled, skulls cracked, their remains pummelled into the dirt.

Yet still they came.

The armed vessels circled overhead, aiding the ground perimeter with fire from above. Shell casings clattered over the line, falling on the wall, sinking into mud.

Brave pilots lowered their vessels, doors and ramps open to let the surrounded army pack on board. With half the fleet dismantled over this attempted construction site, there would not be enough room for everyone, but at least some would survive.

As the evacuation commenced, the outer line drifted back, pulling in towards the rally point where jet after jet touched down. They lifted off seconds later, some with soldiers clinging to storage racks for lack of room.

Drekene backed across the broken ground, feet sinking into mud and cracking chunks of wood. Her sword flashed at the Daem-ans that made it this far, but there were few of those. Between the rifle fire and the turrets from above, little could get through. With a smirk, Drekene recognised the silhouette of the Hawk hovering above, its turret spewing death at anything that approached the Deathless. They were a good crew. Impulsive at times, but dedicated.

Then the fire faltered. One by one, the guns above fell silent, ammo belts running dry. The hail of casings ceased.

Sensing their moment, the underworld's beasts surged once more. Rifle fire lit the dark, the remaining soldiers emptying clips into the oncoming mass of mangled flesh, but nothing could stem the tide.

Once again, Drekene found her blade covered in sweet, disgusting ichor. The sulphur of Daem blood mixed with the copper of that from 'an. Black and red mixed over the mud, all caught in the white glow of searchlights.

Without ammunition, the hovering aircraft had no reason to remain so high. They dropped to the ground, landing in amongst the ground forces, doors open. The Hawk descended fifty metres behind Drekene. Xia stood at the open ramp, rifle firing. Pleading, she shouted at Drekene, waving her towards the ramp.

Instead, Drekene tapped a young Elf-an crouched beside her and jutted a finger towards the hoverjet, never breaking her Song. The man did not hesitate, sprinting to the waiting jet, hurrying other beleaguered troops. Good. Drekene would be the last to leave this field. Other Deathless may have forgotten why they had made their dark pact, but she remembered. She stood here only to protect others. Fighting Daem-ans to keep them away from the innocent was what Deathless were reborn for. This was her purpose.

Just off the Hawk's wing, the Albatross landed. The vessel was more of a transport than a combat craft, but the Thorns had decided to keep it rather than recycle its metal for fortification. As the second vessel in the fleet, the first to volunteer, it held a special place in the hearts of this army. It was a symbol of their resistance, a civilian ship turned into a weapon of war.

And it was a symbol that the Daem-ans would not abide. A emaciated monster—half Hum-an, half ogre, the size of a house—forced its way through the wavering perimeter. Too far for Drekene to reach, the beast shrugged off rifle wounds like gnat stings, and crashed into the Albatross. With a screech of metal the converted hoverjet shuddered at the impact, crumpled. A fuel line broke, then ignited. In an instant the fire spread, belching orange flames from the cabin. The men and women inside were reduced to agonised screams.

A volley of rifle fire cut down the Daem-an—too late, the Albatross nothing but a smouldering crypt. The other hoverjet pilots realised the danger as a second jet was torn in two by a towering scorpion-horse. With a wash of hot exhaust, the aircraft pulled away, ropes dropping from doors. It would take longer to evacuate using ropes, but it was better than losing any more aircraft.

The few remaining troops clustered around the dangling lines', gripping them in squads to be winched up while their comrades held the enemy back. Drekene backed towards the ropes lowered from the Hawk, blade swinging. She was drenched in ichor, corpses of man and beast piled high all over the field. Still, she held her ground, felling Daem-an after Daem-an.

Soon, she found herself alone. Other pockets still fought, but she had no way to break through to those desperate soldiers. The area was awash with Daem-ans, some injured, some dead, far too many unharmed.

Singing through a hoarse throat to keep the nearby Daem-ans slowed, Drekene jumped onto the one remaining rope, seizing it in one hand while the other gripped her sword. The line jolted and began to lift. Looking upward, she could see Xia peering over the Hawk's ramp. The joy on the girl's face warmed Drekene's heart.

The joy evaporated.

The Elf-an cried out in horror.

Pain wracked Drekene's leg, the force tugging at her almost enough to dislodge her grip. She looked down—a Daem-an had its reptilian jaws locked around her leg and rope both, fangs deep in her thigh.

With a whine, the Hawk dipped. The Daem-an was half the size of the hoverjet, too fat for the engines to overcome.

The beast shook its head, fresh pain tearing through her thigh. The Hawk wavered, thrown about by the mass tugging on the line. Another strong pull could bring the hoverjet down, could doom her remaining crew. No time to kill the creature. Not even time to cut through her own leg. Drekene had but one choice.

Giving Xia one last nod, she swung her sword

through the rope above her head, freeing the Hawk from herself and the Daem-an both. She fell, the jaws tightening around her.

The impact on a broken log knocked the wind from her lungs, her battleSong cut short. Not that it mattered. The Hawk had survived, hovering safely twenty feet from the ground. Cadden and Xia were alive. That would suffice.

Drekene blinked as light bloomed above. The sun peaked past Watcher, illuminating the land once more. As the Daem-an came to its feet, stalking over her, the Deathless refused to meet its gaze. She knew what awaited her. Knew the darkness and pain that would become her existence. For now, she would bask in the sun one last time.

Chapter 28

A cry escaped Xia's lips as the Daem-an lunged. Drekene, that towering woman, that paragon of strength, was snuffed out in a blur of gnashing teeth and ripping claws. The leader of the Thorns was dead.

Hands gripped her shoulders, pulled her away from the ramp's edge. Xia turned to see the Elf-an—about her age—who Drekene had ordered back to the Hawk in her stead. In her last act in this life, Drekene had proven herself to be the most noble person Xia had ever known.

Pushing through the crowded cabin, Xia forced her way to the cockpit, collapsing to her chair. Rikk clambered onto her lap, his normal spot on her bunk currently occupied by a bloodied Gobl woman. Hands flicking over his array of controls, Cadden gave orders to the Thorn jets, guiding their retreat.

Xia's nose wrinkled. The stench of blood and sulphur filled the cabin, clung to the clothes of all those they rescued. Drekene would have been coated in the same stink as she died. And for what? Her reward was not some glorious place at the side of her god, not an everlasting peace with her family. No, the woman would be reborn as one of *them*, cursed to throw her broken form at the surface again and again, dying over and over until the end of days.

Pulling Rikk close, Xia breathed deep into his soft fur. He smelled of damp and soup—far better than the reek that pervaded the hoverjet. Picking up on her mood, he whined. As the sunbathed forest rushed by, she held him close, clinging to his warmth.

Cadden pitched the Hawk, flying in a long arc over a field. Debris, muddy paths and scorched fire pits marked this clearing as one they had recently used. Led by the Hawk, the fleet settled onto the grass. With so many vessels left behind, they had an abundance of space. It had been weeks since she had seen the fleet spread so thin.

She briefly wondered how many survivors could possibly fit in the fragmented remains of the fleet, but she already knew the answer.

Far too few.

'Ket's alive.'

Xia turned to see Cadden climbing to join her and Rikk atop the Hawk. The vulfik dozed, head and paws dangling over the wing's edge.

Cadden dropped alongside her, muddy boots and legs swinging from the metal rim. 'Though I doubt he's going to be happy to find us sat on his ship.'

She just grimaced. 'I doubt he's going to be happy about a lot of things.'

With a sigh, he followed her gaze over the clearing, where the remaining Thorn vessels lay parked. 'No. This has been hard for us all.'

Today, there were no smiles on the faces of the Thorns. Some shed fresh tears over comrades, friends and loved ones lost. Others just stared into the distance. Too many bore bandages. The lilting melody of lifeSinging filled the air as those Elf-ans with the skill rushed between the critical patients. Others would have to make do with the few medical supplies they had left.

At least the hoverjets dotting the meadow were relatively intact. Rusted and modified as ever, but in much the same condition as they had been the previous day. Of course, there were far fewer aircraft this evening. Last night this field would have been packed, barely enough room between jets to squeeze through. Now, with half the fleet left behind at the aborted defences, the remaining craft sat in an abundance of space. Lonely. Isolated.

Even though Xia could see so many people, especially now with fewer obscuring jets, she knew that many were missing. She grimaced. Not missing. They lay dead on and around the ruins of the fortification.

Xia turned to Cadden. 'How many did we lose?'

He shrugged. 'I don't know. Kriss is trying to get the numbers. Everyone's mixed up on different transports. A lot of sergeants stayed behind while their squads evacuated, so we're having issues tracking-'

'What's the estimate?'

'A fifth of our force.'

Ten thousand. Xia closed her eyes, warm tears wetting her cheeks. Ten thousand men and women dead, their bodies torn apart and scattered by those beasts. They were volunteers. Brave civilians, barely trained to hold weapons but determined to protect their land.

And what now? If they had not held back the Daem-ans before, how could they do so after such losses? Looking out at the broken army, the tired faces, the open wounds, Xia knew the truth. They had failed. Drekene's quest had died with her.

The fact had not yet dawned on Cadden. 'Xia, once Kriss is back, we need to organise again, come up with a plan.'

'Good luck with that.' Her words were far more bitter than she intended.

'What's that supposed to mean?'

'What plan can you possibly come up with that can save us from this disaster?'

Cadden looked into the distance. 'The last plan still could work.'

'It failed once. What makes you think it won't do so again?'

Muscles in his neck tensed as he forced words out. 'But we didn't follow the plan.'

Xia frowned. 'Yes we did.'

He snapped his gaze to her, intense. 'No, we didn't. We abandoned the front.'

'We went to save the crew of the Fury.'

He smirked. 'We went to fight.'

'You would rather we left those people to die? That we didn't protect our own?'

His gaze became a glare. 'Damnit, Xia, stop lying to yourself. We did not go to save anyone, and you know it.'

She winced at his vehemence. 'What do you mean?'

'For shet sake, Xia, are you really that deep in denial?' At her blank expression, he pressed on. 'You didn't go out there to save 'an. You ordered us off-mission so that you could fight, so that you could kill more Daem-ans.'

'That's not true.'

'Yes it is. By every last 'az, Xia, I love you, but for

you this has never been about protecting anyone.'
Rikk whimpered, but Cadden continued his abrupt
tirade, unleashing a flurry of pent-up frustration.
'Hunting the first Daem-an. Sealing the first breach.
Travelling with us to raise reinforcements. Being on
the front of every battle since we returned to Vandar.
You're fooling yourself if you think you've been
doing all that for the people of Vandar. You've been
doing this for yourself. For revenge.'

Her voice was barely audible. 'Revenge for what?'

Emerald eyes bored into hers. 'For making you kill
your brother.'

'I didn't…'

'It was their fault, but you pulled the trigger. Your
bullet killed him. Not the Daem-ans. Since then,
you've hated them for it, for what they made you do.
Xia, I know you. I've seen your expression when you
face them, when you speak of them. You want to make
them pay. It's what's driven you since we met.'

Fresh tears stung her eyes. 'Why are you saying
this?'

'For a long time, there seemed no harm. Seemed
like you just needed to work through this. Every
Thorn has their own reasons to be here. As long as
you were by our side, it didn't matter to anyone why
you chose to stand with us. But now…'

She did not need him to finish. A sick realisation
shook her to the core. 'But now I've cost ten thousand
lives.'

His silence was all the confirmation she needed.
The truth of his words tore into her stomach. There
was no point denying what she now knew was true.
The fate of Vandar had never been what drove her into

battle. It certainly was not the reason she insisted on going to the Fury's Dawn. No, she had wanted to hurt the Daem-ans, had needed them to suffer.

Her hands were drenched in her brother's blood. *She* had led the Daem-an to her home. *She* had pulled the trigger. Father may have been right—there may have been another way to save Eddan. But she had made a snap decision, a decision that claimed her brother's life, a decision that she would never have had to make if not for those twisted monsters.

Now they had taken even more. She had let her desire for revenge draw her away from the front. If her reinforcements had been in position, they could have held back the Daem attack. The battle would have been tough, but it would not have descended into a rout.

Looking out at the Thorns, Xia saw their pain in a new light. The moans of the injured sounded more intense. Grief-stricken faces seemed to stare at her. These men and women had relied on her for protection. And she had abandoned them to spill more Daem blood.

'I'm sorry,' she muttered.

'Don't be sorry. Be better.'

'What can I do?'

Turning to the landing site, Cadden pointed. 'Help us lead them. With Drekene and Tallic gone, the remaining leaders of the Thorn must come together. That includes you. Like it or not, the scouts look up to you. The Elf-ans follow you—the first volunteer. The girl who stood up when wardens and governments and armies turned their backs. If we're to salvage this, to honour Drekene, we need you with us.'

Conviction growing, Xia nodded. 'I will.' And she meant it. She could not give up her hatred for the Daem-ans, but she had to care more for those around her. How had she been so foolish? So selfish? This war was not to punish the monsters of the underworld, but to protect this land from destruction. For all the 'an out there, for Drekene, for Eddan, she would do better.

A strange calm washed over her, and she found herself laughing at a thought.

'What?' Cadden raised an eyebrow. His anger had faded, and now he just looked tired.

She gave a bitter smile. 'You… said you loved me. You've never said that before.'

'Oh.' He chuckled awkwardly. 'Not exactly how I imagined telling you. Just sort of slipped out.'

Smile warming, she cautiously scooted over to rest her head on his shoulder. 'I love you too.'

Hesitant, an arm wrapped around her. In silence they sat, staring at the battered army. Her selfish desire for revenge had cost these people so much, but she was more determined than ever to make things right. Somehow, she would find a way to protect the forest, protect this army, no matter the cost.

Xia stared into the fire, listening to the pop and hiss of branches being devoured by the flames. Alongside her, Kriss, Ket and Cadden sat on folding chairs around the fire. Similar campfires burned across the night-shrouded field, small clusters of Thorns trying to recover. In the morning, all those men and women would look to Xia and her three companions for orders, for direction, for hope.

They had none to give.

Kriss leaned forward, continuing the debate that had raged for an hour. 'We just don't have the soldiers. No matter how we juggle the numbers, something is left short. We send enough troops to hold the perimeters and we'll have nothing held in reserve. It'll just be a repeat of today.'

'Yeah.' Ket scowled. 'And if we pull my engineers to hold the perimeters, we'll never get the wall up.'

Xia sighed. They had been going around in circles. 'And if we hold all my scouts in reserve, then the perimeter will be too thin, will break at every point. But if we evenly spread out our troops, we'll be open to another concentrated strike.'

Rikk chimed in with a whine. The poor mutt wanted to sleep, but couldn't when surrounded by so many uncertain 'an. Of course, he'd never think of leaving Xia's side to sleep in the Hawk.

'Let's face it.' Cadden tossed a twig into the fire, watching it writhe beneath the flames. 'We've missed our shot. This morning we had the numbers to pull this off. Today too many Thorns died, and not enough Daem-ans. Drekene's plan was good, but it was made for a larger army.' He held up a hand to forestall Xia's fifth apology of the night. 'No, we need to stop throwing blame. We need a plan.'

Kriss hissed, a terrifying sound from a man almost as large as Drekene. 'The 'az take the Daem-ans. They knew exactly where to hit us and when. If I didn't know better, I'd say that they attacked the Fury's Dawn to draw our reinforcements away. That they knew our plan.'

'Perhaps they did.' Xia grimaced. 'Drekene was

the only one of us who knew anything about those beasts. And even she didn't know it all. Who knows what they're capable of?'

Ket spat into the fire. 'They sure as shet do seem far too devious.' He gave a dark cackle. 'Well this's great. We're out-manned 'n' outsmarted. Anyone else feel we should just scarper to the Obsidian Isle? Let this damn continent burn, take our chances with the Dragons. Kriss here's a Drak-an, he can speak to them women, right?'

'Even you don't mean that,' Cadden muttered.

'Eh, maybe not. Still'd feel good to watch Bulwark deal with the pile of shet they created.'

Grunts of agreement. Even Cadden had lost his loyalty for his home fort. The Thorns were not Bulwark, not Vandar, but something else. An independent army, left fighting a war that others refused to acknowledge, saving a land all had abandoned.

'Well, if we don't have numbers, then we only have one option left.' Cadden looked around the campfire. 'We go back to what we were doing before. Fight the Daem-ans in the forest. Protect outlying settlements. Ask for volunteers. Build up our manpower.'

Kriss shook his head. 'Still left with all the problems we had before. More frequent attacks. Larger area. Dwindling supplies.'

'Yeah.' Ket barked a cackle. 'Not to mention there's more Daem-ans out there than ever. Shetting hundreds of the things.'

Cadden threw up his hands. 'Then what-'

A siren cut him off—a distant alarm, taken up by a

dozen repeaters scattered over the Thorn fleet.

The perimeter alert.

Uttering curses, the group scattered, Kriss towards his aircraft, the others to the Hawk. Rikk reached the ramp first, bounding up to cower in Xia's bunk. Cadden was close behind, taking the cockpit stairs in one leap to begin the start-up procedure. Lagging on her shorter legs, Xia sprinted up the ramp and reached the weapon rack, grabbing and loading her rifle, Ket pushing behind her to help Cadden.

After pocketing a spare magazine, Xia keyed her earpiece. 'Xia to scouts. What direction is the attack?'

'Erm, not an attack. I think.' The reply was uncertain, as if the speaker doubted her own words. 'We've got an airborne radar contact in the north. Big one.'

'Flying Daem-ans?'

'I don't think so. There's… transponders. Hundreds of them.'

Disbelieving, Xia hurried out, staring north. A roar built, sounding over the whine of spooling jet engines. The tree line glowed, rear-lit, then burst into dazzling white. Jets flew over the field, searchlights washing over the Thorn fleet. The sky filled with the blue glow of jets, the roar deafening as the hundreds of aircraft circled the field.

A gruff voice barked over Xia's earpiece, 'This is the warden craft Vixen, please state the nature of your emergency.'

'Uh, no emergency here,' Cadden replied.

'Then perhaps you should deactivate your emergency transponders. Permission to land?'

'Uh, granted?' Cadden seemed as lost as Xia.

The circling craft began to descend, finding space between Thorn vessels. Illuminated by each other's searchlights, the newcomers flew a disparate mix of aircraft—tankers landing beside sports jets, cargo shuttles and compact airliners.

One ovoid jet, aluminium hull painted dark green, set down on the grass before Xia. A wash of hot air, rich in jet fuel, flowed over the field. Light bloomed from its side as a ramp descended. Lit from behind, a man strolled down the ramp, rifle over shoulder, confidence in his step.

Father.

Stunned into silence, Xia could only stare as the man who raised her strolled down the ramp.

'Quite an army you've gathered,' he said off-handed. 'Puts my five thousand to shame.'

'Father?'

He smiled softly. 'I said I'd gather the wardens, and I did, plus a few thousand more volunteers sick of the government's games.'

Ket and Kriss in tow, Cadden ran over. 'Why didn't you signal us? Let us know you were on your way?'

Father's face darkened. 'Vandar's government set up jamming stations weeks ago. "To prevent panic." Made our job all the harder.' He glanced around, taking in the wounded, the weary faces, the fresh graves. 'I'm sorry it has taken us so long. You look like you've been to the underworld and back.'

'Could say that.' Ket grinned. 'Well, we needed numbers. A few thousand rifles certainly wouldn't hurt.'

Father laughed as Rikk bounded over to nuzzle

into his chest. 'Not just any rifles. I've brought every warden in Vandar. No finer shots in the world.'

'This could work.' Cadden couldn't hide his excitement. 'It's not the ten thousand we lost this morning, but it might just be enough. We can reclaim the construction site, can contain the Daem-ans here, now.'

He was right, this was their chance. If they held to the plan, they could actually turn this around, complete the wall, end the threat to Vandar. These thoughts buzzed in the back of her mind, but Xia paid them no attention. Only one thing mattered right now.

She threw her arms around Farther, thankful for his return, thankful for his reinforcements, thankful for the love she saw in his eyes in place of earlier resentment. With him at her side, there was hope.

Chapter 29

The familiar hum of the Hawk's engines reverberated through the cockpit. Illuminated by the first rays of dawn, the forest canopy opened before Xia. The green peaks of pines and oaks gave way to a crater of devastation. Trunks lay scattered over the bare circle, littered with corpses of 'an and beast alike.

But the dead were not the only occupants of the area around the breach. In a range of twisted shapes, Daem-ans clawed their way from the soil, which was now riddled with openings. A few mangled beasts paused as the Thorn fleet came into view, and on hooves and hands and flagella they fled, making for the tree line. Just to regroup, Xia knew. They would return.

In the middle of the battlefield stood the skeletal remains of the fortification. The ring of metal had barely been touched by the Daem-ans, only a few sections knocked down—to make room for beasts to scatter into the forest, judging by the deep tracks. Most of the structure remained, a series of half-built walls and partially dismantled hoverjets. Ket would have the material he needed, if only they managed to protect his engineers from another slaughter.

Cadden turned a dial on his communication panel. 'Hawk to all Thorn vessels, prepare to drop ordinance. Thermal devices over the breach. Shrapnel charges over the rest. Gunners, hold fire, conserve ammo.'

As before, the Hawk hurtled to the centre of the

field. Xia primed the bombs under the Hawk's wings. Ket and his engineers had worked tirelessly through the night to restock the charges, aided by the supplies Father had brought. No one had slept, but had instead spent the hours preparing or healing or grieving. Even given their exhaustion, it was clear they had made the right decision to not hesitate. The Daem-ans were pouring out the ground faster than ever. Even a day's delay would have left them hopelessly outnumbered.

One by one, the transponders on Cadden's radar display turned red. Even the wardens had admitted that abusing the emergency signal this way had its use.

Cadden brought the Hawk to a hover. 'Everyone's in position. All Thorn jets, release ordinance.'

Xia slammed the switches into position, and the bomb's fastenings released with a satisfying clunk. Unobscured by trees, the collective blast from the hundreds of Thorn craft was mesmerising. Directly below white light burned, scorching the ground, crumpling warrens and hardening the soil. Across the rest of the construction zone, small flashes unleashed waves of shrapnel. Glinting red in the morning light, the metal shards ripped into soil, bark and Daem flesh. The writhing mass of otherworldly creatures fell still in the spray of death, fresh ichor flowing into mud.

'All craft, begin landing operations.' Cadden pushed his control stick, forcing the Hawk into a dive over the chaos. Meters above the bloody ground he guided the jet to the Gate, a section of the wall left purposefully open to lure the Daem-ans. The towers either side were mere shells, fingers of steel that needed to be turned into the strongest gun emplacements in Vandar.

Ket leapt atop the back of Xia's chair. 'I best be going. Got a shet lot of work while you lot hover about. Oh, and Xia, do try not to piss it all up this time.' Despite his words, he grinned with a wink.

'Take care, Ket,' Xia replied.

'Oh don't say that.' The Greml-an hopped down with a cackle. 'That's what you said to Drekene, 'n' look what it got her!'

As the ramp swung down, releasing Ket and his band of engineers, Xia could only shake her head. The Greml-an meant well, in his own way. If he actually blamed her, he'd have been civil.

Above the heads of her scouts—who remained on the Hawk—a gust blew in the smell of the battlefield. Rotting flesh and gunpowder melded with the thick stench of sulphur, fresh from their latest kills.

The ramp groaned shut and the Hawk lifted into the sky. Across the construction zone, Thorn ground troops fell into positions. Engineers hurried to the wall, metalSingers already at work moulding jets into barricades while other mechanics made do with blow torches. Either side of the wall the lines fanned out, taking positions behind the debris, ready for the inevitable assault. Father and the wardens went to the outer perimeter, facing the tree line. They had the best eyes for movement in the forest, were the finest shots. They would face the hordes of Daem-ans that had broken through.

No one had any doubt. They would face another massed Daem attack. All the army could do was wait.

The morning dragged on with no contact. Xia was not fooled. She focused her attention on the cameras, listened to the occasional comments on the communication channels, waited for the attack they all knew was drawing near.

A voice nagged at the back of her mind, tempting her to break with the plan, to go out in search of the Daem army. Perhaps it was not waiting in ambush, but taking this chance to head out, to lunge towards the more populated cities, perhaps Enall itself. Her scouts could be the only chance of stopping the Daem horde.

With a grimace, she silenced that voice. Cadden had been right—her desire to fight the Daem-ans was behind such impulses. She wanted to be on the front, in the thick of combat, the one pulling the trigger, spilling black blood.

But this battle was about more than her. No, she would remain in reserve for as long as needed. If the Daem-ans did not show, then the walls would be complete. She would have her revenge in their failure, if not their deaths. Her actions had already cost the Thorns far too high a price.

As if sensing her mood, Cadden turned. 'Don't worry, Xia, this will work.'

'We've got fewer troops than before.'

'Yes, but we're going to stick together. Besides, those are wardens down there. I've seen how well you can shoot. A thousand of you? Sounds good to me. Not to mention that your father even managed to get some Bulwark troops together—even if they're all AWOL and probably classed as deserters.'

Xia smirked. 'Bark calling the mud brown there. Aren't you a deserter too?'

'Not at all,' he replied, jovial. 'We are on official business, carrying out the final orders of a Deathless.

We'll get a medal for this.'

'And if Bulwark gets communications through and orders you back?'

He grinned. '*Then* we'll go AWOL. Not before.'

Xia laughed, but had no time to reply before the sky darkened. As Watcher dipped in front of the sun, the noon eclipse began, a shadow blanketing the landscape, turning the verdant canopy a looming black.

Seemingly on cue, dirt sprayed from the ground. Illuminated by a hundred overhead searchlights, the soil moved, squirmed, then fell away. Legs, talons, wings, jaws and claws smashed through the dirt. As one, a pack of Daem-ans dragged themselves from the newly opened ground. Without a pause they launched themselves at the perimeter defences, only to be cut down by a volley of rifle rounds.

The battle had begun.

Cadden cut through the contact reports. 'All air units, conserve ammunition. Keep monitoring for the focal point of the attack.'

More creatures hauled themselves from the ground, matched on the far side of the wall by similar figures sprinting from the tree line. Looking at the beasts through the turret's camera, Xia's fingers itched to pull the trigger, rain death on those monsters, but Cadden was right—again. They needed to save what little ammunition the jets could carry for dealing with a focused attack. For now, she could only watch the ground forces fight, giving them what aid she could by directing the Hawk's searchlight to help them line up shot after shot.

It did not take long for the focus of the Daem-an's

rage to become clear. Although Daem-ans scattered to all points of the perimeter, more than half threw themselves towards the Gate and its two incomplete towers.

Through the opening in the wall, Xia could see the trees shake in the distance. Birds took flight. Trunks toppled. Then the forest disgorged an army. Misshapen beasts, twisted monsters and sinister reflections of 'an clambered over one another, pushing toward the Gate from the outside.

The wardens did not waver, firing with deadly accuracy. Knowing how the Daem-ans hid their vital organs, the wardens instead targeted clearly vulnerable areas. Knees shattered, heads were decapitated, slashing claws were blunted. Every shot counted, if not taking a life, at least crippling a Daem-an.

But they could not hold back the sheer numbers. It seemed as if every creature that escaped the field yesterday was focused there, pushing towards the Gate, charging to meet their new comrades from the breach.

Xia could not let that happen. 'To the west!'

Cadden was already rolling the Hawk. 'All Thorn air support, head to the Gate. Weapons free.'

'All scouts,' Xia barked into her own earpiece. 'Those of you not manning gunnery stations, drop over the Gate. Use grav-belts. Reinforce the line. We have to hold.'

As the Hawk careened to a stop above the gates, the scouts in the rear cabin slapped the ramp controls. Without second thought, they leapt into the air. Xia longed to join them, hated the thought of not standing by their side, but she was more valuable here.

Turning to the weapon console, she aimed the Hawk's turret at the onrushing mass of blackened flesh. Cadden nodded. She pulled the trigger. With a hundred other jets, the Hawk's guns opened fire. The cockpit shook at the recoil, the rasping sound grating behind Xia's eyes. White lines of tracers streaked through the dark, ploughing into the Daem pack.

Keeping up her onslaught, she fired in short bursts, partially to conserve ammo, partially to allow Cadden to steady the Hawk between shots. Ket had done a great job over the past weeks, building ingenious mechanisms to help balance the craft when firing, but it was far from perfect. Each burst sent the Hawk lurching back, the pilot having to fight to keep it from tumbling from the sky.

The Daem-ans died in droves. Like at Bulwark, they were cut to pieces by the automatic weapon fire, beasts large and tiny smashed into a pulp. And like at Bulwark, the tide did not relent.

As Xia pulled the trigger once more she was not answered by the brain-numbing rattle, but a click. Shet. Out of ammo. Despite all of Ket's modifications, the Hawk was only so large, only had so much room to store rounds. His metalSingers and the Drak flameSingers had toiled through the night to restock the various aircraft, but even they had limits. With its rounds spent, the Hawk was toothless.

Time for Xia to join the fight in person.

Leaping to her feet, she met Cadden's gaze. He opened his mouth to speak, but she already knew what he wanted to say.

'I'll be careful,' she promised. They kissed, all too briefly, then she hurried down the cockpit steps. Her rifle was tucked into the rack. Tugging it free, she caressed its smooth handle, strong barrel. After slamming in a fresh magazine, she filled her coarse flightsuit's pockets with all the remaining ammunition on board. Had a feeling she'd need it all.

Rikk followed from the cockpit, whimpering as he fought to keep his stance on the wavering aircraft.

'No.' Xia bent to ruffle the vulfik's snout. 'You stay here. Guard Cadden. Stay safe.'

Rikk get a whimper of protest, but hunkered down. He was a good boy, a loyal companion. At least he would not have to brave the insanity outside.

Sparing a final look to the cockpit, she ran to the rear of the Hawk. The ramp still hung open and she did not pause before flinging herself into the air, one hand on her rifle, the other on her grav-belt.

The darkness below was lit with gunfire and tracers. Catching handheld torches and airborne spotlights, two great masses charged the wall. Untold numbers of Daem-ans, pushing through from both sides. Between them, either side of the Gate, the Thorns fought. A thousand sounds overlapped— gunfire, screams, snarls, thundering footsteps, the crash of a Daem-an hitting the ground, the chant of metalSinging.

Leaving her grav-belt off, Xia plunged towards the chaos. The smell of battle swamped her. Sulphur. Gunpowder. Blood. The fighting was heaviest on the inside, gunfire barely staving off the mass of disjointed flesh that poured from the breach.

Xia activated her belt at the last moment and slammed into the mud, the soft surface cushioning as she collapsed onto her side. Covered in muck, she pushed to her feet and sprinted towards the breach, towards the constant flashes of a hundred rifles.

Wounded 'an staggered away from the front, some helped by friends to get to safety. Many would be fine, superficial cuts from glancing blows, needing only a bandage before they would be able to return to the fight. Others would never be the same, limbs missing or simply too damaged for even a lifeSigner to recover. And then there were the walking dead, men and women with wounds so grave that they would never again see the sun.

Xia's heart twisted at the sight, made all the more potent by those who clearly still clung to the hope of surviving their mortal wounds, but she had no time to dwell on their plight. She pushed to the front, dropping to a knee behind a scratched and torn trunk, and raised her rifle.

With the airships providing glaring illumination, she had no need for her scope's night vision. Before her Daem-ans lumbered in a mass, their black and broken skin glistening in the burning light.

She picked her target, a beast that looked like a giant porcupine, only those spines were made of shattered bone, oozing from their tips. Her first shot cracked its skull. Her second punctured the wound that was its neck. The third brought it crashing into the dirt.

Next she felled a two-headed snake the size of a vulfik. Then what appeared to be the front half of a goat, tottering on its two legs. A dragon-fly with only a lone wing. A Drak-an without a face. A whale dragging itself across the battlefield on fanged flippers. The endless variations of Daem-an assaulted her, one horror crawling over the carcass of the last.

Round after round she fired. As magazines emptied, she replaced them with practised efficiency. Around her, the Thorns did likewise, pouring death without mercy. Even the wounded—reeling from a Daem-an that burst through despite the mass of fire— had the forethought to leave their ammunition to their comrades before running, limping or crawling to safety.

Gradually, impossibly, the flow of Daem-ans eased. Gunshots lessened as fewer and fewer monsters broke through the dirt. The battlefield fell still. It seemed every 'an held a collective breath, expecting the next wave at any moment.

Nothing.

Sergeants gave wary shouts, warning their squads to stay alert. Engineers toiled behind, their welding and metalSinging now clear in the relative quiet, only having to compete with the moans of the wounded and uneasy shuffling.

Uneased by the stillness, Xia looked over the line. Everywhere the guns had fallen silent. Behind her, through the still-unfinished gate, the wardens' guns let out a few last barks, finishing the wounded, then joined the silent chorus. One at a time, grins broke out. Unbelieving prayers of thanks. Cries of joy. It was over. They had stood in the path of the otherworldly tide and held their ground. When Vandar and Bulwark, 'an and 'az had given up all hope, the Thorns had emerged victorious. A cheer began to fill the air, weak at first, then louder, resounding off the enclosing metal walls.

Then the ground shook.

Xia frowned, wondering if her sleep-deprived mind had imagined it, but no, another rumble through the dirt. Was the breach collapsing in on itself? Dare she hope for such fortune?

Another tremor, this one accompanied by a fresh stink of sulphur. The cheers died. Her heart froze as she stared towards the breach. In the centre of the battlefield, perfectly ringed by the wall, the soil bulged, rose. In place of a crater, a new hill stood at the heart of their round perimeter.

The hill burst upward. Clods of dirt fell away, filling the air with debris. Xia squinted through the murk, eyes focused on a massive form highlighted by the hovering searchlights.

As the dust settled, disbelieving cries filled the air. At the centre of the battlefield towered… something. A Daem-an. It was a worm with the head of a beetle, jaws flaring, half its face seeming melted. It would have been just another beast from the underworld if not for its size. Easily as wide as a house, it rose twenty meters from the ground, squirming under the glare of surrounding lights.

But it was not done. What she had first assumed were spines littering its body, she now realised were legs—thousands of them. They flailed at the ground, trying to force its mass up. This was just its head, she realised, the tip of an impossibly large monster.

Around its edge, smaller creatures struggled through, pushing past its bulk to fling themselves towards the line. Some took flight, others sprinted across the soil. Heart sinking, she realised the attack was not over, not even close. This leviathan had just been blocking the tunnel from the underworld. Who knew how many beasts were piled behind it, just waiting for this giant to clear the breach?

'Fire,' she yelled. 'Bring it down.'

They must stop it before it freed itself from the ground. It was not the colossus that she feared, but the untold masses waiting below. If they killed it in the hole, they had a chance, time to recover before the rest dug past. If it broke free, it could crush the wall like paper, opening the way for its comrades to pour over the Thorns, ending the world's last hope for salvation.

But how did one kill *that*? She fired round after round, ignoring the smaller creatures that scuttled, crawled or flew towards the perimeter, focused only on the worm. Some rounds bounced off, barely scratching the thick bone hide. Other bullets found weak points, breaking through flesh with a satisfying spray of ichor.

The beast did not react. Even with thousands of round impacting its skin, digging into its body, it seemed more frustrated at being stuck in the ground than at this onslaught.

Xia had fought many Daem-ans, and knew them well. Even small beasts could shrug off horrific injuries, only dying if you pierced a major organ—the heart, the brain. But where would such be on a creature this size? Her rounds were no more than pinpricks, marring small sections of flesh. There was no logic to Daem physiology, no pattern. She was far more likely to damage useless fatty tissue than ever find this thing's heart.

Gritting her teeth, she continued to fire, praying to Elf-az, to any god, for help.

Instead she was answered by a shadow. Strange.

What could cast a shadow between her and the searchlights?

Pain slammed into her back. A crack resounded from her neck. She was thrown to the dirt as a mass smashed into her from behind, fire blooming in her spine. Uselessly, she struggled to roll over, but her muscles would not obey. Below her head, she could not feel anything but agony.

Her vision span. Something flung her like a doll across the dirt. Blood suffused the air, her face feeling cold as she landed on her back, only bringing fresh pain. She couldn't move her head, her body, just look around with terrified eyes. A black mass filled her vision—a Daem-an looming over her, black wings flaring, bone talons striking into the soil. On its mangled face, she could swear that she saw a grin.

Then it struck, a talon piercing her chest. There was no more pain, she could not even feel the impact, but the gouts of blood told her that it had hit a major artery. The world faded. Silent grey surrounded her. A clarity filled her awareness.

Xia died.

Formless nothingness surrounded Xia. This was not how she expected to feel, realising she was dead. She would have anticipated terror, dismay, anger. Instead, she simply felt calm. At peace. In the surrounding grey, she felt two pathways tug her, luring her onward. The first felt warm, joyful. She focused on it, finding radiance at the end of a tunnel. The light was bright, but not blinding. It welcomed her, drawing her towards its glow. Greenery spread out beyond, perfect trees, an endless forest. The realm of Elf-az.

And there, waiting at the gates to the afterlife, stood Mother and Eddan.

Bodiless, she somehow still gave a cry of joy. She moved towards them, towards her family. They would be reunited. They would wait for Father, then all would be together again. An eternity without pain, without Daem-ans, without suffering.

She froze. Something buzzed in the back of her awareness. A shadow of the future played over those loving faces, an hint of what awaited the world if she went to Mother, to Eddan. In an endless heartbeat, she saw it all. Saw that worm struggle free and unleash a massive wave of monsters in its wake. Saw them rip apart the Thorns, shatter Ket's defences, overwhelm the defenders whose guns ran dry, who faltered with exhaustion. Saw the black mass spread into the forest, an unstoppable army of destruction that would reach every corner of the continent. Then take to the sea. The Dragons of Obsidian Isle would put up a fight, but fall. The Archipelago would be demolished. All life would end.

Revolted, she turned her attention to the other path, where she saw only darkness. A horrendous, crippling black that would fill her. Another future played before her awareness, starting so sweet. She could be reborn, become Deathless. She would be one of Daem-az's minions, yes, but that connection worked both ways. She would see into the dark god's mind, would know how to bring down the worm. She would kill it before it escaped, leaving its corpse to block the breach. It would be the delay the thorns needed, giving them time to dig in, ready the defences, save the forest.

But that sweetness would turn to ash. She would

not age, just endure. She would watch Father die, see Cadden grow old and be buried. Life would lose its lustre. Friends would just be more people to lose. Each day would just become a step closer to the inevitable dark. And that dark was all-encompassing. Some day, she would fall, and be reborn again, but as a Daem-an. She would throw herself to the surface, hating the world, trying to slaughter innocents before she was killed, only to be born again. And again. The cycle of death would never stop. She would murder soldiers, families, children, and be killed in turn.

It was a dark future. A hopeless future. But it was the only future in which the forest survived. She froze, caught between the two paths, the two fates. Suffering filled both. Guilt. Heartache. By turning her back on the world, she would save herself from grief. By protecting the forest, would condemn herself to endless torture.

It was an impossible decision. A cruel decision, but one she had to make. One that, in this moment, became so clear. There was only one true option, one future she would embrace.

Turning back one last time to the light, to the welcoming gaze of her family, her heart hardened. This was not about her. This was about the forest, the world. There was but one route that led to the Thorns surviving, that led to her redemption. One dark, hateful choice.

She would be reborn.

Facing the darkness, she allowed Daem-az to take her, to work his dark power, to return her soul to the world.

She became Deathless.

Air filled Xia's lungs. Coated in her own blood, she took the first breath of her new life. Fire burned in her neck, her chest. A cold breeze blew into the opening in her heart, but she could already feel her wounds healing.

The battle still raged around her, only seconds having passed. The Daem-an that had killed her lay dead a few paces away, torn apart by rifle fire from her comrades. Those men and women stared at her in disbelief as she came to her feet and grasped her rifle.

She ignored their horror, turning to the worm struggling to free itself. She saw the beast in a new light, felt a part of it. There was beauty in its form, its rejection of order. It was not random, but free. Its melted face not a mistake in its creation but a denial of symmetry. There was sanity in its twisted body, a chaotic plan that seemed so obvious now.

Raising her rifle, she targeted a patch of its flesh near the dirt. How she had not located its heart before, she did not know. She fired a single round. There was no need for a second. A bellow echoed through the air, sweet sulphur belched from the dying worm's maw. Glorious ichor slopped out from where her bullet had landed, its heart beating out its blood in great globs.

With one last, fearful, lovely death-rattle, the thing collapsed, falling back into the ground. It settled down, the scream of Daem-ans trapped below music to Xia's ears. The battle fell silent, the fighting finished.

Eventually, the Daem-ans would dig through, would tear their way through the worm's corpse, carving its carcass into a stairway to the surface, but that grim, delicious work would take them days. By then, the defences would be ready. The fort would be strong—harsh order that would cage the Daem attacks.

A wash of jet exhaust buffeted her, the warmth seeming distant, weak. She turned to see the Hawk settling down over the sick, charming tableau of corpses. The ramp descended, and she forced herself to smile as Rikk and Cadden sprinted down.

'Xia,' Cadden panted, hurrying over the blood and gore. 'Thank every 'az. I thought we'd lost you when you fell, but-'

He froze, his eyes meeting hers, taking in the blackness there, the emptiness. Rikk saw it too. The vulfik whined, ears back, as he sheltered behind Cadden. At the sight of their horror, Xia felt ill, hopeless, alone.

And full of joy.

Epilogue

Hand-in-hand with Cadden, Xia walked along the walls of Thicket—the name they had given to the Thorn's fort. That morning, on the first anniversary of Xia's rebirth, the Daem-ans had mounted their greatest attack to date. Like all their assaults, it had been crushed. Under Ket's cannons and the guns of Xia's scouts, every last Daem-an had fallen. They had damaged the wall, of course, killed defenders, but that was just life out here on the new front line.

Now she strolled through the carnage, the gloriously disturbing smells of blood and sulphur filling her senses. After a year like this, of being half-alive, half-damned, Xia felt no more at peace. Every sight, every smell, every taste brought two responses, both seemingly natural, one that gave her hope, the other made her know only horror.

The cries of the wounded sent a shiver down her spine, while putting a smile on her face. A dismembered hand—buried under a collapsed section of tower—turned her stomach and made her salivate. The neat rows of tarp-covered bodies awaiting incineration made her tearful, made her proud.

Even Cadden was a paradox. He had stayed by her side, loved her more intensely than she could have ever hoped, and for it she loved him back, and hated him to the core. His smile brought her delight, while his beauty brought her disgust. The warmth of his touch was at once joyful and agonising. When they kissed she was filled with calm and turmoil. He relaxed her. He tormented her.

In some ways, she was thankful that Rikk refused to get close. She could hold onto her memories of him, unblemished. Alone and sleepless at night, she could still remember what it had felt like to hold his fur close and feel nothing but joy. She still constantly saw the mutt—who had adopted Cadden—but he kept his distance. A sweet, tainted reminder of life.

Father had been the same for a while—thankfully avoiding Xia while he came to terms with her choice, her sacrifice, her greatest error. Then a month ago he had turned up at the door, ready to accept her, to make the most of the time they had together before they would be forever separated by his death. She loved him for that. She hated him. Now her every childhood memory was tainted with the revulsion, fear and anger that his presence elicited. His acceptance gave her hope, brought her closure, and tore her to pieces.

They walked towards the most damaged section of Thicket, where the Daem-ans had managed to shatter Ket's largest gun through sheer numbers. Thicket was huge now. After months of hunting, they had cleared the forest of remaining Daem-ans, and none had managed to break through the circular defences. The outside was now filled with barracks, factories, landing fields.

The Thorn fleet still flew constantly, not hunting, but trading. Explosives were exported, tankers coming back with food and supplies. With the number of lifeSingers in the Thorns, they needed little extra. Orchards filled the region between the wall and the tree line. Tended by teams of lifeSingers, they provided a bounty.

Vandar objected, of course, not wanting so much of their land to be annexed by the Thorns. But they had no choice. By the time they had finally responded to the breach with a token force, the Thorns were already legend. Volunteers flocked from across the world. She hated to give the Deathless Council credit, but they had been right. This breach had reminded the world why they needed defences like Bulwark, like Thicket. Funding poured in. The world respected them. For now.

Ahead, the shattered turret lay surrounded by bodies—Elf-ans, Daem-ans and the unidentifiable. Crimson blood blended with black ichor, a horrendous, awe-inspiring pattern of death.

Something shifted. In an instant, Xia's rifle was in her hands, scope on, weapon trained. Her life was now torture, but she was determined to use her stolen time to make the Daem-ans pay for doing this to her, causing her such pain. If one of those monsters had survived, she would send it straight back to the underworld.

A figure rose, but not a Daem-an. A young Elf-an stood, his back shattered, bloody, a metal shard the size of a plate cutting into his ribs. With a shaking hand, he reached behind him, tugging the metal. In a flow of blood and gristle, the shard tore free.

Even before he turned, Xia knew the truth. There was no way anyone could survive those wounds, and this young man was no exception. He staggered around, black eyes meeting hers.

And for him, she wept.

ACKNOWLEDGEMENTS

First of all, I would like to thank Laurence King. His mentorship has turned me into the writer I am today. Without his patient advice, editing and proof reading, none of this would be possible.

Thank you to Neil Rankin, who put designed the covers. His work is absolutely stunning, unique and professional. I could not be happier with how they came together.

A big thank you goes to my parents, for always encouraging my writing from the days when it was just paper stapled together to make books, all the way through to now.

I would also like to thank all of my other beta-readers—Charlotte, Fiona and Michael. Thank you for putting up with some very rusty work and giving invaluable feedback.

Most of all, I would like to thank my wife, Emma. Without her help, support and constant encouragement, I would have given up a long time ago.

Soul Thief

by K. J. T. Carr

Now available on Kindle

The morning sun shone through the curtains of Takket's waystation room. By the time the sun rose again, either he'd have proven himself to be the greatest thief in the Imperium, or he would have been burned to ash.

A hundred thieves, some Mages, most Mundanes, had tried to steal the bones of the angel of Southreach. All had been immolated. The Soulshards left in the ash now adorned the temple that housed the bones--a warning against other thieves foolish enough to repeat the attempt.

His predecessors had all failed for the same reason—lack of patience. They tried to break into the temple in a single night, or brute force their way through the guards. They opted for the exact methods the priests expected. Takket had a different plan. Today, the priests would invite him inside.

Staring into the mirror, Takket neatened his elegant beard. He would miss it when he shaved, but it was too memorable to keep. High Priest Innavonus was well known for his exquisite beard, and, for today only, Takket would become that man.

The previous evening, he had arrived in this

waystation with a beard bushy, and dirty in the battered tunic and riding boots of a horse messenger. Now, the neat beard was matched by slicked back hair. His clothing had been replaced with the immaculate red cloak of a Circlist priest. He had completed his transformation by smearing a pigment through his greying brown hair, turning it a pure white. Annoyed, he realised these days there was no need to accentuate his wrinkles.

The time and expense he had invested in this day astonished him. The cloak alone had cost a year's wages in Soulshard flakes. The investment would be worth every Shard. No one would doubt his disguise. No one would remember his average build, brown eyes or fair complexion. No, they would remember the grey hair, the beard, the fine clothing. Give people something remarkable yet replaceable to remember, and the trivial details would be forgotten.

Casting one last glance to the mirror, Takket shouldered his leather travelling bag--now containing the plain clothes he had arrived in and a long length of rope--and strode out through the door into a hallway of varnished mahogany floorboards and wall panels, flanked by oil paintings exhibiting religious and historical scenes--all lit from above with the ever-shifting red glow of Shard chandeliers. So close to the city of Southreach, this waystation must attract many important guests.

He descended the curling staircase at the end on the corridor, running a hand down the banister, to the main reception hall. The early morning light was just breaking through the stained-glass windows at the front of the building, the images of angels and demons scattering the room with multicoloured light. A lone attendant snoozed at the desk.

Takket strode towards the man, his riding boots thudding over an extravagant maroon rug, startling the attendant. The man's face fell as he saw Takket's cloak.

'Pardon, sir,' he stammered apologetically, straightening his brass-buttoned jacket. 'They didn't tell me we had a high priest staying with us.'

Takket raised his nose imperiously and lied in his best high-class Indspire accent. 'Yes, well I don't like having to deal with the...' he waved a hand towards the man '...help. My driver booked us in yesterday. During my mediation last night, it seems the dullard decided to help himself rather freely to your bar here. He's sleeping it off upstairs.'

The attendant's smile was quickly hidden as he caught Takket's glare. 'My apologies if our staff encouraged him in any way. I'll have words with restaurant manager. Is there anything I can do to help you today?'

'Yes. I have an appointment in the high temple in an hour, and it seems I am in need of a new driver. Can you organise one for me? I'll settle the bill when I return--demons know how much I already owe for that man's bar fees.'

'Of course, sir. Horse or Shard?'

Takket glared at the man as if he had just spat on his cloak. 'Shard, of course.'

'Right away.' The man scuttled towards the main doors. Takket followed at a more sedate pace. He took no joy from tormenting the poor man, but it was good to get into character. Besides, lying was a skill like any other, and to hone a skill you had to practice. He made sure to lie at least once a day, warming up with an easy falsehood.

Takket heaved open the stained-glass doors and was greeted by the brisk southern wind, which carried a metallic smell. The low sun glared through the Sharddust kicked up by the wind, casting a red hue over the cobbled driveway of the waystation. The dust was thick here, so close to the major city of Southreach. Fine red particles mixed with the morning mist to surround the waystation like soup. He could barely see to the end of the drive, let alone the landscape beyond. The only indication that anything existed within the all-concealing haze was the muffled call of unseen birds.

The crunch of a cart rolling over dust-caked cobbles drew Takket's attention. A tall horseless carriage pulled up--its wooden frame layered in black paint--and its driver hopped down from his seat in front of the enclosed passenger cabin.

'Where to?' The man lowered his red-stained woollen face covering to give Takket an obviously forced smile. All Mages were terrible at covering their emotions.

'The Circlist Temple of the Angel of Southreach,' Takket replied with an air of authority. 'As quick as you can.'

'As you say.' The driver pulled open the carriage's door for Takket to climb aboard. The passenger cabin was plush, red velvet cushions overlaying the blackened wood frame. Clear glass windows looked out at all angles into the red haze. Not the cheap kind either, these were modern Mage-crafted windows that barely distorted the light at all. If this was the class of carriage in the waystations, Southreach really was trying to compete with the capital for luxury.

The driver tugged a set of riding goggles over his eyes and slammed the door. Just the other side of the front window, he climbed onto his perch.

Takket set his bag to one side and took a seat along one of the benches inside the cabin. Yanking his woollen scarf back over his face with his right hand, the driver reached down with his left. From a compartment below, he drew out a Soulshard about the size of a finger. The Shard responded to the Mage's gloved touch by amplifying its glow from a dull twinkle to a radiant red.

Its brightness increased further as the carriage lurched into motion. Takket settled back into his surprisingly soft bench as the coachman guided the vehicle out of the driveway, the Mage steering with one hand while drawing on the Shard's power with the other. The cart creaked and shook its way over the cobbles. Thankfully, it was not long before they joined the smoothed main road leading to Southreach.

No sooner had they cleared the drive than the Soulshard in the driver's hand disintegrated into fine red dust, its power exhausted. The driver cast the dust to the side, the handful joining the sea of red Sharddust floating in the wind.

The cart slowed little in the time it took the driver to retrieve a new Shard, this one the size of an adult's hand. The cart began to accelerate rapidly to speeds faster than a horse in full gallop.

The large Soulshard rock would probably have enough power to reach Southreach--assuming the driver was a competent Mage. Even then, the price would be exorbitant. Shard carriages were a luxury afforded only by the very rich, far less efficient than the Shardrails, but travelling on a train packed with passengers would just draw attention to Takket's disguise. Besides, it was not like he was actually going to pay for this journey.

A murky landscape whipped by. Fields of root vegetables braced the road, interspersed with ramshackle pig farms and the occasional hamlet. As the sun burned off the morning fog, the view became clearer, but the red persisted. Sharddust hovered near the ground, slowly settling into piles by trees and houses, only to be kicked up by the slightest breeze. The rivers that crossed the road under stone bridges were stained blood red. The dust was a constant in the world, but it was always thicker this close to major cities.

By the time they reached the outskirts of Southreach, the sun was high enough in the sky to no longer be completely filtered by the layer of Sharddust. Although a general redness still dominated, other colours now became visible--bright yellows of tree leaves, deep purples of hedgerows along the roadside, dark greys of buildings.

Those buildings grew ever more frequent. First they were single-floor cottages at the very edge of the city, the hovels of the poorest of Mundanes. They steadily rose in height to two, three, then four storeys, the space between them constricting into only the narrowest of alleyways. Traffic increased at the same rate, horse carts and pedestrians rapidly filling the road, forcing Takket's driver to slow to a crawl. Mundanes of all ages packed the streets. Their heavy woollen cloaks were tucked tightly against the bitter southern cold, the drab fabric decorated only in the unwanted dusting of the red haze. Muffled through the cart's windows came the cries of shopkeepers, shouts of men and women dodging carts, and screams of infants.

Eventually, Takket's cart clattered its way to the old city walls, passing under the archway that had once stood as a battle-ready gatehouse, now nothing more than a marker for the wealthy core of Southreach. Once through, the houses were more widely separated, and were constructed in an archaic style. One or two levels at their base, each had a narrow tower rising up to various heights, imitations of the ancient Magetower that loomed high above the rest of the city.

That tower dwarfed the rest of Southreach. At least thirty storeys high, and as wide as a hamlet at its base, it gently narrowed to a crowned peak. Far above the layer of Sharddust, the view from the top would be breathtaking. It still stood as a wonder, centuries after its creator had died. Takket had to give the long-dead man grudging respect--few knew the name of the Magelord who had constructed the tower, but his legacy stood the test of time.

They rolled their way towards its base, moving much faster now that the traffic had thinned to only a scattering of Shard carts.

The driver guided the carriage around the corner of a mansion and their destination came into view: a red-stone building that would have been imposing had it not sat at the foot of the much larger Magetower. The structure--the Circlist Temple of the Angel--was fronted with two small replicas of the Magetower, each about four floors high. Between them hung a massive black granite ring, through which the morning sun now peeked.

The cart stopped by the stairs leading up to the temple. Hopping from his perch, the driver pulled down his face mask and opened the door. Shouldering his pack, Takket was greeted by the stench of the city. The coppery tang of Sharddust was almost overpowering, contrasting with the background odour of the waste of thousands upon thousands of people. Unfortunately, he frequently had to endure major cities in his profession. Priceless artefacts were seldom found in hilltop monasteries.

With the smell came the gentle sounds of the inner city. Carts crunched over the Sharddust on the roads, birds chirped in gardens, and people engaged in pleasant conversation. All of this was muffled by the red haze, the Sharddust filtering sound and light alike.

Turning his attention to the matter at hand, Takket began making his leisurely way to the temple. The hem of his cloak dragged over the smoothed marble staircase, picking up the fine red Sharddust that collected on the edges of the steps.

At the top of the stairs, he was greeted by a young acolyte in a rough-spun black cloak, who--on seeing Takket's clothing--bowed low, hand over heart.

'High Priest Innavonus,' the young man greeted. 'We are honoured to have you here.'

'I am here to meet High Priest Instantino,' Takket said regally.

'The High Priest is expecting you in the angel's shrine. Follow me, please. May I take your pack?'

'No, thank you,' Takket replied. 'Sloth is the ally of the demons. I will not allow myself to become pampered.'

The young man nodded thoughtfully and pushed open the two great doors to the temple. Takket followed him into a vaulted hallway, lit from above with Soulshard chandeliers. A gaggle of acolytes hurried to the entrance, sweeping the polished stone floor to clear Sharddust that drifted in from outside. Keeping a building this large free of the red haze was a full time job for the lowest ranked in the temple.

Takket's guide took a right at a branch in the hallway, following a gently curving corridor. The temple had the same layout as all Circlist temples, the bulk of the building forming a large ring enclosing a circular courtyard. The scale of this temple, however, put most others to shame. The ceiling towered so far above that there was a notable delay between footstep and echo. The glass windows to the side stretched up to meet the ceiling, alternating between stained glass masterpieces and clear panes to allow natural light to bathe the hallway.

Through the windows, Takket could see the ceremonial courtyard. Not the simple gravel or stone courtyards that most temples made do with, but a lush green paradise, with tall trees and even grass. Takket had to admit he was impressed that they managed to cultivate the grass with so much Sharddust outside the temple walls, but the tall building surely kept the majority of the low-lying dust at bay. Set against the green background were red marble statues of angels and demons engaging in their unending battle.

The building was meant to impress, to show the

power of the Circlists, demonstrate the skill of their
Mage architects. Takket would have been overawed,
had his mind not been focused on his impending
crime.

The acolyte pushed aside a polished mahogany
door and ushered Takket into a darkened chapel. As
the door creaked shut behind him, the only natural
light filtered through a stained glass window high on
the far wall. His attention was drawn to a pool of
flickering red light in the centre of the room, where an
object rested on a pedestal made of interlocked
Soulshards. Silhouetted against their combined light, a
figure rose from a crouch.

'High Priest Innavonus, I presume,' a strong voice
called out, echoing through the expansive shrine.

'Yes.' Takket crossed to the man. 'High Priest
Instantino, it is good to finally meet you in person.'

'It is.' Instantino gave a bow, which Takket
returned. 'Though it feels as if I already know you
better than I know some of my colleagues.'

'It does.' Takket flashed a fond smile as he walked
up to the other man in the uneven light of the
Soulshards. He looked older than Takket had
expected, only a few strands of hair clinging to his
head. Small eyes looked out under bushy eyebrows.
The man wore an identical robe to Takket, the bright
red glittering in the unsteady light.

Takket really did feel he knew Instantino, though
their relationship was rather more one-sided than the
priest suspected. Takket had been intercepting the
messages between the two high priests for the past
year, and editing the responses for three months. The
real High Priest Innavonus had no intention of ever

making the strenuous journey to visit Southreach, but so far as Instantino knew, this was a lifelong dream.

Playing the part, Takket turned to gaze at the object atop the pedestal. There, illuminated by the Soulshards, suspended in a cylinder of solid glass, rested the bones of an infant. Not just any child, this skeleton proudly displayed a pair of wings rising from its shoulders. As Takket approached, he could see other abnormalities: the skull was disproportionately large--even for a child--the forehead strangely grooved, the limbs too short.

'The Angel of Southreach,' Takket breathed.

'Stillborn from a human woman,' the priest intoned. 'Proof of Circlist doctrine.'

Takket suppressed a smirk. It proved nothing, certainly not circular reincarnation. It could be a natural malformation. It could be an elaborate fake. It mattered little. The bones were famous across the globe, priceless, sought after by collectors, fanatics, Circlists and Scalists alike. Wars had started and had been ended by these bones. Magelords of old had died in their pursuit. Empires had crumbled, and the Imperium had risen in their name. They had sat here in this temple for almost a century, guarded by the Mages that filled this building.

Tonight, those bones would belong to Takket.

It was well into the night by the time Takket extricated himself from Instantino and the rest of the priesthood. Shortly after meeting the High Priest, Takket had been whisked away on a grand tour of the temple. His parade through room after stuffy room had given way to a roast lunch with the senior priests, most of whom quizzed him about life in the capital and the health of Arcane-lord Venning Indel.

The afternoon had proved the most challenging part of the day, as Takket was expected to deliver a sermon to the temple's resident priesthood. Takket had never been an overly religious man, and he viewed the various sects with equal scepticism, so he doubted a lecture on religious doctrine would be convincing. Instead he spoke of politics. He had spent more than enough time infiltrating high society to have become adept at discussing taxes, the authority of the Arcane-lord, the rights of Mundanes. Takket had launched into a tirade against the New World across the seas, urging action to spread Circlism to replace the dominant Scalist views there. If it was the one commonality to all people, it was the love of having their views reinforced publicly. His speech was met with a standing ovation.

Takket had spent the banquet dinner asking questions that he knew would illicit lengthy responses. He nodded along quietly, sampling the range of parsnips, carrots and pork on offer, speaking only to draw more information from his companions. Long ago, he had found that the easiest way to avoid giving away a disguise was to allow others to do the talking. Thankfully, talking was a favoured pastime of priests. After the meal, Instantino had granted Takket permission to pray privately before the angel's bones.

Exhausted from a day of lying and play-acting, he now finally stood alone in the angel's shrine. The sun had set long ago, and only the occasional flicker of a street lamp highlighted the lone window. Otherwise the only source of light was the pedestal, casting its ever-shifting light over the room.

Takket crossed to the pedestal and examined the bones. The glass encasement was strong, formed by a Mage to survive rough handling. The pedestal itself looked stronger still--imported Soulshard batons, each the size of a forearm, banded together with lead and driven into the ground. They would be worth a fortune, but Takket could not hope to lift them all, and prying apart the lead lining would cause too much of a din.

No, he could not steal the pedestal, but he could use it to aid his escape. He set his travel pack to one side and hauled out the length of rope. Made of modern artificial fibres, forged by the latest advances in Mage-crafting, the rope was strangely soft yet more than strong enough to hold his weight despite being the thickness of his thumb.

He wrapped the rope around the pedestal, tying his best knot in the dancing light. Satisfied, he shifted the contents of the bag--now only his cheap travelling clothes--and turned to the bones.

He would have given a quick prayer to the angels, but somehow doubted they would aid him in this task. Instead, he asked the demons to help him with this act of mischief, and hefted the cold glass block containing the bones. Not as heavy as he feared, though he still felt a strain in his legs as he lowered the bones into his satchel.

He secured the loose end of the rope around his waist and shouldered his pack. Hurrying over to the far wall, he looked up to the reflected light of the window. The lower window sill was a good fifteen feet high, but thankfully the gaps between the red marble wall sections were large enough to use as handholds.

The climb was not easy, the sharp marble corners cutting into his fingers, his heavy pack dragging him down, the polished surface giving poor grip, but it was hardly the most difficult climb he had ever attempted. Scaling the ancient tower of Iggranious had been far more challenging. Getting down again had been worse.

With a grunt, he pulled himself onto the narrow window sill, the marble platform icy to the touch. The stained glass twinkled with the glow of street lamps and the reflected Soulshard light. He could try to twist away the lead lining holding together the panes, lower them softly to the ground one by one, but that would take time--time enough for a passer-by outside to notice the disappearing window and sound an alarm.

No. Takket would go for the direct approach. He untied the rope around his waist and secured it to the bag. With a quick plea to the demons, he closed his eyes and flung the pack through the glass. The heavy block within his pack made short work of the decorative panes, punching a sizable hole through the window.

Takket grabbed the rope to slow the bag's decent, as the sound of glass on cobbles echoed across the city. After lowering his pack to the floor, he flung himself out into the chilling wind and rapidly descended the rope to the street below.

Takket shivered as the wind buffeted him, smells of coal fires and gas lanterns carried in the night's breeze. Hands already beginning to shake, he untied his pack and sprinted towards a nearby alleyway. Gas lamps stood as pools of red light in the haze, acting as markers for the streets rather than giving any real visibility. Sharddust persisted through the day and night alike, swallowing the city in this persistent fog. As shouts of alarm chased from behind, he lost himself in the maze of houses.

Allowing himself a grin, Takket sprinted in the direction of the old city gates. He had done it. He had stolen the sacred jewel of one of the Indel Imperium's great cities. Now all he had to do was escape.

Takket's cloak billowed as he sprinted towards the gatehouse, leather satchel weighing heavily over his shoulder, the strap creaking with each step. From behind, shouts of alarm had given way to a bell summoning aid from nearby watchmen. The guards at the gate were already peering curiously towards the noise, their monotonous duty finally interrupted by excitement. There was no way they would simply let Takket pass through, not when a chance to fulfil their role as law keepers had finally presented itself. They would search Takket's pack, question him for hours, anything to avoid going back to dully monitoring the gate.

Takket would have to offer them something more intriguing.

'Demons below, what are you doing?' he shouted. 'Can't you hear the alarms?'

The tallest of the guards straightened, the buttons on his high-collared blue uniform glistening under the gatehouse's gas lamps.

'We can hear it,' he replied sternly, 'but we have a duty to guard this post.'

'For the sake of the angels, this is an emergency. Vandals are attacking the temple. Didn't you hear the smashing windows? Scalist zealots, I'm sure. The priests are in danger. Demons below, the *bones* are in danger. They need all the help they can get.'

The watchmen shared a look, worry giving way to anticipation.

'We should go to the barracks to raise more men,' the shorter guard said reluctantly.

'No use soldiers delivering a message when I can,' Takket persisted. 'I'll run to the barracks, you get to the temple. Hurry, before it's too late.'

The taller watchman nodded once. 'With me, Harling. We'll teach those Scalist demon-puppets to stay in the New World.'

The two sprinted away, gripping their ornate flintlock rifles. Takket took off through the gatehouse, heading towards the barracks further up the main road until the two guards disappeared into the Sharddust. Satisfied, he darted into the narrow alleyways.

The further he ran from the city walls, the more decrepit Southreach became. Arcanes and Mages kept to the old city, their wealth supporting pleasant gardens, fine structures and expert sewage systems. Here, where the Mundanes lived, the locals made do with what they could put together. Rickety houses showing signs of multiple amateur repairs leaned precariously against one another. The paving under his feet turned from stone to gravel and finally to bare mud. Every wall was lined with thick Sharddust--the city cleaners were paid only to keep the Mage's areas clear. At least the grime was harder to see with the lack of gas lamps, the only light coming from the stars overhead. The reek was the worst of it--without a decent sewer system, waste was just tossed into the alleyways, covering the area in a choking stench.

Despite the late hour, the alleys echoed with noise. Screams of children. Drunken conversations. Shouts of rage, passion and fear. The sound of a thousand families crammed into the buildings around him contrasted sharply with the inner city's tranquillity.

Takket turned into a particularly dark alleyway, thankful that he could not see exactly what the soft, sticking floor was coated in. Finding a relatively clean section of gravelled street, he threw down his pack and retrieved his small wash bag, drawing his razor. Shivering in the darkness, he hacked off his beard, then shaved the stubble down smooth, gritting his teeth at the occasional cut.

Once finished, he threw off his cloak and pulled out the travelling clothes from his pack. He changed as quickly into the scratching cotton tunic and trousers, the cold stabbing into his arms. He wrapped his cloak around the glass block containing the angel's bones and strapped his bag shut. The cloak would be as incriminating as the bones, but at least it would provide padding.

Finally, he reached into a pile of what he hoped was Sharddust resting against a wall. He rubbed the fine powder through his hair, leaving it stained and dishevelled. For good measure, he patted more dust over his face and clothing. To any passer-by, he would look like an overworked courier, too poor to afford shaving cream, a regular bath or even a change of tunic. Just another Mundane, like the thousands of others packed into the surrounding tenements.

Shouldering his satchel, he headed downhill towards the waterfront. He stuck to the side streets and alleyways. The theft would have been discovered by now and, although they would likely be looking for an elderly man with a long beard, Takket did not want to take any chances. By now, the Mage sergeants would be out assisting the Mundane watchmen, and Mages needed no excuse to hassle a lone Mundane. Sticking to the poorest areas would keep him relatively safe-- what Mage would want to pick their way through this squalor?

His progress was slow through the winding streets, but he was in no rush. The Shardrail would not be opening until dawn, and he would need its speed to put enough distance between him and the city before the thief hunt intensified.

He had always considered himself to have a good sense of direction, but even he repeatedly got turned around by the mismatched buildings and seemingly random arrangement of alleys. Thankfully, whenever he became truly lost, he just had to follow his nose. The fresh wind from the harbour brought with it blessed relief from the waste around him.

Eventually, the tenements began to give way to warehouses and factories as he reached the waterfront. Ships sat in the harbour, their lights bobbing with the gentle waves. To one side lay the Shardrail station, its lines stretching away into the distance, to freedom.

Turning into a darkened alleyway between a textile mill and a Shard-cutters, he lay down against a set of empty crates. Leaning back, he felt the weariness of the day settle over him. All that was left was to wait until dawn, and pray he would next be sleeping in a

Shardrail cabin, not a dungeon.

Takket woke to sounds of hammering. The sun had barely risen, but the industrial area was already alive with activity. Mage-driven machines began to wind up. Men and women shouted back and forth, calling over the din. The thud of crates being moved was punctuated by the sound of chisels striking Soulshards.

Takket stretched, immediately regretting the action as his leg cried out in pain. Once he had been able to sleep in a cobbled alley and rise feeling spry and ready to face the day. Now his every joint complained at the uneven surface. It took a conscious effort to avoid limping as he strode out of the alleyway, dusting off the fresh layer of Sharddust that had settled on him overnight.

Outside the alley the red haze filled the street, the mist and Sharddust dancing in the wake of the horse-driven carts shuttling their loads between the factories, Shardrail station and harbour. Takket dodged between the carriages and foot traffic, steadily making his way towards the station. The odour of the harbour was strong here, the smell of salt water, seaweed and fish a welcome change from the stench of the city.

He reached the row of houses adjacent to the station and looked through the billowing red haze to the fence at the rail yard's edge. He swore to himself as he noticed the watchmen at the gates pedantically sifting through bags. They were stopping every male coming through, thoroughly searching their luggage.

Peering through the haze, he could see lines forming at the waterfront. No doubt more watchmen were searching passengers leaving on the morning ships. If this was the response here, the roads out of the city were certain to be monitored. He had hoped it would take the city longer to block off the exits, but Southreach clearly did not take the theft of the bones lightly.

Takket looked around for other options. The rail yard was surrounded by fencing, there to keep away the fare-dodgers. The fence was some eight feet tall, topped with sharpened points. Still, he could climb it. In the thick haze, it was unlikely anyone would spot him.

Taking a step towards the fence, he was quickly brought to a stop by the cry of protest in his leg. He was having a hard enough time walking after his uncomfortable sleep. Even his arms ached from last night's climb. As much as he wanted to deny it, his age was taking its toll. He was in no shape to vault a low wall, let alone this fence.

He chewed his lip in growing frustration. The longer he lingered here, the more time he gave the watchmen to notice him. A man hovering at the edge of the station was bound to draw suspicion. Still, he needed to get out of the city. The watch would be out in force as the news spread. Bounties would be offered. It would take just one person to notice a foreigner lingering in the city, and Takket's life would be forfeit.

Stealing this relic was meant to be his greatest heist. With all routes of escape blocked, he feared this theft would be his final failure.

Printed in Great Britain
by Amazon